PRAISE FOR
THE VALENTINE'S ARRANGEMENT

"*The Valentine's Arrangement* was sexy as hell and kept me up all night. I couldn't put it down. Kale is my favorite kind of hot."
—*New York Times* bestselling author Abbi Glines

"Hot, sexy, and steamy. A very well-written story that flowed smoothly. The chemistry between Ronnie and Kale was palpable, and I was hooked from the first page until the last."
—Sydney Landon, *New York Times* bestselling author of *Fighting for You*

"Kelsie Leverich serves up fun, sexy and hot."
—Flirty and Dirty Book Blog

"I could feel the sizzle in the pages." —Into the Night Reviews

"Fast-paced and sexy as all get-out." —Let's Get Romantical

"A great, fast, sexy story . . . it is a love story that was not all hearts and flowers and gushing and overkill." —Book Crush

continued . . .

ALSO AVAILABLE FROM
KELSIE LEVERICH

The Valentine's Arrangement: A Hard Feelings Novel

Pretending She's His: A Penguin Special Novella

FEEL the Rush

A Hard Feelings Novel

KELSIE LEVERICH

A SIGNET ECLIPSE BOOK

SIGNET ECLIPSE
Published by the Penguin Group
Penguin Group (USA) LLC, 375 Hudson Street,
New York, New York 10014

USA | Canada | UK | Ireland | Australia | New Zealand | India | South Africa | China
penguin.com
A Penguin Random House Company

Published by Signet Eclipse, an imprint of New American Library, a division of
Penguin Group (USA) LLC. Previously published in an InterMix edition.

First Signet Eclipse Printing, March 2014

LIBRARY OF CONGRESS CATALOGING-IN-PUBLICATION DATA:
Leverich, Kelsie.
Feel the rush: a hard feelings novel/Kelsie Leverich.
p. cm.
ISBN 978-0-451-46666-2 (pbk.)
1. Single women—Fiction. 2. Airmen—Fiction. I. Title.
PS3612.E923455F44 2014
813'.6—dc23   2013038341

Printed in the United States of America
10 9 8 7 6 5 4 3 2 1

Set in New Caledonia
Designed by Spring Hoteling

To my husband,
my Mr. All of the Above

FEEL the Rush

CHAPTER ONE

There was not enough alcohol in this bar to get her up on that stage. No way in hell was she singing. She would rather strip down to her bra and panties and dance on the bar stripper-style than get up there and sing karaoke. It was like a string of bad outtakes from *American Idol* auditions, and, as entertaining as it was to watch, she was not going to partake in the self-humiliation.

Meagan Mitchell licked the salt off the rim of her margarita glass before she pressed it to her lips and took a sip, observing her girlfriends as they attempted to pick out a song for her to sing.

"Oh, what about 'Black Velvet'?"

"Okay, first of all, that's your typical clichéd karaoke song right there. Second, I'm. Not. Singing."

"Meg, you need—"

"Nope," she said, interrupting her friend Brittany, who was already two margaritas ahead of her, but Meagan couldn't blame her for letting loose a little bit. The woman's husband was deployed to Afghanistan and she rarely got out.

What with three kids all under the age of five at home, Meagan was lucky she ever saw her anymore.

"I love you, but my singing would clear this place faster than the DJ would be able to turn the music off."

Her best friend, Eva, was sitting next to her, so she was in clear range of Eva's elbow to the ribs. "You're such a chickenshit."

Meagan's mouth puckered and she feigned a wince as she rubbed her side. "Nooo. I'm not scared, but I'm also not delusional—I can't hold a note to save my life."

"Which is what makes it fun."

"Exactly, it's fun to watch people make complete asses of themselves, but I for one choose not to be the ass in this scenario." Meagan put her glass to her lips and finished the delicious tequila-induced heaven in two long sips. "I'm going to get another drink, you girls want anything?"

"No, but don't think you're getting out of this so easily," Eva said.

Meagan shrugged. "Sorry, pretty lady."

"Allie will be here soon, she'll get your ass up there to sing."

Meagan pushed her blond hair over her shoulder as she stood up. "Don't hold your breath."

Meagan sauntered up to one of the empty stools at the bar and ordered a drink from a woman who looked like she needed a drink herself.

She felt a pair of eyes roam over her body. A slither slid up her back, causing goose bumps to prickle on her freshly shaved legs—and unfortunately they weren't the good kind of goose bumps.

Meagan's gaze landed briefly on the roaming-eyed guy sitting a few stools down. "Hey," he said, paired with the standard guy head-nod. She smiled faintly and turned her head back toward the rows of alcohol bottles lining the wall in front of her. Maybe if she ignored him he would go away.

The guy stood up and slid into the stool next to her. Guess the ignoring tactic wasn't going to work. "Can I buy you a drink?"

Seriously? Okay, first of all, this guy didn't even look old enough to buy her a drink. Even if he was of the legal drinking age, it was just barely, and she was pushing thirty. *Okay, Meagan, don't go there again*, she thought, blinking her eyes to push aside the ever-present nagging reminder of her age that had seemed to keep popping up since the dreadful day was getting closer.

Against her better judgment, she chanced another quick glance at him. She didn't want her gaze to linger on him and give him the wrong idea. He had some boyish charm and the build of a man, but his blunt flirting and body language when she was clearly uninterested gave him a neon light above his head flashing the word *egocentric* with an arrow pointing straight to his penis. Having had her fair share of selfish one-nighters, she knew the type. You know, the kind that were in and out. The wham-bam-thank-you-ma'am fucks—and, usually, the ma'am was left high and dry. Plus, he was screaming inexperience, and as fun as it would be to take a newbie to bed and teach him the tricks of the trade, she didn't see him as being a perceptive learner.

Yes, she got all this just by looking at him. But when

you've dated every Mr. Wrong and Mr. Bad in the book, you learn a few tricks of the trade yourself. Besides, she wasn't here for sex, she was here to spend a night out with her girl-friends, something she didn't get to do often now that Britt had her hands full playing the role of single momma while her husband was deployed and Allie was as pregnant as they came—Meagan was surprised she was even going to come out tonight.

"No, I'm fine, thanks," she said, not fully meeting the guy's eyes. It's better if she didn't. Sometimes you give them that little inch and they feel like they can take the whole damn mile.

She saw him smile from the corner of her eye and she fought back the urge to roll her eyes. "What's your name?"

She should have taken her chances with the karaoke ma-chine.

"Hey, sexy," a familiar voice said behind her as he slid his large hands around her waist and pressed his palms against her stomach, pushing her back into his chest. His lips were hovering close to her ear, and his warm breath tickled the bare flesh of her neck.

Meagan rolled her neck to the side, allowing Trevor to nuzzle the curve above her shoulder. "Hey, handsome," she replied. He pressed his lips to her skin and kissed it softly. Just a peck, just a single brush of his lips over her neck—but she could feel the tension start to pull between him and the young guy who was now watching intently. It was like a rub-ber band stretched to its max and you didn't want to be the one holding on to it when the other let go.

"Is there a reason you're still sitting there?" Trevor said, standing up straight and moving his palm to the small of Meagan's back. Her body sagged back against him and she turned her head away from the pissing match that was unfolding. She pressed her lips together, trying her hardest not to laugh.

No more words were said, but she could imagine the scowls and narrowed eyes on the expressions of the guys as they stood there exuding their "me Tarzan" alpha mojo. What seemed like a full sixty seconds later, she heard the sound of the stool sliding back against the hard floor.

Trevor's hand dropped from the small of her back and she turned back around as he sat down on the now empty stool next to her, grinning like an idiot.

Meagan leaned in and rocked her shoulder into Trevor's. "Thanks for coming to my rescue." Although she hadn't needed his help and was perfectly capable of rejecting a barely legal man-child, watching a testosterone pissing match was always amusing. Besides, Trevor seemed to get the job done faster.

Trevor gave her his signature wink. "Anytime. I could feel your rejection the second I walked in the door. That kid clearly needed a *bigger* clue to back off." Yes, Trevor was big and built and attractive. If Ken and G.I. Joe had a love child, it would be Trevor.

Meagan was sure his little public display of fake affection had broken a couple of hearts in the room tonight, although she knew he would be more than happy to mend them. Trevor was a man-whore and a self-proclaimed flirt, but never once had he tried to get Meagan into his bed. Actually, she didn't know whether to be grateful or offended by that little fact. It just wasn't like that between them, though—it never had been.

Meagan and Trevor went to high school together when their parents were stationed at Fort Bragg in North Carolina. Meagan always had a huge circle of friends, girls and guys alike, and Trevor happened to be one of them. He was the guy everyone wanted to be around. He was fun and outgoing, smart and athletic, funny and always entertaining. He and Meagan became close, and Trevor instantly stepped into the big-brother role. It was nice, having that type of a friendship with him—no pressure to have anything other than that. Hell, Trevor had even seen her damn near naked more times than she could count—and not one of those times was sexual. He had seen her ugly-cry—we're talking blotchy-faced sobs, snotty nose and all—and had held her hair on more than one occasion while she was taking a trip down hangover lane. He was a keeper, but just in that high-five, not-afraid-to-fart-in-front-of-him friend kind of way.

After high school he joined the army, following in his dad's footsteps, and he and Meagan made sure to stay in touch. When she found out Trevor was getting stationed at Fort Drum in New York, she did her very own version of a touchdown happy dance in the middle of her work's break room, and the second he got there, they picked right back up from where they had left off—nothing had changed. He was still her overprotective, big brother–like best friend.

"I think you just like to intimidate the hell out of any guy that comes around me, anyway," she teased. "It's like you get some twisted enjoyment out of it."

He propped his elbow on the bar and leaned against it. "What'd I tell you, Meg? If they're not willing to fight for you—not willing to fight *me* for you—then they're not fucking worth it anyway."

She rolled her eyes—she'd heard that one before. "Did you just get here?" she asked, changing the subject.

"Yeah, I came with Mike and Allie."

Meagan turned around and looked back over to the table where her friends were sitting and waved at Allie. Luckily the bars in New York were nonsmoking, or Allie never would have agreed to their little girls' night out. "Well, thanks again for coming to my rescue." She stood up, grabbed her margarita that the bartender had apparently put in front of her at some point, and leaned down to kiss him on the cheek. "I'm gonna go say hi to Allie. I will leave you to hunt down your latest prey for the night."

"Ah, you know me too well, honey—it's scary," he said, giving her another wink before he stood and made his way to the back of the bar.

"Did Trevor scare that poor guy away?" Allie said through her laugh when Meagan got back to the table.

Meagan groaned. "Yes, thank God."

"He was kinda cute," Britt said.

Meagan tilted her head to the side and pursed her lips. "Uh, Britt, I know it's been a while with Craig gone and all, but no. Sure, the kid had that puppy dog kind of thing going for him, but I'm a cat person." Hopefully she wouldn't end up the single crazy cat lady.

"Yeah, but when's the last time you've had sex?" Eva asked.

"You mean other than with myself?" She sighed.

Eva rolled her eyes and laughed before turning her ever-present mocking stare at Meagan. "Yes, when was the last time you got hot and sweaty between the sheets with some-one other than Mr. Dildo?"

Meagan's head shifted toward her friend, her pain-in-the-ass friend who she loved more than anything, even if she liked to pry into every aspect of anything that had to do with Mea-gan's sex life or love life—or in this case lack thereof. Between Eva, who thought it was her life mission to make sure Meagan had a healthy sexual appetite, and her mother, whose voice was a constant tick in her ear, reminding her of the sand in her hourglass, it was no wonder Meagan was still single.

"That would be when I dated Mr. Sexy. God, that man was beautiful." The very thought of Jax, the last man she dated, made her chest flutter in excitement. His chocolate eyes and his smile were enough to make her hormones go out of whack, but when the clothes came off and she was staring at his hard black body, all thick and masculine . . . she was ready without even needing him to touch her. "Now that man was good in bed. I definitely wouldn't mind getting hot and sweaty with him again."

"Jax? Ugh, you and every other female in a thirty-mile radius. That's why you *dated* him, as in past tense, as in no more. The man was a player."

Meagan blushed and attempted to remove the image of

Jax naked in her bed from her mind. "Yeah, MVP." She laughed.

"Gross," Allie chimed in.

"Oh, shut up. You know he was gorgeous. Yes, he was a two-timing asshole, but I gotta give it to the man."

Eva bit her teeth together. "Why the hell aren't you more pissed about his cheating ass?"

"Because I didn't love him. It's not like I would have married the guy, we just dated."

Eva rolled her eyes. Meagan didn't know what was worse: the fact that her overprotective friend was still pissed at her ex—if you could even really call him that—for cheating on her or the fact that her overprotective friend was throwing a hissy fit. "Whatever you say. Now Joey, he was a good candidate."

"Mr. Bad? Yeah, *you* would think so," Meagan managed to say through her sudden burst of laughter. Eva thought Jax was bad, yet at the same time thought Joey was in the running for husband-potential boyfriend? That girl had a twisted image of what good meant. Eva was always going for the bad guy, the guy with a little bit of danger to him, but unfortunately she wasn't alone in that little area—hence Mr. Bad, aka Joey. Why did girls always want the bad boys, anyway? It was like they were bred with a specific pheromone that attracted women by one single sweep of the eyes. It was a universal bad-boy trick that seemed to work 99 percent of the time—and Meagan was guilty of falling for it 100 percent of the time.

An elated smile fanned over Eva's cheeks. "Ah yes, Mr. Bad. Tell me again why you dumped him."

"Because dating a guy that had monthly bar fights, and cared more about his car than he did about me, wasn't on my priority list. Plus, I was always worried Trevor was going to kick his ass. It stressed me out." Needless to say, Trevor didn't like Joey either. Maybe saying that her friends were overprotective was an understatement.

"Yes, but that man was sexy," Eva purred. Meagan could see the flush in her cheeks and could only imagine her stretching her claws out like a vixen cat, waiting to pounce.

She shook her head and sighed, suppressing a laugh. "I'm not arguing with you there, but no."

Eva hung her head slightly, feigning disappointment. "Mm, mm, mm, that's too bad."

"Who did you date before Joey?" Britt asked innocently, but the question had Meagan's hackles standing up. She didn't want to travel down that particular road tonight. Not so close to her dreaded birthday and definitely not two margaritas in.

The mood around the table instantly shifted and Meagan jerked her head toward Brittany. "Why are we rehashing my list of failed relationships?"

Poor Britt looked like she was ready to burst into tears at Meagan's little lash out.

"We're not hashing," Allie said, knowing good and well who Meagan dated before Joey. "You haven't talked about Kale much lately, where's your head at?"

Britt's eyes widened as realization struck and she mouthed the word *sorry* to Meagan.

Kale was admirable and honest. He was an amazing man

and an even more amazing soldier, and he had become a good friend of Meagan's. No one seemed to understand their relationship, though. She cared about him, yes. But with Kale, it was just sex. He wasn't interested in diving into anything more than that, and he was honest about it. He didn't lead her on and he treated her better than most guys she actually had relationships with. But when he found a woman who made him want more, she couldn't help but feel a tiny bit jealous. She wasn't going to play the typical why-wasn't-it-me card, but she'd be lying if she said the thought never crossed her mind. "My head is nowhere. We were just friends who liked to sleep together every now and again," she said, heat reaching the surface of her cheeks as the memory of nights tangled in his arms came into view. Ugh, his arms. And that damn dimple in his cheek when he smiled. . . .

"I miss him, though," she admitted, her voice going a little soft as a proverbial knife plunged into her stomach.

Shortly after he had come home from his last deployment and climbed back into the bed of the first woman he ever fell in love with, he had come down on orders to Fort Hood. She hadn't talked to him in a while, and she missed him.

Meagan scrunched her nose and shook her head, trying to shake off the damn chest pang that seemed to creep in every time she thought of Kale. "But seriously, thank you girls for reminding me of all the great sex I *was* having," she whined, putting an end to the Kale conversation.

Allie swatted her hand in the air. "Oh, quit your damn whining." Her brows tilted upward, causing tiny little wrinkles to appear across her forehead. "When you have a human being growing in your stomach, kicking you in the ribs, and using your bladder as a trampoline, then you can whine," she said as she looked down at her huge pregnant belly. "Do you know how badly I would kill for a margarita right now? And sex, oh my God. Mike won't even consider it. I'm telling you, this kid better come out soon or I'm likely to go all *Desperate Housewives* and screw the pool boy."

"You don't have a pool or a pool boy." Meagan laughed.

"I'll find one."

Meagan swiped her tongue across the rim of the glass then took a long drink. "It can't be that bad."

"Yeah, let's put a pin in it and visit this topic of conversation when you can no longer see your vagina and can map out the entire state of New York on the stretch marks covering your ass."

"Please, someone change the conversation," Britt said, laughing, her words slightly slurred. Allie rolled her eyes and laughed.

"I'll change it," Eva volunteered. "I have something to tell you anyway. But where's Carmen? I wanted to tell you all together."

Britt set down her near-empty glass. "The hoochie has a date with that Special Forces guy that she met last weekend."

"Well, at least one of us will be getting some tonight," Allie whined in mock annoyance.

Britt picked up her glass and raised it out in front of her. "Amen to that."

"That's the truth."

"I'll drink to that," Meagan said, putting her glass to the other two hovering above the middle of the table. Yeah, Meagan would drink to that, maybe it would bring her some luck.

They all clanked their glasses together; then Meagan took a long sip before she turned in her seat to face Eva. "All right, spill it," she said, instantly holding her breath for the inevitable.

Eva sighed, and Meagan knew exactly where this was going. Eva was a medic in the army and had been stationed at Fort Drum for four years now. It was about time for her to come down on orders to another duty station. Meagan had been waiting for the bomb to drop for a while now. One thing she'd learned quickly growing up as an army brat was that in the army, you changed states—and friends—almost as often as you did panties.

They had been best friends since Eva first got stationed there and started working with Meagan in the medical clinic on post. Meagan was one of the civilian nurses who worked at the clinic, and Eva was one of the enlisted medics who she ended up working almost every shift with. The thought of not having her badass wingman at her side every day was enough to make her consider kidnapping, or she supposed it would be friendnapping. Either way, she was willing to do it.

Eva glanced around the table before landing her eyes on Meagan. Dammit, she was right; she knew what Eva was going to say even before the words left her lips. "I got orders to Fort Benning, Georgia. I'm leaving in three weeks."

Meagan's eyes widened and her mouth fell open. Okay, so she hadn't been completely on target. "Three weeks? How is that enough time for you to clear Fort Drum?" she asked, panic working its way into her voice. She'd figured she would have at least a few months before her best friend had to up and leave. But three weeks?

Eva picked up her glass and took another drink, acting as if she hadn't just dropped a world of shit on Meagan's lap. Three weeks? Seriously?

"I've been going through out-processing already. I got my orders a few months ago," she finally said, the hiccup in her voice spilling over with guilt. Yeah, she knew she should have said something sooner. This was bullshit.

Britt's eyes shifted between her and Eva, probably because Meagan had a look of death on her face. "I have a few friends whose husbands are stationed at Fort Benning. You will love Geor—"

"A few months? Why didn't you tell me, Eva?" Meagan said, interrupting Britt's attempt at lightening the pissy mood that suddenly infected the space around Meagan. She sat forward on the edge of her chair, her back rigid and her body stiff as she ignored everyone at the table and kept her eyes focused on her best friend.

"Because I knew you would be upset. And I came down on orders right when you found out that Kale and Ronnie—" She halted her words, biting her lower lip. "I didn't want to burst your fragile bubble."

"My bubble isn't fragile," she said, the volume of her words making a couple of people around them look their way. She took a deep breath. She had an array of emotions swelling up inside her, the tequila bringing them nice and cozy to the surface, heating her blood at the same time. Was she really mad at Eva, or was she just mad at the whole damn situation? She rolled back her head onto her shoulders and released her breath. "I just would have liked to have had a little more of a heads-up that my best friend was moving."

Yes, she'd known Eva was going to come down on orders sooner or later, but she also thought that she would have had a little more time to get used to the idea. Almost thirty—with no husband, no kids, and no best friend. That crazy cat-lady scenario seemed more and more like a very real possibility.

"What the hell am I going to do without you?" She felt a prickling sensation at the back of her eyes, the tequila bringing out her emotional side. Damn margaritas, they were a doubled-edged sword.

"You still have us," Britt said with a full tipsy smile planted on her ivory cheeks.

Meagan couldn't help but smile back. "I know." She stood up. "Look, girls, I'm gonna head home."

"Really, Meagan?" Eva was pissed. Meagan could tell by the way her nostrils were flaring and how her neck was starting to match the red color of her hair.

"Yes, really. My best friend just dropped a load of shit my way." The alcohol in her veins was starting to block the path from her brain to her mouth. "I'm sorry, but Britt has her three boys, Allie has Mike and will soon have her new baby. It was you and me, Eva. You're my wingman, my best friend, and now you'll be gone. Sorry if I'm not in the mood to sit around and play nice. I'm going home."

Meagan headed toward the back of the bar, where Trevor was leaning in dangerously close to a blonde with boobs that could put Dolly Parton's to shame and an ass that was in the running with Kim Kardashian's. Meagan's sour face instantly smoothed out. Trevor genuinely loved all women, big, small, blue, or purple. She stopped and started to turn around—she wasn't going to break up what looked like a possible hookup—when he spotted her. His face dropped when he locked eyes with her and he gave her that goofy-ass wink of his before he whispered something in Dolly Kardashian's ear and then started walking her way.

"You okay?" he asked, swinging an arm around her shoulder when he reached her.

"Not overly."

Trevor placed his hand palm up in front of Meagan. She loved that he knew her just as much as she knew him. She dropped her car keys in his hand. "Come on, honey. Let's get your drunk ass home."

The drive home was quiet, and that was one thing she loved about having Trevor. Men didn't pry. Trev was there for her—always—and he dished out the advice when she needed it, even if it was unwanted, but he never pried. He knew she would talk if she wanted to—but she didn't. He wouldn't get it.

"You sure you don't want me to come up and spend the night? I'll even do that spooning thing you love," he said, pulling up to her apartment building.

"I love you for offering, but no. You go back to the bar and take that blonde you were talking to home—do more than just spoon," she said before she leaned over and pecked him on the cheek. "Thanks for driving me."

His smile wavered and he opened his mouth to say something but shut it again. She knew he was struggling with leaving her.

Meagan got out of her car and shut the door, peeking through the window at him. "Go."

He sighed and lifted his lips back up, but it wasn't sincere. "All right. Call me if you need me. Otherwise, I'll bring your car to you tomorrow."

"Yeah, you look pretty sexy driving around in my Bug." She laughed.

"Honey, I make anything look sexy." He winked at her again and then pulled away.

Ten minutes later Meagan was in her ratty sweats, sitting on her plush couch in her two-bedroom apartment, her two furry cats on either side of her, and a bottle of merlot in her hand. Yes, a bottle. She had given up on the glass a couple of self-pity sips ago. This better not be what her future had in store for her. Lonely nights curled up on the couch with nothing to warm her body but two cats. Seriously, thirty had a way of creeping up on you and then when you least expect it—BAM, you were no longer in your twenties and you were staring at the only men in your life and they happened to have four legs, a tail, and they peed in a litter box.

Meagan's phone took that moment to ring, making her jump and breaking through her mental pity party. She looked at the incoming number and groaned. She was really not in the mood to hash this out with her right now. . . .

"Hi, Mom."

"Hi, sweetie. What are you doing?"

"Not a whole lot, it's almost midnight." Meagan knew

better than to tell her mom she was sitting on her couch drinking a bottle of wine by herself. No, not by herself, with her cats. "What are you doing up so late?"

"Your dad and I just got home from the Legion." Her dad was a retired army major and commander of one of the American Legions in Fort Pierce, Florida—their new snowbird home they had made permanent.

"Sounds fun. How's Dad?"

"He's good, sweetie. We want to know how you are. . . ."

Oh great, here it comes, the never-ending conversation about her nonexistent love life. She was really not in the mood for this tonight.

"I'm good, Mom," she said, slouching down in the corner of the couch, snuggling in, and taking another sip of her wine.

"No date tonight?"

Ah, so that's why she'd called. Knowing her mom, she was calling hoping to catch her in the middle of a date. She was so nosey.

"Nope."

Her mom paused and there was an awkward moment of silence that stretched between them. It was only maybe four seconds, but in those four seconds Meagan knew her mom was trying hard to hold back the lecture that was at the tip of her tongue, begging to be let out.

"Mom?" Meagan asked, rolling her eyes as she imagined the scowl that was on her sweet old mother's face.

"Sweetie, I know that you don't like it when I talk to you about your—"

"Then don't, Mom," she interrupted.

"Okay, okay. So what do you have planned for your birthday this year?" Subtlety was not her mother's strong suit.

"I think I would rather go back to talking about my miserable, nonexistent love life."

"What about that nice boy, Kale?" Obviously the nonexistent part didn't register with her mother. "Maybe you two should do something special for your birthday since it's such a big one." Unfortunately, the excitement in her mom's voice wasn't forced—and the single mention of Kale's name sent that pesky knife in a little more.

"Mom, I thought I told you already, but I will let you off the hook, considering you are ancient—Kale moved. The last time I talked to him was when he called to tell me that he and Ronnie got engaged." Knife . . . twisting . . . deeper.

"Ronnie? Now what kind of name is that? What in the world was that poor girl's mother thinking naming her a boy's name?"

Meagan giggled. Her mom was a pretty "hip" seventy-year-old, but she let her true age shine through every now and again.

"Sweetie?" The low, hushed sincerity in her mother's voice sliced through Meagan's laughter, stopping her cold. "I'm sorry. I know you really cared about that man."

Meagan pulled in a deep breath through her nose—it didn't seem to help, that damn chest pang still came back. "It's fine, Mom."

"It's just, you're almost thirty, sweetie."

"Yes, I'm completely aware of the sand in my hourglass."

"Oh, now, Meagan. I just want you to have someone—to have a family. I want you to find a good man, not those usual men you seem to get wrapped up in."

Meagan giggled again—she wasn't normally a giggler, but apparently the wine was starting to kick in. "Okay, so what type of man do you suggest I get wrapped up in then?" Meagan pressed the bottle of wine to her lips and took a long sip—all right, more like a couple unladylike swallows.

Her mother sighed, the worry and exasperation apparent, even through the phone. "You need a man who has his head on straight, who has a bright future and a clean past. You don't want any momma drama eith—"

"Mom, have you been watching *Real Housewives* again?" Meagan interrupted. She couldn't help smiling at the thought of her seventy-year-old mother with a reality TV show addiction.

"Oh, you hush. Anyway, you don't need that. You need a man who is stable and who is settled."

"And how do you suggest I find this stable man with no momma drama and a promising future?"

"By staying away from those troublemakers who think with the head between their legs."

Meagan laughed. She could picture her tiny mom sitting at the kitchen table with her feet tucked up in the chair next to her small body, her short silver hair tucked behind her ears—talking about men's penises. She might be an older mom, but she had spunk, she always had. Even as Meagan was growing up, all her girlfriends would sit at the counter while her mom cooked, or baked, or just drank her coffee, and chatted with her like they were all friends. Everyone envied the relationship Meagan had with her mom. She was the type of mom that you would actually call to come pick your underage ass up from a party when you were drunk and needed a ride. She was the type of mom that you would honestly tell when you started having sex so you could get on the Pill. She was always there when Meagan needed her, and more often than not she was there when Meagan's friends needed her too. She was the kind of mom Meagan hoped she could be someday—if that day ever came.

"Don't pretend that you don't get caught up in the fun of it all. I was young once, I remember. I may have only been with your father, but when he was your age he was a pistol in the bedroom."

"Okay, thank you, Mom, for putting that oh so pleasant image in my head."

"You are a grown woman, nothing to be embarrassed about. You're almost thirty."

"Again with the age thing, seriously?"

"All I'm trying to say is you need someone safe."

Safe?

"But I'm heading to bed now, sweetie."

"All right, Mom. Love you."

Meagan hung up the phone, pulled her legs underneath her, and leaned against the armrest of the couch. "Harry, what would I do without you?" she said as her long-haired black cat climbed onto her lap. "It's just you, me, and Weasley." She rubbed the head of the orange tabby that was purring next to her and then tipped back her bottle of wine—again.

Dammit, her mom was right. If she wanted to fall in love and have a family before she started sprouting gray hairs and before gravity took ahold of her boobs, she needed to stop screwing around, literally. Her five-year plan was up. There were only so many times she could flip over that damn hourglass and get away with it.

"Oh, please tell me you are not sitting on your couch drinking wine with your cats?"

Meagan turned her head toward the front door as Eva came barging in, kicking off her flip-flops at the door.

"Okay, I won't tell you."

"What the hell is your problem? You didn't need to bail on us just because you got your panties in a bunch."

Meagan blinked hard. "Do you realize that in one month from today I will be turning thirty? Thirty, Eva."

"Yes, you will be turning thirty. So what?"

"Easy for you to say, you still have three more years before the threatening thirty comes knocking at your door."

"Oh my God, you're acting like you are about to turn to dust or something. What's going on?"

"My time's up. My five-year plan is—"

"What five-year plan?" Eva interrupted, sitting down in the chair across from Meagan.

"The five-year plan I had. You know, find Mr. Right, get married, have two-point-five kids, a house, the picket fence, the whole nine yards—all before I hit thirty. So much for that plan." Meagan pressed the wine bottle to her lips and just as she was tilting it back to let the smooth liquid into her mouth, the bottle was ripped out of her hands.

"Are you kidding me? Let me guess: You've been talking to your mom again, haven't you? You are not going to sit here and wallow in your ridiculous plan that didn't follow through."

"Yes, I am going to wallow. Look around, Eva. I live in a shitty apartment by myself with my two cats. I'm single and I'm almost thirty. Top that off with the fact that I just found out my best friend is moving and I think I'm entitled to some wallowing."

"You really should have taken that young guy up on his flirting. What you need is sex."

Meagan threw her head back and laughed. "Mark my words: I'm officially done dating Mr. Sexy, Mr. Bad, and especially Mr. Unavailable. That also includes Mr. Puppy."

Eva laughed. "Good luck with that, honey. Who does that leave you? Mr. Boring?"

"No, Mr. Safe."

"Mr. Safe? What the hell does that mean?"

"It means no more guys that just want to fuck me senseless or pick me up at a bar and especially no more guys that will break my heart."

"So, no more fun?"

Meagan inhaled deeply. "It . . . can still be . . . fun," she said haltingly, trying to make the idea sound more appealing, even if she didn't have a damn clue what she was talking about. "But just because it's fun doesn't mean that it has to be reckless. I'm ready to start my forever, Eva."

"Sooo"—Eva leaned back in the chair and folded her arms across her chest—"Mr. Safe, huh?"

Meagan returned a full, toothy smile. "Yes, find Mr. Safe. That's the plan."

"You know what your plan needs?" she said with a little too much perk in her voice for Meagan's current mood. When Eva started plotting, it usually didn't end well.

Meagan groaned. "And what's that?"

"A change in scenery. Come with me." Eva's words trailed off in a high-pitched tone, which was definitely not a sound that usually came out of her mouth. It was like the sudden thought had to escape before it passed by, and it came out in an excited screech.

Meagan's brows darted up toward her hairline and her baby blues rounded even more. "To Benning?"

"Why the hell not? You have nothing tying you down here anymore. Your parents moved to Florida last year, you live in a shitty-ass apartment, you will have no problem finding another nursing job, you're single, and the topper—I'll be there."

"Well, damn, don't sugarcoat it or anything."

"Okay, I hit below the belt, I'm sorry. But it would be great, Meggy. Come on, come with me. You said you wanted a new plan, why not get a new start?"

That actually wasn't a bad idea.

CHAPTER TWO

Meagan loved summer nights. It was nine o'clock and only now starting to get dark. The sky was still that dim blue, like it was holding its breath for daylight before the night smothered it. And the Southern air was beautiful—just the right amount of warmth to make it perfect.

Meagan pulled her feet out of the open passenger-side window of Eva's truck as they pulled into their new apartment building in Columbus, Georgia, and sat back up so she could get a better look. It was a small community, just eight apartment buildings forming a square surrounded by the parking lot. It seemed almost cold, isolated. There was only a small section of grass extending from the buildings to the sidewalk—other than that it was empty, plain, and very unimpressive. But it was nighttime—maybe it would look better during the day. Here's for hoping.

Eva parked in a couple of parking spots. Luckily she owned an oversized monster of a truck, and it was able to pull Meagan's little Volkswagen Beetle on a trailer. It would have been complete hell driving the entire nineteen hours in the car by herself, although having complete control of the music would have been nice. If Meagan never had to listen to another country song, it would be too soon—and she didn't even mind country music, but nineteen hours of straight twang was torture.

Meagan hopped out of the truck to stretch her legs. She brought up her ankle to her butt to stretch out her thighs, which had cramped up somewhere in North Carolina, and the pull she felt in her muscles was delicious.

Eva walked around the front of the truck and stopped in front of Meagan. "So, what do you think?"

"It's great."

"Don't lie to me. I can tell by the complete look of panic on your face that you think it sucks. Well, don't get your panties in a bunch, princess. The pictures on their Web site looked great." That wasn't completely promising. "I'm meeting the landlord at his apartment to get our key since the office is closed. I'll be right back."

"Um, Eva, that sounds a little sketchy," she said, leaning against the side of the truck. "I'm going to stay here and watch our stuff. If you're not back in ten minutes, I'm going to assume that you've been offed by the landlord and I'm taking the truck and getting the hell out of here."

Eva tossed Meagan the truck keys. "You wouldn't come looking for me?"

"Hell no, this feels like the beginning to a cheap horror movie—it would be called *Tenants*. But I will be the smart one that gets away in the end, you will be the stupid one that goes running to the killer in the middle of the night looking for your damn apartment key." She shook her head and laughed as Eva looked completely amused. "It's your funeral."

"You're such a bitch; I can't believe you wouldn't come save me. I'll remember that!" she shouted as she walked toward the apartment building in front of them.

Meagan smiled and then opened up the door to the truck and grabbed two very noisy crates from the backseat. "Hopefully we will be inside soon so you guys can get out of there," she said, peeking in to look at her cats, who sounded like they were dying—they really hated those damn things.

Within a few minutes, Eva was jogging back to the truck with a couple of keys dangling from her fingers. "Did the boogeyman come while I was gone?"

"Shut up. Which one's ours?" she asked, handing Eva a litter box and a container of litter.

"This way."

Meagan picked up the crates and followed Eva down the walkway in between the two buildings that were in front of them. When they got to the back side of the buildings it was like they were in a completely different world. It was absolutely beautiful. It was set up like a courtyard, with a stone fountain surrounded by a circular stone walkway placed in the center of the enormous grounds. The lawn was beautiful, professionally landscaped to perfection. It was the middle of June, and flowers were blooming everywhere, and there was a handful of surprisingly mature trees throughout. There was a huge pool at the far side of the courtyard, complete with a diving board and a twirly slide—and, yes, the twirly slide got her the most excited. When she looked at the backs of the buildings, there were small patios and decks that faced the courtyard.

"This is amazing, Eva."

"No shit," she murmured, slightly surprised as well. "This is even better than the Web site let on. Now I'm dying to see the inside. We should be this one right over here." She walked to the building to the right of the fountain, stuck her key into the patio door of apartment 2C, and pushed it open.

Meagan was more than pleasantly surprised when she walked in. Actually, that was putting it mildly. Going off the opinion she had from looking at the outside of the building, she was completely prepared for molded carpet, broken cabinets, crusty bathrooms, and maybe even one of those chalk outlines of a dead body on the kitchen floor.

Instead, she saw beautiful hardwood floors—okay, so they were probably laminate floors, but they sure as hell were better than nasty carpet—stainless-steel appliances, beautiful mocha-colored cabinets, and the bathrooms—there were three! This place made her old apartment look like a college dorm room, which actually wasn't too far off from the truth, to be honest. This apartment was clean and spacious with a huge eat-in kitchen and a separate dining room. The bedrooms were large with walk-in closets and each one had its own bathroom.

"So what do you think?" Eva asked, looking around the large, open living room.

"I'm thinking this is a hell of a lot better than my old apartment."

"We're splitting the rent, roomie. You can afford a big-girl apartment now."

"Point taken. In that case, I'm glad I left all the planning to you. This is perfect."

Eva headed toward the front door, which Meagan assumed led to the outside of the apartment building. "I'm not gonna say, 'I told you so'... well, yep ... I am ... 'I told you so'. I'm gonna go grab a couple boxes."

Meagan rolled her eyes. "Okay, I will be out to help in a minute. I'm going to let Harry and Weasley out and get their litter box set up real quick."

"Okay," Eva said before shutting the door behind her.

Meagan opened up the crate. You would have thought they got bit in the ass by the way they bolted out. Meagan laughed. "Not too bad, huh?"

Meagan stepped back and looked around her new home. Sure, there was nothing filling it yet, and there probably wouldn't be anything for another couple of weeks until the movers got there, but oddly enough it already felt like a place she could settle in to. She still had slight reservations about packing up her entire life and moving, all within a matter of weeks, but just being here eased those up a little bit. Moving without any plan was probably the most irresponsible thing she had ever done, but if she wanted to change, if she wanted to find her forever, why not get a fresh start? She swept her eyes around the empty apartment again. This was it—her fresh start.

"Hey, Meggy, grab the door for me, will ya?" she heard Eva holler from the living room as she walked out of the laundry room.

Meagan hurried to Eva, who had her hands full of boxes

stacked one on top of the other. That little shit was strong. "Seriously, I'm about to drop. . . ."

The top box fell from her hands. Luckily the army was moving most of their stuff and all they had packed with them were mostly clothes, but the sound of the box hitting the hard floor scared the crap out of Harry and he bolted out the patio door.

"Shit!"

Meagan ran after him. This was great; they had been here a total of ten minutes and her cat was already lost. Looking for a black cat at nighttime was difficult, add the fact that they were in a new place and the cat had just been spooked to the equation, and Meagan knew it was going to be hard to find him.

"Here, kitty, kitty, kitty," she said over and over as she frantically searched the courtyard. As she was coming up to the fountain she heard a deathly screech, one that could only be her cat, followed by a bark that more resembled thunder.

Great.

There was a dog—no, this wasn't a dog, it looked more like a bear—barking at one of the larger trees in the courtyard. Meagan ran to the tree and sure enough, Harry was halfway up, hissing like a trooper at the devil dog below.

"Dammit," she said under her breath. "Go. Shoo. Get out of here. Get the hell out of here, Cujo."

"Actually, his name's Tiny," a low Southern voice said from behind her, making her spine stiffen and her pulse accelerate.

"You've got to be kidding me," the blonde said as she turned around and saw Reed standing there. He grabbed ahold of his dog's leash, which was trailing behind him, and hooked it around his wrist.

"I'm sorry. He caught me by surprise. I wasn't expecting him to take off like that. He's harmless."

"Yeah, tell that to my cat," she said, looking up in the tree to where a black cat crouched, hissing at Tiny.

Reed laughed. "Ah, makes sense now. He saw something he liked." And Reed saw something he liked as well. This woman had curves that could make a man dizzy, and the thin cotton pants left little to his imagination on the way her hips gave way to her luscious ass. He had to keep himself from staring—and it was a hard task to do.

"Well, any possible way you could put him inside? I've got to try to get my cat down before he climbs up any higher." She tucked a piece of her blond hair behind her ears as she gave him an annoyed glance.

"Yeah, hold on and I'll help you." He jogged back to his apartment and let Tiny inside. Rescuing a cat out of a tree, now that's not how he saw the start of his Friday night going.

"I haven't seen you around. You just move in?" Reed asked as he jogged back to her. Her eyes traveled over him, and at first he thought she might be checking him out, which—he wasn't going to lie—turned him on, but then she lifted her gaze and sent him another annoyed look, her blond eyebrows creasing over her round eyes as she frowned.

"Yes. We just got here, as in, like, fifteen minutes ago, and I've already managed to lose my cat—this better not be a sign."

"A sign? Eh, if anything it's a good sign. You got to meet your next-door neighbor on the first night you were here, and it just so happens that this awesome new neighbor of yours is a pro at climbing trees." Reed slipped off his flip-flops and flashed her a megawatt smile that caused her golden cheeks to tint a shade of pink.

"That's good, I don't do heights and I was coming up short on ideas to get him down."

"You don't do heights? Ah, I think you just broke my heart a little bit there. . . . I'm sorry. What's your name?"

Those eyebrows of hers danced up again and those pretty blue eyes seemed to enjoy narrowing into a glare. "I'm Meagan," she said, although it might have been more like a hiss—he was new to the female species acting like this around him, so he couldn't be sure.

"So, Meagan, what do you have against heights?" he asked as he jumped up and grabbed onto the lowest branch so he was dangling from the tree in front of her.

Her eyes followed to where his hands gripped the branch. "Oh, pretty much everything. The way I feel like I'm going to throw up as I start getting higher, and then there is the big fear of falling to my death that gets me a little, oh, I don't know, terrified."

Reed let a low laugh escape from his chest before he swung his legs up and wrapped them around the branch, pulling himself into a sitting position. "See, everything you just explained right there—that's why I love it." He stood up and jumped to the neighboring branch. The second his feet left the tree an audible gasp left Meagan's mouth. He couldn't help but smirk at her sweet reaction. "Did I happen to mention that I'm a pro at climbing trees?"

"You might have mentioned that, yes. But you never mentioned that you were a complete lunatic. You could have missed that branch and fallen, or what if it didn't support your weight? Do you want me to have to witness a suicide on my first night here? Because that's what it would be, suicide!" she hollered up at him.

Reed reached up and grabbed onto the branch above him and pulled himself up. He was almost to the cat.

Smiling to himself and ignoring her little rant, he continued. "So, Meagan, what brings you to our nice little community here?"

"Small talk? Really? I'm kind of having a panic attack down here watching you. Think we can save the chitchat until you are back on the ground?"

Oh, he liked her. She was funny with just the right amount of sweet to make her sarcasm adorable.

"I'm a good multitasker too." He could hear the soft sigh curl from her lips and he could almost bet that an eye roll went right along with it.

"I moved here with my friend Eva. She's stationed at Benning. We just got here from Fort Drum."

Reed was just about there. He stepped his right foot over to the next branch and pushed himself up just enough until he could reach the cat. He slid his forearm under the cat, gaining more than a couple of puncture wounds as it dug its claws into his skin, and pressed it against his chest. Getting down was always much faster. He weaved his body in and out of the branches until he was low enough to hand the cat over to Meagan. She wrapped her hands around the cat and clutched him against her. Lucky bastard.

Reed jumped down from the tree and landed in front of Meagan. "So your friend's a soldier, huh?" he said, slipping his sandals back on.

"Yep."

"I am too. I'm the captain of Charlie Company 507th Parachute Regiment."

"Ah, airborne. That would explain the insane lack of fear of heights." Her smile extended a little more, but it didn't quite reach her eyes—not the way he was sure it could.

"What do you say you put that little guy up and come on over for a drink? I'm afraid all I've got is beer, though." There was something about her, something about that smile that had his mind working in overdrive. She intrigued him, that was for damn sure, and he wasn't ready to say good night.

"Beer's good, but I'm gonna pass. I've got lots of unpacking to do. Thanks for saving my cat." She smiled again, the corners of her pouty lips barely tilting upward, and started to walk away. He got the impression that she was blowing him off.

"All right. Well, it was nice to meet you," he hollered after her.

She stopped and turned back around. Her eyes looked over him again, like she was studying him, before she frowned. "It was nice . . . meeting you too."

Seriously? Reed Porter? Of all the people she could have possibly run into, she ran into him. And to top it off she looked like she had just walked out of the homeless shelter. Her yoga pants should have seen the rag pile more than a couple of washes ago and her hair was piled on top of her head in a massive case of truck-bed-head. Running into the sexy bad-boy charmer that she had her first one-night stand with years ago wasn't ideal. Oh, and he didn't even remember her! That was an ego-bruiser right there. Didn't say much for the impression she had left on him.

And of course he looked good. Better than before. Funny how age made men better. He'd had that boyish thing going for him back when she had met him before, but now he had the sex appeal of a man. His face had a five o'clock shadow and the angle of his jaw was a little sharper, but his dark hair had that same short cut, and his eyes were that same riveting color that couldn't decide if they wanted to be brown or green or gold. They were a little bit of all of the above. Light brown, ringed with green, and flecked with gold—beautiful. And his mouth. Dammit, if that wasn't the sexiest mouth she had ever seen on a man in her life. The sharp angle of his top lip made her want to bite it, and his bottom lip was slightly fuller than the top. That mouth sure knew how to lay on a smile too—and she was pretty sure he knew the effect that smile of his had. Damn, Reed Porter was her neighbor.

Meagan opened the patio door, walked in, and sat Harry down inside.

"I was just getting ready to come on the hunt with you," Eva said, rounding the corner from the hall that led to the bedrooms. "I snatched Weasley and locked him in the bathroom until we get done bringing our stuff in." She nodded toward the black fur ball that was now sniffing out every square inch of the living room. "I'm glad you found him."

"Yes, found and retrieved by our new neighbor," Meagan said, plopping down on the empty living room floor.

"You met one of our neighbors already?" Eva asked, taking a seat on the floor across from her.

"Yep, our next-door neighbor, but I've met him before. Actually, I've more than met him."

"Okay, you're going to need to explain a little better than that."

"His name is Reed Porter, and I met him the night he graduated Officer Basic Leader Course when I was at Fort Leonard Wood with my dad, gosh, almost eight years ago."

Eva pulled her hair back with her hands and wrapped her long curls into a ponytail, pulling the mass of red hair out of her face. "And I'm guessing by the way your face is turning into a cheesy grin right now that you did more than just meet him?"

"Yes, he flirted his way into my bed. Well, actually, he flirted his way into his motel bed with me in tow." Meagan huffed out a breath through her mouth and tilted her head toward the ceiling for a moment before looking back at Eva. "We had a one-night stand, a really good one-night stand."

Eva laughed. "How perfect is this? You already have a booty-call and we haven't even been here an hour—bonus that he lives next door. What did he say when he saw you?"

"Oh, that's the kicker. He didn't remember me."

Eva's face fell and her eyes bugged out of her head. "You're fucking kidding me."

"I wish I was, my friend. He even checked me out like I was a new piece of meat. And get this, he invited me back to his apartment for a drink."

"And you didn't tell him who you are?"

"What was I supposed to say? 'Hi, remember me? You fucked my brains out eight years ago in your motel room.' No, it's embarrassing enough that he doesn't remember me. I don't need to feed the humiliation fire by adding his own embarrassment to it."

"Good point. So what's the game plan? Revenge sex? Best friend revenge sex?"

Meagan laughed. Leave it to Eva to start scheming. "No, I'm not plotting anything."

"You're no fun. Come on, let's at least torture him a little. You need to get him all hot and bothered again and then shut him down. You said he was checking you out. Play with him a little. Give me some fun."

"You're cruel—you know that?"

"Guilty. But seriously, you need to tease him until his memory comes back in full swing."

"That's not really my style, Eva."

"I know, but it's my style and I need to live vicariously through you. Will you just think about it?"

"Yes, in an attempt to shut you up I will agree to think about it. But don't hold your breath. And on a serious note, what the hell are we going to sleep on while we wait for our stuff to get here?"

Eva pulled her legs underneath her and stood up. "I have air mattresses in the truck. I'll go get them," she said, walking to the patio door.

Meagan quickly got up and followed her. "I'll come with you. And this time, don't let the cat out."

CHAPTER THREE

Reed hadn't seen his sexy new neighbor around the apartments all week and it wasn't for lack of trying. She had lit a fire under him. There was something about her and he couldn't quite put his finger on it, but there was just . . . something. Like a word on the tip of your tongue. Like an itch you can't scratch, but you needed to so damn bad. That was what the small amount of time he spent with Meagan the other night had done to him, given him an itch. She had crawled under his skin when she gave him those narrow-eyed stares that were challenging him in a way she couldn't possibly even know. She didn't seem like a woman who liked to play cat-and-mouse games, and it wasn't his thing either. He liked a challenge, there was no doubt about that—but he didn't do the chase. However, he just might be willing to chase after Meagan—if she would let him catch her—and as of right now, that hadn't yet been determined.

It was the final day of Jump Week, the last time his soldiers would jump before they graduated Airborne School. He loved jumping out of a C-130 aircraft at twelve hundred feet in the air, feeling the rush of the fall before landing, and he loved jumping with his soldiers. The fun part was the first jump. He loved listening to the other jumpmasters tell their horror stories—trying their damndest to put the fear of God in each and every one of the jumpers, especially the young, cocky sergeants who thought they had something to prove. The instructors would tell stories of how they broke legs or how they thought they pissed themselves. He got a morbid thrill out of watching his instructors scare the shit out of the soldiers as they went around, checking off each soldier on their Kevlar with chalk once their equipment was cleared, giving them hell. Fuck, they all had to go through it, it was fun to dish it back out. It was tradition.

The last jump was his favorite, though. The first-jump jitters were all but gone, and the thrill of the fall vibrated through every soldiers' bones as the plane took off from the ground. By jump five the men knew what to expect—that small ounce of fear still lit up behind their eyes, but at that point the men got to enjoy it for what it was.

Reed also enjoyed watching his jumpmasters in action. It gave him a sense of pride watching the noncommissioned officers of his company do their job. Reed wasn't your typical company commander—he didn't just sit back in an office somewhere running the groundwork behind the scenes, wishing like hell he was out with his men. No, he made sure to be with his men. He made sure to form those relationships with the soldiers who were there for school. He made sure that they knew just who the hell their CO was.

The plane had just taken off and Reed's eyes circumnavigated around him, taking in all the soldiers who were sitting, waiting to reach the drop zone to jump for the last time before their wings were pinned.

"You still getting that cabin this weekend for the Fourth?" one of Reed's first sergeants, Murano, asked as they stood at the back of the plane.

"Yeah, I've got it Sunday and Monday night. I took a four-day pass. You still comin'?"

"Yeah, unless Bridgette comes to town."

"Really, man? You're still hung up on her? Life is too fucking short, move on. You're acting like a whiney-ass girl."

"You say that because you've never had anyone stick around long enough to care about. I'm tellin' you, you find that one and she leaves you high and dry—you'll be crawling back to her every chance she gives you too. No fucking lie." Murano stepped forward. "Two minutes!" he shouted through the plane, and the words ricocheted back to him as the soldiers repeated it.

The large door at the back of the plane opened up, and Murano hooked into the plane and leaned out to check for the drop zone and to ensure there was nothing on the aircraft that would cut the static line when the soldiers jumped. This was all true, but he also did it to show off in front of the soldiers.

"We all good?" Reed asked as Murano pulled himself back into the plane.

"Yep."

"Good."

"Stand up!" Murano shouted over the sound of rushing air that now filled the plane.

The soldiers all stood and faced the rear of the plane.

"All right, hook up!"

Everyone took the static lines that were attached to their parachutes and hooked them up to the retention wire above their heads, including Reed, who, since he was the company commander, was always the first one out of the aircraft. Each soldier checked his equipment, then did the same to the guy in front of him—checking reserve chutes and Kevlar.

"Thirty seconds!"

Reed looked back and drank in the moment like he did before every jump. Everyone's adrenaline was pumping—the feeling of knowing that you were about to do something completely crazy, but knowing it was completely worth it, was humming through their minds. It was the best fucking feeling, and seeing it across every single soldier's face as they stood waiting like little kids ready to tear open their birthday presents never got old.

The green light turned on and a wicked smile pulled on Reed's lips. "See you on the ground, Murano," he said, right before his NCO shouted, "GO, GO, GO." Then Reed was soaring through the air.

Reed pressed his feet and knees together as he rolled his head to his chest. The warm air that pricked against Reed's face was soothing and comforting as he counted, *one thousand, two thousand, three thousand, four,* to the sound of the static line pulling his chute open.

Reed looked up and checked his chute. All was good—it was open, and he was able to enjoy the twenty-second ride back to the ground. He looked around, deciding the direction of the wind and looking for the smoke pits that indicated the drop zone. Unfortunately, there was never a soft landing, but Reed knew how to anticipate the vibrations that ricocheted through his body from the impact—it was that good kind of hurt, that addictive pain.

Reed landed on the ground and rolled to a stop and within seconds was packing up his chute.

"Hey, CO!"

Reed turned his head toward the smoke pit to his left where a big silver truck was parked. Standing next to it was a cocky, arrogant jumpmaster who just so happened to be Reed's best friend. He gathered his bag into his hands and jogged toward the truck.

"Hey, Sanders," he said after he threw his bag and Kevlar in the bed of the truck. "Weren't you supposed to be with the next plane?"

"Nah, not today, I'm on ground duty, and I come bearing gifts." Sanders tossed Reed a Monster. Fuck, getting up at 3:30 in the morning on jump days, he needed something a hell of a lot stronger than an energy drink, but he wasn't going to complain.

"Thanks," he said, popping the tab and taking a couple of swigs.

"Fuck, we got a cigarette roll," Sanders said.

Reed snapped around and sure as shit one of his soldiers' chutes hadn't opened. He absentmindedly held his breath. His body straightened and his hands clenched and unclenched at his sides.

Reed could see the soldier kicking his legs like he was

running in the air, just like he was supposed to, as he spun around and around. A lot of times the chute would catch wind and open up, and Reed prayed like hell it would, but as the soldier got closer and closer to the ground, it wouldn't matter anyway.

"Fuck, pull your reserve," Reed said out loud.

"He's gonna hit hard, Porter." Sanders reached in through the window of the truck and grabbed the handheld radio. God, Reed hoped like hell they wouldn't have to use it.

"Dammit, pull your reserve!" Reed yelled, knowing good and well the soldier couldn't hear him, but the need to do something, anything, to help the guy out was clawing at him.

Just as the soldier was reaching the top of the trees, his reserve chute shot up—but it wouldn't do much to soften the land.

Reed and Sanders both sucked in a breath in unison, cringing as they watched the soldier hit the ground.

"Oh, fuck," Sanders said as he released the breath he was holding.

They both stood there for what seemed like forever when in fact it was no more than a second or two, waiting for the soldier to hit his knees, to give the "All okay, jumpmaster." But he didn't.

"Let's go!" Reed said, jumping in the truck. Sanders tossed him the radio and then hopped in behind the wheel.

"We need a medic on-site, now. Soldier's chute didn't open; reserve was pulled at about two hundred feet. We are on our way to him now, about one hundred and forty yards out," Reed said into the radio. His words were calm, even, and completely in control—the complete opposite of what he was feeling inside, but he was the company commander; it was his job to stay in control.

The truck pulled up next to the solider and Reed was out of the cab before it rolled to a complete stop. There was blood covering the guy's pants across his thigh and Reed didn't need to cut through them to know that he'd broken his femur. The way his leg was bulging through the material and the way the fabric was stained crimson was evidence enough.

"Hey, Sergeant," Reed said, the level of his voice lowered to a tone you would use to sooth a child. "You'll be fine, my man, we gotcha."

The young soldier was in shock, his screams turning into moans, but there was nothing Reed could do but wait for the medics to pull up.

*I*t was Meagan's second day working in the emergency room at the Martin Army Community Hospital on post. She was lucky to even have this job. She didn't know what the hell she was thinking when she up and quit her job at Fort Drum to move here. Sure, she'd wanted a change of scenery, but it was kind of reckless. Thankfully they hired her on and she was able to start immediately. She loved being a nurse, and working in the ER was going to be a nice change from the clinic back at Drum. She was just *rolling* in the changes these days.

"So, Meagan, how's your second day treating you?" Zoe, a tall, voluptuous brunette with legs that went all the way up to her eyeballs, asked as she leaned against the nurses' station.

"It's going really well."

"Yeah, the staff showing you the ropes okay?" An extremely tall, dark, and handsome doctor said as he walked up and leaned against the desk next to Zoe. Okay, so if this were an episode of *Grey's Anatomy* she would have most definitely been staring at McSteamy or McDreamy—she never remembered which one was which—but it didn't matter because this doctor was all of the above. He was tall and lean, but what she could see of his arms gave her a clear idea of how chiseled his body was underneath his ACU pants and his scrub top and let's just say she was fighting back the heat that was threatening to rise in her cheeks.

"Yeah, they've been great."

"Good. I'm Dr. Ryan, by the way," he said, reaching out his hand to Meagan. "But please, call me Jason."

Well, damn, the blushing came. "Hi, Jason, I'm Meagan," she said, smiling like the band nerd who just got asked to prom by the star quarterback.

Somewhere in the midst of the ten seconds of the Mc-Dreamy introduction, Meagan missed the phone ringing at the nurses' station. It wasn't until Zoe rushed around the desk and stopped in front of them that she registered it. "We've got a soldier coming in with a broken femur." Dr. Ryan instantly dropped Meagan's hand and they both turned to Zoe as she continued. "Airborne student, his chute didn't open and his reserve went up at tree level. He has a lot of blood loss. The medics gave him morphine."

They were all rushing to the ER doors, and it took Meagan a second to realize it. She was so caught up in the moment that she was unaware her feet were even moving.

"Zoe, call OR and have them prep room one."

Not even a moment later, the ER doors were opening and two medics were pushing a now unconscious soldier into the hospital—and behind them was Reed.

The medics started talking to Dr. Ryan as they set up the soldier in one of the empty ER rooms. Another doctor and another nurse came to assist Dr. Ryan, and Meagan stepped out of the room to where Reed was pacing the hall.

"Hey," she said calmly, placing her hand on the back of his shoulder. The soft touch of her fingers startled him and he spun around to face her.

"Meagan, hi," he said, almost surprised. "I didn't know you worked here."

"It's only my second shift," she replied, but it was like she was talking to a wall. He wasn't paying attention to her. Sure, his eyes were looking at her, but it was as if none of the words that she said reached his ears. His head was elsewhere at that moment.

"Reed . . . ," she said again when he picked back up his task of wearing down the hall floors.

"Is he going to be okay?"

"The doctor is taking him up to surgery as soon as the OR is ready. We'll take good care of him, I promise."

He stopped back in front of her and shoved his hands down into the pockets of his ACU pants as he threw his head back. "Fuck, surgery? I need to call his parents."

He lowered his head and his eyes landed directly on

Meagan's, which hadn't left him since he stopped moving.
"Can I see him real quick?"

"Reed, you know you can't—"

"Captain Porter?"

Reed looked to the side of Meagan as Dr. Ryan spoke
from behind her.

"Yes?"

"We're taking Sergeant Brewer to the OR now. We will
contact your battalion when he's out of surgery."

"Thank you, sir."

Dr. Ryan turned and headed back down the hall. There
was nothing that Reed could do other than wait. She was
actually surprised that he came with the medics at all. It
wasn't typical for the company commander to ride in an am-
bulance with an injured soldier—but she had a tugging in-
kling in the back of her mind that he was anything but
typical. He might have lost a handful of brownie points when
he didn't recognize her, but she tossed a couple back. He
cared about his soldier, he was worried, and the sight of this
sexy, strong man going out of his way for his soldier earned
him a few gold stars in her book.

"Look, Meg. . . ." Her nickname coming out of his mouth
reminded her of Trevor, instantly flipping her switch and pissing her off. It was genuine, sweet almost, which made it worse,
because he didn't even remember her. Her friends called her
Meg; the people she was close to called her Meg. Neither one
of those things described the man in front of her.

His expression flinched and Meagan realized that her
face was now twisted into a scowl. He was worried. One of

his men was about to be taken to surgery. He was putting up a facade, but she knew better—she could see through it. She forced herself to be Nurse Meagan, not the ego-bruised Meagan he took home from a bar eight years ago. Her face softened and she smiled.

Relief rolled through his shoulders as he cracked a smile. Not a full one, but a relieved one, and of course it had to make her want to do the whole swoon-and-sigh thing. "Would you do me a favor? Would you just keep me updated throughout the surgery? I've got to get back, I have my company's graduation tomorrow to get ready for, but I can be back here in five minutes if you need me. Please?"

Dammit. She was hoping that she would find out that Reed Porter was some grade-A asshole who would make her want to avoid him at every turn, especially given the case of memory loss he was apparently privy to having—but it wasn't looking like that was going to happen.

"I'm sorry. I won't be able to give you specific updates, but we will make sure to contact your battalion as soon as he's out of surgery."

The depth of anguish that folded over his face sent her heart into her stomach. This man was truly concerned for his soldier, and there was nothing she could do to ease his worry—and even with the loud warning sirens blaring in her mind, she hated seeing him like this.

She internally sighed and pulled out her phone. She wanted to pout and hold a grudge against him, but dammit, he was making it difficult. "What's your number? I will call you directly and let you know when he is out of surgery, but that's the best I can do."

A grateful flash skimmed over his eyes. Yes, he was making this grudge thing extremely hard.

He reached forward and slipped the phone from her hand. His fingers made contact with hers, and she cringed inwardly at her schoolgirl reaction, that giddy flutter that pricks in your chest for half a second. Not long enough to get worked up about, but long enough to notice.

"There," he said, placing the phone back in her hand. "I texted my phone, so now I have your number too." He smiled, and it was one that was attempting to be real, but an emotion that was embedded in the creases of his eyes weighed down the small tilt of his lips. Was it fear, or sorrow? Maybe a little bit of both, and whatever it was, Meagan instantly wanted to take it away. She wanted to wrap her arms around this man that she didn't know anything about and hold him against her.

"Okay," she replied, not really knowing what else to say at that moment.

"Thanks," he said, and then he turned around and left.

Meagan made her way back toward the nurses' station. She looked at the clock. She'd been there for four hours already. She had forgotten how quickly time could pass with an ER full of patients. The health clinic she had worked at on post at Fort Drum wasn't exactly a hustle-and-bustle environment.

She knocked on the slightly ajar door to one of her patients' rooms before she pushed it the rest of the way open. A woman in ACUs, probably around Meagan's age, was sitting on the hospital bed, her tan boots kicked up and crossed at the ankles as she cradled a sleeping toddler in her arms.

His little face was flushed and blotchy from apparent crying. His head was full of tight little curls, and his tiny bare feet were dangling over his mom's lap. His Thomas the Tank Engine sandals were on the floor next to the bed, along with a blue blanket that looked like it had been dragged through space and back, washed, and repeated about a million times.

Meagan smiled as she eyed the blanket; she'd had one of those growing up too. The stinkier and dirtier, the better.

"Would you mind handing me that scrap of disgusting fabric before he wakes up and has a meltdown?" the woman whispered. Her body was frozen like she was afraid to even breathe, afraid that he would wake up.

"Sure," Meagan whispered back, picking up the blanket and handing it to her. She tucked it up next to his cheek and his little face instantly nestled into it.

"I just want to make sure Braden's temp has gone down." Meagan was instantly grateful to whoever invented those handy little forehead thermometers. She didn't want the little man to wake up either. She had been the one to get his temp when he first arrived to the ER screaming in agony—it was 105. She had almost started crying for him too, he had to have been miserable.

"Looks like the Motrin has kicked in. 99.2."

The woman kissed the top of her son's head. "Thank God. I don't know how it spiked so quickly like that. He seemed fine this morning, other than that constant runny nose of his. When the daycare called me, his temp was 101.

By the time I got there not even thirty minutes later it was 104." She sighed and Meagan could see the apparent fear in her eyes.

She gave the woman a reassuring smile. "The doctor will be in here shortly to talk to you about his meds for his ear infections, but it won't be long, and then we can get you two outta here. He will be back up, bouncing off the walls and driving you crazy, in no time flat."

"Ha, ain't that the truth." She smirked.

Meagan smiled and gently ran her hand over the top of his blond ringlets. "Enjoy his cuddle moments. Even though it stinks when they are sick, they always cuddle better when they don't feel well."

She gave a knowing nod. "How old are your spawn?"

"Oh, I don't have any children yet." Meagan wrote his temperature on the patient chart. For some reason she was afraid to meet the woman's eyes. Which was stupid, she knew that. But her question just added to the nagging in her ear.

"Well, for the record, he likes to color on my walls and poop in the bathtub while I happen to be in there with him, he tries to eat dirt, and at the ripe age of three, has managed to destroy every piece of furniture in my house, so even though I hate it when my baby doesn't feel well—I definitely cherish these snuggle-bug moments. Drool and all." She snickered, looking down at her chest, which had a nice wet spot right under little Braden's mouth.

Meagan laughed quietly, attempting to keep from waking him. Lord knew his mom needed a few more minutes of quiet after the wave of panic she went through when her son had a dangerously high fever. And sleeping it off was the best thing for him too.

Meagan's eyes shifted from the little boy to his mom, and she was just staring at Meagan with a smile on her face.

"Oh, just you wait till you have kids. You'll see. They only look sweet when they sleep," she teased, kissing his head again.

Meagan made sure they didn't need anything else before she headed to check on her next patient.

"Back again?" the soldier asked when he looked up from his phone to acknowledge Meagan as she walked in his room.

"Yes, I know. I'm a pain in the butt, but I just wanted to check in on you again real quick. How's the hand?"

"It's starting to throb again, but I've had worse."

Meagan shook her head. Men and their pride. Scratch that—*soldiers* and their pride. He probably wouldn't tell her if it felt like it was about to fall off. "All right, tough guy. I'll be back to check on you *again* and I promise the doctor will be in here as soon as possible to go over your X-rays."

He just nodded and looked back at his phone. If he wasn't in pain, she might have told him to shove that phone in his ass. She just might check in on him a few more times, just to push his buttons.

The rest of Meagan's shift went by even more quickly. She made sure to keep tabs on Reed's soldier during his surgery, and she kept her word and called him as soon as he got out. The surgery went well, thank God, and now Sergeant Brewer was recovering in the medical surgical unit.

Meagan leaned over the nurses' station and whispered to Zoe, who was on the phone. "I'll see you tomorrow."

She nodded and smiled her reply and Meagan made her way to the elevators to head on up to the med surg unit. She wanted to check on Sergeant Brewer one last time before she left. She had popped in a few times after he was out of surgery, and he was sleeping like a baby—well, more like a heavily drugged oversize baby. He was a good-looking guy, shaved head, long lashes that brushed the tops of his cheeks as he slept, and from what little she could tell from the hospital gown he was wearing, he wasn't lacking points in the build department either. But something about this guy triggered the motherly, sisterly, whateverly instinct that was coiled up inside her to come out, more so than usual. Meagan was always the friend who took care of everyone when they were sick, or, hell, just drunk or hungover—and that definitely carried over to her job, but for some unknown reason, Meagan had a pull to this guy that made her instinct kick into overdrive. She just needed to make sure he was okay. For no other reason than she just needed to know.

She walked down the hall and stopped outside his door. There was laughter coming from inside the room and it instantly made her cheeks tighten into a grin. He was awake, and from the sounds of it, he was enjoying his medical cocktail.

"Knock, knock," Meagan said as she opened up the door. Two sets of eyes turned her way, and one of those sets happened to involuntarily make her insides turn to a quivering mess.

Reed's mouth fell open. "Well, how in the hell did you get so lucky to have this beautiful woman come visit you?"

The not so coherent soldier rolled his head to the side as he lay back on his pillow and looked Meagan's way. "Hell if I know, are you sure I haven't died and gone to heaven?"

Reed shook his head and laughed. "Really, Brewer? That's the best you got? Come on now, a sexy blond nurse just walked into your room. . . . Give her something better than that."

His eyes glinted wickedly as if Reed had just thrown out the challenge of a lifetime, and Meagan was the prize. She pressed her lips together to keep from laughing at Brewer, who was high as a kite. She lifted her hands to her hips and waited for the punches to start rolling.

"If I had a nickel for every time I saw someone as beautiful as you, I'd have five cents."

She shook her head back and forth but was unable to keep the smirk from appearing on her face. "Surely you can do better than that," Meagan said, walking farther into the room and setting her purse down in the chair next to the bed.

He shifted his upper body slightly and his face twisted tightly as he fell back onto the pillows again. "I don't know," he huffed, struggling to even speak. "I'm in a lot of pain right now."

Her face dropped and she glanced back at the door. "Do you want me to go grab your nurse? What can I do?"

"I'm not sure, I think there's something wrong with my eyes."

Meagan frowned. "Your eyes?"

A slow, deliberate smile pulled across Brewer's cheeks

and she knew she had just fallen right into his trap. "Yeah, because I can't seem to take them off of you."

"If you weren't so drugged up and injured right now I would hit you."

Reed couldn't stop laughing.

"Really, you think that one was funny?"

"Hell no, but it's funny you fell for it. I knew where he was going the second he said he was in pain. Good one, my man."

"Hey, nurse," Brewer slurred.

Meagan rolled her eyes at Reed before turning back to Brewer. "My name's Meagan."

"My beautiful nurse Meagan, can I use your phone?"

Meagan reached for her purse and pulled out her phone. "Um, sure."

"Thanks. My mom told me to call her when I found the woman of my dreams."

She snatched the phone back out of his hands and rolled her eyes. Reed reached around Meagan and fist-bumped Brewer. Seriously? Did grown men actually still do that? "Did you really just fist-bump over a pickup line? You two are something else."

"And you can do better?"

She arched her eyebrow, meeting Reed's playful eyes with her own challenging stare. "I'm here, aren't I? Now, you've got two wishes left."

"I do believe we've met our match," Brewer said, his words slurring even more.

She looked back over at Brewer, who was starting to slip into dreamland. "Did he just get a round of meds?"

"Yeah, about five minutes before you came in. Looks like they're starting to kick in."

"Yeah, looks like—"

Her words were cut short as Reed moved closer, invading the immediate space that encircled her. She was now surrounded by him and the look in his eyes was lacking all the playfulness that had been there moments ago. His jaw was set tight, and he hovered over her, his tall body framing her as he stood so close they were touching, save a thin slice of air between them. His hand reached up and brushed away the strands of hair that had fallen loose around her face. His fingertips were rough, callused, but his touch was so light that it caused tingles to erupt all over her scalp.

He squinted his eyes and tilted his head to the side as if he was studying her. Holy hell, did he remember her? Meagan's palms clammed up and she took a few quick breaths to try and steady her damn body, which was acting on its own accord. "Hey, hold still, sugar," he said, moving his hand to cup her face. His accent rumbled through her ears and sent shivers across her skin. "I think you've got something in your eye," he said, so low it was more of a whisper. The rough pad of his thumb traced the thin skin underneath her left eye as he leaned in closer to her, his warm breath now bouncing between them—and damn it if her mind didn't wander back to the way his lips had felt moving over hers that night that seemed like a lifetime ago. And damn it if she didn't want to feel them again at that very moment.

His hand left her face and dropped back to his side. "Nope, just a sparkle." His mouth twisted, and beautiful as it was, it caused Meagan's eyes to almost completely disappear behind her lids.

The back of her palm connected with a thud against his chest. "Smooth, real smooth," she mocked, taking a step back in the hopes of regaining her composure.

"I know." That's all he said. No, "Yeah, I know, I'm good," or "I got this," or whatever else cocky and annoying things men like to say. Nope, just "I know." Simple as that. And that alone was in fact smooth.

Meagan leaned over and picked her purse up off the chair. "I think it's safe to say that you have won this round. But let it be known that I don't give up that easily, and I'm pretty good with the comebacks."

"Is that so?"

"Yes. And since our friend here has hit the snooze button, I'm gonna head home." She smiled and turned to walk out the door, but he called out her name, and she turned back around to face him. When she looked at him again, she saw something she couldn't quite put her finger on—it was like she was seeing layers lifting around his eyes, and this particular one was solemn.

"Thanks for checking in on him. He's gonna be on his own the next couple weeks until he can get back to Fort Carson."

"It's no problem, I kinda like the guy."

"Uh-oh, should I be threatened?"

Meagan rolled her eyes. His flirty, playful banter was back up and running—it was cute, and it reminded her exactly why she got sucked in so easily eight years ago. "Bye, Reed, see ya around."

"Meagan," Brewer mumbled from his bed, apparently drifting in and out of sleep.

"Yeah?"

"You forgot something."

"What?"

"Me."

She and Reed laughed in unison. "Go to sleep, Brewer."

And he didn't reply, because he already had.

CHAPTER FOUR

Meagan turned on the shower and waited for the water to heat up as she stripped out of her clothes. The day had taken an unexpected turn. Seeing Reed at the hospital was—a surprise. And the way he was with his soldier was adorable. It was like there was no sign of the company commander in him, just a buddy coming to see a buddy. She could imagine all of his men liked him and respected him for how involved he was with them. He was so relatable—not stuck-up on some high horse with a rank power complex. No, he treated his soldier just like any other guy, and she admired that about him. Meagan had lived around soldiers her entire life; hell, she had been raised by a soldier, so she knew a thing or two about a good leader when she saw one, and Reed—he was one of the good ones, but in a way like no other. He was so different. Whereas Kale took no shit and had a balls-to-the-wall mentality with his men, Reed seemed more laid-back, more compassionate, and more patient. And it didn't surprise her in the least. He was a big goofball wrapped up in a sexy package of solid masculine authority. His silliness was what had attracted her to him—well, along with the fact that his entire body seemed to send shivers down her spine every time he came in close proximity of her. But when she pushed that silliness aside there was an intensity to him that she couldn't escape. It roped her in and tied her in knots, leaving her to wonder—what was shifting underneath all that carefree playfulness that wanted to claw its way to the surface? What layers of Reed had she yet to see?

"Hey, Meggy?" Eva said, knocking on the bathroom door.

Meagan cracked the door open and peeked her head out. "Yeah?"

"I'm going to the gym. I'll be back in a little bit."

"All righty, see you later," Meagan said before she shut the door.

She turned on her iPod, setting it down on the counter, and stepped into the shower, singing as she stood there, letting the water run over her. There was something about taking a shower at night that made everything better. Her mom always said it was washing the day away—not that she had a bad day to wash away, but old habits die hard. Meagan closed her eyes, enjoying the light spray of the shower hitting her skin. Her limbs instantly loosened and her muscles went slack, the blood slowing in her veins as she relaxed—maybe she should have taken a bath instead.

"Um, Meagan?" a deep voice said from the other room. Outside her bedroom maybe? The hall?

Crap.

Meagan stopped humming and froze. The warm water

did nothing against the chill that suddenly slid down her spine. She just stood there for a moment, listening.

After a few erratic heartbeats, Meagan turned off the water and grabbed the towel from the hook on the wall, wrapping it around her as she quickly went to the bathroom door and opened it just a crack. She heard someone, didn't she? And she was pretty sure it sounded a lot like Reed. Oh gosh, if her imagination was starting to hear his voice when she wasn't asleep—yes, she had dreamed about him. . . once. Dammit, twice. But he was just so damn sexy, and unfortunately, every time she closed her eyes since she had seen him again that first night, her mind—conscious or not—automatically went to him as she remembered the way his stomach and his thighs looked without clothes on. . . .

"Hello?" she called out, stepping into her bedroom. She didn't see anyone—or hear anyone, for that matter. Great, she really was imagining it. She needed to get laid, this finding-Mr.-Safe thing was starting to mess with her. If she didn't find Mr. Safe soon, she was going to have to invest in a new Mr. Dildo.

She pulled the towel tighter around her as it started slipping down her breasts and walked into the hall that led to the living room and kitchen. Still no one. See, if this were a horror film she would be Dumb Blonde Number One, going to investigate a voice she heard in the other room while she was showering in her empty apartment. *Smart, Meagan. Real smart*, she said to herself as she padded barefoot and wet down the hall.

When she stepped into the living room, her feet automatically shuffled a few steps back and she damn near dropped her towel. Luckily, all the muscles in her body seemed to go on high alert, stiffening like stone, including the muscles of her fingers that were now wrapped around the towel in a death grip. Reed was standing with his back to her, leaning over the kitchen counter. He was wearing a pair of black gym shorts that hung down past his knees and a light gray cutoff army PT shirt. And of course he had to look amazing in it.

After the shock of seeing him standing in her kitchen diminished, she cleared her throat. "Reed?" she asked, the sound of her voice causing him to spin around to face her. She clutched onto the towel that separated her naked body from Reed's stare, which was now locked on her like he had on X-ray vision goggles—and dammit, it was hot.

"Hey, Meagan." His eyes shifted over her and he dropped his arms to his side and licked his lips. Whether or not he did it knowingly, she didn't know, but the slow, subtle movement had Meagan's thighs pressing together. He might not remember her, but she sure as hell remembered him—especially her body. It was like the memory of him hovering over her left a physical imprint on her skin, and it was walking the line with torture. No matter how many sexy looks he sent her, or how many times that tongue of his reached out and swiped across his perfect lips, she was not going to go there again. He was Mr. Safe's arch nemesis—her plan's arch nemesis. He was anything but safe; she already knew that.

When she didn't say anything, he continued. "Sorry. I didn't realize you were taking a shower. I was just writing you a note. I passed your roommate in the hall and she told me you were home and to walk on in. I'm sorry." His eyes squinted slightly, garnished with a flash of mischief. Yeah, his words might have said he was sorry, but the slight pull to the corners of his mouth paired with the intensity in his eyes said that he was anything but. The asshole was amused.

Meagan was sure her face was about ten different shades of red at that very moment. She had no doubt in her mind that Eva had given him the go-ahead to come in the apartment. The little tramp was plotting something, Meagan just knew it, and when Eva had something up her sleeve it never ended well.

Meagan didn't respond; she just looked at him, puzzled.

Reed smiled, that damn mouth of his perfectly crafted into what was now a cocky smirk that made Meagan want to shake her head in exasperation, yet at the same time it made her want to drop her towel and give him something to smirk about—but she wasn't that ballsy.

Reed reached around the counter and lifted a large brown paper bag. "You like Mexican food?"

He had brought Mexican food? Okay, first off, major brownie points scored right there, Mexican food was her favorite. And second, he was surprising her with dinner? Hmm.

"It just so happens that I love Mexican food." She started walking toward him, curious to see how much more this guy could get right. "What'd ya bring me?"

Reed's eyes were unashamed, slowly traveling down the length of her body as she got closer to him. She tightened her hold on the towel that was wrapped around her; it just barely closed completely. If she took too long strides, he wouldn't need any X-ray vision.

She watched as his eyes, which seemed to be more liquid gold than brown at the moment, returned to hers. He swallowed a few times and wet his lips again. She was affecting him—she could tell, and she liked it. It gave her a sense of power that suddenly made her want to strut around the whole damn apartment in nothing more than the towel, just so his eyes could continue to warm her body from the inside out, just like they were at that very moment—but again, not that ballsy.

"Well, I didn't know what you liked, so I hoped for the best and bought the basics and my favorites. We got your chicken fajita quesadilla, a couple supreme tacos, and my personal favorite, the loaded loco burrito. I've got enough queso here to last us until next week and"—he walked around the counter and picked up a milk jug filled with a lime-colored liquid—"margaritas."

Meagan scrunched her nose at the jug in his hands and his persona instantly shifted. The intensity was gone, and his playfulness was back in full swing, and although Meagan was relieved to know that her body might stand a chance at being in the same room with him without feeling the need to take a walk down memory lane, she was also slightly disappointed. She shouldn't, but she liked the way he was looking at her moments ago. It'd been a while since a man looked at her like she was his favorite dessert.

"What? You don't like margaritas?" he asked when he

saw her face contort into a disgusted scowl. He looked slightly wounded, like his puppy had just died or something, and Meagan couldn't help but laugh.

"Oh no, I love margaritas, but I'm really picky. I'm a tough critic when it comes to my margaritas, and that jug of juice you've got there, my friend, does *not* seem appealing."

"Okay, well, I was going to let you finish your shower in peace and leave this nice food here for you to enjoy by yourself"—he grabbed the note he was writing off the counter and raised it for her to see. Sure enough, it said he was going to leave the food and head home since she was in the shower—"but now I want you to get your cute ass in there and change, because, quite frankly, you're very distracting in that towel, and then come back in here and I will wow you with my margarita-making abilities."

Cute ass? Distracting?

She smiled at him, an unexpected flutter pattering against her stomach, and turned on her heels knowing good and well she shouldn't. She should just tell him to leave and go finish her shower—but she caved. "On the rocks with lots of salt," she said over her shoulder before she picked up the pace and trotted down the hall to her room.

*W*ell, fuck. He didn't expect her to be in the shower when he walked into her house. And he sure as hell didn't expect her to come walking out of the hall looking surprised with her big, round eyes, her blond hair clinging to the side of her face and neck, and her body dripping wet from head to toe—but it was a sight he wouldn't mind seeing again.

He had wanted to surprise her—to thank her. He knew good and well that she shouldn't have called him after Brewer's surgery, and he definitely didn't expect to see her check up on him after her shift. She was going out of her way for him, and for his soldier, and that said a hell of a lot about her. Brewer didn't have anyone here, and a pretty face like Meagan checking in on him every now and again would be good for the kid—keep his spirits up.

"I hope you don't mind sitting on the floor, our stuff hasn't gotten here yet," Meagan said as she returned to the kitchen. She had her hair wrapped up in a towel, which was unusually adorable, and she was wearing a pair of shorts that put Daisy Duke's to shame, paired with a snug-fit plain black tank top.

There was still something about her that had his head swimming. His body responded to her, but hell, he was a man, he didn't think it was possible for any man to be near her without their dick getting a little rise from the way she looked when she scrunched her nose or twirled the tuft of hair at the nape of her neck. This woman was oozing with sex appeal that she didn't even realize she had. She was sweet, but in the way that made him feel like she could be anything but sweet, given the right opportunity, and he would most definitely like to give her that opportunity.

His mouth became moist, his lips parting slightly as he allowed himself to toy with the thoughts that entered his mind as his eyes traveled over her dulcet body again. She fidgeted with her fingernails and shifted her weight from side to side, waiting for his response—but he was enjoying taking the time to breathe her in, watching as she grew eager. "Nah, I don't mind at all," he finally said, deciding to put the poor woman out of her misery.

She threw a couple of pillows down on the floor. "Good."

"All right, I need you to taste this for me," he said, handing her a red Solo cup filled with his margarita. "And when you're done tasting it, you can give me a big fat thank-you followed by the words 'Reed, you're the best.'"

Meagan laughed. "Is that so?"

Cracking a smile, he nodded. "Yes. Now try it."

Her tongue flicked out and skimmed across a small section of the Solo cup, lapping up the salt before she pressed the rim of the cup to her lips and took a sip. Which was sexy as hell, and he was sure she didn't have a damn clue.

The instant she pulled the cup away, a smile broke out across her face. She was trying desperately not to, but it was a lost cause. Her full lips parted and her white teeth went on display as her lips turned up in a smile that reached all the way to her eyes. "Dammit, Reed," she said, shaking her head, apparently surprised, and sighed. "You're the best."

Reed clasped his hands together. "Ah, I knew you would love it. No woman can resist my margaritas."

She cocked her head to the side and lifted her blond eyebrows. "Oh, is that so?"

He looked at her and stumbled over his words. Fuck, that didn't sound good. He opened his mouth to say something—what, he wasn't exactly sure. He just knew women were sensitive about that shit and he needed to try to divert the situation to a different direction. But before he could get a single sound out of his throat, she spoke up. "It's fine, Reed. You can put away the ghostly guilt look," she said as she pulled the towel down from around her head and ran her fingers through the damp blond waves.

His shoulders slumped and he grinned, grabbing the paper sack off the counter and bringing it into their makeshift dining room where Meagan had retreated, sitting on one of the pillows she had thrown down. "So, what'll it be? Taco, burrito, or quesadilla?" he asked, sitting down next to her.

"Well, I'm usually a burrito girl, but since that's your favorite I will let you have it and I will take the taco."

"Nope, here"—he handed her the burrito wrapped in foil—"you have it."

She took it from him, crossed her legs Indian-style on the floor, and started opening the burrito. "You don't have to twist my arm when it comes to Mexican food and margaritas." She took a large bite, sour cream and cheese spilling out of her mouth.

Reed laughed; he loved a woman that could put away food like a grown-ass man. "Good?"

"Uh-huh," she mumbled and nodded her head, lifting her hands to cover her full mouth as she laughed. Reed was still watching her a few moments later when she swallowed, wiping her mouth off with a paper towel. "What?"

"Nothing."

"Well, you're looking at me like I just grew a second head, so spill."

Reed released a long, low sigh mixed with a deep chuckle. "I like watching you eat."

Meagan smiled knowingly, picking up her burrito, slowly bringing it to her lips, and bit off another impressive-size bite.

Reed blinked his eyes slowly and shook his head. This damn woman seemed to enjoy testing his self-control. "Tease," he admonished, but the word came out in a throaty laugh—and sounded more like a plea than a warning.

Meagan gave him smile around a mouthful, reaching out the burrito for him to take. "Want some?"

She didn't know how badly he wanted some, but not the fucking burrito.

"Nah, you seem to enjoy it."

She shrugged. "Suit yourself," she said before taking another bite.

Reed dug into one of the tacos. "So this roommate of yours, what's up with her? I kind of got the impression she wanted to twist my testicles off when I talked to her earlier."

Meagan erupted in a fit of laughter that was contagious. Her hand covered her mouth as her small body shook and her eyes disappeared beneath her lashes, and Reed couldn't help but join in. The sound of their combined laughter echoed through the empty apartment. Meagan lowered her head to her lap as her laughter tapered off. When she lifted it again she wiped the tears that had accumulated and sighed.

Reed had a pain in his ribs, the good kind that you only got on the rare occasions that you laughed so hard it hurt. He missed laughing like that, it had been a very long time since someone made him laugh that way, but now that he had, he welcomed it. "Something funny I should know about?" Reed asked, his eyes wide as he watched Meagan's face slowly return to its original color.

She sighed again and smiled. "She is a spitfire. You might need to watch out for her. She may be tiny but she is tough as nails and if you piss her off I have no doubt in my mind that she would, in fact, attempt to twist off your testicles."

"Well, fuck. What did I do to piss off the fire-breathing dragon?"

She pressed her lips together, suppressing another laugh as the corners of her mouth twitched. "She's not pissed, she wouldn't have let you in if she was. She's plotting."

"Plotting?"

Meagan rolled her eyes and shook her head. "Yes, just ignore her." She pushed the nearly demolished burrito aside and stretched her perfectly tanned legs out in front of her. Yes, self-control was something of his she seemed to push, knowingly or not.

"If you say so, sugar."

"There you go with the 'sugar' again."

"What? You don't like it when I call you 'sugar'?" He lowered his voice and made sure to let his thick Alabama accent stroke his words before they left his mouth. Why? Because he could tell she liked it—he could tell by the way her face heated up and her legs brushed together, and anything he could do to get that kind of reaction from her, he would do it.

A soft flush spread across her cheeks, only making her

look that much more beautiful. She didn't come across to him as someone who got embarrassed easily, but he was definitely doing the job nicely.

"It doesn't bother me either way," she said, meeting his eyes directly. There was that confidence he liked. Her face may say she was affected, but her eyes—they weren't going to tell him so easily, and that was okay—he liked a challenge. "I do like your accent though, where are you from?"

Yep, that Southern drawl hadn't let him down yet. "I'm from Birmingham. What about you, *sugar*?" He intentionally let the sound of the *r* fall short.

Meagan cocked her head, her mouth parting in a slight smile. "I'm from everywhere." She lifted her finger and pointed to herself. "Army brat."

"Oh, yeah? You been stationed here with your family before?"

She shook her head and picked up her drink. She pressed it to her mouth, brushing her bottom lip across the rim of the cup, and then she pulled her bottom lip into her mouth, sucking off the salt before she took a drink. Reed needed that bottom lip in his mouth. He wanted to lean in and pull it between his teeth, then suck on it until it was swollen, and if she kept doing little things like that he might just do it.

She lowered the cup from her mouth and paused. Her head tilted a little to the side, her eyebrows furrowing before she blinked and continued to set her cup down. Reed was pretty sure he had the hand-caught-in-the-cookie-jar expression on his face and she more than likely knew why. "Nope, this is the first time I've ever been to Georgia," she said, letting him off the hook from his involuntary staring that he couldn't seem to control.

"And what do you think so far?"

"Well, in the week I've been here I haven't really seen much to gather an opinion. I mean, I like it just fine. It's beautiful here."

"Have you ever been white-water rafting? They just opened up an urban course here not too long ago."

"No, I've never been."

"Oh, I will take you sometime. It's a blast."

"Okay, that could possibly be fun."

Reed flinched. "Possibly? Oh, sugar, you just broke my heart a little."

Meagan rolled her big blue eyes at him, then pushed her bottom lip out in a pout, mocking him. "Do you need a Band-Aid?"

"Ouch, woman," he said, clutching his chest.

Her lips tightened into a line, and she scrunched her nose, causing her eyes to disappear behind her long lashes. "You just strike me as the type of guy who would take the boat over a waterfall or something equally as insane, just for kicks, and I don't know how much fun that would be."

Reed smiled. She had him there—that was exactly something he would do. "Nah, with you, sugar, I would take it easy. That is, unless you like it rough."

Her eyebrows darted to her hairline and her wide eyes stared at him incredulously.

Reed threw his head back and laughed; he liked this

woman. He liked making her blush and he liked shocking the hell out of her, even if he didn't mean to that time. "Get your head out of the gutter, woman. I was talking about the courses. There are several different levels, and some are rougher than others."

"Uh-huh. Nice cover."

"Think what you think, but it's nice to know where your head keeps going."

Her mouth gaped open and she made a little noise that caused his dick to twitch beneath his shorts. It was going to be a long night.

CHAPTER FIVE

Meagan didn't know how to respond to that—because he was right. Her head kept going back to that night eight years ago when she'd followed him back to his hotel room like a dog in heat. She had just gotten home from college for the summer, packing with her a broken heart. Her dad was stationed at Fort Leonard Wood at the time and she didn't know anyone there yet other than the neighbors' daughter, Courtney, and she was a little on the wild side. Courtney had taken her out to a small hole-in-the-wall bar that played a mix of eighties rock music and country—not the best bar, but there wasn't much to choose from at Leonard Wood. The atmosphere was mixed, young and old alike, and they sat at the bar as Courtney flirted with the bartender and obsessed about getting out from underneath her parents.

Meagan had made a trip to the restroom and was making her way back to the bar when she ran into Reed—literally. Yes, it was kind of like one of those typical romance movies where the girl runs into the guy and he spills his drink on her and tries to wipe it off with his hand, conveniently brushing over her boobs in the meantime, and when they lock eyes it was all love at first sight, yada, yada, yada. It was exactly like that, minus the whole love-at-first-sight thing. It was more like turned on at first sight. Reed was sexy, and he had this playfulness to him that instantly roped her in—and she needed roped in, she needed the distraction he was so easily giving her. He seemed like the cure-all for her newly broken heart, standing there flirting with her in his worn pair of jeans and solid black T-shirt, (again, typical, and, yes, she remembered what he was wearing), his mouth tilting up in that cocky smile, the Cupid's bow tempting her, just like it was at that very moment.

Needless to say, they both had a little more to drink than they should have had to make morally correct decisions, but at twenty-two, decisions based on morals weren't high on the priority list. She left with him, and he took her back to his motel room. She had never had a one-night stand before Reed, and she didn't care. She had just come out of a relationship that left her numb to the idea of caring, and besides, the things he did to her body made any regrets she was afraid she would have later vanish. And she never once regretted it.

She'd anticipated this raw, intense . . . fuck . . . for lack of a better word, but it was anything but that. He was silly and playful. Their foreplay was more wrestling around and flirting, play-bites between kisses, and tickling between undressing. It was lighthearted and fun; and she let him sweep her up and carry her away in it.

The Reed she saw sitting before her now still had that

playfulness to him that she adored. But there was a new harshness that hung on his shoulders, like something had eroded away a thin layer of his carefree demeanor and left a rough patch in its place. It wasn't something that was obvious or noticeable, and she didn't understand why after only spending such a short time with him back then that she could see this subtle change in him, especially when he didn't even remember her at all—but she did.

The small amount of silence that lingered between them as Meagan's mind wandered into the past was strangely comfortable. She didn't feel the need to fill the quiet with small talk, and the little fact that she was already this comfortable around him startled her. She shouldn't be getting comfortable or taking walks down memory lane—not with Reed.

She looked over at him and smiled, but he only shifted on his pillow and dropped his head a little. Obviously his mind was working during their little moment of quiet as well. She could feel the shift in his mood like a cloud of smoke was somehow permeating the air around them. It was thick and almost suffocating. His eyes lifted to hers and they were ringed with a sincerity that she had seen earlier today—when he was in the hospital—and she knew what had somehow entered his mind.

"Hey, you okay?" she asked softly.

His finger reached up and stroked his eyebrow. "Yeah, I'm fine. I just wanted to thank you again—for taking care of Brewer."

Meagan reached over and placed her hand on his forearm and the muscles under his skin tightened. "He'll be fine. I promise."

He lifted his lips in an attempt to smile at her, probably more for her reassurance than anything, but they didn't make it too far before they fell again. "I've seen my fair share of injuries. Hell, I've been deployed three times and have seen more life-threatening injuries than I can count—but this is different. This is one of my students. I've heard the horror stories of jump injuries, and I've witnessed a lot of them, but it's never been this bad. One of my guys has never needed surgery from a jump injury before. It's my company, they're my men—if he had died it would have been my fault."

She remembered the concern that was engraved on his face when he walked into the emergency room with the medics. He was a completely composed wreck. He was keeping up the facade of the in-control company commander, but when he looked at her, the reflection he shielded behind his eyes slipped away, and she got a glimpse at the distress he was working so hard to hide. It wasn't like he was just concerned for one of his soldiers, it was like he was hurting with him, fear and anger threatening to consume him—but only on the inside.

"Reed, there's no way you can possibly blame yourself for what happened. It was completely out of your control, there was nothing you could have done to change the outcome. His chute didn't open. He just landed wrong."

"And what if that wrong landing had cost him his life? It's our job to make sure these guys know how to jump safely, how to land safely. It's my job." His eyes went blank as he fixed them on a spot behind her. "It was just a moment, one single moment, but it was the longest fucking moment. . . ."

He finally blinked and pulled his eyes back to Meagan's and held them with a vise grip that startled her. "Someone's always to blame."

Her heart stopped for a moment—the moment he seemed to slip away, his mind traveling somewhere she couldn't reach. He felt responsible—and that was not a burden he should take on—but there was something else tightening in his jaw, tensing in his muscles—guilt. And if she couldn't erase the guilt that was eating away at him from somewhere far away, maybe she could ease the guilt that was right in front of her.

"Reed." She scooted closer to him and grasped his face between her hands, the stubble on his face tickling the skin on her palms. His eyes searched her as she looked at him. He drew his eyebrows together, a small crease forming between his gold eyes. His breathing started to calm as his mind seemed to find its way back to her. "You and your instructors teach these soldiers everything you possibly can to prepare them. But there are things that are out of your control. Once they leave that plane, it's up to them—and even then things happen. You can't beat yourself up over this." He swallowed and shut his eyes briefly. When his lids lifted, his eyes were back on hers, never wavering from the hold they had on her. "He will be fine," she whispered.

"You're right. I know, I'm sorry." He attempted another smile, his face still between her hands. "I didn't mean to go all mopey on you."

"You can mope to me anytime."

His eyes held hers, and in that moment when his guard

was lowered and his playfulness was in hiding, she saw the full layer of Reed that he kept tucked tightly away, not just a glimpse, and it was intense and consuming—and intimate.

Meagan cleared her throat and dropped her hands, leaning away from Reed. She had to get out of his stare, out of his reach, because if she didn't she would give in—and she couldn't give in. She needed to stick to the plan. She could tell Reed was a great man, and she already knew he was great in other aspects as well, but she also knew that he wasn't what she needed. And she didn't need to throw into the mix the little fact that he didn't even remember who she was. Her ego was already slightly bruised—okay, it was every ugly shade of blue and green and purple there was—she just needed him to leave.

Meagan stood up, picking up the discarded food on the floor, and Reed jumped up after her. "Thank you so much for dinner," she said, setting the food down on the kitchen counter.

Reed ran his hand over the top of his head, messing up the short cluster of hair, making him seem disheveled and sloppy and, dammit, sexy. His brows pinched together as he watched her quickly pick up their mess.

She started walking toward the front door. He needed to leave. "Next time, I'm buying dinner."

She felt Reed following close behind her, his body only mere inches away from her back. She wanted to stop. She wanted to feel his chest crash into her. She wanted to spin around and push her breasts against him and feel his large palms splayed across her back. She wanted to feel his annoyingly perfect lips softly smooth over the skin below her ear. And she wanted to reach her hand down and feel the solid length she knew would be beneath his shorts. But she didn't, and this was exactly why he needed to leave. Her self-control was faltering.

Meagan grabbed the doorknob, and just as she opened the door, Reed's hand reached above her head and pushed it shut again.

Her head jerked up to look at him and her eyes immediately searched his face—his eyes did the same. "Did I do something wrong?" he said quietly, obviously taking notice of her whiplash mood swing. His body was so close that his chest brushed against her. His arm was still raised, his hand was still pressed against the door, and his head was lowered, looking down at her. She felt consumed by his proximity. He was hovering over her, his expression intense and worried, and all she could think about was him leaning down just a little bit more. . . .

She closed her eyes briefly and sighed. "You really don't remember, do you?" she asked, exasperated.

His eyes narrowed in concentration. "Remember what?"

She pressed her lips together and inhaled deeply, then let out her breath slowly, trying to gain the courage to endure the humiliation that was about to take place. "Me."

His eyes widened, and small lines formed across his forehead as he looked at her, then a slow, very slow, almost agonizingly slow, smile pulled up on the corners of his mouth. His impish eyes gleamed with mischief.

Ah hell, he remembered.

He was a fucking idiot. How in the hell did he not put two and two together and realize that this was

Meagan? Well shit, probably because he didn't remember the name of the girl he slept with on the night before he graduated OBC eight years ago, but still, he knew there was something about her, something his mind just couldn't grasp. She looked different. Her blond hair had been short and sleek, just below her chin before, now it tumbled down her back and over her shoulders. She had more confidence now, too. The woman he'd met all those years ago was a little shy and unsure of herself—that was definitely not the woman he saw now. Sure, she still didn't realize how every little thing she did dripped with a sex appeal that made him want to rip the clothes from her body, but the way her eyes were unafraid to meet his, the way her shoulders pulled back straight, and the way she was so relaxed around him was completely new.

Reed didn't know what to say to rectify the fact that he hadn't recognized a woman he had had sex with. He knew that was a blow to her ego, and that was the last thing he wanted. He had been just a young, stupid, horny-ass guy who was looking to have a good night before he left. Now that his memory was back in working order, he remembered just how sweet she tasted, he remembered just how she sounded when she moaned into his mouth, and he remembered exactly how she felt beneath him.

Meagan didn't look pissed, and she didn't look embarrassed, she looked almost hurt—and there was no way in hell he was going to hurt this woman because of his stupidity, especially since he had wanted her since he first saw her that night in the courtyard. There was only one way Reed knew to reassure her.

His hand dropped from the door and he wrapped it around her waist. He almost pulled his hand from her body just so he could do it again, because the surprised little look that crossed over her face was the sexiest damn look she had given him all night.

He pulled her body against him and she sucked in a quick breath—ah yes, he very much liked surprising her. His other hand lifted to her face and he pushed back the damp hair that was resting next to her cheek and his thumb skimmed over the smooth skin and traced her jawline. He leaned over her and his shoulders curled forward as he moved his face in close to hers. Her eyes stayed stoic, locked on his as if she were held in a trance. Her mouth parted slightly, and he could feel the smooth, soft puffs of air that were streaming from her lips, caressing his mouth. He smiled again. "I may not have recognized you, but I never forgot you," he whispered, and then his mouth crushed against hers before she had a moment to respond.

He expected her to hesitate, to maybe even push him away, but her lips connected with his with a ferocity that caused a deep moan to hum in the back of his throat. Her hands flew to the back of his neck, and he felt the small pinch of her fingernails digging into his flesh as her fingers curled around his neck.

His tongue invaded her mouth, her taste encasing his senses in her sweetness, and it was fucking delicious. Her eagerness was hitting him with a force that would make even the strongest of men weak.

"Hell," he said against her lips, "I could never forget

this." His fingers reached around and threaded through her wet hair, and he tugged her head back, deepening the kiss.

No, he remembered her perfectly now, and the memory of her naked body pressed against him mixed with the melodic whimpers undulating from her mouth at that very moment had his dick rising.

Her legs seemed to give slightly, and she molded her body to his and he gladly held her firmly to him, supporting her weight as she fit her small body against him. She was sweet—sweet and spicy at the same time. Her soft moans and her body's gentle delicate reaction to his touch tugged at him, sending a possessive shrill through his body, but the way her mouth moved over his, taking what she wanted from him, the way her nails bit into his skin, and the way she made his own body quiver above her was anything but sweet—it was sexy as hell. How this woman could give him two totally different sensations at one time was testing new waters for him.

Reed rotated his body, moving her along with him as he firmly pushed her back into the wall. She let out a surprised gasp before he felt her lips tug up into a smile against his mouth. Oh, hell. This woman had no idea what she was getting herself into. If she kept responding to him like that he was bound to have to show her the other ways he would like to make her gasp—but he didn't think she was ready for that, not yet.

He couldn't take it anymore; her kiss was like drinking an expensive brandy. It was smooth and rich, slightly sweet— just enough to allow it to go down smoothly, but it had that bite to it that he craved, that little bit of edge that caused him to anticipate its effect. He could easily get drunk on this woman, besotted by the mere taste lingering on his tongue. Fuck, if her mouth had this effect on him, he was dying to taste the rest of her.

He broke their kiss, and Meagan's head rolled back against the wall as she tried to catch her breath. Her long neck was stretched out and exposed in front of him, the thin skin at the hollow tapping rapidly along with the beat of her heart. Reed slipped a hand up the inside of her tank top, splaying his palm out across her flat stomach as he fastened his mouth on the curve of her neck, sucking gently. It was like sucking on sugarcane.

He released the hold his mouth had on her neck before it left a mark—although he wouldn't mind seeing proof of his mouth on her skin—and continued his way down her body. He rained easy kisses across her shoulder and down her arm, pulling a slender finger into his mouth when he reached her hand.

His own fingers inched upward until he reached the lace covering her ample breasts. In one quick tug, he freed her tits from the cups of her bra and moaned when her back arched against the wall, begging for his hands to cover her. His thumb brushed across her smooth, taut nipple, rolling it between his fingers before he palmed her full tit in his hand. His mouth retreated back to hers and a deep, gratifying sigh heaved from her chest. Reed smiled again, his lips curving up around hers—there was that little reaction he loved, and it might just get him in trouble.

There was no use in trying to stifle the moan that had worked its way up her throat. His fingers were like magic, working her breasts with his rough hands, the sensation brushing across her skin was gentle but eager—and exactly what she wanted.

She lifted her leg and wrapped it around his waist, the evidence of his arousal pressing against her, and she had to force herself not to crumble from the fervor running though her body. His arm almost instantly slid under her thigh and lifted her other leg off the ground so she could wrap it around him. The second her legs locked together above his ass, a groan that sounded more animal than man rumbled deep in his chest—the raw sexual tension that vibrated through his body was almost terrifying. She hadn't felt this turned on in a long time, and his intensity was overwhelming—terrifying and overwhelming in the best possible way.

Why was she doing this? *Be strong, be strong, tell him to stop,* Meagan thought to herself as she laced her arms around the hard torso that was pressing into her. But as quickly as the thought entered her mind, Reed's tongue snaked out and traced her bottom lip, causing the thought to melt away with the warmth of his mouth. She felt almost out of control—she couldn't stop. She didn't realize how much she was craving sex, craving Reed, until that very moment.

Reed's weight pressed into her, her spine molding to the wall as his teeth tugged on her lips, his tongue fighting with hers for dominance. His hands crept forward until they skimmed over the material of her shorts, teasing the sensitive ache between her thighs. The soft pressure of his fingers caused the rough denim to rub against her clit, and she involuntarily rolled her hips down to intensify the pressure.

"Fuck," he groaned, moving his mouth close to her ear. "Drop your legs."

She did, but only because she was trembling so badly that her legs could no longer hold on to him. She had never been so close to climax from so little stimulation before. Her bare feet hit the floor, and luckily Reed still had his hands wrapped around her waist, or she might have collapsed. He leaned back and looked at her, his gaze taking its time as it navigated down her body. It was as if his stare was burning her skin, leaving a trail of flames.

He crouched down, trailing his hands along the outside of her thighs all the way down to her ankles as he lowered to the ground. "Let's get these off you," he said as he raised his fingers to the clasp of her shorts, toying with the button.

His eyes looked expectantly at her, and she knew he was waiting for permission to undress her, but . . . she couldn't give it to him. She wanted to, God, she wanted to. But as he lowered himself in front of her, his lips no longer causing her to lose focus of her self-control, she was finally able to form a logical thought—one that wasn't compromised by the addictive taste of his lips moving over hers. If she allowed his hands to unbutton her shorts and slide down her legs—she would be a goner. She would sleep with him, there was no doubt about it. She wanted him, and he clearly wanted her too, but then what? They have yet another one-night stand? She'd been down this path with him before, and dammit, it would be worth every ounce of pleasure she knew he would give her, but would it be worth it tomorrow? She wanted safe, and this wasn't safe. This was everything she was trying to get away from. It was spontaneous, and reckless, and . . . damn . . .

"Reed, stop." His hands halted instantly, his mouth went slack, and his eyes went blank before they squinted behind his thick lashes.

Meagan stepped to the side and lifted her bra back in place as she watched Reed slowly stand back up. He just looked at her and she felt this rush of guilt sweep through her at rejecting him after she so obviously wanted him—she knew he could tell, it was written clear as day on his confused face. She wished like hell she could go back in time five minutes. She would have never said a damn thing. The last thing she wanted was for things to get awkward, because, let's face it, not only did he remember her now, but she had to go all moan-y and come close to orgasm—*great*. Friends, she could do friends. She needed to do friends, because whatever the hell just happened, she couldn't do that again.

Her face and neck heated up as she looked at Reed, who had gone from confused to cocky in about two seconds flat. His eyes flitted over hers and he stepped to the side so he was standing in front of her again.

"You sure you want me to do that, sugar?" His voice was low, deep, and that subtle arch in his words—that sexy hint of an accent—slithered across her skin as they left his mouth, that damn perfect mouth. On the plus side, she no longer felt guilty.

Meagan cleared her throat, unfortunately sounding just as unsure about his question as she felt. "Yes."

Reed's lips pursed together; the jackass was trying not to laugh.

"What?" she said, furrowing her brows and making a conscious note to stand up straight and look him dead in the eyes, when all she wanted to do was grab onto him again.

"Nothing." He chuckled.

Meagan sighed. "Reed, we both know that whatever that was . . . was . . . fun, but I don't really think it was a good idea. Just because we slept together one night eight long years ago doesn't give us a pass to do it again."

"You don't want to do it again?"

"No," she responded, a little too quickly to be believable.

Reed laughed, and Meagan's eyes about came out of her head.

"What the hell is so damn funny?" She went from turned on, to guilty, to annoyed.

"You are, sugar." He winked at her. "Okay, we won't do it again."

Meagan cocked her brows up and her head bobbed downward.

Reed threw his hands in the air in surrender, his playfulness in full swing. "I swear not to make your body quiver and shake," he said slowly, deep, like he was using his words to touch her body as he stepped closer, "and I promise not to kiss the smooth skin below your ear—"

"Reed," Meagan admonished, cutting him off before he could do any more damage to her . . . willpower, hormones . . . hell, pride. She pushed her hands against his chest, causing him to stumble back. Now that was self-control at its finest, right there.

Reed laughed. "I'm kidding, damn, woman." His lips curved upward, and that megawatt smile beamed at her.

"Look, we live next door to each other, and I don't know a lot of people here. Can't we just be friends?"

Reed cocked his head to the side as Meagan held out her hand in front of her, and, yes, she knew she looked like an idiot. "Friends?" she asked, her hand still dangling from her outstretched arm.

Fortunately Reed let her off the hook and took her hand in his and gave it one quick shake. Just as she was about to let go, he jerked on her hand and pulled her flush against him again, moving his hand to the small of her back, pinning her to him. She gasped, suddenly feeling like all the air was knocked out of her lungs.

His head leaned to the side, his nose pressed against the damp hair that clung to the side of her face, and he inhaled deeply before he pulled back around to look at her. Her heart had picked up the twelve-year-old-at-a-Bieber-concert pace again, and she couldn't do anything but look into his liquid gold eyes that had gone intense—tempting.

"We can be friends, only because you're too sweet and funny to not want to be around you all the damn time, and we won't fuck again—not if you don't want to, but that doesn't mean that *I* won't want to"—he leaned down and ran his mouth along her jaw, nipping her chin, then swiping his tongue lightly over the gentle bite—"but I'll respect what you want."

He released his hold on her and stepped in front of the

door. "See ya around, friend." He winked and opened the door, and Meagan just stared after him as he walked out, closing the door behind him. *Friends.* That's what they were going to be. From now on he was hands-off, completely hands-off. He was definitely not Mr. Safe—Mr. All-of-the-Above, yes, but Mr. Safe, no. *He's definitely not part of the plan,* Meagan said to herself as she ran her finger over the luscious tingling sensation he left on her chin.

CHAPTER SIX

"Y ou have big plans this weekend?"

Meagan was standing in front of the elevator waiting to go up to the med surg unit before she headed home for the evening when she heard Doctor Ryan sneak up behind her. "No, nothing," she said, turning around to look at him. She completely planned on hiding out in her apartment the rest of the weekend until she had to crawl out and head back to work on Thursday. Working three twelve-hour shifts a week definitely had its perks.

"Really? No big fireworks bash or party?" he asked, stepping up beside her. He was attractive, and Meagan always seemed to get those fluttery butterflies in her stomach whenever he was around.

Meagan smiled at him and wrinkled her nose. "Nope, and considering it's Saturday, I will probably just lie around all day tomorrow, and I don't plan on leaving the house on Monday either," she admitted.

"Aw, that just won't do. How about you come out to dinner with me on Sunday and we can plot your Monday Fourth of July plans while we eat sushi?" The elevator doors opened, and Meagan stepped inside, and Dr. Ryan held his arm against the door, preventing it from closing.

"You want to plot?" she asked, crossing her arms over her chest.

Dr. Ryan—Jason—lowered his head and smiled. It wasn't that same cocky, lopsided grin that she loved to see pulled on Reed's face. No, Jason's was sweet, almost shy— she liked it.

He raised his eyes back to her, and she dropped her arms to her side and smiled. "No, I actually just want to spend some time with you, alone, outside of the hospital."

His little bashful admittance was cute, and it gave her another wave of flutters. "Sushi sounds great," she said.

Jason pulled his phone out of his pocket, and Meagan rattled off her phone number to him. "I'll call you tomorrow and we can work out the details?"

"Sounds good."

He pulled his arm away from the elevator, and the door almost immediately started shutting. "Have a good night," he said, flashing that sweet smile her way again, just as the elevator door closed completely.

Jason was definitely one she could see working the "safe" angle. He was a doctor in the army, he was sexy and handsome and sweet all bundled into one. And from what little she knew about him, she got the impression that he had his shit together. So he was a little shy. That's okay, she could work with that—it was cute. She just typically went for the assertive type, the slightly cocky I-know-what-I-want-and-I-want-you type of men, but look where that had gotten her—nowhere. So the bashful, sweet, I'm-nervous-to-ask-you-out type might be exactly what she needed.

The elevator smelled of hospital food and antiseptic cleaner, which you'd think Meagan would be used to by now, but it still made her hold her breath. As soon as the door opened she stepped off, inhaling deeply only to breathe in another gust of sterile hospital air. She made her way down the narrow hall that led to Brewer's room, passing room after room of patients, all there for different reasons, of course, but she couldn't keep her mind from wandering back to Kale. Knowing that at one point not too long ago, he was one of the soldiers who was sitting in a cold, empty hospital room, with no one to visit him while he was recovering from an injury—from an attack on him and his men—was heartbreaking. It was one reason she loved working in a military hospital. Not only did she get to help military families, but she got to be there for the soldiers—especially the ones who didn't have anyone, like Brewer. His parents lived clear across the country and couldn't afford to make a trip down here while he was recovering. It damn near broke her heart. Here was this young soldier that would never again be able to do what he loved, never again be able to jump, possibly never be able to return to combat, and he was alone. Day in, day out, sitting in a hospital room with no one or nothing but his thoughts. But that was why she was there, that was what made her love her job—she could make sure he wasn't alone.

Meagan tapped on the hospital room door that was slightly ajar and pushed it open when she heard Brewer's voice telling her to come in. The room was dark, only the dim light creeping in through the open blinds was illuminating the room.

"Hey, how are you feeling today?" she asked, plopping down in the chair next to the bed.

"Much better now that you're here."

Meagan laughed. She liked this kid, and she gathered that the drugs he was heavily on yesterday didn't bring out his flirty side like she had originally thought—this was just him. Another cocky, flirty bad boy with a big heart who could easily rope her in. She could already see herself getting attached to him, only in the little-brother sense.

"Well, good. Did you eat yet?"

"Not that shit they tried to bring me from the cafeteria," he said, attempting to scoot up in his bed a little. Meagan wanted to help him, but she knew firsthand that injured soldiers had more pride than anyone else, so she just sat there, twisting the handle of her purse as he struggled to sit up.

"Do you want me to run and grab you something?" she asked as he situated himself in the bed.

"I'll gladly have you for dessert, but Captain Porter already brought me dinner."

The single mention of Reed's name caused mini heart palpitations to take off in her chest. She was trying hard not to think of him, what with everything that went on between them last night, but it was a near impossible task. Her mind drifted to the way he pinned her against the wall, and the way his fingers felt brushing across her bare breasts, nearly every other minute of the damn day.

"Oh," she said, unable to find anything else to say now that Reed was clouding her mind again.

Brewer sighed heavily then smiled. "Well, fuck."

She lifted her brows. "What are you well-fucking about?"

"Ah, that pretty mouth saying dirty words, mm, mm, mm."

Meagan rolled her eyes and reached over and slapped him on the arm. "Spill it."

"You have a thing for CO." It wasn't a question, just a simple statement.

"You think I like Reed?" she asked, making sure to keep her voice even as the words left her mouth. She didn't like him—not in that way—she knew better than to like him. It just so happened that her body didn't give a shit what she thought.

"Oh, my sweet and beautifully sexy nurse Meagan, I don't think, I unfortunately know. And don't think for one second that it doesn't piss me off knowing that my chance with you is pretty much shot now."

She pressed her lips together to keep from laughing. "Brewer, you never had a shot to begin with. You may be incredibly good-looking," she said to soften the blow, although it was completely true, "but, you're what, twenty? Twenty-one?" What was with these young guys hitting on her lately anyway? Well, hell, she might as well take it as a compliment, considering she was about to enter cougar territory—okay, not really.

Brewer threw his head back against the pillow and blew out a long breath from his mouth, causing his lips to pucker. "I'm not gonna lie—that stung a little. I'm twenty-three." He lifted his head from the pillow and looked her dead in the eyes. His were a hard gray—bursts of blue shooting throughout, like gunmetal, like the freshly polished and oiled barrel of a revolver. They were still light, silly almost, but there was an intense sincerity ringing them that made him instantly appear much older than twenty-three, and if Meagan didn't already have him set to the little-brother burner, she may had easily gotten sucked in by that stare. "Age has never been an issue with women, and I don't play with girls," he said, his words sure and firm and . . . hell . . . sexy. Then, just like that, he dropped his stare and the air surrounding them returned to its presexy state.

"He told me to tell you 'hi' by the way."

Meagan blinked. "Who?"

"Who do you think? Captain Porter."

"What do you mean he told you to tell me 'hi'? He didn't know I was going to come see you."

"Ah, but you see, he knew you wouldn't be able to stay away from me long—surprising, I know, considering he's got his balls all twisted in a knot over you, but yeah, he knew you would come."

"And he just said, 'Tell Meagan hi'?"

"No, he said 'When that sexy-ass nurse from yesterday comes back to check on you tonight, you tell her I say "Hi, friend." And you also tell her to get her cute butt to my apartment to see me when she gets home.'"

Meagan laughed. Reed was using one of his soldiers as a messenger boy?

"See, I wasn't going to tell you to go see him tonight.

Fuck, if he wants to see you, then he can tell you himself. But seeing as you are just as twisted up for him as he is for you, I thought I would tell you—and seeing that I have no chance in hell left with you."

Meagan laughed again. If she kept this up she was going to start getting side cramps. She wanted to wrap Brewer up and take him home with her. But she didn't want to let Eva loose on him, she would tear him to shreds—actually she didn't want to let Brewer loose on Eva, he would probably be all over her. Hell, mental note—never let those two near each other.

"What are you grinning about?" Brewer asked when she didn't respond. "Trying to figure out a way to let CO down easy, huh? Tell him I'm the one you really want?"

She shook her head and rolled her eyes. "No, I was actually thinking how you and my roommate can absolutely never meet each other."

"Oh, yeah? Tell me about this roommate," he said, his eyes gleaming with a mischief that gave her another glance into the sexier Sergeant Brewer. "Tell me she's a redhead."

Meagan's eyes widened, and he laughed. "Ah, hell, she is, isn't she? I love me a feisty redhead, almost as much as I love me a sexy blond nurse." He winked.

"Oh, no, you two will definitely not be meeting each other now." Meagan stood up. "Can I do anything for you before I leave—and keep that mind out of the gutter, please. Soda, snack, movie?"

His eyes shifted downward, dropping his chin to his chest. She knew the look; she had come across more proud men in her lifetime than she could possibly count. A soldier asking for help when they were hurt was like pulling teeth. She knew he was in pain, she could tell the second she walked into the room, but the light way he held himself made it easy for her to forget.

Meagan leaned over the side of the bed and lightly pressed her lips to his cheek. "All right, Casanova, I'm going to send your real nurse in here to give you some meds so you can sleep. And don't argue with me, I know what's best. Also"—she grabbed an old receipt out of her purse and wrote down her phone number on the back, slipping it into his hand—"call me if you need anything. Seriously, even if you want me to come here and watch stupid old movies with you in the middle of the night, I'll do it."

He grabbed her hand and looked up at her, and the young guy who was hurt and alone was staring back at her. "Thanks, Meg."

"No problem."

Reed was waiting outside Meagan's front door when he saw her pull up in her ridiculous Volkswagen Beetle, but if anyone could make that car look good it was her. It was five till eight, and if Meagan had the same schedule she did yesterday, she would have gotten off work at seven, which meant that she had probably gone to see Brewer, just like he assumed she would. Hopefully the little shit gave her his message.

She stepped out of her car, grabbing her purse before she

shut the door. When she turned toward the apartment building she spotted him instantly and a sweet smile tugged on her face.

"Hi, friend," she said to him as she walked up to her door.

"Good, I see Brewer gave you my little message."

Meagan put her key in the door and unlocked it, pushing it open and stepping inside. "Yes. Well, I'm home and I see you. What'd ya want?" She turned around and stepped to the side, giving him the nonverbal invitation to come in—so he did.

"I want to take you somewhere," he said, stepping into the empty apartment.

"And where would that be?"

"What fun would it be if I told you? Go change into something comfortable and grab extra clothes, I'll stick them in my bag."

Her lips parted like she was about to say something but changed her mind instead. She turned around and headed down her hallway without saying another word.

A few minutes later she was walking back into the living room wearing a pair of skintight black cotton pants that hit just below her knees and a red tank top. This woman sure knew how to make comfortable look sexy.

"You ready?" he asked, taking a pair of shorts and a sheer top out of her hands and stuffing them into his bag along with a pair of sandals before he threw it over his shoulder.

Meagan cocked up a blond eyebrow. "For what exactly?"

Reed winked at her before he made his way toward the back door. He wasn't going to divulge his information that easily. She might have had a way of crawling under his skin, but he was still holding on strong. "Ah, you'll have to wait and see."

They walked through the courtyard toward the parking lot. It was eight o'clock, but the summer night allowed the hazy sun to sneak over the horizon and the mix of colors it created played against the color of Meagan's hair, and her blue eyes seemed to reflect the pink and yellow hues. Seeing her in this lighting was picture worthy, hell, any lighting this woman was in was picture worthy—but seeing her now, it seemed as if she was encased in a warm glow, and it was fucking beautiful.

A slight shade of pink rose on Meagan's cheeks when she noticed him staring, but he wasn't going to pretend he wasn't. He told her yesterday that he would respect what she wanted, but he also told her that it didn't mean he wouldn't want her—she better just get used to it now because he was sure staring at her was going to be a common occurrence when they were together. He just needed to learn to get his dick under control. He wasn't keen on being miserable all the time.

"You're really not going to tell me?" she asked from behind him.

"Nope."

"Well, as long as I'm not jumping out of any airplanes, I think I'll be fine."

Reed stopped abruptly and spun around to face her and she damn near ran straight into him. Her feet shuffled a step back, only causing him to take another step toward her. He was much taller than her, and his shoulders rolled forward as he hovered over her, trying to get closer. He fixed his strong gaze on her and lowered his head so he was mere inches from her face. The close proximity did nothing but intensify the need he had to pull this woman hard against his body. He took in a steady breath. "Sometimes, the things we're afraid of"—his words dropped off as he took the time to move a stray strand of hair that had fallen loose over her face—"the things that scare us the most, are the things that give us the biggest rush," he said slowly, his words low and thick.

He watched the thin skin at the dip in her throat move as she swallowed hard. He loved watching those little subtle reactions that her body involuntarily had, because she sure as hell wasn't going to give anything away with her eyes. "Is that why you do it? For a rush?" She breathed, the sound leaving her mouth was soft and gravely.

Reed lifted the corners of his mouth. "It's why I do every-thing. If it doesn't make you hold your breath and shut your eyes the moment before you do it, then it's not worth doing." He winked and turned back around and started walking to-ward the parking lot again. "What's better than feeling your heart beating so hard in your chest that you can't breathe, feel-ing your adrenaline pumping through your veins? It's the unknown—it's a rush," he said as Meagan stepped up next to him, her body so close that it was hard for him not to reach out and touch her, just for the sake of doing so.

"So you're an adrenaline junkie?"

Reed huffed out a short chuckle. "You could say that. I

like to think of myself as more of a thrill seeker. But yeah, I'm addicted. I'm addicted to the feel of the rush. I need it."

This time Meagan released a soft chuckle. "Mr. Thrill," she mumbled.

He snapped his head in her direction. "What?"

She rolled her eyes and smiled. "Nothing. So what are some of these breath-holding activities?"

"Well, a few years back I took my kayak down Palouse Falls in Washington. That was a little more than three seconds of breath-holding free-falling right there."

"I knew you were crazy enough to take a boat over a waterfall."

Reed laughed. "I also love to hang glide. The best place to go is Chattanooga, Tennessee. I go a couple times a year."

"Yep, insane."

His head cocked to the side, and he peered at her from the corner of his eye. He liked seeing that lighthearted smile spread across her cheeks, and he sure as hell liked being the one to put it there. "You think that's risky, you should see someone wing-walk."

"Okay, and what the hell is wing-walking?"

"It's when you're strapped to the top of a vintage biplane, flying through the sky at one hundred and thirty-five miles per hour."

Megan's round eyes widened to the size of golf balls. "Oh hell no, I don't think I could even watch that. You've done it?"

"Done it and loved it," he said, making sure to drop his voice to get that little eye roll and head shake from her.

"Ok, I'm declaring it official: You're insane."

Reed belted out a laugh. "I've also been cliff diving in Acapulco, Mexico, and ice climbing in Colorado, just to name a few. There are still some things on my bucket list, though."

"Yeah, like what?"

"I would love to go wingsuit jumping in Switzerland. It's the most intense free-fall jump and the closest thing to natural flight as humanly possible."

"I'll gladly go to Switzerland, but there is no way I would do that."

"What about the death drop in Zambia?"

"Oh gosh, do I even want to know?"

"Probably not." He chuckled as he stopped in front of his motorcycle and stuffed his bag into the saddlebag behind the seat.

"Does everything you enjoy have to do with heights?" Meagan said behind him.

He turned to face her again. "Pretty much. That or water. My brother and I had plans to surf Ship Stern Bluff in Australia. It's one of the most dangerous places to surf in the world."

"Okay, water I can do. As long as I'm not going over any waterfalls or cliffs, I'm good."

"I'm glad you said that." He swung his leg over the bike and sat down, picking up the extra helmet. "Get on," he said, reaching the helmet out for Meagan to take.

"Wait. What?" She hoisted her hands up on her hips. "Reed Porter, where in the hell are you taking me?"

He cracked a smile, he couldn't help it—he had to tell her. She was just too damn cute all flustered and nervous, it was easy to give in. "White-water rafting, now get on."

She blew out a long breath that caused her shoulders to slump. She yanked the helmet out of his hands, pulled her hair out of whatever it was that was keeping it piled on top of her head, and put on the helmet. "I swear to you, if you even think about taking me over some damn waterfall, I'll kill you." She lifted her leg and climbed on behind him.

He laughed, which he was starting to realize was something she made him do often. It had been a long time since he let loose and laughed with someone like this. It was just another reason he liked being around her. Even if she only wanted to be friends, he would try to learn to deal with that. He'd take her anyway he could have her—although, he would still have rather had her in his bed. "There are no waterfalls on the Chattahoochee River. At least not where we're going."

"Oh, that's reassuring."

Her small body slid against him, and she wrapped her arms around his waist. He wanted to laugh at the death grip she had locked on him, but he resorted to a smile instead. He loved the way she felt clinging onto him, and he wasn't about to ruin it by making some smart-ass joke. No, she could hold on to him like this anytime she wanted to.

He turned his head over his shoulder to look at her. "You okay?"

She nodded. "Just don't go popping wheelies or get the speedometer over one hundred and I'll be fine."

"I've got to one hundred, huh?"

Meagan tilted her head to the side, and although he couldn't see her brows beneath the helmet, he was sure they were pressed all the way to her hairline.

"I'm kidding," he managed to say through yet another laugh. He reached down and placed his hand over hers, which were folded together against his stomach. He peeled her hands apart and wrapped his own around them—never once moving his eyes from her. "I may like to take risks, but I would never risk your safety. Not ever." The concern that lined her expression smoothed out as she stared into his eyes . . . as she realized he was serious. He squeezed her hands gently. "You're safe with me."

CHAPTER SEVEN

"So, what'd ya think?" Reed asked as they got back to his motorcycle. It was just now dark out and the night air was perfect for a ride.

"I loved it."

"So you would do it again with me?" he asked, straddling the bike. He grabbed Meagan's hand and helped her on behind him. She had changed into her jean shorts, and his palm brushed against the top of her thigh as she lifted her leg behind him.

"Absolutely," she said, sliding back behind him, a place her body very much liked to be. She'd loved watching Reed as he guided them down the river. It was like all the playfulness that was inside of him seeped into his expression. It gave her that little pitter-patter that was happening more and more often around him.

"All right, sugar. I'm holding you to that."

"You do that." She smiled. "I'm going to text Eva and tell her I'm on my way home, she probably thinks I've gotten lost or something."

"Better yet, why don't you text her and have her meet us over at the Oasis for a drink?"

"I don't know—"

"Come on, one drink, sugar."

"Fine, one drink . . . and food . . . then you're taking my ass home."

"One drink and I will take your sexy ass anywhere."

Meagan grinned and sent a quick text to Eva but didn't wait for her reply. Instead she just leaned forward and pressed her body against Reed. The insides of her thighs molded around his hips, and a dull throb crept through her core. She was going to have to get a handle on this effect he had on her, and quick, but some subconscious part of her didn't care, and that same subconscious part of her allowed her to press her thighs against him, almost squeezing him with her legs as she locked her hands around his stomach again. She could easily feel every single ridge and valley of every single muscle that made up his hard stomach. If memory served her right, she could just shut her eyes, lean her cheek against his back, and picture his naked body as she felt him beneath her fingertips. But what good would that do her? Absolutely nothing.

He was hands off, well, so to speak; she wasn't particularly hands off at that very moment, but allowing herself to go back there, to think about what had happened last night, or eight years ago for that matter, would do nothing but weaken her. Dammit, she wasn't going to get wrapped up in Reed. She wasn't going to get wrapped up in him, she wasn't, she wasn't . . . she just needed to keep telling herself that.

"You holding on, sugar?" Reed asked as the motorcycle roared to life, the vibrations rumbling underneath her.

"Let's go."

Reed took off, and she wrapped her arms tighter around his hard stomach. The wind was warm, and it bathed her skin in a layer of comfort as she relaxed against Reed's back. She enjoyed feeling the flex of his muscles beneath her fingers, the subtle movement of his hips between her legs, and the faint expanse of his back moving beneath her chest as he breathed. Every once in a while she would feel him turn his head over his shoulder to look at her, but she kept her head to the side, watching the street blur past her in an array of reds and greens as the lights flashed around them.

Ten minutes later they were pulling into a sports bar. It was your typical "beer, fried food, TV screens everywhere, and more pool tables than actual tables" kind of place. She just hoped like hell no one was singing karaoke.

Meagan climbed off the bike, using Reed's shoulders for balance as she swung her leg around. "You like burgers?" he asked, tucking the keys in the pocket of his jeans as he climbed off after her. The man could pull off jeans and a shirt better than any other man she knew.

"Am I American?"

A smile lifted at the corners of that damn mouth of his. It was a smile that lit up his eyes, making them greener now. Why did he have to look so adorable and hot at the same time? "Ah, you're a woman after my own heart. Beer?"

She tilted her head to the side. "Guinness draft."

"I think I'm in love," he said, swinging his arm around

her shoulder. It was a casual gesture—simple—there was nothing romantic or sexy about it. Hell, it was something Trevor would do. But she still couldn't stop the flutter that picked up in her chest.

They walked in, chatter and laughter bouncing through the open room. There wasn't a single table available, and the seats along the bar were all full as well. "Well, I'm not sure we're gonna be getting a burger here," Meagan said, scanning the room.

"Nah, some of my guys are here. We'll take over their table. That okay?" He was cute, concerned, like she might have a problem sitting at a table with a bunch of men.

She nodded. "Why wouldn't it be okay?"

"All right." He led her to the side of the bar—smack-dab in front of where the Cubs were playing the Braves on a large TV hanging on the wall. No wonder it was packed.

"And who do we have here?" a guy with a Braves baseball hat on said with just a little too much innuendo. He was cute, and he would be even cuter if he took off that Braves hat. Okay, so, yes, they were in Georgia, but the Braves, really? She was a Cubs fan through and through, just like her dad.

"Guys, this is Meagan, my new neighbor," Reed said, yanking the seat out from under Baseball Hat Guy.

The guy hopped off his stool before he fell to the ground and not so nonchalantly bounced his dark eyebrows up and down at Reed. "So this is the new neighbor, huh?"

"Aw, you've been talking about me?" she asked teasingly, helping herself to the now-empty stool and picking up a menu. "All good things, I hope." She kept her eyes on the menu.

Reed slapped Braves hat guy on the back of the head. "Nothing but good, sugar."

"Damn, brother. How in the hell you forgot a woman that looked like her is something I will never understand." He shook his head.

"I didn't forget her, prick. I just didn't recognize her. Not at first." Meagan pressed her lips into a tight line to keep from smiling as Reed tore his hands through his hair. Okay, so she gathered that he felt bad about his little memory loss, but was it so wrong for her to enjoy his inner turmoil as his friends give him shit about it? Nah, she didn't think so.

Meagan looked up and smirked across the table at Braves guy. "Thanks."

Dimples drilled into his cheeks as he smiled one of those I-just-one-upped-my-buddy smiles. "Hey, all I'm sayin' is, I wouldn't have forgotten you."

Meagan didn't need to turn her head to the side to see that Reed was sending his buddy a look that was lethal, she could basically feel the tension ready to snap. Mental note—sore subject for Reed. Okay, fun over . . . for now.

His buddy just laughed and shifted his head toward the ground. He obviously got the shut-the-hell-up memo from Reed's stare, but whether or not he was laughing at the fact that Reed didn't recognize her or if he was laughing at Reed's reaction to his little rib to the ego, she didn't know.

"So this pain in the ass right here is Sanders, or Luke—whichever you want to call him. Prick usually works too."

"Nice to meet you, Meagan," Sanders said, reaching his thick arm out for her to shake. Damn, the guy was like sex on steroids. *Big* didn't even come close to describing him. She thought Trevor was huge, and Kale was huge, but this guy made them look like weenies. She couldn't help but wonder if he had little-dick syndrome. Someone that big had to be lacking in other areas, it just wouldn't be fair if he wasn't.

"You, too."

"And this guy over here is Murano," Reed said, gesturing to the olive-skinned man sitting across from her. He had a hard line to his jaw and a faint scar across his bottom lip that extended down his neck. He was wearing a plain white T-shirt that made his dark skin look even darker. And his arms were something to take notice of. Not only were they big and defined—just the way she liked them, okay, just the way every warm-blooded female liked them—but they were covered in tattoos that went almost completely to his wrists. He looked like your typical Mr. Bad, with his short hair and hard eyes that were so dark, they smoldered. And that scar. She had seen her fair share of scars like that one, and she would bet money that it was evidence of his deployments. But she liked it, it made him even more attractive.

"Hi," he said, and Meagan was shocked at the warmth in his voice. She had to admit, she was half expecting him to give her the guy-nod and leave it at that.

Meagan smiled back at him. She had a feeling she was going to like these guys.

Her phone buzzed in her pocket and she pulled it out to see a text from Eva. "Eva's here, I'll be right back."

Meagan got up and headed for the front of the bar, her itty-bitty friend walking in just as she got there. Eva was short, really short, barely reaching five four, and her curly red hair was bigger than she was. The girl had a body on her, too. She looked like a gymnast with firm thighs and arms, and a tummy Meagan would kill for. If you took away her collection of push-up bras which transformed her Bs to full Cs, then she would be the ideal image of a gold medal gymnast. Her low-cut tank top showed off just how good Victoria's little secret could be for a pair of boobs, and her jeans clung to her body perfectly from her hips all the way to her ankles.

"Hey, babe," Eva said when she saw Meagan. "Where the hell have you been all night?"

"Reed took me white-water rafting."

Her body perked up a little as she focused her gaze on Meagan. "With Reed, huh? And I suppose he's here with you now?"

"Yes, and a couple of his friends. Fair warning: They look like they need to be up onstage at that Chippendales show we went to in Vegas last summer."

A hint of a twinkle sparkled in Eva's eyes and Meagan could see her perverted mind reeling. "Really?"

"Yes, really, and I know how you operate, so keep it clean," she warned.

Eva shook her head. "I'm slightly offended." Meagan narrowed her eyes. One thing Eva rarely got was offended. "You're right. I'm not. But don't worry. I have no plans to scoop up one of your neighbor/old one-night stand/new hookup boy's friends. Rest assured, I will be on my best behavior."

Meagan frowned. "His name's Reed. Please refrain from

calling him *old one-night stand* or *new hookup boy*. I'm try-ing to move away from that, remember?" she said, pulling a tuft of hair from the nape of her neck and twirling it around her finger.

"Honey, I don't know why you are fighting it. He's beau-tiful, he puts a cheesy-ass grin on your face, and after what you told me about last night—he does a lot more than that. I don't see the problem."

"You know what the problem is. He's everything that I usually go for. Sexy, funny, carefree, silly, reckless—"

"I don't see how any of this is helping your case. You're just making *me* want to date him."

Meagan sighed. She needed Eva to be on her side, to cheer her on and keep her on track. Not push her in the op-posite direction. She was supposed to be her wingman. "I'm looking for stable, settled, mature—Reed's like this giant man-boy who wants to play all the time."

"I forgot, you are turning thirty and now you want Mr. Boring."

"Mr. Safe. Come on," Meagan said, changing the subject. She and Eva could go at it all night, and Meagan was hungry.

Eva followed behind Meagan, through the crammed bar and back to the table. Meagan stepped to the side, allowing room for Eva to squeeze in, and she couldn't help the laugh that escaped from her mouth when she saw Sanders' face as he looked at Eva.

"Down, boy," Meagan said as she sat down on her stool, earning a round of laughter from Murano and Reed—but all it did was fuel the fire. Sanders laid on the smile, nice and thick, and introduced himself to Eva. Meagan was pretty sure Eva swooned a little, which shocked the hell out of her. Eva didn't swoon. She gawked, flirted, and sometimes even harassed—but never swooned. She seriously swayed a little in her peep-toe pumps (Eva was the girliest tomboy Meagan knew) as she shook Sanders' hand. He got up and offered Eva his stool and she took it, sitting down next to Meagan. Eva smiled, and Meagan knew exactly what was going through her best friend's mind at that very moment. They might as well been speaking telepathically to each other—Eva had a new game, and it was called Sanders.

"Scratch the burger, I'm getting the Chicago-style hot dog," Meagan said, closing her menu and handing it to the waiter who had finally made his way to the table. Reed didn't like the way his eyes lingered on Meagan a little longer than necessary, and he didn't like the smile he was giving her either. Jealousy was not one of Reed's many attributes, but he was feeling all sorts of jealous at that very moment. He chalked it up to being the result of her not wanting *him* to look at her that way—a result of the fucking "friend" title she had labeled him with. He could be her friend, hell, he wanted that—but being restrained from getting her beneath him when that seemed to be all he could think about was making that damn "friend" title a scarlet letter. What made it even worse was that he couldn't do a damn thing about the waiter looking at her like he was picturing her naked—and Reed wanted to pluck his eyeballs out of their fucking sockets.

Sanders snagged a couple of chairs over from the neighboring table as the people left, scooting one over to Reed. "So, Meagan, you ladies coming to the cabin with us tomorrow?"

"The cabin? No," she said as she brought the tall frosted glass to her lips. She took a sip of her beer and set it back down in front of her, her fingerprints lingering on the chilled glass.

"Why the hell not?"

"Maybe because no one asked her," Eva said, pointing her accusing stare at Reed while she arched those red eyebrows of hers. Reed was just waiting for her to start breathing fire. She obviously was also aware of the unfortunate lapse in his memory when it came to her best friend. He'd duck when the fire came—he brought that heat on himself. He threw his hands up in the air. "I had complete intentions on asking her and you," he said, nodding toward Eva. "But I got a little distracted."

Meagan turned his way, no smile, no typical narrow-eyed glance. She just looked at him, like she knew exactly the distraction he was talking about—almost like she hoped she was the distraction he was talking about.

"You gonna make me drop to my knees and beg?" He winked at Meagan.

"That doesn't sound like a bad idea. I like to see a man beg."

"Do you now?"

"Gutter, Reed. Out. Of. The. Gutter."

Reed laughed. "But you make it too damn easy, woman."

Meagan shrugged her shoulders, putting her I-don't-know-what-you're-talking-about smile on as she once again brought that frosty glass to her lips. The froth of the beer fuzzed on her top lip, and her tongue lifted from her lips to lick it off—and Reed watched carefully as she did. If he kept this up he was bound to move from friend status to creep status.

She set her glass back down. "I'm just gonna stay home, though."

"What?" Eva whined, and Meagan sent her a look that even Reed knew meant to drop it, but Eva either didn't get the memo or didn't care. "Stay home and do what? Stare at the wall? Watch our nonexistent TV? Come on, go. I will tag along."

"That sounds like a good plan to me," Sanders chimed in. Of course he thought it was a good idea, the guy hadn't stopped drooling over Eva since she had gotten there. Reed was about ready to suggest he tuck a damn napkin in the top of his shirt.

"Eva," Meagan warned. Okay, it was Reed's turn to take a swing at this.

"Come on, it will be fun. It's got an in-ground pool surrounded by a huge deck, we're gonna float the river too. Plus, the firework show you can see from the cabin is amazing. It's the Fourth of July. Come."

Meagan inhaled a deep breath and bit her bottom lip as she blew it out in a rush of air that shook her shoulders. Yep, Reed was pretty much calling this a win.

She glanced at Eva again then sighed. "Fine, we'll go. But I have full intentions on staying in that pool the entire time—just to warn you," she said, sending a knowing glance toward Reed.

"Why you looking at me? I don't care if you sleep in the pool, just so long as you come with me . . . us."

She smiled, a sweet one, almost a shy one. Hell, this woman had him in all sorts of knots. Her challenging looks and her sarcasm had him daydreaming about bending her over his bed, but those sweet looks, like the one she just gave him, had him thinking about holding himself above her, slowly kissing that sweet neck. Reed cleared his throat and shifted slightly in his chair.

"All right, just so we're clear, that means no crazy cliff diving or tree climbing or white-water rafting, just relaxing," she said.

Sanders laughed. "Dude, she's got you down solid."

She did.

Reed ignored Sanders' comment and instead kept his eyes on Meagan, who was sending him a look that not only caused his dick to twitch in his jeans but also sent a possessive ache through his bones. Never before had he wanted to be with a woman so damn bad, and not just in the physical sense. He just wanted to be near her, close to her, around her. He didn't know the last time he'd felt this way about a woman. Sure, he'd been in love before, a few times, not that he was even close to feeling that way about Meagan—but he never liked them like he liked her. She was real. She was funny and sweet, with just enough sass. Hell, maybe it was the challenge of it all that had him on edge and ready to snap. Maybe it was because he remembered so well from that night eight years ago the taste of her skin on his tongue and the feel of her wet pussy clamping around his fingers as he bit the soft pad of her ear.

"You can relax to your heart's content, sugar."

"What time are we leaving?"

"I'm driving my bike, it's kind of tradition."

The blue of Meagan's eyes nearly disappeared as she squinted and tilted her head to the side, baffled. This woman knew how to read him. She had him mapped out and had figured out the easiest route. Just like last night—she saw through him. Reed was pretty fucking good at locking away the crap that lurked in the deep crevices of his mind, but Meagan, she had a way of slipping through. But he didn't feel like getting into that discussion at that very moment, so he mustered up as much of a smile as he could, given the sudden brick that slammed against his chest as certain memories lifted to the surface, and said, "I usually ride by myself, but I would love it if you rode with me."

He could see his buddies' heads out of the corner of his eye as they shifted from him to each other, then back to him, their eyes trying to connect the dots of the paint by numbers that had suddenly made up Reed's decision making.

Meagan shifted her eyes between Eva and Reed and started twisting the blond strands of hair at the nape of her neck. "Um, well, I would, but what about Eva? She and I will just drive down there together."

Hell no, if she was coming, he wanted her with him.

He shook his head. "Nah, Sanders can pick up Eva."

"Yeah, you can ride with me and Murano," Sanders agreed.

"See, it's settled, you'll ride with me. We'll leave around three."

"Is that okay with you, Eva?" she asked.

Eva winked at her. "Fine with me, babe."

"Okay, three it is."

CHAPTER EIGHT

Meagan set her bag down by the front door so Eva wouldn't forget to take it with them when they headed to the cabin. Ugh, she was not particularly looking forward to this little trip. Okay, so she knew she needed to get out of the empty apartment and do something, Eva was right, there was no point to sitting on the air mattress all day staring at the wall. But she wasn't in the celebrating mood. She always loved the Fourth of July, it was always her favorite holiday, but not this year. . . .

"Hey, woman, you ready?" Reed shouted as he walked in through the patio door.

"Yeah, I'm in the kitchen."

Reed walked in and laid on that smile that could probably make a screaming baby stop crying. It was soothing, almost hypnotic. Reed just had this ease about him that was contagious, you couldn't help but enjoy it.

"What are you doing?"

"Packing food for Eva to take."

He grabbed the container out of her hand, opened the

fridge, and put it away. "I've got you girls covered. We're completely prepared."

She cocked her eyebrow at him. Somehow the idea of a bunch of men getting everything ready for a weekend away didn't strike her as likely. "Okay . . ." she said, dragging out the word. "What about chips?"

"Got it."

"Hot dogs? You can't have Fourth of July without hot dogs."

"Already got it."

"Okay, what about stuff for s'mores? I've got my traditions too, ya know," she challenged, trying hard to keep a straight face, but it was extremely difficult, especially when Reed was smirking with that sexy, lopsided grin—that try-me smile.

"Already taken care of. Give me a little credit, sugar. I've spent every single Fourth of July that I've been in the States either camping or at a cabin on some lake for as long as I can remember. I've got this packing thing down."

"Yeah, your family does the Fourth up big too, huh?"

Reed's eyes went a little distant, and his smile faltered. She felt a chill crawl over her skin as his expression hardened. "They used to," he said.

Meagan cleared her throat and quickly spun around to the fridge, needing a distraction from the apparent distortion that came over Reed—it was more so that *he* needed the distraction. She pulled open the bottom drawer of the fridge and lifted her lips into a smile. She turned around to face Reed, her legs planted firmly apart as she raised her hands to her hips. She nodded her head toward the fridge. "What about these?"

Meagan watched as Reed's body loosened and he tilted

his head to the side. The fog lifted from his eyes, and she was staring again at the perplexed shades of brown and gold and green that had no problem holding her hostage with their riveting colors.

Reed closed the short distance between him and the fridge, his body standing a little closer than necessary as he looked down at the drawer Meagan had pulled open.

He laughed. A good, heavy, thick rumble that started in his chest and bounced from his mouth, saturating the space around her. She was glad to hear it too. "Jell-O shots?"

"Hell yes, Jell-O shots," she said as she glanced back down to the drawer that was damn near overflowing with tiny plastic cups of vodka-infused Jell-O. "Who can have the Fourth of July without Jell-O shots? I've got a few things to teach you, my friend."

"I like the way you think, woman. Now *that* is one thing we didn't bring."

"See, sometimes I'm good for something."

He stepped back from the fridge and pinned her with a look that immobilized her, petrifying her limbs. The only thing moving was the quickening thud of her heart bouncing off of her ribs. Her eyes shifted upward, easily finding his in the spilt second before he pulled his lips up ever so slightly on the corners. "You're good for a lot of things." That sultry baritone accent of his was taking its time rolling over every syllable—and she was beginning to realize he was doing it on purpose. This was his little trick, his signature. Trevor had his wink, Kale had his dimple, and Reed had his accent. Each one used their little trademark move to weaken the stronger female species, casting some sort of spell that caused all rational thought to leave the brain, leaving only the thoughts that seemed to be geared toward anything and everything that had to do with removing clothing. Okay, so basically it was a weapon for temporarily tricking a woman's mind by her body's reaction. Smart, clever, and inspiring. She needed one of these trademark moves for herself. And she needed to figure out a way to become oblivious to Reed's.

Meagan rocked back on her heels, crossing her arms across her chest. "That's not going to work, ya know."

Reed's smile lowered, but only just slightly—he was going to attempt to play the innocent card. "What?"

"Uh-huh. You know what I'm talking about, Mr. Sexy Accent—just let me deliberately speak low and slow. Nope, not gonna work, my friend."

"You sure?" he said, overexaggerating the arch in his voice as he leaned in close to her.

The back of her hand conveniently found his chest. "Dammit, Reed. Yes, I'm sure."

A roar of impish laughter exploded from Reed's frustratingly perfect mouth, causing Meagan to sigh and roll her eyes and shake her head all at once. He was exasperating.

"Come on," he said, latching his arm around her shoulders and leading her to the front door. "Let's go."

It wasn't a long trip to the cabin, not as long as Reed would have liked. This was a trip that always seemed to tip the scale, to shift the so-called balance he attempted to put back into his life to the side of blissful hell. It was a ride that was not only cathartic but one that he resented and loved and needed all at the same time. He took all his pent-up, bitter fucking frustration and just rode.

There was a fraction of time in Reed's life when he was complete, when he felt whole. After losing that feeling—that part of you—some people never recover, some people never feel restored. Reed was one of those people. You can't possibly lose a piece of yourself and expect to feel the same ever again. It was impossible. Pain didn't work that way. Pain doesn't heal that way. It heals, but only for small periods of time, because nothing can last forever. It was this time, this moment, that healed him. It was doing this one simple thing every year that made that irreplaceable part of himself feel the shadow of its missing piece. It made him feel closer to the person he once was. It made him yearn for the life he once lived, and it made him crave the love he once had—because there was no other love like family, and when Reed lost that piece of himself three years ago, he essentially lost his family.

This ride was what made him feel the reminder of the joy he once shared with them—it's where he felt himself the most.

Reed breathed in the thick summer air as the memory flooded him. The same daily ounce of sorrow still bled from his veins, still seeped from his pores, but it was laced with a joy that was numbing.

This year was different from the last two though, and he didn't know if time played a part in that or if it had to do with the body that was clinging to him. Meagan's arm pressed into him and brought him to a place where reality wasn't suffocating him. Where the memory didn't weave a pattern of regret and guilt. She pulled him to the present—back to now.

Gravel crunched and popped under the tires as Reed pulled his bike up a long driveway that led to the same cabin that Reed had rented for the fourth year in a row. It was one of the largest cabins on the river and it was also built into the side of a hill, making for the best view.

The bike rolled to a stop and Meagan leaned back and released her arms from around his waist. "You said you rented a cabin. I expected a house made of logs surrounded by lots of trees, not a two-story lodge built into the side of a cliff." She placed her palms on his back and gave him a little shove. "Reed, this is amazing."

Reed looked over his shoulder to see a wide-eyed Meagan gawking at the house. She liked it, and pleasing her, making her happy, gave him a new excitement that he wasn't accustomed to. He'd seen his buddies go all romantic and out of their way to do those small gestures that women were so intent on having done for them. He didn't see the big deal. He understood the need to make the wife or the girlfriend happy, but to take the time to think and plan and execute said gestures seemed like a lot of unnecessary work. But then seeing the elated look that came across Meagan's face as she looked at the cabin he had rented for them made him understand exactly why they did it. It was a rush. Seeing her happy from something he did gave him a small thrill, and he would do anything for a thrill.

"Well, come on, let me show you the inside."

Her smile grew into her eyes as she climbed off the bike. Reed swung his leg over and stood by Meagan as she looked at the cabin. It was all beautiful red-cedar logs, with rich oak decks that wrapped around the two levels of the cabin. The fireplace was a mixture of gray and tan and brown bricks, forming a wide, impressive tower that made up the chimney. Behind the cabin were lush woods that lined the banks of the river that could be seen from any and all of the back windows of the cabin. He loved this place.

Meagan pulled her stare away from the cabin long enough to shift her head toward Reed and she gave him a titillated grin as she bounced on her toes. They had started up the few steps that led to the front door of the cabin when a large SUV pulled up.

Reed turned around and jogged back down the steps toward the SUV as the driver's-side door opened up. "Hey, Conner!" he exclaimed as he wrapped his arms around him.

"Hey, bro. It's good to see you. It's been way too fucking long."

Reed released Conner from his death-grip embrace and latched onto his shoulder with his hand. "It has been way too fucking long."

"Oh, you two act like you never see each other, you just saw each other at Christmas," Reed's sister said as she walked around the front of the car. Her hair was cut short, and although Reed was used to seeing it long, he liked it. She had always had a healthy figure, but recently it had been her mission to lose weight and get back to her "prebaby" body, and Reed for one thought she was getting too thin. He rushed to her and scooped her up in his arms. "Hey, Beck," he said as he squeezed her.

"Reed . . . you . . . are crushing . . . me."

He set her feet back down on the gravel and laughed. "Sorry, sis. You're just too damn skinny."

Her smile shot out and lit up her eyes. "I will take that as a compliment."

"Mom and Dad still not coming?"

She blinked slowly and offered him a weak smile as she squeezed his hand and Reed returned an understanding nod.

They weren't coming.

As much as he had hoped they would show, it wasn't surprising that they weren't. And he couldn't blame them.

He felt a presence closing in behind him and he didn't need to turn around to know that Meagan had left the front steps to join them, but he wasn't going to waste an opportunity to look at her. He turned his head over his shoulder and winked, causing her to scrunch her nose in response. It was not a response he was happy about getting—and only because the effect it had on him was not something he wanted his little sister to see.

"Hi, I'm Meagan," she said, reaching her hand out to Becky as she stepped up next to Reed.

He pressed his lips into a tight line, waiting for the look of death to cross over his baby sister's face. She was one hell of a woman, and she didn't like women sniffing around her brother, not that Meagan was doing any sniffing. Something told him that Becky was going to have a run for it with this woman.

Becky folded her hand around Meagan's and gave it a firm

shake. "I'm Becky, Reed's sister," she said with a disdain that made Reed angry. His eyes narrowed at his sister. He knew she could be a little tough to the women he brought around, not that there were ever many, but like hell was he going to let her be rude. She dropped her hand from Meagan's and pointed her accusing stare at Reed—her eyes flinching a little when she saw the look he was returning to her—but she continued talking to Meagan. "And, Meagan, you are . . ."

"Ah." She nudged Reed with her shoulder and he relaxed a little. "You've got a protective sister, huh? I like that." Meagan looked back and smiled—strangely enough, a genuine smile—at Becky. "I'm just a friend."

Becky shifted glances between Reed and Meagan, the proverbial wheel spinning in her head as she tried to determine the situation in front of her. Becky's body seemed to relax some and a smile somehow made its way into her expression. "Okay," she said flatly, although she didn't sound completely convinced.

Conner walked up carrying the most beautiful girl Reed had ever laid eyes on. "Baby, I'm pretty sure Addie is ready to eat."

Becky turned toward her husband and reached out her hands to the brown-eyed baby girl who was nothing but a one-toothed smile and drool.

"What happened to my niece?"

"Six months happened. You finally ready to hold her?"

Reed took off his baseball hat and ran his hands through the short mess of hair on top of his head then put it securely back in place. "Yeah, let me see the little rug rat." He held his arms out and Becky placed Addie in his hands. His whole body went completely stiff and his arms moved into an awkward position as he held the baby against his chest.

"She's not gonna break, Reed," Conner said, amused at Reed's apparent lack of confidence.

"Easy for you to say, she's your kid."

Meagan reached out and placed her finger in the baby's little hand. "She's adorable," she cooed, winning a grateful grin from Becky, who had yet to take her eyes off of her big brother, who probably looked like he was as comfortable as a hooker on a church corner.

"Thank you," she said warmly.

Reed looked over at Meagan, who was smiling at him with complete adoration.

"All right, Uncle Reed, I think that's enough torture for now," Becky said, lifting the baby from his arms.

"Hey, it wasn't torture, I was actually just starting to get used to it."

"I was referring to you torturing my poor baby girl, holding her like she was made of glass and carrying the plague."

"It wasn't that bad, was it?"

Meagan laughed. "Oh, it was." Becky shot Meagan a smile before she turned and headed toward the cabin. That didn't go so bad after all.

The inside of the cabin was just as amazing as the outside, if not more so. There was a beautiful great room with windows that lined the back wall, overlooking the river. The kitchen was huge, all beautiful wood cabinets and an island large enough to use as a dinner table. It was furnished with a cherry-brown leather sectional and a couple of cream-colored overstuffed chairs that faced the fireplace, which took up nearly half of the wall. The fixtures and the simple accents of the cabin were rustic, but the rest of the sleek and modern décor made for a blend that was astounding.

"Okay, which room is mine? I'm ready to test out the pool."

Reed bounced his eyebrows up and down, insinuating things Meagan was not wanting to think about. It was going to be hard enough spending an entire two nights under the same roof without wanting to give into every irresponsible desire her body was having for him. She didn't need any not so subtle innuendos to add to the temptation.

"This way."

Meagan followed him up an open staircase that led to the top level of the cabin. There was an open landing that looked down to the main level with two hallways extending from either side of it.

She followed him down the first hall, past a couple of empty rooms, to the bedroom at the back of the hall. It was simple enough, a large king-size bed, dresser, mirror, closet—oh yeah, and it was also beautiful. Reed had completely outdone himself, this wasn't a cabin—it was like staying in a five-star resort.

"Seriously, Reed, this is—" Meagan's phone buzzed in the back pocket of her shorts, cutting her words off short. She pulled the phone out and a wrinkle formed in between her eyes; she didn't recognize the number.

"Hello?"

"Meagan? Hi, it's Jason—uh, Dr. Ryan."

Meagan's eyes bugged out of her head and her jaw nearly hit the ground as her oh-shit moment slapped her in the face. She had completely forgotten about her dinner date with Jason.

She didn't wait for him to say anything else, she just jumped on the apology wagon. "Oh my gosh, Jason, I am so sorry. I completely forgot about our dinner date and I let some friends talk me into going away for the Fourth." The second the words left her lips she saw Reed's face turn to hers as an array of emotions flitted across his expression—and she instantly felt guilty. She was turning Reed down like he had two heads, waving the white "friends" flag in his face, yet accepting a date from a handsome doctor—a slap in the face, she knew, and she felt like shit that he had to hear her conversation.

She turned her back to Reed and lowered her voice slightly. "I can't tell you how sorry I am."

"Hey, it's not a big deal. How about you make it up to me next Saturday? Dinner *and* a movie."

"Yeah? That sounds great," she said, relieved that he was still willing to go out with her after she had completely and unintentionally stood him up.

"Good." She could hear the smile in his voice and it sent a flutter of pesky butterflies dancing around in her stomach. "How about you give me a call when you get back into town?"

"I can do that."

"All right, enjoy your trip."

"Thanks, bye." She pressed End and slowly turned back

around. Reed was leaning against the doorframe, his arms folded across his chest, an impassive look covering his scruffy face from eyes that almost looked like worn leather—hard and flat and dark, something she had never seen in them before—boring into her like he was trying to read her thoughts. Like they were written out in the flecks of her eyes. It was terrifying, yet it caused a subtle ache to travel throughout her body, tickling her skin and heating her blood.

"Doesn't say a lot that you forgot, does it?" His face remained stoic, but he had a hard edge to his voice, one that was so unlike him that it startled her.

She opened her mouth to say something. What, she hadn't quite figured out yet because she felt slightly guilty, yes. But now she was also a little bit pissed. The problem was, she didn't know if she was mad that he seemed angry or if she was mad that the little speck of jealousy in his voice excited her.

But she didn't have a chance to say anything anyway, because in the infinitesimal second she hesitated, he turned around and walked away.

CHAPTER NINE

He knew he was out of line. Fuck, he also knew he sounded like a jealous prick, but whatever part of him that seemed to acquire this new and vexatious little emotion was also the same part of him that was finding it hard to keep to the "friends" side of things where Meagan was concerned. It was fucking stupid to be so twisted up over a woman, but dammit, he was. And why? He hadn't the slightest clue what she had done to inch herself in so deep to cause him to act like a completely different person when it came to her.

No, he didn't like the thought of her out with another man, but what claim did he have over her to prevent that from happening? Not a fucking one. One thing was for sure: He was balancing on a tightrope, he was no good at it, and it was hard as hell, but unless he wanted to fall off, unless he wanted to possibly lose the friendship he had with this woman, then he needed to keep his head forward, no looking down.

Reed was sitting outside on the back deck with his

brother-in-law when Meagan finally came out. She had spent a good twenty minutes up in her room, and Reed knew it was because he had crossed the line.

"Hey," she said sweetly. Dammit, that soft, sweet side of her was becoming the hardest one to resist.

Reed stood up and gently grabbed onto her elbow, leading her to the far side of the deck next to the pool and away from Conner. She didn't protest or jerk away from his grasp, she just followed him. He turned around to face her, placing both hands on her arms just below her shoulders. "I'm sorry for being a prick."

"You're not a prick, Reed. Maybe an idiot, but not a prick."

"I shouldn't have walked away from you."

"You were mad, I get it."

"You're right, I was." He searched her face, looking for anything that gave her away, but she wasn't giving in. Her eyes stayed on his, focused and soft, but there was nothing in them that told him anything.

His hand moved to the side of her neck, brushing back the stands of hair that were loose from her ponytail. She gently inhaled a breath. It wasn't intentional, and it wasn't exaggerated, but he noticed it nonetheless. Her body had never been able to hide the way it felt from him, even though her eyes were perfectly capable of doing so.

She smiled up at him; the glint in her eyes, the little hint of mischief that he fucking loved, made an appearance, and it eased him in a way he didn't know was possible.

"Friends?" she asked, with a little too much smirk for his liking.

He cocked an eyebrow at her and frowned. He felt a little trapped by this question, feeling like it was a double-edged sword, but also feeling like she needed to hear the words. She needed confirmation, and he wanted to give it to her—for no other reason but to give her a little ease and a little control, because he knew she wanted it.

"Friends."

"Good," she said. Her feet rolled up onto her toes. "I was hoping you would say that."

Reed couldn't help but smile. That one little word changed her entire demeanor, and her ease was contagious. "Yeah, and why is that?"

A roguish gleam took over her big, round eyes. "Because only a friend could get away with doing this." She thrust her palms against his side, and in that spilt second, realization struck, and Reed knew he was going in the pool—but in that same split second of realization, his hand wrapped around her wrist. If he was going in, she sure as hell was going in with him.

She let out a delighted scream as they both went crashing into the water.

Reed pushed himself back to the surface and laughed when he saw Meagan's head emerge. "You didn't honestly think you were going to get away with that, did you?"

"Well, obviously I did or I wouldn't have done it," she said, laughing as she flicked her hand in his direction, splashing water in his face.

"You wanna go there too? Because I'm telling you right now, I. Will. Win."

"Pretty cocky, aren't you?"

"You have no idea, sugar."

Reed started swimming toward her, and she retreated, swimming as fast as she could toward the steps. "Reed Porter, I don't know what you are about to do, but I suggest you think before you act!"

"What fun would that be?"

She laughed as he gained on her and latched onto her waist. She spun around in his arms. Water trickled down her face, over her lips, and all Reed wanted to do was press his lips to hers and lick the moisture that clung to them. His dick started to harden as his eyes looked down at the tank top that was now clinging to her generous tits. Tits he already knew fit perfectly in his palms with just the right amount of soft flesh spilling over.

Reed tightened the hold he had on her waist as she tried to squirm out of his grasp. The way her wet skin slipped over his as she wiggled in his arms, laughing as she struggled to break free, turned him on, and she didn't have a damn clue how sexy she was when she wrestled against him, which only made it worse. He started to lift her body out of the water, and she squealed—it was a sweet sound, a playful sound, and he very much liked her reaction that went along with it.

She bit her fingers into his shoulders, holding on tight. "Reed, don't do it," she warned, her already big, round eyes widening. Ah, but that only made him want to do it more.

He lifted her a little higher, and just as he was about to toss her across the pool, she wrapped her legs around his waist and locked her ankles above his ass, squeezing his hips with the insides of her thighs. He felt her center nestle against him, and he knew she could feel the way his body was responding to her. She fit so perfectly to him, their bodies molding to each other as she clung onto his waist.

She gave him a little squeeze with her legs. "Now, if I let you go, you promise not to throw me?" She pressed her lips together and lifted her eyebrows, waiting for him to respond.

Reed let go of her waist and lifted his hands in the air. "I'm not promising anything, woman."

Her mouth fell open and her eyes widened slightly. She was pouting, and it was damn sexy.

He slipped his hands back beneath the water and smoothed them over her small waist again. She rocked her hips downward, more than likely without even realizing it given her body's track record, but the way she felt pressing against his hardened dick was almost too much to bear. There was only so much willpower and self-control a man could have before falling off the tightrope, and Reed already had one foot dangling over the side.

His fingers trailed south, tracing the curves of her sides, her hips, until they touched the bare flesh of her smooth thighs. He splayed his palms out over her legs, his thumbs bushing gently over the insides of her thighs as he worked his way toward her knees. Her legs relaxed under his touch and her eyes moved over his as she slowly pulled her bottom lip into her mouth, and it took everything Reed had in him not to pull that lip from her mouth and suck on it himself, because he sure as hell knew how good it would taste.

He continued his journey down her legs, moving his fingers over her calves until he found her ankles, still crossed, pressing into the small of his back. His fingers wrapped around her delicate ankles, and in one slow, gentle movement, he pulled them apart and slid out from in between her legs.

Fuck, he deserved some sort of medal.

Meagan was sure that her face had turned about fifty shades of red within the matter of a single heartbeat. Her face felt on fire as she stared at Reed, who she knew was just as turned on as she was, because she felt how hard and ready he was for her when her body sunk down onto his. Dammit, it was a thin line, and Reed was doing a hell of a lot better staying on his side of it than she was.

A big splash splattered from the pool as a giant dog jumped in and paddled its way over to Reed, whose expression had went from intense and turned on to happy and excited. "Hey, Tiny!"

"How in the world did you get the name Tiny for that dog?" she asked as she joined Reed, rubbing the giant mop of wet black hair.

Reed just smiled.

"Hey, you two, I thought it was supposed to be more fun to swim with your clothes off, not on."

Meagan instantly snapped her head to the side when Eva's voice penetrated through the self-humiliation wall she had stupidly put up when she had to go and wrap her legs around Reed. Ugh . . .

Luke stepped up next to her, a mischievous smirk taking

over his face. "Yeah, that's what I've heard too. Wanna try it out?"

"You think that was gonna work on me? Really, big guy? You may be hot as hell, but I'm gonna need a little something extra before I let you talk me into skinny-dipping in a pool with you, just saying." Eva patted him on the back, which looked hilarious all in itself because he was so much taller than her. "Better luck next time." She winked.

"I think I may be in love with this woman," Luke said, watching as Eva walked to the edge of the pool and sat down, slipping her feet in. By the look Eva had plastered on her round face, she'd heard Luke's little joking admission.

"You're gonna have to do better than that too," she hollered behind her, gaining a grin from Luke as he walked back into the cabin. Yep, Meagan was right.

Meagan swam to the edge of the pool next to Eva and pulled herself out, her light pink tank top clinging to her stomach, and her black, high-waisted shorts sticking to her thighs. "What took you so long?"

"Oh, we had to wait for Murano, he was waiting to hear from some woman who has him wrapped around her little finger, tied up on a leash in the backyard, and quite possibly has his balls in her back pocket."

Meagan clenched her teeth and sucked in a sharp breath between them. "That bad, huh? Did he enlighten you on what was going on?"

"Nope."

Tiny climbed the steps of the pool and got out, shaking his long black fur, spraying water drops everywhere. It reminded her of that scene from *Beethoven* when the dog shook his wet, dirty body, getting drool and water and mud all over the walls of the room.

Reed swam over to Meagan and Eva, Tiny making his way to Eva as well, and leaned his forearms over the side of the pool, resting his chin. "There was this woman that used to live at Benning, she's married."

"S-she's . . . what?" Eva stuttered.

"Yeah, her husband was stationed at Benning, but he came down on orders to Fort Campbell, I think. Murano's dumb ass met her at the gym one day and had her in his bed later on that same night. They made it a thing, and in his defense, he didn't know she was married at first, and the stupid fucker got attached. He waits around for her now. They meet up every now and again whenever she can get away, but she's got kids, too."

"What the hell is he thinking?" Eva spat, discord spilling over the sides of her words.

Reed shook his head, and it relieved Meagan to see the same emotions cross over his face—he wasn't happy about the affair either. "Fuck if I know."

"So, what, she's in love with him?"

He shrugged. "I don't think so, but I don't know."

"Well, if not, he's gotta be fucking amazing in bed."

"Eva!" Meagan admonished.

"What? Oh, don't act like you weren't thinking the same exact thing."

She was.

"Murano's a good guy, just a little bit sappy, and unfortunately he's in love with a married woman." Reed pulled himself out of the pool, dripping water all over Eva as he climbed out next to her.

Eva shook her head like she was thoroughly disappointed. "I would have never pictured Murano to be a sucker for love. Could I picture him with some whips, maybe some rope and a blindfold, yes—"

Meagan just rolled her eyes.

"Don't you roll your eyes at me. I had the pleasure of seeing him half naked in nothing but his boxer briefs today when we picked him up, and, babe, that man with that body—which was covered in ink, by the way—was made to be naughty. Like I said before, he's got to be amazing in bed."

"I think that's my cue to go. You girls getting hungry?"

Meagan laughed. "You cooking?"

"Yep."

"Then yes." Meagan stood up and lifted her soaking wet tank top over her head, peeling it from her skin. Reed's lips curved up as he watched her and it sent a thrill through her body knowing that she was getting to him. She unbuttoned her shorts and stepped out of them, standing in her black polka-dot bikini.

Reed clucked his tongue and shook his head, unashamed as he allowed his gaze to skim over every inch of Meagan's near-naked body. Okay, so this probably wasn't smart. She was already torturing herself with the "no sleeping with Reed" rule while she was on her self-proclaimed hunt for Mr. Safe, and stripping down in front of him, knowing good and well that he would watch and enjoy every moment of it, was going to add a notch to the difficulty meter on her temptation chart.

His greenish-gold eyes melted and took over the dark hues of brown as his expression shifted. He was no longer looking at her, enjoying the view. Now he was looking at her as if his eyes could physically touch her body. The intimate way it made her feel not only had the blood rushing to the surface of her cheeks but it also caused her to shift her gaze to the two people around them. She hoped like hell they weren't privy to the little moment that seemed to be hanging in the small space between her and Reed.

"That's just evil," he said. And just like that his buoyant demeanor smothered the intensity that he had just thrown at Meagan. She was learning to have a love-hate relationship with his apparent split personality. She loved both the playful, silly, light-hearted Reed who was present 99.9 percent of the time, but she also unfortunately loved seeing the side of Reed that was intense and powerful and raw. It made her feel wanton and sexy and needed—all feelings she had been lacking as of late. But that was why she hated it too. Because she didn't want to feel those things from Reed. He was a wild card. Not safe.

Reed headed back toward the cabin and Eva stood up, stepping closer to Meagan. "Nice moves, babe. You basically have him eating out of the palm of your hand. But I'm going to give you a little piece of advice, and I suggest you take it. Either get over yourself and your ridiculous so-called plan to find your Mr. Safe, your forever, and let that sexy-ass man fuck you senseless, or stop playing these stupid little games with him."

Meagan's mouth fell open and her brows furrowed tightly. "What the hell, Eva?"

"I'm sorry, Meggy. I know—shocker coming from me, right? But you're fucking with him, babe. You tell him you don't want him, that you just want to be friends, yet you're sending him all the signals that say you want to do a lot more things to him than your typical friendship allows. Make up your mind. Either have sex or don't. Either be friends, or fuck-buddies, or get married for all I care, but just make up your mind. You're torturing the poor guy."

Meagan threw her head back, huffing a frustrated breath out of her mouth as she focused her eyes on the fluff of white clouds that was slowly moving across the sky. Dammit, Eva was right. And she hated when Eva was right.

She dropped her head back down. "It's so damn hard."

"Because you're making it hard."

She was. Meagan was letting her body have a mind of its own. She had told Reed that she wanted to be friends, and he was being so respectful of that. Hell, he even pulled away in the pool when she obviously was lacking the restraint to do it herself, and when he so clearly didn't want to either. She just needed to figure out a way to line the boundaries—to draw a line in the proverbial sand. And she needed to figure out a way to do it soon—if anything, this weekend should be like a thread tied around her pinkie, reminding her exactly what she needed to do—stick to her plan. Reed had a way of throwing her off course, changing the speed limit, and whipping in a couple of U-turns. She didn't have time for his detour. . . .

"I would listen to your friend."

Meagan's head snapped around to see Becky walking up behind her. Had she heard their entire conversation?

"I'm sorry?" Meagan retorted. She was trying not to sound annoyed, but she couldn't help the small dose that seeped through. This woman didn't care for her—she'd gathered that little tidbit—but that didn't mean she had to be a bitch. Meagan didn't care if she was Reed's sister or not, she wasn't going to let her intimidate her.

"You say you're friends, and that's fine. Tell me whatever you need to to make yourself sleep better at night. But I know my brother. Just listen to your friend. Don't play games with him, okay?" She pressed her lips together briefly, like she was sifting through her memory, and when she spoke again her voice was softer—sad. "Especially not here—not this weekend." She turned on her tiny bare feet and headed back to the door to the cabin before Meagan had a single chance to get a word in.

Meagan's brows furrowed. What was with her? And what was so significant about this damn weekend?

"You bleeding?" Eva asked.

Meagan blinked and pulled her eyes off of a retreating Becky and looked over at Eva. "What?"

"She was spitting daggers. Cold, sharp daggers. What the hell did I miss?"

She sighed. "You didn't miss anything. She gave me the evil eye when she first got here, but I thought she was just playing the overprotective sister."

"Um, I think it's safe to say you assumed correct, babe."

"Yeah, but I think there's more to it."

Eva threw her hands onto her little waist. "Well, whatever it is, we're not going to let it ruin your big weekend."

Meagan rolled her eyes. Becky wasn't going to ruin her weekend, it was already ruined by default. "Shut up, go get your swimsuit on, and get your ass in this pool with me then."

"You don't have to tell me twice." Eva leaned forward and smacked Meagan on the ass before she bounced off toward the cabin. "You want a beer?" she hollered over her shoulder.

"Do you really need to ask?"

Eva winked. "Be right back."

CHAPTER TEN

Reed woke up the next morning to the smell of bacon frying and coffee brewing and his stomach rumbled in gratitude. He sat up in his bed, his hand instantly slamming against the throb that was pulsing in his forehead. Hangover headache, just what he needed, although it was nothing a couple of aspirin couldn't cure. After the amount of alcohol he consumed last night he was lucky all he had was a headache.

Meagan had been acting weird all night, and it did nothing but frustrate the shit out of him. She wasn't her typical cute, sweet, comfortable self around him. Actually she wasn't around him much at all. After they ate dinner—which she maybe said a total of two words during—she spent the rest of the evening playing poker on the back deck with Sanders, Murano, and Eva, drinking beer, and downing her Jell-O shots. She had offered him a few smiles here and there, but that was it. So what did he do instead? Pouted like a pussy-whipped moron and drank until he damn near couldn't walk. He was amazed he made it up to his bed. Whatever the hell he did wrong, whatever he did to cause him to fall off that fucking tightrope, he was fixing it—today.

Reed clumsily walked down the stairs, using the railing as his support as he felt the full effect of his alcohol consumption.

"Well, good morning, Reedster. How ya feeling?" Becky said from the couch where she was sitting, nursing Addie, whose tiny baby feet were the only things Reed could see poking out from the blanket Becky had draped over her.

"I feel like a million bucks, how about you?" He yawned, scratching his bare chest.

"Well, considering I didn't drink until I passed out, I'm doing great." Becky's eyes softened around the edges. "You good, Reed?" Her tone was gentle, concerned.

He gave her a knowing glance. "Yeah, I'm good." He shook his head quickly. "It's not that."

She nodded her head, then peeked under the blanket to check on Addie. "Well, whatever it is, I'm here."

He winked and gave her a reassuring smile. "I'm good."

Reed padded barefoot toward the kitchen. He needed water—a gallon of it. He had a full day planned for them. He wanted to float the river—there was a lake that branched out from the Chattahoochee, and they usually took his buddy, Finn's, speedboat out, but he wasn't able to get a pass this year, and he was stuck at battalion pulling staff duty—so floating the river was the next best thing.

Reed and his brother had always spent the Fourth out on the water for as long as he could remember—it was their tradition. He and his brother were two peas in the pod when it came to pretty much everything. They liked the same foods, enjoyed the same activities, had the same friends, and even, at times, unknowingly had the same woman, which earned them a few matching black eyes. His brother wasn't here—but he wasn't going to let that stop him from holding on to those things, to their traditions.

"Well, look who is up and moving. Morning, sunshine." Eva was standing at the stove, flipping pancakes and frying bacon.

Reed opened the fridge and pulled out a jug of water. "Morning." He put the jug to his mouth and tilted his head back, the cold fluid soothing his throat as the water flowed down, quenching his hangover thirst.

He set the jug down and reached for a pancake that was on top of a stack a foot high, but Eva swatted his hand away with catlike reflexes. "Hands off. Those are for Meagan, it's her birthday."

Meagan groggily moped out of her room and dragged her feet along the plush, thick carpet as she headed downstairs. She had been trying to avoid this day for more than a month now. Good-bye, twenties; hello, thirties. Meagan always used to love her birthday being on the Fourth of July, celebrating with fireworks, cornhole, and hot dogs on the grill. She loved her birthday, and she usually did it up big. But this year she just wanted to crawl back into bed and pretend it never happened. But she couldn't—she had let Eva and Reed talk her into this trip and now she was forced to put on her happy face and celebrate.

When she walked into the kitchen and saw the huge stack of pancakes, complete with thirty lit candles poking from the top, she wanted to cringe and laugh and quite possibly die. Birthday pancakes, she should have known. Eva had made them for her for the last four years.

"Happy birthday!" Eva exclaimed with a little bit too much enthusiasm for before noon. She handed Meagan a mimosa and Meagan smiled. It was faint, and it probably looked ridiculous spread across her face, but it was all she had in her at the moment.

Her head shifted to the side when she saw movement out of the corner of her eye—a half-naked Reed was taking the few short strides to her. He swung an arm around her shoulders, pulled her against his side in that half-hug sorta way, and kissed the top of her head. "Happy birthday, sugar." The warmth from his bare chest seeped into her skin at the comforting contact, but just as quickly and easily as he had embraced her, he released her.

"Ah, hell yes, pancakes," Luke said, walking up behind Meagan as he and Murano entered the kitchen. She watched as Eva's face contorted into a cheesy-ass grin the second she saw Luke. She did believe that her pain-in-the-ass, tough-as-nails friend had a little crush.

"Not just pancakes, birthday pancakes, and you can have some after Meagan blows out her candles."

"It's your birthday, Meagan?" Becky asked, joining them with Conner by her side and Addie in her arms.

"Yes."

"Well, happy birthday. Reed, why didn't you tell us?"

"Because, I didn't know." He pointed his accusing eyes at Meagan and she shrugged, shifting her eyes toward the ceiling in that don't-blame-me way.

Eva carried the stack of pancakes, which looked like it was about ready to burst into a ball of flames from the abundance of candles that were lit on top of them, over to Meagan and set them down on the island in the middle of the kitchen. Everyone started singing "Happy Birthday" to her while she attempted to keep a grateful smile on her face for the duration of the time. She could already tell she was going to need something stronger than a mimosa to get through the day.

CHAPTER ELEVEN

Eva pulled her fiery red curls back into a ponytail. "You can't just ignore him and hope that it goes away."

Meagan looked over at Eva as she slipped her swimsuit cover-up over her head. It looked more like a lightweight black dress than a swimsuit cover-up, though. "Hope that what goes away?"

"Your attraction to him. I told you to stop torturing the poor guy and instead you go and add a notch to his misery and ignore him the entire night. That's even worse than teasing the hell out of him, Meggy. I'm probably going to regret what I'm about to say, but cut the man some slack."

Meagan pulled her hair out of the messy bun that was on top of her head and let it fall down over her shoulders. "Since when did you become the Yoda of all things men- and sex-related?"

"I've always been your Yoda, you just never listen to me."

"Yeah, because if I did that I would have been having little Joey babies."

A shiver shook Eva's shoulders. "Ah, Joey . . . don't get me all excited—and don't try to distract me from my lecture," she reprimanded. "You may be thirty now, but you're still young and single and sexy. Take advantage of what you've got, babe. Reed is gorgeous, he has a body that I would love to crawl on top of, and his eyes—oh, and that mouth. How can you keep away from those lips? I can only imagine what they can do."

"Believe me, I'm having trouble keeping away. I just don't want to get suckered in."

"Then don't. If you want to keep your relationship sex-free, then by all means, it's your potential orgasm you're wasting, not mine—but don't ignore the guy. He looked like a lost, sad little puppy last night, I could barely stand it. He obviously knew something was up with you, hence the drunken stupor he slipped into. Enough with the games."

"Coming from the woman who was all for torturing him—I believe the game you were plotting was to get him hot and bothered then shut him down."

"You're right, but that was when the idiot didn't remember having sex with you. It's different now."

Meagan crossed her arms over her chest, waiting for Eva to volunteer her words of Eva-wisdom, because Meagan was dizzy from trying to keep up with her.

Eva sighed. "That was before I saw the way he looked at you—"

"What way?"

"You may be a blonde, but I know you're not dumb. That man has no desire to be your friend."

"You're right, I'm not stupid. It doesn't take a genius to know that Reed wants to dive into the past and get me back in his bed—hell, he would probably even admit it."

"Okay, I take back my 'you're not dumb' comment, because clearly you are." She picked up the SPF lotion and tossed it to Meagan. "I'm gonna let you off the hook today since it's your birthday, but do me a favor, no more ignoring him. I don't think I can handle a full day of pouty Reed."

Meagan laughed at the thought of Reed sulking in the hammock on the deck last night, drinking like a fish. It wasn't funny, and she shouldn't be laughing at him—but she couldn't help but think his little temper tantrum was cute. She just definitely didn't want to be the cause of another one. Besides, Eva was right—again. She couldn't keep playing games with him, and she couldn't just ignore him for the rest of the trip either. She liked him, she really did. He made her laugh and he was fun to be around. He was like chicken noodle soup on a cold day. He was like her favorite song that she hadn't heard in a long time—the one that made her smile regardless of the mood she was in—and he was like her favorite movie when she needed a good laugh. He was soothing, and comforting, and just—easy. Being around him was easy—except, she didn't just want to be around him, she wanted to be with him. Could she do that? Could she keep her feelings locked away and enjoy him for what he was offering? She'd done it with Kale, why couldn't she do it with Reed? But then what? She would be right back to where she started—no closer to finding her forever than when she was dating all the other Mr. Wrongs that had come into her life. Mr. Thrill was no exception. She needed to keep him separate, she had to.

"You girls ready?" Luke stuck his head in the doorway to

their room, giving Eva a once-over as she stood in her shorts and bikini top.

"Yep." She slipped a T-shirt on and stepped into her flip-flops.

"Good, then get your little asses downstairs so we can go, you women take longer getting ready than my men do on the first day of jump school—and that's not saying much."

"Oh, quit your whining, we will be down in two minutes," Eva mumbled.

Luke looked at a nonexistent watch on his wrist. "I'm timing you, and if you're not down here in two minutes, I'm coming up after you."

Eva cocked her head to the side. "Is that supposed to be a threat or a promise?"

Luke leaned his Hulk-like shoulder into the frame of the door and crossed his arms over his massive chest. "What do you want it to be?"

Meagan cleared her throat. "You guys realize that I'm still standing right here, don't you?"

"Aw, sweetheart. We wouldn't leave you out. You're more than welcome to join us."

"How very generous of you, but thanks. I've seen Eva butt-ass-naked more times than I can count"—she smiled at Eva—"and I promise, you won't be disappointed, but I will let you enjoy her all by yourself. Besides, I live with her, I can have her anytime I want her."

Meagan struggled to keep the seriousness even on her face as she watched Luke's mouth part slightly and his eyes widen. He was too easy.

Meagan winked at Eva then walked past Luke, stopping in the doorway to give him a friendly pat on the back. "She likes her hair pulled, just not too hard. Oh, and she gets extra feisty when you spank her ass."

A fit of laughter was caught in the back of Meagan's throat as Luke looked down at her, trying to determine whether or not she was serious. Her little white lie was worth it too, she had him all twisted up and it was hilarious. Oh, the power women had over men was sometimes unbelievable.

"No, I get extra feisty when I spank *your* ass, remember?"

"Reed!" Luke turned his head into the hall and hollered. "These women are fucking with me something good!" He looked back at Meagan, who was still standing next to him, and then to Eva, who was standing conveniently next to the bed. "You two are fucking with me, right?"

That was it, Meagan couldn't hold back the laughter that was starting to strangle her. Her mouth opened and the most soothing laugh erupted from her throat. Eva crossed the room and stopped in front of Luke, more like stopped *on* Luke, her small body brushing against him. Eva smiled at him and then snaked her arm out and slid it around Meagan's waist, pulling her in close. "Wouldn't you like to know?"

She then walked past Luke, who was now frozen solid in the doorway, pulling Meagan along with her. When they got halfway down the hall Meagan turned her head over her shoulder to see an oversize Luke staring after them.

"He was like putty." Eva giggled.

"Jeez, mention a little girl-on-girl action and men lose all rational thoughts they possess in their usual one-track minds."

"Well played, babe. That should make for a more interesting night. I can almost promise you I get a hair tug here or there and more than likely a couple good ass spankings."

Meagan hip-checked Eva. "Yes, I'm dying to know if his penis is as big as the rest of him," she whispered.

"I shall let you know."

"You're such a little slut," Meagan teased.

"No, unlike you, I'm going to enjoy myself. There is absolutely nothing wrong with two consensual adults enjoying a night of casual sex at its finest. And besides, Luke has those lift-me-like-a-rag-doll-and-pin-me-to-the-wall arms. How could I possibly resist?"

Meagan rolled her eyes and smiled. Eva was a spitfire, but that's why she loved her.

Luke's feet hit the bottom of the stairs just as they were turning the corner into the great room. "Reed," he said, shaking his head back and forth like he was extremely disappointed, although Meagan knew he was anything but. "These women are up to no fucking good."

"These two? Nah." Reed winked at Meagan. "Y'all ready to go?"

"Yep," Eva said, glancing back at Luke. He walked past, keeping a watchful eye on her as he continued to shake his head, and picked up the cooler next to the island in the kitchen.

"Where's everyone else?" Meagan asked.

"Beck and Conner are going to hang out at the pool here with Addie, and Murano is waiting for us out by the truck, I think he's on the phone."

Megan lifted her head slowly in understanding. Murano was talking to his married girlfriend. . . .

"All right, let's go." Luke said, walking toward the front door, cooler in hand.

They all followed. Meagan was actually looking forward to this. She hadn't gone on a float trip since she was a teenager. Relaxing in a giant tube while drinking an ungodly amount of beer sounded like the perfect way to spend her birthday. Especially the beer part.

They loaded in the truck, Meagan sitting between Eva and Reed in the backseat.

"You feeling okay, lush?" Meagan asked as she nudged Reed with her shoulder.

"Are you kidding? I'm perfect. Nothing a little bacon grease and a couple aspirin couldn't fix."

"Good." She smiled and for some reason Reed seemed to relax a little bit. Whatever it was that had him so uptight seemed to settle under his skin—and unfortunately, she had a feeling it was her.

The water was the perfect temperature as Reed walked into the river, pushing his tube and the beer tube on each side of him. Everyone followed and soon enough they were all tied up to the beer tube that was carrying their cooler.

Eva, Murano, and Luke were floating up ahead of him, and Meagan's tube lingered in the back with Reed's—and he was grateful for the alone time. He needed to get inside this woman's head, because lately she was confusing the hell out of him. Sending him death looks one day, moaning in his mouth the next, calling the friend card, making dates with other guys, teasing the hell out of him, and then ignoring him altogether. Fuck, he knew women were temperamental but this woman was taking it to a whole new level.

He leaned up a little in the tube, supporting his weight with his arms, as he turned his head to the side to look at her. She was temptation in the flesh, wearing her skimpy yellow bikini that sat so low on her hips, it wouldn't take much to pull it down just slightly and he would be able to see her in the way he had been picturing for nights. She had tits that were made to be worshipped. They were full and soft and the ample flesh was beautiful, barely hidden by a thin scrap of fabric. He wanted—no, he needed—to reach over and pull the string that tied around her neck, to let the material fall away, so he could feast his eyes on what his hands had been lucky enough to touch the other night.

But he wasn't going to trample down that fucking path. Something was off with her last night, and as badly as he wanted to ask her what the hell was going on, he didn't want to ruin the mood she seemed to be basking in at the moment. She was better today, she was back to herself, back to the confident woman who had embedded herself in his life when she sent him those narrow-eyed glances that first night.

Her head was leaning back against the back of the tube, her hair spilling over, skimming across the top of the water. Her beautiful golden legs were hanging over the edge, her pink-polished toes dipping into the river. He stuck his hand into the cool, flowing water and paddled himself closer to her until he was able to reach out and latch onto the handle of her tube. The subtle jerk as his tube bounced against hers made her eyes pop open.

She smiled at him. "Hey, you."

"Hey, birthday girl, you need another beer?"

"Ugh, don't remind me." She pressed her beer can to her lips and took a sip. Obviously she didn't need another one.

Reed continued to hold on to her tube, keeping them right next to each other. "Yeah, so about this birthday thing, why didn't you tell me it was today?"

"Because"—she lifted her head up off the tube and looked at him—"I'm thirty today."

"Yeah, and?"

She sighed and dropped her head back against the tube. "I had hoped to have a lot more going for me by now, turning thirty just put this whole new ticking clock to the mix."

Reed laughed, she was being ridiculous. "What the hell are you talking about?"

She rolled her head to the side, her baby blue eyes blinking slowly before she fixed them on his. She parted her lips, then shut them again—seeming to be deciding her next words. He could see the indecision flicker through her eyes before a heavy sigh heaved from her chest and relaxed her shoulders. "I wanted to be married," she said, turning her head so she was looking back up to the sky. "I wanted to have kids. I wanted to be settled and happy by now. Instead I'm thirty and single. It's just not what I pictured for myself, and turning thirty was a not so subtle reminder of everything I wanted and everything that I don't have."

"Why the hell did you give yourself a deadline anyway, sugar? So you're thirty, big deal. Welcome to the club."

Her eyes snapped back at him. "I don't want in the club."

"It's not so bad."

"Says the big, overgrown man-boy."

He pinched his brows together, pretending to be offended. "Hey, now. What's that supposed to mean?"

"You have this addictive energy for life, for the exciting spontaneous thrill. You like to play."

"Yeah, and is that a bad thing?"

"No, not at all," she said quickly, obviously trying to soften her unintentional insult. He smiled, letting her off the hook, and she relaxed. "I love that about you. But let me ask you, do you want a family? Do you want to get married and settle down?"

Reed thought about it for a minute. Did he want a family? Yes. He wanted the family that wasn't here, the family that basically refused to see him. But did he want to get married and settle down? Why should he have that? It wouldn't be fair.

"See," she said when he didn't respond. "You're fine with your life the way it is, so you don't understand where I'm coming from."

He wanted to understand her. Fuck, he wanted to know everything about her, even her crazy-ass ticking-clock theory.

"Help me to understand, baby."

Her eyes widened at the endearment he slipped out. He didn't even mean for it to happen, but he couldn't help but like the way it sounded rolling off his tongue.

A tingle coursed through Meagan's bones when Reed called her *baby*. She hadn't been called that in a very long time. Actually, she hadn't been called that by anyone other than Daniel, the man who broke her heart eight long years ago, right before she met Reed.

Reed winked at her. "Sorry, sugar."

"No, it's okay. It just caught me off guard. A man hasn't called me that for a long time."

"I'd be lying if I told you I wasn't happy about that."

She splashed water on his face. "Be serious."

His eyes glazed over, and he looked at her like he could see through her, and it scared the living hell out of her. "I am being serious. Tell me about him."

"About who?" Her subconscious instinct was to evade his question, to dodge the bullet that was aimed at her memory. She repositioned herself in the tube, letting her lower body submerge into the water as she latched her upper body over the side of the tube.

Reed brushed his thumb across her arm, gaining her attention from where she was previously focused, skimming her fingers across the top of the water. "About the man who broke your heart."

She swallowed hard as she felt the color drain from her face. A sense of betrayal rocked through her mind as it lingered over the small fissure that was still visible on her heart. "There's not much to tell," she lied. "He was the first and last man I have ever loved." The fact of the matter was, she just didn't want to talk about it. Bringing up the man she thought she would spend forever with—bringing up Daniel—was like opening up an old wound and pouring in salt and whiskey. It hurt . . . still.

She and Daniel had dated all of her junior and part of her senior years in college. They were inseparable, and she'd loved him more than she ever thought possible. He was sweet, and handsome, and funny. He was also silly and playful, and if she took a step back and thought about it—he was a lot like Reed.

Daniel was a football player for the University of Florida, with hopes of going pro. They met at a frat party that she had basically dragged her roommate to. He spotted her the moment she walked in the door, and she knew in that one instant that she needed him. Meagan was a little shy back in college, but that all seemed to change when a little tequila was thrown into the mix. It didn't take her long to gain the liquid courage to make her move. They danced and talked the remainder of the party, and before the sun came up that next morning, she was fast asleep cradled against his naked chest, wrapped in his strong arms. Those same arms held her nearly every night after that. She fell so hard and so fast that it blinded her. She didn't even see it coming. . . .

She was waiting for him outside the locker room. The loud voices that filled the locker room had finally started to taper off. The Gators had just claimed their victory over the Illini, and the guys were more than a little revved up.

Meagan knew how to read Danny. She knew how to see through him. It was a practiced skill, one she had loved learning. But when he walked through the locker room doors, she wished like hell she could read the emotion that was written on his face. It was one she had never seen before, and the worry it caused to course through her put her on edge.

"Hey," she said as he stalked toward her. His eyes were hard, cold, and angry. She had never seen him like this. Never.

"Let's go," he barked. He never talked to her that way.

"Danny, what's wrong?" She reached her arm up and placed her hand on his hard bicep. She felt the tension in his muscles, the rigidness in his body. Something was wrong.

He jerked away and stormed into his truck, throwing his duffel behind his seat before he slammed his door. Meagan had a moment of hesitation. A tiny part of her was afraid to get in that truck with him, afraid to know what had happened that seemed to take over the man she loved. But she loved him—she had to know what was wrong. She wanted to fix it.

Her body moved before her brain had a chance to catch up and she climbed into the truck. Daniel didn't say a word, he just put the truck in reverse and peeled out of the parking lot.

She didn't know where they were going. She didn't know if they were going to the usual post-game party or if they were going back to her house or his. He wasn't driving in a familiar direction, and she didn't even think he knew where they were going.

"Baby, what's going on?" she finally asked after what seemed like forever of silence. They had just won another game, he killed it out there on the field. He should be basking in the afterglow of victory, not sulking.

His head shifted to hers for the first time since they had gotten into the truck. Remember that reading him thing she was so good at? She wished like hell that she couldn't read him at the moment, because the look he gave her sent her heart to the pit of her stomach.

"What is it?" she demanded.

"Fucking Jo," he huffed.

Jo? Jo, Jo . . . oh Jo. Beautiful blond cheerleader who had been dating the QB, Avery.

"Avery's girlfriend?"

"Yes," he spat.

"What about her?"

"She's fucking pregnant."

Meagan's eyes widened. Avery's girlfriend was pregnant?

"Well, I don't understand why that's such horrible news. Sure they're young, but they seem to really care about each other. It's not the end of the world."

Daniel shot her a glance that might as well have pierced her chest with a knife. He had never looked at her with such anger, maybe even hate. "Why the hell are you so fucking mad?" she snapped. Whatever was going through his mind, he needed to tell her, because this pissed-off stunt he was pulling was getting real old, real fast.

"Why am I mad?" He was shouting, another thing he had never done to her. "His fucking life is over. What's it going to be like with a knocked-up girlfriend? And the draft is soon. Fuck!"

"Calm down, Danny. They will figure it out."

Daniel finally pulled onto a familiar road after his sulking detour. They were heading to his house.

"She needs to get an abortion." The words left his mouth in a cold, dead sweep that had Meagan second-guessing them.

"What?"

His face momentarily turned to her, but it was long enough. She had heard him correctly. At least he had the decency to look guilty.

"You did not just say that," she whispered. That volume even sounded like a stretch.

"Meagan, she's fucking pregnant," he said as he pulled up in front of his house. His roommates were already gathering on the front lawn with a couple of girls on their arms. Looked like the after party was here tonight.

"What if it was me, huh? What if I was pregnant?"

He didn't flinch, he didn't blink. His face remained stoic—like the answer had always been there. Like he didn't even need to think about it. *"You don't want me to answer that right now, M."*

"Like hell I don't!" She shook her head, unable to wrap her mind around the words he was saying. This wasn't the man she loved. This wasn't the man that she thought she was going to spend the rest of her life with. He wouldn't want that. He couldn't . . .

"So you're telling me that you would want me to kill the life inside me? Kill your baby?" Meagan was supportive of women's rights and their choice to do what was best for them. But that would never be Meagan's choice.

Her eyes stayed locked on his. She needed to see his face, she needed to see his reaction. The first reaction was always the most honest form of the truth. In that split second when your mind didn't have time to wrap around whatever it was that was thrown at you, that's when your true colors showed—your first reaction didn't lie.

"It is my baby!" he blurted as his fist flew into the dashboard.

That's when her world decided to flip on its axis.

That was when she found out that everything she wanted, everything she loved, was a complete lie.

She had lost the ability to breathe. She just sat there looking at him as he stared out the windshield. He was so consumed with his own fear that he didn't even see Meagan crumbling right in front of him. The longer she looked at the man she loved, the more she hated him.

"Look at me," she demanded.

The coward that he was took his sweet little time shifting his body toward her. His eyes met hers and there was only a tinge of remorse in them—the rest was fear, and she knew that fear wasn't a fear of losing her. It was a fear of losing himself.

His jaw clenched tightly under his skin and his voice was cold when he finally spoke again.

"It is my baby."

And she saw her future ripped from her hands with those four words.

"I beg to differ," Reed said, his voice bringing her mind back to the present.

"What?"

"I think there's a lot to tell about this asshole, he obviously fucked with your heart. I can see it on your face right now."

Meagan pinched her lips together, forcing herself to maintain eye contact with Reed as she tensed her body, trying miserably to ward off the chill that seemed to seep into her bones, regardless of the July heat. Reed was reading her more easily than she felt comfortable with. She didn't know if she wanted him to have that power over her.

She blinked her eyes slowly. "He just didn't want the same things I wanted. End of story."

Reed nodded his head. "Ah, he didn't want kids?"

"Nope."

"And that's a deal breaker for you, huh?"

"It is." She never thought she would have a deal breaker. She never thought that a man she loved wouldn't want the same things out of life that she did. But now she knew better. She couldn't risk it. She didn't want to feel the way she felt that night ever again.

Reed lowered his body into the water like Meagan had, leaning his arms over the side of his tube, still holding on to hers. "But what I still don't understand is, what's the rush, sugar? You have plenty of time."

Meagan didn't want to get into her life story with Reed. She didn't want to hash out all the miserable details of her failed relationships and her reasoning for wanting what she wanted, but Reed was as stubborn as they came. And she wanted him to understand. She wanted to wipe that too-much-life-to-live-before-settling-down look off his face.

"You're right, I could have plenty of time. But I might not. My mom and dad thought the same thing. They thought that they had all the time in the world to start a family. But when they finally decided to try to have a baby, it was too late. My mom was unable to get pregnant."

Reed looked at her, the question written plainly on his frustratingly handsome face. "I'm adopted," she said.

"You're like this amazing, intricate puzzle, and you're finally giving me some pieces to put together."

Megan laughed, and Reed was relieved to see the flush creep back into her cheeks. He thought he had lost her there for a minute. He thought the Meagan that he loved to see had slipped into the fucking past with that son of a bitch who hurt her. And that was the last thing he wanted. He wanted her here with him, he wanted her good thoughts, he wanted to see that smile pull across her face, and he wanted to see those pearly whites shine at him while her body unknowingly flirted with his own thoughts. Thoughts he was trying to not have, but he was failing—miserably. Good news was, he was back on that fucking tightrope—both feet balancing, unsteadily, but he was back on. And that was all that mattered at the moment.

"I think that's a first. I've never been referred to as a puzzle before."

"Yeah, well, you're taking a while for me to figure out, but I like that you're finally showing me."

"So you don't think I'm crazy?"

"Now, don't go putting any words in my mouth, woman," he teased.

She laughed and took another drink of her beer.

Reed was in no hurry to settle down, he had too much life to live before he did that. But he admired how Meagan wasn't going to apologize for what she wanted. He loved how she put him in his place and let him know it too. If they'd been in a relationship, her thoughts for her future would have had him running fast in the opposite direction. But now the fact of the matter was, the way she wasn't afraid to go after what she wanted, and the way she wasn't going to let anyone hold her back, made him like her that much more.

CHAPTER TWELVE

So, the day wasn't a complete bust. Yes, she was the age we shall not mention, but she'd enjoyed her birthday. From waking up feeling like all she wanted to do was to crawl back in bed and sleep the day away, she had to say that it turned around pretty well. Staring at Reed with his shirt off for the majority of the time probably had a great deal to do with the appeal of the day as well.

Meagan was lounging in the free-standing hammock that was on the back deck, her hair still damp from her recent shower. Everyone had long since gone to bed, and she was enjoying the quiet. Tiny had rested his enormous head in her lap and she raked her fingers through his dense, soft fur.

She was staring out at the river, watching the soft ripples move across the calm water. She pressed the wineglass that rested in her hand to her mouth and savored the robust flavor of the cabernet that settled on her tongue before she let it coat her throat. The night had finally completely taken over the sky, no more fading blue hues lingering around in the late hours, no. Now it was completely dark. The few remaining fireworks would occasionally light up the night sky from somewhere distant along the river—but other than that, it was black. It was peaceful, the only sound was the faint trickle of the river down below, the soft breaths from a satisfied Tiny, and the occasional crackle of fireworks as they faded away.

Tiny's head popped up off her lap the second before she heard the door to the house open up.

Reed walked into view and she smiled up at him as he stood over her, nothing on but a pair of gym shorts hanging low from that perfect V in his hips. Dammit, there he was again with no shirt on. She pulled her eyes away and took another drink of her wine.

"Hey, whatcha doin' out here all by yourself?" he asked as he sat down on the oversize patio chair that was next to her. Tiny clumsily made his way to Reed and lowered his head onto his lap.

"Just enjoying the last of the lingering fireworks."

Reed took up the hypnotic task of rubbing the top of the dog's head. "Yeah, have you had a good birthday?"

"I have. Thank you for making the dreadful three-oh not so dreadful."

"Anything for you, sugar." His voice had that soft, sleepy, sexy rasp to it, and paired with the Southern drawl that really seemed to make an appearance when he was tired, Meagan was done for—that voice sent a shiver through her body, prickling goose bumps all over her legs—the good kind. "Where's Eva?"

"Up in our room, more than likely getting her hair pulled."

Reed narrowed his eyes in confusion. "Luke's with her," Meagan explained, and Reed cracked an approving grin as he gave an understanding nod. She returned her own form of an approving smile, hell, she was happy for Eva. "I've offered to take the couch tonight."

Reed's jaw set tight, his strong eyes boring into hers. "You're not sleeping on the couch," he declared, his tone not leaving much room for argument.

"Yes, I am," she protested. "It's fine. I'm a hard sleeper, I can pretty much crash anywhere."

Reed lifted his hand from Tiny and leaned back in his chair, crossing his arms over his bare chest. "Okay, then you can crash in my bed with me."

She sucked in a sharp breath between her teeth. "I don't think so, Reed."

He leaned forward again, resting his forearms on the tops of his thighs. The thick muscles of his shoulder flexed, causing Meagan to gawk like a hormone-crazed teenager. *Great.*

Reed smiled, apparently privy to her little drunken, gaping eyes. Damn wine . . .

"Look, it's late. Come to bed. I will be a complete gentleman." He lifted his fingers in the air. "Scout's honor."

Meagan debated her options as she finished the last of her third glass of wine. She toyed with the idea of her body curled next to him. It was tempting, and the thought was very appealing. She had slept in the same bed as Trevor many times—but she was afraid it wouldn't be the same when she was lying next to Reed. Trevor could curl up behind her and wrap her up in his arms and she would feel nothing but content—no flutter of excitement, no wanton desire to feel more of him. But what if she did with Reed? Actually, she already knew the answer to that question—she would feel those things with Reed, she didn't need to be in his arms to feel them either. But ultimately, her body's cravings won out against her pesky internal need to weigh the repercussions. She wanted that contact, even if it was just lying in the same space as him, sleeping.

"Fine," she said. "But I'm warning you, I'm a kicker. And I sometimes talk in my sleep too."

Reed stood up and reached out for her hand. "That's okay, I snore."

"Well, good thing I'm a hard sleeper then," she said, placing her hand in his, allowing him to help her up. Her legs swayed under her, causing Reed to move his grip from her hand to her elbow as he steadied her.

"How much wine did you have, birthday girl?"

"A glass or two . . . or three . . ."

Reed chuckled and shook his head. "Come on."

Reed led Meagan to his room and she smirked when she heard the soft mumbles and cries coming from the room at the end of the hall. That little hair-pulling assumption was probably right.

She followed Reed down the other hall, which led to his bedroom. Reed flipped the switch to his room and Meagan had to squint her eyes from the sudden blinding light. "Oh, shit, sorry," he said, quickly turning it back off.

Meagan walked to the far side of the room where the

wall was completely made of glass from ceiling to floor. The view was breathtaking, even in the dark of night when she couldn't make out much other than the shine from the water and the crackle of colors sparking up the night sky in the distance.

She felt Reed walk up behind her. "Great view, huh?" His body was close, close enough that she could feel the faint heat radiating from his naked chest onto her back, but far enough away that they weren't touching.

"It's beautiful. And you can see the deck and the pool from your room too."

His head moved forward, his mouth hovering dangerously close to her ear. "How do you think I knew you were down there?"

Meagan turned around, their nearness knocking the breath from her lungs. She had to tilt her head back to look into his eyes, and she almost regretted doing it—almost. They stared at hers with a rawness that held her captive, an intensity that she knew he possessed, but she hadn't been sure until that very moment how much it could consume him. He was looking down at her like he was unable to do anything but that—like she was the one holding him captive instead.

She involuntarily licked her lips, and when the little action registered with her now clouded mind, she took a step back. The small distance she had put between them cooled the moment that had penetrated the air, and with that small distance, Reed's body seemed to soften, his muscles relaxing and his breathing evening out.

"Here," he said, holding out a T-shirt to her.

She took it from his hands. "Thanks."

He turned around, keeping his back toward her as she pulled off her tank top and unsnapped her bra, letting them both drop to the floor.

"Better hurry up, sugar. I'm trying hard not to sneak a peek here."

She laughed, relieved that whatever moment had passed between them wasn't going to make this little sleeping arrangement any weirder, or more difficult, than it was already going to be. She pulled his T-shirt over her head and narrowed her eyes when he glanced over his shoulder.

"Damn," he said, hanging his head between his shoulders when he saw that she was already in his shirt, a wicked grin fanning his face.

"I thought you were going to be the perfect gentleman?"

Reed winked at her before he threw himself on the bed, pulling the covers down and spreading out on his back.

Meagan rolled her eyes, unable to suppress the smile that was threatening to take over her face. He had flipped the switch, and carefree Reed was back in full swing. She shimmied out of her shorts, leaving them discarded on the floor with the rest of her clothes.

She crawled into bed and curled up in a ball on her side facing him. His head was turned toward her and a slow and sweet smile tugged on his lips. It was cute and honest. It was lacking the impish pull or that playful smirk. It was just a genuine, sweet smile, and she couldn't help but return it. Reed lifted his arm up above her pillow and patted his chest. "Come here."

Meagan didn't hesitate. She could use a warm body to hold on to, even if that's all it was. Reed was comfort—and she let him encase her in it.

Her head nestled in next to his shoulder, and his arm left the pillow and wrapped around her back, holding her close to him.

"See, not so bad, huh? What'd I tell ya? Perfect gentleman."

She tucked in closer, it felt too good not to. "Uh-huh. Perfect."

Reed huffed a short, soft chuckle, then pressed his cheek to the top of her head and sighed as he tightened his hold on her.

"Reed?" Meagan whispered, after a few moments of silence passed.

"Yeah?"

"We're friends, right? I mean, friends that are clearly attracted to each other, but friends, right?"

He laughed, a deep, authentic, sexy laugh—his warm breath spreading across the top of her head. "You could say that."

"Okay, so I need you to be honest." She lifted her head to look at him. "I'm tough, you're not going to hurt my feelings. I just want you to answer honestly. And none of that bullshit tell-her-what-she-wants-to-hear crap that men always do."

"Shoot."

"Am I wife material?" She lowered her head again, relaxing it back on his chest.

"What in the hell kind of question is that?"

"An important one."

He took a deep breath in, her head rising and falling with his chest. "I think you've had a little too much wine."

"Probably so, but really. Am I? I mean, if you weren't so fly-with-the-birds, bungee-jumping, wing-flying-walking-whatever-it-is crazy that you are. If you were to slow down—could you see yourself with someone like me?"

His hands started lightly skimming over her back with the tips of his fingers, and the feeling was delicious. "I don't know, Meg. I've never thought of my life like that. It's never been in my cards, so I've never played my hand. But I'll tell you, no lie, that, yes, you are absolutely wife material."

She rolled out of his arms and propped herself up on her elbow so she could look at him. The faint light from the moon that was seeping into the room did little to aid her eyes in the darkness, but she could still make out those handsome features she loved to look at, and he was smiling.

"So what the hell is the problem?"

He rolled to his side and leaned up on his elbow as well. "You're not the problem."

"I know. It's the good-looking, up-to-no-good, panty-dropping, sweet-talking, don't-want-a-relationship Mr. Wrongs that I've been dating. I've established that." She dropped her arm and fell back onto the pillow.

"Panty-dropping? Did you really just say that?"

She rolled her head to the side to look at him. "Yes, I really just said that."

He inched closer to her as she lay on her back until he was pressed up against the side of her body. His hand reached out and smoothed the hair away from her face. "You will have it all one day, Meg."

She swallowed hard, unable to take her eyes off of him as he looked at her with such assurance that she was almost forced to believe him. "And what makes you so sure?"

A smile cracked open his lips and lines creased around his eyes. "Do you need me to make a list?"

She wiggled on her back, situating herself under the covers. "I would love for you to make a list, why thank you."

"Smart-ass."

She shrugged.

"Look, sugar. You're the fucking package. You're funny as hell, and half the time I don't even think you mean to be. You're strong, you're not afraid to go for what you want, and you're not ashamed to let everyone know it either. You're witty and sarcastic, which makes for a hell of a good time being around you, and you're a knockout. You have this sweet, gentle beauty about you paired with this crazy sex appeal that you seem to use even when you have no fucking clue that you are, and it's even sexier when you do it on purpose." He paused and leaned over her. "You're everything good and bad and interesting mixed up into one. You've got it all."

She lay there, her eyes unable to shift from the riveting ones staring back at her. His words left a wave of longing trailing after them. Hearing him tell her she was everything, that she had it all, not only shocked her, but it swayed her. It tipped her thin needle, pointing to the scale that was weighed down with everything she tried to ignore—and every single thing was a part of Reed. But she couldn't ignore the way he was making her feel at that very moment, and she didn't want to. Her arms lifted and wrapped around his neck, her fingers brushing over the short hair on the back of his head. His eyes stayed fixed on hers, never moving, never wavering from the hold he had on her. She waited for him to crack that cocky smile, but nothing. It was like he was afraid to move, afraid to break his contact with her, like she was going to bolt from him at any moment.

Her fingers crept around to his jaw, and she ran the pads of her thumbs over the fresh stubble that was prickling his face. She could feel the tension in his muscles working under his skin. She smiled to herself, he was trying so hard to hold true to his gentleman promise, and she would definitely give him credit where credit was due, but right now—she just wanted him to kiss her.

The moment her fingers pressed against the side of his face, he felt an overwhelming need to cover her mouth with his until he could no longer feel or taste or smell anything other than her. But he couldn't. He knew where she stood. He knew what she wanted—what she needed. And he also knew he wasn't it. He wasn't crossing that line, because if he did, he was afraid there would be no going back.

But then her shoulders left the mattress, her blond hair tumbling down until the ends were skimming across the sheets as she lifted her head to meet his. She hovered there for a moment, waiting, almost begging him to kiss her—so he did.

He pressed his lips to hers and all the pent-up cravings he'd been having the last few days started building pressure in his chest. He waited to see if she would hesitate or push him away—but she didn't. And when he felt her lips soften under his at the same time a satisfied sigh moved her shoulders, that pressure exploded and his lips crushed against hers, tasting, feeling, exploring every part of her mouth and she matched him with an eagerness he was unaware she possessed.

Her arms immediately lowered and linked around his shoulders, her fingers digging into his back as he lowered his chest down on top of her, pressing her deep into the mattress. Somewhere in the back of his mind he knew that he probably shouldn't be doing this, but he couldn't stop—not with her nibbling on his lip with her teeth, and not when her fingers slid down his back, scraping her nails on his skin. No, he didn't have any intentions of stopping.

His fingers toyed with the hem of the T-shirt covering her beautiful body—it wasn't what he'd had in mind when he handed it to her to put on, but he was suddenly very grateful for the ease it allowed his fingers. He slipped the tips of his fingers over the outside of her thighs, feeling goose bumps pop up along the path he was making toward her hips. Her skin was so soft and flawless, and he had the urge to rip the shirt from her body, tear the panties that were covering her, and drink in the sight of her naked beneath him.

She was an eager little thing beneath him too. Her thighs rubbed together and her body squirmed against him as her tongue devoured his mouth. He could feel the obvious need that her body was craving from him, and he was more than willing to satisfy it.

When his fingers finally reached their anticipated destination, he slipped his index finger under the thin lace strap that rested on her hip and followed the path that little strap took—across her smooth stomach, over to her other hip, and down the inside curve of her thigh—skimming across the top of her pussy as his fingers went back for a round-trip.

His mouth left her lips, but only so he could brush them down the center of her throat. His lips absorbed the vibrations that penetrated through her skin as a moan undulated through her chest, up her throat, and out of her mouth.

His hands were still enjoying the feel of her soft flesh beneath his fingertips and the way the muscles of her stomach trembled every time he brushed over the skin right above her pussy.

"Reed."

His name came out of her mouth, breathy and hurried—and for a brief moment, an ache pressed against his chest as a fear that she was going to tell him to stop entered his mind. But when his fingers stopped their seductive journey, and his eyes lifted to hers, she smiled, lifted her hips off the mattress, and pushed the damned panties down her thighs.

A wicked smile splayed across the width of Reed's face—a very contented, relieved smile. "Damn, sugar. I would have been happy to do that for you."

He lowered his hands to the fabric still resting on her knees and pulled it the rest of the way off. She squirmed, as if the material was a burden and her body was finally free from it.

Placing a knee on the mattress between her legs, he reached his hands under her back, and pulled her up into a sitting position. Her hands instantly raised above her head, and the fact that her mind was so in sync with his, turned him on in a completely new way.

He lifted the T-shirt over her head and tossed it to the ground. Then he took a moment to just look at her. The woman who had taken up residence in his mind—in his dreams—for the last week was right in front of him, and he wanted to make sure to embed the real image of her in his mind, because the memory of her from that night long ago did nothing to exemplify what was in front of him now.

"You're staring," she whispered shyly.

"I know."

She slid her legs behind her and raised to her knees in front of him. Her tits were right in his reach, her nipples pink and taut, and he wanted to lean down and pull one into his mouth and roll it between his lips—but he didn't. He was more interested to see what Meagan had planned now that she was on her knees in front of him.

She inched her body closer to him, but even then she still wasn't close enough—not as close as Reed needed her to be. Reaching out, she grabbed his hands in hers then slowly brought one to her mouth and pulled his thumb between her lips, sucking it gently. His eyes were fixated on her plump lips as she swirled her tongue around his thumb, then released it from her warm mouth. She moved his hands down, splaying his palms over her collarbone, down over her tits—barely giving him time to enjoy the soft mounds before she skimmed them over her stomach. Just as he thought she was leading him to her sweet spot, to where he was itching to touch—to feel her warm and wet, coating his fingers—she wrapped his hands around her waist and pressed her body against him.

The closeness he was craving seeped into him as her soft, bare skin fluttered over his.

"Isn't it more fun to touch than to look?"

Oh, hell, he was in for it with this woman.

"I like to use all my senses," he said. "Sight." He slowly and deliberately trailed his eyes over every inch of her that was visible to him without pulling away from her. "Smell." He buried his nose in the curve of her shoulder and breathed her in. Her skin was sweet, clean, and it encased him in the scent that was hers and hers alone. "Taste." He slicked out his tongue over his lips and licked a path up to the soft skin below her ear, causing a delicate, soft moan to trickle from her lips. He smiled against her neck. "Sound," he whispered, loving the little noises he was producing from her. "And touch." His hands gently gripped the tender skin right below her ass, slipping his finger between her thighs and over the warm lips of her pussy. He gently spread her open and slowly rubbed the bud of her clit.

Her head fell back and her hair brushed the top of his arm that was wrapped around her waist. Her body gave a little as she quivered, and Reed moved his hand down and pressed onto the small of her back, holding her firmly against him as he continued to circle her with his thumb. "Try to hold still, baby," he whispered, his mouth still lingering over her neck.

"I don't think I can."

"Yes, you can."

He angled his wrist, leaving her tender clit, slowly and easily slipping a finger inside her. She instantly clamped around him and her body bucked against him.

"Reed—"

"Not yet," he whispered. He had been waiting for too fucking long to feel her body tremble beneath his touch. "Let me take you on this ride, baby. I will get you there, but I'm going to take my time." He twisted his fingers until he found that spot deep inside her, that smooth little spot that sent a pleading moan into his ear. "That's it, let me find all your sweet spots, sugar."

Her body trembled against him and he continued to hold her tightly to him, immobilizing her, forcing her to feel only what he wanted her to feel. When her breaths became heavy and when he felt her quickening, he withdrew his fingers and released her from his chest.

Her eyes lazily opened and met his with a wanton need that matched his own. "Lie down."

She sank down onto the bed, slinking her legs out on either side of Reed's. "You've seen me, now let me see you," she said.

His head cocked to the side and he smirked. "All you had to do was ask, baby," he said, pulling his shorts and boxers down, his erection springing free. He lifted his knees, then pushed his clothes to the floor. "Now, where was I?"

The sight of Reed between her legs, his thick, hard cock an inch away from the ache that he came so close to soothing, had her licking her lips and arching her back—begging for him to take her.

"Patience," he said with a smirk. Damn him.

He lowered himself on the bed and realization of what he was about to do entered her hazy mind. Her internal muscles pulsed along with the beat of her heart, the very idea of his mouth on her was sending her close to the edge of no return.

She felt him settle between her thighs; then she felt his fingers biting into the flesh below her ass—and then she felt his tongue gently swiping over her opening, up to her clit, and back down again. Her body shook and her hips moved in unison with the rhythm of his mouth, bringing her closer and closer. He dipped his tongue in, and the wet warmth was heavenly, but it only intensified the need she had to feel his cock buried deep inside her.

"Reed, I want you—inside me."

"Fuck, baby. Don't tempt me."

"Reed—"

He slipped two fingers inside her and hooked them into her G-spot and she absentmindedly grinded down against him. "I'm going to stoke you slowly, carefully," he said, gently easing his fingers in and out of her then hooking them, hitting that little spot that she loved. "I'm going to bring you so close that you feel like your body won't possibly survive without release." He spoke in time with the pleasure he was giving her body, telling her word for word what he was doing, and it was the hottest thing a man had ever done to her. The sound of his voice alone had the ability to create shivers that would cause her to slip, shivers that would make her fall headfirst with blindfolds on in order to reach the nirvana he was capable of creating. But when that lush, thick voice was combined with his mouth and his hands and his body—all on her, all at once—it made for a combination that not only created shivers that shook her to her core, but it made her not want to slip and fall, it made her want to jump. He was taking her someplace she couldn't reach, but when she got there, she would definitely jump.

A tingle was building low in her stomach, pulling her insides tighter around his fingers. "Good girl," he whispered as his mouth moved over her ear. "And now I'm going to give you what you need, and you're going to scream my name."

His words sent a fresh batch of tingles rippling through her. She needed to let go. Every part of her was on edge. Her body felt irritable, eager, and anxious. It was like she was going through withdrawal at the same time that she was experiencing the most intense, blissful high her body had ever had—and Reed was the drug.

He leaned back down and breathed his warm breath over her clit as he continued to slowly and relentlessly bring her closer and closer to ecstasy. His mouth closed around her all-too-sensitive clit and he sucked gently—and that was it. Her body exploded beneath his touch and his name bounced from her lips, ricocheting through the room. His mouth left her, but he continued to slowly bring her back down with his fingers.

"And now"—he lifted himself over her—"I'm going to do it all over again." His fingers left her body and he placed his hands on either side of her head as he leaned down and crushed his lips to hers. The tip of his cock nestled against her entrance and she wrapped her legs around him, using her thighs to bring him in closer—begging him to fill her.

A deep rumble escaped from Reed's chest as his lips left hers. "Easy, baby."

"I want you—now, Reed."

His forehead fell against her shoulder, and he kissed it softly.

Her eyes were closed—it was too hard to open them. She was too sensitive. She had shattered against his mouth, and now she needed him to consume her. The only thing that would satisfy the dull ache that reached deep was to feel him inside her—pressing his weight on top of her as he filled her completely. She let that vision warm her as a chill blanketed across her naked body when Reed left the bed. A few heartbeats later she felt the bed dip and she felt thick, warm thighs moving between her hips. The anticipation was torture, and she forced the weight of her lids to lift. Reed's eyes raised to hers as he quickly rolled down a condom. He searched her face; then he carefully lowered his hips. He hovered there for a moment, his eyes staring into hers, indecision passing through them. Why was he unsure about this? She wanted it. She needed it, and she knew he needed it too.

"You're staring," she said again, trying to pull him from his mind.

The corners of his mouth tilted and he ran his knuckles down the side of her cheek. "That's because I've never seen anything as beautiful and sexy as seeing you beneath me. I wasn't sure I was ever going to be able to see this again. I want to burn this moment into my mind. I want to see every emotion that crosses your face when I bury myself inside you."

The thought of him inside her made her writhe beneath him. "Want to make sure you'll remember me this time?" she teased, lifting her hips to try to coax him inside her, but the second the words left her lips, he tensed. She was just kidding, but the way his mouth instantly fell from its beautiful smile made her curse herself for saying it.

His thumb brushed against her brows, which were now pinched together, thanks to her loose lips. The tip of his cock stretched her as it slowly entered her, and the surprise sensation caused her to gasp.

"Baby, I could never forget you. Even if I wanted to." He sank into her a little more, but not enough. His mouth latched onto the curve of her neck and sucked before he pressed an openmouthed kiss to her skin. "I will never forget your sweet taste, or the way your tight pussy feels when I slide into you." He pulled away from her neck and looked her in the eyes as he slowly pushed in a little farther. "And I will never forget this beautiful face. Not a chance in hell. Not now, not ever."

She felt the same way. He had sucked her in.

His lips fell to hers and the gentle touch scorched a path to her chest. She moved her mouth against his, molding her lips to his perfect ones as he started to easily push farther inside her. She clung to him. She could feel her insides involuntarily tighten around him—and he hummed low in his chest.

"Fuck, baby," he growled as he continued his slow, torturous journey filling her.

"More," she breathed. She didn't want him to be gentle with her. Not tonight.

He groaned. "I don't want to hurt you."

She didn't care at that moment if it hurt. Right now, she just wanted to feel the force of him deep inside her. She needed it. "More," she repeated, squeezing his hips with her legs. "And hard. Please."

And that was all he needed. She sighed as a happily defeated growl left his throat in a deep, raspy moan that vibrated through his entire body, and in the very next heartbeat, he thrust hard inside her.

She gasped. It was sharp and quick, and the fullness that took over her was exactly what she was craving. Her muscles pulled as she stretched to accommodate his thick, long cock. It was a mix of pain and pleasure that was weaved together so tightly it was hard to differentiate between the two. Whether it was painfully pleasurable or pleasurably painful, she didn't know. And she didn't care.

"God, baby," he said against her mouth as his lips kissed her and his body slammed into her with a force that rocked her body back and forth. She couldn't keep the moans locked away, not when he was sending her through hell wrapped in angel wings—it was blissful, iniquitous pleasure, and she was completely lost in it.

Somewhere in the midst of it all she slipped away. Her mind left any and all realms of thought, and all she did was feel—that's all she could do. He consumed her so completely that it left nothing but the way he was making her body feel as he sent her closer again. She clenched tightly around Reed as his hands dug into her thighs, pushing her legs closer to her chest, allowing him deeper still. He wasn't holding back, he was giving her just what she had wanted, just want she had asked for.

She arched against the bed, her hands clinging to his biceps for support as another orgasm reverberated through her body. This time she didn't scream out his name, she didn't moan or cry out—she couldn't. The pleasure took everything she had in her and she was left with nothing, nothing but the feel of Reed releasing his own pleasure inside her before he collapsed onto the bed, pulling her into his arms.

She molded against him, her body tangling with his as they both struggled to catch their breath. He lifted her chin with his fingers and sweetly pressed his lips to hers. The kiss was soft and easy, completely different from the raw, intense, passionate ride he had just taken her on. She melted into his kiss as his hands lightly skimmed up and down her body, soothing the aches that lingered in her spent muscles.

"That was a nice puzzle piece," he said when he broke their kiss. "Happy birthday," he whispered. Then he tucked her in his arms, and she drifted to sleep.

CHAPTER THIRTEEN

The sun was streaming through the glass wall, warming her naked skin, as Meagan stretched her aching legs. She opened her eyes to see a sleeping Reed wrapped around her like she was a security blanket. She rolled over, struggling to shift under the weight of his arm that was draped across her, and pressed her back against his naked chest, wedging herself in close. She tucked her head back, nestling under his chin and he automatically pulled her in against him.

She smiled. "You're awake?"

"I've been awake."

Meagan grabbed onto his hand and wrapped it around her tighter—if that was even possible. "For how long?"

"Long enough to see you drool, kick me a few times, and mumble something that sounded a lot like 'Reed is a sex God.' I couldn't be sure, though."

She thrust her elbow back. "I don't drool."

He pressed his lips to the back of her head as a sleepy laugh escaped. "You do, baby."

"Damn it, Reed," she whined.

"Sorry, sugar."

A knock on the door broke through their combined laughter. "Hey, you two, you planning on coming down any-time today? Becky made lunch and we're getting ready to load up the truck," Murano hollered through the door.

She turned in Reed's arms, a lazy, sex-induced smile on her face. "What time is it?"

Reed reached for his phone on the nightstand. "Damn, it's after one o'clock."

"Nuh-uh."

"Yep." Reed leaned over and kissed her forehead. "We better get up and get moving."

Meagan climbed out of bed and made her way to where her clothes were lying disheveled on the floor, Reed never once taking his eyes off of her. He scooted toward the end of the bed, reached out, and pulled her in between his legs. "I think you're right, it's definitely more fun to touch than to look."

He traced the curves of her body with his hands, his cock rising as he leaned forward and kissed the swell of her breast.

Meagan's hands braced on his shoulders, pushing him back. "I'm usually always right," she teased. She stepped out of his embrace and pick up her clothes, quickly getting dressed before Reed had a chance to distract her again.

Reed pulled on a pair of worn jeans up over his hips, threw on a T-shirt, and then walked barefoot toward Mea-gan, who was raking her fingers through her tangled hair. There was something about the determination in his steps that made her . . . anxious . . . excited . . . unsure.

"You hungry?" he asked, stopping in front of her.

"Starving. Feed me."

Reed's lips turned up, and she didn't like the crooked angle of his grin or the impish gleam in his eyes. "Reed—," she warned.

He bent over and wrapped his arms under her butt and threw her over his shoulder.

"Reed Porter, what the hell are you doing?"

"Taking you downstairs to feed you, sugar." He smacked her ass—hard—making her jerk in his arms, then turned and jogged out of the room.

She was still laughing like a kid when he paraded into the kitchen with her flung over his shoulder. He sat her feet down on the floor and the back of her hand instantly made contact with his chest. "Thanks."

He winked. "Welcome. Eat. I'm gonna go grab a shower."

Reed came back downstairs carrying his bag in his hands. As he stepped into the great room, Becky appeared in front of him, blocking his path.

"Hey, sis."

"Don't hey me. I thought you said she was just a friend." Becky nodded toward the living room, and Reed followed her gesture with his eyes to where Meagan was cradling a cooing Addie in her arms.

Reed's brows furrowed. "We are friends, Beck."

"Reed, the entire cabin heard you two last night."

He smiled as the thought of that woman screaming out

his name loud enough for everyone to hear raked through his memory. And he liked it.

"Wipe that smirk off your face, Reed. That was *not* something I wanted to hear."

Reed's shoulders shook with a suppressed laugh. "I wish I could say I'm sorry, but I'm not."

Becky rolled her eyes and slapped him on the back of the head. "Well, Addie seems to like her. So she's got me there."

Reed tilted his head to the side of his sister so he could look at Meagan again. He leaned his shoulder into the wall and watched her.

Meagan tilted her head forward and rubbed her nose against Addie's little stub of a nose, and Addie reached up her tiny hands, grabbing a fistful of Meagan's blond hair. Reed heard her soft laugh as she carefully untangled her hair from the baby's grasp. Lifting her in the air, she tickled Addie's tummy with her mouth, earning a sweet belly laugh from his niece. She tenderly kissed her head and held her close, swaying her hips back and forth as she talked softly to her.

She looked so happy, so natural. So this was the Meagan that she saw for herself. This was the Meagan she wanted to be, the future she wanted to have. And seeing her now, it was a future that would fit her perfectly—one she deserved.

Reed ran his hands through his hair as a tightness took over his chest. The wave of happiness that encased him this morning when he woke with that beautiful woman in his arms suddenly seemed wrong—it seemed selfish. She had laid it out there for him. She had told him she wanted to be friends. She had made it perfectly clear what she was looking for—what she wanted. And Reed knew he wasn't it. He wasn't whole—not anymore. That part of him was ripped away four years ago. The only way he knew to fill that void was to let the adrenaline seep into his wounds—help him remember while allowing him to forget at the same time. How could he be a part of the life Meagan wanted? He didn't deserve it.

Becky's eyes shifted between him and Meagan, and she sighed. "You really like her, don't you?" she asked, her voice penetrating his thoughts.

"I do."

"So what's with the sad face?"

"I'm not what she wants—or what she needs."

Meagan took that moment to look at him and smile, Addie still tugging on the blond strands of hair that hung down in front of her shoulder. He smiled back then turned to Becky. "It was good to see you, sis. Tell Conner bye for me."

She frowned, her face lined with worry. "Reed?"

"I've got to go, Beck." His voice had thickened. He leaned down and kissed his sister on the forehead, never making eye contact with her as he lowered his head. Then he made his way to the living room.

Reed stopped and stood in front of the woman who he knew was too good for him, the woman who deserved more than he could give her. He didn't know if he would ever be able to give her the things she wanted. And he knew her terms—it was a deal breaker.

"Reed, I think Addie needs to come stay the weekend with her uncle sometime so I can love on her some more. She's the sweetest baby, and I'm already in love with her."

If only he could go back in time twelve hours and offer to take the couch instead. If only he could rewind time and take back what went on between them—then maybe what he was about to do wouldn't feel like it was ripping him open from the inside out. But he'd be lying if he said he wanted to change even one fucking second of the time he had had with her last night.

Reed lifted his hand and gently stroked the top of Addie's head. Meagan's eyes scanned his face and her smile instantly faltered.

"Hey, look, I'm gonna ride back alone. I'm so sorry, sugar. Luke will take you home."

Meagan's eyes connected with his, a long, pained stare forming ice in her big blue eyes as the distance he was wedging between them settled over her. She swallowed hard as she slowly nodded her head, tucking her chin to her chest as she bounced Addie in her arms.

"That's probably for the best," she said, and her words sliced through him like a thousand sharp daggers, splintering parts of him that he didn't even know could hurt.

The tightrope snapped, and he was tumbling fast.

He opened his mouth to say he was sorry, to try to ease the hurt that was forming in every facet of her expression, but she pinned him with a look that stopped his words cold, lodging them in the back of his throat. Then she turned from him and walked away. And he did the same.

CHAPTER FOURTEEN

Reed didn't see Meagan much the rest of the week, and it wasn't for lack of trying. He had fucked up—he knew that. He selfishly took what he wanted, knowing good and well that what she wanted he couldn't give her. And now, that little moment of weakness had cost him—it had cost him her.

Sure, she would wave to him if she passed him as she was leaving the apartment, and she always said hi to him if she saw him in the courtyard with Tiny, but that was the extent of it. Every time he tried to take their conversation past the greeting stage, she cut him short. The last thing he wanted was this giant space between them that was full of awkward tension and regret. He liked her too much for that. He missed her.

After a Saturday spent out on the lake with his buddies, Reed headed back to his apartment to bring Tiny home and to get cleaned up to head back over to Murano's for their monthly poker night. He was looking forward to a night of nothing but his guys and a case of beer. He needed a night that would distract him from the desperate need he had to walk next door, barge into Meagan's apartment, and demand that she talk to him. He didn't fucking deserve that, though. He'd walked away from her. He'd pulled out of that cabin, alone on his bike—leaving her behind.

He hadn't wanted to walk away from her that day, but he'd needed to. He needed to put that small amount of space between them to strengthen his willpower, to revert his status back to the one he claimed before he slept with her again. And if he would have stayed, if he felt her slender body slide against his, if he felt her cradle him from behind with her legs, and if he felt her arms clinging to his waist as she rested against his back—he would have caved. He wouldn't have been able to hold true to the friends title he accepted any more than he could when she was wrapped in his arms in his bed.

He didn't blame her for pushing him away either. He didn't blame her for cutting his legs out from under him and ignoring him as he so desperately tried to mend the fucking crater he created between them.

Why should she talk to him? Why should she forgive him and give him a second chance at the friendship she offered him? She shouldn't. But he fucking wanted it—because not having her at all was pure hell.

Reed walked out of his apartment to head to Murano's. He was locking up as a tall man strode down the narrow walkway toward his building, and Reed got that gut-twisting intuition that caused a red haze to fuzz the edge of his vision. It was the ER doctor, the one who took care of Brewer. He hoped he would turn the corner and head toward the stairs that led to the apartments above him—because if he didn't, then there was only one other place he was going.

"Hey, man," he said, nodding his head casually at Reed as he passed him and walked toward the front door of the only other lower-level apartment in that building—Meagan's.

He knocked on the door and it almost instantly opened. The guy's face lit up and Reed hoped like hell Eva was standing on the other side of that door, because if she wasn't, Reed didn't know what the hell he would do. But he knew better than that. The man worked with Meagan—he was there to see her.

There was that fucking jealousy thing again, rearing its ugly head when it didn't have a damn claim to do so—but that didn't change the fact that his heart started pounding in his chest and small beads of sweat clung to his hairline, as he stood there and waited, unable to peel his eyes from the scene unfolding in front of him. It was like driving past a horrible car accident. You didn't want to look, you knew it would make your stomach drop if you saw the evidence of life slipping away, but you couldn't help but drive by slowly and turn you head to see as much as you possibly could.

A sound reached Reed's ear, clouding any and all thoughts that were previously taking up the space of his mind. It was Meagan, it was her laugh. Fuck, it'd been one goddamned week, and the sound of her voice meeting his ears quenched a thirst he didn't realize he had.

He watched as she stepped out of her apartment. She was wearing a gray dress that clung to every curve and dip of her body, and he imagined running his fingers over the seams, testing the feel of the fabric under his fingers as he trailed them along her body. It cinched her generous breasts, cutting low, showing a beautiful amount of soft, supple, golden cleavage. It stopped at the middle of her smooth thighs, giving him a view of the legs he had had wrapped around him not too long ago. Her small feet were arched, standing in a sexy pair of soft pale pink heels. She was absolutely stunning.

The guy opened his hand to her and she slipped her fingers through his without hesitating. Her cheeks gained a rosy tint as he leaned down and pressed a kiss to her cheek in greeting. Reed's hands clenched into fists at his sides as a burning feeling crept through his veins. Seeing her with him was like swallowing a splintered rock—it didn't go down easily and it didn't settle well.

They walked hand in hand down the pathway, and when her eyes fell over Reed's, he saw her breath hitch. Her eyes stayed on him and she offered a sweet smile, but it was that subtle moment when her chest expanded slightly and the hollow of her throat caved inward that gave her away. Like always, her body couldn't lie to him.

"Hey, sugar," he said, stepping onto the sidewalk that led to the parking lot—intercepting her.

She frowned a little. "Hi, Reed. This is Jason." Her words were rushed—she was uncomfortable.

Reed didn't acknowledge her introduction, he heard her, but he wasn't going to acknowledge it—instead he just looked at her, not willing to drop his eyes—but she was. She shifted her gaze to the ground for a brief moment, and when she looked back up an indifferent smile—an imposter of the sweet, genuine one he knew her lips were capable of producing—was set in place.

She swallowed hard. "Good to see you," she lied.

Reed tore his hand through his hair. "Meagan—"

She shook her head quickly, the movement barely noticeable.

Meagan stepped around Reed, but he only shifted back in front of her. Her head lifted, the skin around her eyes bunching as she released a deep, aggravated sigh. She closed her eyes briefly as if she was forcing herself to calm down. Good. He wanted her to be mad at him, he wanted her to open those hauntingly perfect blue eyes and tell him to go fuck himself. He wanted her to get mad, because mad he could fix, mad he could handle. But her ignoring him—he couldn't fucking take that anymore.

"Jason, can I meet you at the car, please?" Her voice was sweet as she smiled her reassurance at him.

"You okay?"

"I'm fine, I just need to talk to Reed for a second. I'm sorry. I won't be long."

He nodded and released her hand and walked toward his car.

As soon as he was out of immediate earshot, her head snapped back at Reed and she pinned him with a look that could have dropped him dead. "What the hell is your problem, Reed? I'm on a date."

"I see that." The words came out of his mouth with more

accusation than he should have had. He blinked slowly. "I'm sorry, sugar."

"You're sorry." She laughed, and the sarcasm that clung to it was souring the beautiful sound he missed so much. "For fucking me? For leaving me? For what exactly, Reed?" She shook her head. "Look, I'm not getting into this with you. What's done is done." She started to walk away but he grabbed onto her wrist and spun her back around to face him.

"No . . . I'm sorry for hurting you."

Her lips pressed together tightly and her eyes, the eyes that hid everything from him—the eyes that were a beautiful, secret puzzle piece, lowered their protective shield, and he saw the damage. Damage that formed every hole in her heart, and now Reed was part of the infliction.

He reached for her hand but she pulled it away. "I'm not some sad little girl that gets her panties in a bunch over a man she slept with. I've been down that road with you before, Reed, we fucked—it was great. Did I want to travel down that same path I was trying hard to stay away from? No, but it happened—what's done is done." She swallowed hard as her breaths became shallow. "I expected more from you, though, Reed." Her voice got soft. "You weren't the sexy soldier that took me home from a bar this time. You were my friend—I cared about you, and you walked away from me with no explanation. You just left."

"Fuck, Meg." If ever there was a moment that a woman had the power to make a man fall to his knees and beg—it was that moment. The way her voice cracked from the sound of threatening tears damn near brought him to the ground. He had hurt her—not only was he looking into the eyes of the one woman who was capable of slowing him down; he was looking into the eyes of the one woman he couldn't bear hurting. But he fucking had, and he was afraid that she wouldn't let him back in. He needed her in his life—even if it wasn't the way he so desperately wanted.

He ran his hands through his hair as his head lowered. He looked back at her. She was just staring at him with a lost expression on her face, and he felt defeated. "You don't even know how much it kills me that I hurt you. I never wanted to hurt you. But when I saw you with Addie . . ." He blew a heavy breath from his mouth. "You set the terms, you laid down the ground rules, and I broke them—and I'm sorry. But I care about you too fucking much to not have you at all. Can't we just go back? Can we be friends—I need more than just a casual hello from you. Please."

She lifted her hand and smoothed her palm down the side of his face. "I'm sorry. I can't," she said, a soft whimper trailing the end of her words. Then this time, she left him.

"Was everything okay back there?" Jason asked as she slid down into his very nice, respectable, safe car.

Meagan folded her hands in her lap, trying to keep from twisting the strap of her purse as she attempted to calm the irritable swarm of vexation that caused heat to course through her chest and throat. "Yeah, everything's fine."

"Are you sure? Because it seemed like—"

"It's fine, Jason. Reed is just my pain-in-the-ass neighbor."

"Okay," he said, unconvinced, but Meagan didn't care at that moment to try to change his opinion or sooth his battered ego from the obvious tension that was strung between her and Reed. She was too riled from seeing him, too shaken from the penetrating gaze he gave her and the pain that lingered in it. He was hurting, she saw it written in every line on his face—but she couldn't give him what he was asking for. She couldn't go back to friends, as much as she missed his playfulness and the easy comfort he brought her. It would be too hard. She had a glimpse of him—of the sexy lover, of the intense man who had a power to shake her to her core— and she couldn't get it out of her mind. After seeing that part of him, being friends would never work—she would always want more. And he wouldn't.

Jason looked over at her as he shifted his car into reverse and pulled out of the parking lot. It was his shy, worried expression that had her slightly wounded heart softening around the edges.

She lifted her hand and rested it on top of his that was holding on to the gear shift between them. "I'm sorry. I didn't mean to snap. Reed just . . . I'm . . . he . . ."

He flipped his hand over and laced his fingers through hers, giving her hand a reassuring squeeze. "I get it, Meagan," he said, letting her off the hook. "And it's okay. You're with me right now, and that's all I care about."

She sighed and relaxed against the leather of the seat and

forced herself to push Reed from her mind and focus on the man next to her.

She looked at him and squeezed his hand back. This man just got better and better. She could now add understanding to the list of great qualities that he seemed to possess. Oh yes, she was making a list.

Once they were at the restaurant, she felt she needed to whip out said list and start checking things off. Jason was pulling out all the stops.

Opened her car door—check.

Sweetly held her hand—check.

Held open the restaurant door for her—check.

Pulled out her chair—check.

Order a bottle of her favorite wine, yes, a bottle—check.

He was being the perfect date. Sweet and attentive, asking all the right questions and, surprisingly, appearing interested. So their conversation was a little stiff and awkward, that was to be expected on a first date, right? She couldn't check everything off her dating list right away. . . .

Jason poured her another glass of wine—she was on glass number three. Any more and he would be carrying her out of there.

"So," he said, sitting back in his chair after the waiter took their plates and he ordered dessert. "Do you want kids?"

Her eyes lifted from her glass and she was sure that the expression that was written on her face was flirting with shock.

Jason laughed, and it was nice to hear. She was beginning to think he didn't have it in him. "I take it you don't want kids, huh?"

She smiled back. "Oh, no. I do. You just surprised me. Not too many guys ask that question, especially on a first date."

His eyes dropped slightly and he leaned forward in his seat. "Yeah, well, I'm not most guys," he implied, his voice low.

The little hidden innuendo that seemed to sneak into his words gave her the first flinch of excitement all night—that little flutter she was waiting to feel from him again. She had been worried that it wasn't going to come.

Good head on his shoulders—check.

Easy on the eyes—check.

Wants a family—check, check, check.

Not to mention he would make some pretty beautiful babies—not that she was thinking about that. Well, not too much.

Either his little admission or the three glasses of wine was making her feel a little more comfortable and she started to relax. She generously dug into the chocolate cake the waiter had set down in the middle of the table, and she blushed and turned her head to the side when Jason reached over and wiped the icing off the corner of her mouth.

Sweet and sexy—check.

But then her eyes caught a glimpse of something as her head was turned toward the window. Something that gave her more than just a little flutter of excitement. Something that caused her chest to go tight and her palms to clam up. She could feel her heart thud against her ribs and it was threatening to knock the air from her already deflated lungs.

An all-too-familiar motorcycle was parked along the side of the road in front of the restaurant. The same motorcycle that claimed nearly half of her good dreams over the last week—but it was also the same motorcycle that drove off and left her, breaking the small fraction of her heart that she opened up to him—to Reed.

Meagan's head snapped forward as her eyes scanned the open room, looking for him.

"You okay?" Jason asked, following her gaze as it circumnavigated the restaurant.

"I'm . . . not sure."

Then she saw him.

Reed stepped into the room from the waiting area and it was like a magnetic pull forced his eyes to find her—because it didn't take but one single blink and they were on her.

He didn't smile, he didn't wink, or do any of the other common Reed antics—he just walked toward her. Even from a distance she could see that his jaw was set tight, his posture straight and determined. It was intense, and paired with the unknown, with the unpredictable storm that seemed to have taken over his eyes, it was terrifying, but only because she couldn't look away.

She felt a palpable tension emit from Jason, and although her eyes were fixated on the man who was holding her prisoner with the raw power he held in his gaze, she could see a slight movement from the corner of her eye as Jason weaved his arms across his chest. "You've got to be kidding me," she heard him mumble under his breath. Meagan didn't respond, she just slid her chair back and stood, bracing herself for whatever was coming her way. Reed was a wild card, she already knew that.

He stopped in front of the table—no, it was more like he slammed to a stop as his chest collided with her, his hand snaking around her waist, pressing into her lower back, bringing her in tightly to him. His shoulders curved forward as he looked down at her, once again hovering over her like he always seemed to do, overwhelming the proximity of space between them.

He rested his other hand on her neck, his palm splayed out on the side, the warmth from his skin seeping into her pores as he ran the pad of his thumb across her lips.

He wasn't Mr. Safe. He was Mr. Thrill, Mr. Playful, and Mr. Impulsive all rolled into one—and he was wearing her down bit by bit with the tip of his finger as it feathered across her bottom lip.

She tilted her head back to look at him—to see his eyes . . . to tell him to leave. "Reed—"

The word barely finished leaving her mouth before his lips crushed onto hers. He wasn't just kissing her; he was claiming her, taking her with his mouth, which was consuming her in a way she was craving, in a way that she needed—in a way that she needed from him.

His hand slid up her back and gripped the back of her neck, tilting her head slightly so he could deepen the kiss. Her own hands weaved around him, holding him to her as if she was afraid he would turn and walk away if she didn't.

A soft moan of relief hummed against her mouth as Reed's shoulders relaxed and he melted against her—and held her even tighter.

She became breathless and her fingers ached with the need

to reach out and touch him—all of him. She was lightheaded, a sure result of the mixture of wine and the intoxicating taste of Reed's mouth. A shifting feeling swayed around her heart, it almost hurt—but she welcomed it completely, because it was Reed. It was him finding his way back in. And as much as that scared her, and as much as she knew she'd probably pay for it down the road, she didn't care—not at that moment.

Reed's lips stopped moving over hers, but he didn't pull away. He stayed right where he was, his forehead pressing against hers, his hands molding against her body, and his lips skimming the tops of hers. "Hey, sugar."

It was like the little bubble he surrounded her with had popped. She could suddenly hear the soft conversations blend around her from the other people dining. She could smell the aroma of delicious food in the air, and she could feel Jason's eyes burning a hole through her.

She backed away and Reed's brows pinched together.

"You need to leave," she said. She kept her head up, her shoulders back, feigning her strength, because she was about two seconds from caving. Two seconds from wrapping her body around him again.

"What?" he asked. The look on his face was wounded and it crushed her.

"You heard her, man," Jason said, standing up from his chair.

Reed lowered his gaze to Jason and Meagan flinched. That was one look she never imagined Reed could possess.

"Just go, Reed." Her voice betrayed her and the subtle crack caught his attention.

The corners of his mouth started to rise. That half smirk paired with the lift of one eyebrow had an effect on her she wished she could hide from, because his cocky smirk only got bigger. "You sure you want that?" His low Southern drawl bathed her in warmth and she had to fight back a shiver. He stepped closer.

She didn't move, she didn't respond, she just held his eyes.

His smile dropped but there was a challenge in his eyes, like he was daring her to go with him, as if he could feel her body's desire to throw herself back against him. But she couldn't.

She breathed in a steadying breath.

Slowly, he grinned.

And she melted.

"Okay, Meg, I'll go," he said before shooting another lethal glare at Jason. When he looked back at her, his eyes softened around the edges. "But I'm not done with you."

CHAPTER FIFTEEN

The entire drive back to her apartment was tense. She had apologized to Jason more times than she could possibly count. He was sweet and comforting, and if she was still keeping that checklist, she could add understanding to the very top. But she had thrown that list out the window the second Reed walked into that restaurant. He claimed a piece of her that she wasn't ready to admit to, but when he wrapped her in his arms, she was done for. No matter how many things on that list she was able to cross off, Jason would never be Reed. He would never give her that panicky feeling in her chest the moment before he kissed her. Not like Reed did.

Reed made her want to hold her breath and shut her eyes.

"Are you sure you don't want me to walk you to your door?" Jason asked as he pulled into one of the parking spaces in front of her building.

She tilted her head and smiled. "I'm okay, thank you. And thank you for being so great about . . . well, everything. I'm so sorry."

"Don't apologize. I got to see you in that sexy dress and watch your cheeks flush as you got tipsy. It might not have panned out how I hoped, but I'd say it was worth it."

Her head tilted down. "Thank you."

He reached over and grabbed her hand, bringing it to his lips. He softly kissed her knuckles before lowering her hand back down to the seat. It was a sweet gesture. He was trying to make her feel better when she should be the one groveling at his feet. "For what it's worth, that guy is one lucky son of a bitch," he said, looking past her to the apartment building.

Meagan looked out the window and her heart stalled. Reed was leaning against her door, his thick arms crossed over his chest, his eyes fixed directly at her. She was sure he couldn't see her in the dark through the car window, but knowing that he was watching for her, waiting for her, sent a blush that not only hit her face, but every other place as well.

Meagan looked back over at Jason. "Why do you say that?"

He frowned, looking at her like it was the most obvious answer. "Because he's got you."

The sound of her heels echoed quickly through the quiet surrounding her as she walked down the walkway to her apartment. She felt her heart pick up the pace and fall into rhythm with the soft click of her steps.

Reed leaned away from the door as she got closer. She was nervous, her chest felt like it was constricting around her lungs, making it nearly impossible for her to breathe.

She soaked him up as she stepped in front of him. His light blue T-shirt pulled against his chest and hung just below the waist of his worn, tattered jeans. She loved the way he looked in jeans and his brown flip-flops. She smiled.

"Does that smile on your face mean you're happy to see me?" he asked, his eyes raking over her appraisingly. He had never been ashamed to look at her. Never once.

She sighed. "I'm always happy to see you, Reed." No matter how mad she was at him, she couldn't help it.

His face contorted in confusion.

"You shouldn't have come to the restaurant and you—"

"I'm not sorry, Meg," he interrupted. "I'll never be sorry for any moment that I get you pressed against me. Do you know how hard it was for me to leave that restaurant without dragging your ass along next to me? It took every single ounce of restraint I had not to pick you up in my arms and carry you away from him." The muscles of his jaw started working beneath his scruffy face. "Especially with you in that damn dress." His stare grazed her skin, physically heating the path it took, and regardless of the fire that had set flames to her skin, she shivered.

"You told me to go, so I went. But I will never walk away from you willingly." His feet took one step toward her and her pulse picked up. His chest lingered near her beasts and she instantly craved the feeling of it pressed against her.

His fingers slipped through her hair and his palm rested on the side of her cheek. "Never again," he said, his voice low.

She held his eyes, waiting for something to pass through them that would bring her back to solid ground, because she was sinking fast. She was anchored to him, and she was sinking. But nothing in his eyes told her anything other than the words he just spoke.

She sighed and leaned her face into his hand. She was done fighting it. She might hate herself for this down the road; hell, she might hate herself for this in the morning, but she didn't care anymore.

His lips pulled up ever so slightly as she molded her cheek to his palm. Before she could even register what had happened, he had his hand wrapped around hers and was pulling her toward his apartment.

A slight thrill washed over her from the intensity of his movements. Urgent, determined. No more words were spoken between them—and the silence alone spoke volumes. What was there to be said that wasn't being told in the way his fingers curled around her hand, the way he led her up the walkway, making sure to keep little distance between their bodies, or the way he looked at her from the side, as if her very presence was rocking him?

When Reed stepped up to his door, she leaned against his back, her hand still held firmly in his. She waited patiently behind him as he fumbled for his keys and turned the lock. He stepped inside and Meagan's feet helplessly followed—a marionette to her puppeteer.

The place smelled of him—clean, spicy, and masculine. She breathed in deep, taking his scent into her lungs.

Reed's arm reached around her waist and pushed the door closed. The air stiffened around them, thick and heavy, coated with anticipation as Reed's eyes sank into hers. He held them there for a moment—a transparent need possessing her—then his large hands dug into the flesh of her hips. He lifted her up with an ease that shocked her and slammed her back against the wall.

"I know I'm no good for you, baby," he breathed as he pressed his mouth to her ear. "But I want you. I want you so fucking bad it's selfish." Her spine straightened as he used the force of his own body to pin her in place. "You do something to me that twists me up." He ran both hands down the front of her neck—the pressure anything but light—over her breasts, and down her stomach, until they reached the hem of her dress. In an instant it was around her hips and he was lifting her legs around his waist. He leaned forward and swiped his lips across her jaw. "I can't help myself when it comes to you."

She felt so bare, so exposed—nothing but a thin strip of fabric covering her as her legs clung to him. "I want you too," she confessed, and she felt his lips tighten into a smile as they lingered on the skin below her ear.

"That's all I needed to hear."

In the very next breath his mouth connected with hers, his teeth pulling her bottom lip into his mouth. She felt like she was strapped on a roller coaster, her feet dangling over the edge. It's that fear, that feeling as you're *click, click, click*-ing up to the top. It was that feeling that had you begging to get off, wondering why in the world you climbed on in the first place. Then when you reached the top, there was that split second of pause, that one flash of a moment where you could see the ground below and you'd think, "This is it."

This was it.

He was claiming her. He was breaking down the walls and strapping her in. He was lifting her, taking her to a place she'd never been before. But then there was that moment—he pulled away from her, his gaze penetrating her to her core, and he smiled. It was that crooked lift of the lips, that split second of pause where she felt the need to lift her hands in the air and give into the ride he was about to take her on.

Her hands tore at her dress, desperate to remove it from her heated body. She shifted, squirming as she pulled the material up. Reed's hands graciously came to her rescue and he yanked the dress over her head. She needed out of that damn constricting bra too, she needed to feel his hands roam over her bare skin. She wanted to feel her sensitive nipples roll through the rough pads of his fingers. She needed his hot mouth to cover them, then to cool them.

It was like he read her mind. He reached behind her and with one flick of his fingers removed her bra from her body.

Meagan's hands wound around his shoulders and she bunched his T-shirt in her hands, balling it up until it coiled at his neck. His mouth left her collarbone, where he had more than likely left a couple of marks, and he ducked his head, allowing her to pull his shirt off.

"Reed," she pleaded, causing him to lift his eyes to hers.

Without saying a word, he slid his forearms under her ass and carried her the few strides to the couch, depositing her on the cool leather. There was a stillness lurking in his eyes. Like the calm beneath the storm. All that controlled, intense power was forming a rotation, and she was just waiting for the funnel cloud to form.

"Raise your hands above your head."

She did.

"Keep them there, don't move."

She didn't.

The whole time he was barking out his aphrodisiacal demands, he examined her body, gauging her physical responses—her reactions.

Seemingly satisfied, he unbuttoned his jeans, stepping out of his clothes. His shins hit the edge of the couch as he stood above her. Her eyes lingered over his body. The broad width of his shoulders, the impressive roll of his biceps, the hard ridges and valleys of his stomach, the deep V of his hips, the hard swell of his cock. He looked delicious and she wanted to rise up and wrap her mouth around him.

But she didn't.

She stayed on her back, her hands above her head.

His knee fell to the couch, and her legs opened for him, making room for him to settle between. But instead he leaned over her and grabbed her wrists, which were extended over her head, curling his fingers tightly, holding her in place.

"You're mine," he said, his mouth levitating above hers.

There was a spike in her heartbeat. . . .

"Only mine." His mouth lowered to her breast and he pulled her nipple into his warm mouth.

A catch in her breath . . .

"Tell me," he said, but it wasn't a demand—it was a plea. His fingers pushed aside her panties and leisurely entered her, softly, slowly stroking her as his grip on her wrists tightened.

Then a blistering rush of arousal . . .

She exploded around his fingers, her orgasm taking her by surprise as her muscles clamped down on him. She cried out and writhed beneath him, her fingers digging into the leather of the couch above her head.

Reed released her wrists. "Good girl," he said, that pixilated smirk splitting his face.

He pulled the lace from her hips and discarded it on the floor before he lifted her from the couch and sat her down on his lap. She wiggled above his cock as he held it in his hand and rubbed it over her all-too-sensitive clit. She squirmed.

"Hold still."

"You're demanding," she teased. But she liked it.

His brows lifted, his hand bit into the flesh of her ass, the brown in his eyes soaked up the gold flecks that spattered in them, and his addictive mouth—it was almost a sin. "You make me this way," he said, his voice rattling her as he continued to rub his cock down the center of her, never letting it reach her entrance.

Meagan leaned over and swept her tongue across his taunting bottom lip. "Is that a good thing or a bad thing?"

A growl reverberated in his chest, tickling her skin that was pressed against it. "I've never needed this before, baby. I've never felt the need to take what I need to be mine. But you— I saw you leave, I watched you walk away. . . ."

His hand left his cock and grabbed her hip, lifting her, positioning her. Then he slowly lowered her onto him.

She was so slick, so hot, that her body encased him easily. Her head rolled back and Reed's mouth brushed the center of her throat. She lifted slightly, needing to move, needing to feel him stroke the ache that was clinging to him. But his hands gripped her tightly, holding her down—making her take all of him. She flinched—overwhelmed—the sharp sensation of him so deep inside her, stealing her breath. But she knew he needed this.

"You were jealous?" she asked, slinking her hands around the back of his neck.

"I was pissed." He lifted her until her opening ringed the tip of his cock; then he thrust her back down on him, evoking a sharp intake of air into Meagan's lungs from the surprise. Then he lifted her again. . . .

"I was pissed that I let you walk away." And again . . .

He was so different with her, not like the other times. This time it was almost primal. He was staking his claim, making her his own—and she wanted it.

He lifted her again, only this time so slowly it was almost agonizing. She clinched around him. The feel of him sliding against her as her body rose off of him caused a shudder to rake through her back. His fingers squeezed her hips and lowered her back down on him—hard and deep, forcing her to take all of him that she could.

Then he held her there. His hands pinned her to him, preventing any movement from her hips—stilling her body as he took up the tight space inside her. It was fulfilling and overwhelming.

"I'm impulsive. I do what feels right in the moment, regardless of the consequence. I thought leaving without you that day at the cabin was the right thing to do. I had to leave. Seeing you with Addie wrapped in your arms brought every fucking thing you pictured for yourself front and center in my line of vision." His eyes closed, and even though she couldn't see the emotion submerged in them, she could feel it. His shoulders tensed and his chest expanded with his deep breaths. "I was scared of letting you down. But when you walked away from me tonight, the consequence hit me hard. That consequence was you—losing you."

Her mind was reeling with his words. "You didn't let me down until you left."

His forehead fell to hers. "I know, and I'm sorry." His hands left her hips and he held her face between his hands as she took over the delicious rhythm he set in place, rolling her hips up, then lowering herself hard.

"I won't walk away from you again unless you tell me to go." His fingers threaded through her hair and he wrapped the thick strands in his palms. "And even then," he breathed, moving his lips to hers. "I can't promise that I will be able to." Then he tugged his hand back as his mouth crushed hers. Her scalp pricked from the blunt sensation, and an incisive gasp bounced between their connected mouths. He used his hands to hold her head in place as he explored the side of her neck, the dip in her throat, the ridge of her collar, and the swell of her breasts. She was confined to his hands, her body subject to his mouth. It was blissful torment.

Reed's dick twitched inside her as her sweet, slick pussy wrapped around him tightly. Her tender skin below his lips was like satin, and his tongue devoured the texture.

Reed felt her contract around him. She whimpered and shook as a wave of excitement coursed through her, penetrating his own excitement. He released the hold he had on her hair and her head dropped down. The look in her eyes was validating— she needed this from him just as badly as he did from her.

Her head fell to his shoulder and his arms wrapped around her retentively. She latched onto him as a spasm of shudders tore through her body. Reed lifted her head and pulled her mouth to his. He wanted to feel her moans and the vibrations of her cries in his mouth as she came around him— and he did.

She tightened and squeezed around him until he couldn't hold on any longer, and at the same time his mouth filled with the sweet, ragged, sharp breaths of her cries.

Her body collapsed on him and he held her to him as their orgasms slowly climbed back down. When he was feeling the sensation in his legs again, he stood, his dick sliding out of her as he held her in his arms.

She used her toes to push her stilettos off her feet and they fell to the floor. Her head was still weighted down on his shoulder and he couldn't help the smile that cracked on his lips—he loved that he pushed her to the brink of exhaustion.

He carried her back to his room and laid her down on the bed. Her body stretched like a cat, arching her back, pointing her toes as she elongated across the mattress.

"That's incredibly sexy," he said, standing next to her.

A blush crept over her cheeks and she shifted herself underneath the covers.

Reed lowered himself to the bed, lifting the cover so he could wrap himself around her. "I can't promise you the things you will need me to promise," he said against her hair, his breath causing the strands to cling to his lips. He waited for it. He waited for her to run like hell, this was the moment she would realize she deserved more—better.

She turned around in his arms and wedged herself tightly against his chest.

She wasn't running.

"I can't hold up to the bar you've raised," he whispered, brushing the hair back away from her face. "But I sure as hell would like to try."

Meagan just looked directly into his eyes. Her mouth parted slightly as she inhaled a breath—a poor attempt at easing the cluster-fuck of emotions that had piled its way into her chest. She was happy, Reed wanted her, how could she not be happy? She was scared. Scared for her heart and scared for her future. She was also a little angry with herself. She had promised herself that she wouldn't go down this road again, yet here she was, driving full speed down a gravel road with more potholes than she could possibly anticipate. But more than anything, she was nervous. Nervous because everything he was telling her was the truth. He wasn't sugarcoating it and he wasn't trying to tell her what she wanted to hear. He was being honest.

She tucked her head under his chin and lodged her leg in between his thick thighs. "I'd like to try too." She pressed a tight kiss to his chest and he pulled her in close.

She wanted to find Mr. Safe, but instead Mr. Thrill came barging into her life.

CHAPTER SIXTEEN

"All right, I'm a little sick of your cheeky-ass grin. You've been coming in here every day for the last week like you've won the lottery. And if you haven't noticed, I'm a little bit bedridden at the moment. Some fake sympathy or maybe even a frown every now and again would be appreciated."

Reed lowered himself into the plastic chair next to Brewer's hospital bed. "Sorry, man. I will make a note to check my good attitude at the door."

"You're fucking her, aren't you?"

Reed dropped his feet, which were propped up on the lower rail of the bed, the smack of his boots hitting the cold tile echoed through the sterile room. He sat forward in his seat. "Excuse me, Sergeant?"

Brewer's face didn't take on that intimidated pucker some young sergeants had when Reed was about to administer an ass-chewing. He just remained impassive—unaffected. Little shit.

"Sorry, CO. I didn't mean any disrespect."

Yeah, Reed was fucking her, but like hell was he going to

let another man talk about her like that. "Just because I come visit your sorry ass and shoot the shit with you doesn't mean you get a get-out-of-jail-free card."

"Yes, sir."

Reed heard the words come out of Brewer's mouth, and although he knew they were genuine because Brewer wasn't one to disrespect his chain of command, let alone a woman, the flat, monotone response pissed him off. Reed's nostrils flared and his jaw set tight as he looked at his soldier.

Brewer started again. "Let me rephrase that. That nurse, Meagan, she gave into you, didn't she?"

Reed pressed his lips together as they cracked slightly into a smile that he was repressing as his anger dissipated. "You could say that."

Brewer shook his head incredulously. "Lucky."

"Watch it."

Brewer sighed heavily. "Here I am, broken leg, didn't get my wings, there's not a damn thing on TV, I would kill for a beer, and you get to go home with her every night. I will say it again: lucky."

Yeah, Reed would have to agree with him there. He was lucky. He had spent every evening the last week with that woman pressed against him in one way or another—more often than not while she was gloriously naked.

He'd found himself skipping his evening rides and passing up on a few of his regular extracurricular activities just to get back to her quicker.

Brewer's eyes darted past Reed. "Oh, hell. Speaking of the angel."

Reed looked over his shoulder. Meagan was walking in, her hair pulled to the side and braided over her shoulder, giving Reed the desire to tug it. He could see a tired tension tightening in her shoulders underneath her pink scrubs as she walked over to the bed. She flashed Reed a quick smile before she turned her focus on Brewer.

"Isn't the saying 'speaking of the devil'?"

"Oh, my beautiful nurse, Meagan, *angel* is much more fitting for you."

Megan laughed and Reed shook his head and pressed himself to the back of the chair, folding his arms across his chest. It was either that or reach out and pull Meagan onto his lap, and that wouldn't be all he would want to do if her ass was nestled on top of him.

Meagan ignored Brewer, she was probably used to him laying it on thick by now. She had been visiting him after every one of her shifts since he'd been there—three weeks.

She reached into her purse, which was the size of a suitcase, and pulled out a plastic sack, tossing it on Brewer's lap.

"What'd ya bring me?" he asked, opening the sack.

"The greasiest burger I could get my hands on."

"You're a keeper—you know that?" He looked over at Reed. "Seriously, you better hang on tight to this one or I might snag her out from under you."

"I hate to break it to you, man, but if this woman is under me, there is no way I'm letting her go."

Meagan turned around, a fresh blush brushing across her cheeks as she winked at Reed. "So I heard from your nurse that you get to go home in a week or so," she said, changing the subject as she sat down on the edge of Brewer's bed.

"Yeah."

"You don't sound overly happy."

"That's because you won't be there."

"Ah, I see." Meagan laughed. She was used to his excessive flirting, so she didn't seem to realize he was serious. But Reed could see it in his eyes, he had gotten attached to Meagan.

"No, really. I'm gonna hate not seeing you almost every single day." His expression shifted, and he was looking up at Meagan with admiration. Seemed as though she had found a way to wedge herself under his skin as well. Reed knew the feeling, and he sympathized with the guy. If he didn't get to see her every day he would fucking hate it too.

Meagan reached down and grabbed Brewer's hand. "It's the army, we are bound to run into each other again at some point, right, Reed?"

The little suggestive glance she tossed over her shoulder at him sent a rush through his chest. He was sure as shit happy that he ran into her again, that's for damn sure.

Reed leaned forward. "Yeah."

"I'm looking forward to getting back to my squad and seeing everyone again, but fuck, there's been talk about my unit deploying in the next six months or so." His head turned toward Reed. "What if I'm not cleared for combat?"

Ah, there lay his true fears. It was a fear that floated in the back of every good soldier's mind—not being in the game. It was why Reed enlisted. After 9/11, he and his brother were ready to sign their contracts in blood, ready to join the fight. To serve their country. Being told that you could no longer do so, that you weren't fit for combat, was like telling a country singer she could no longer play the guitar or like telling a baseball player he could no longer bat. It was a part of their job—a part of them. If you took away the chance to go to combat, to fight for what you believed in, you might as well tell them they were no longer a soldier, because they would no longer feel like one.

"You've gotta hit the physical therapy hard," Reed suggested.

Meagan's eyes darted toward Reed's for a split second, and they were narrowed behind her lids as her mouth puckered into a line. "But don't overdo it. Your body needs to rest and heal just as much as it needs to regain strength."

Brewer sent him a knowing glance, and Reed understood it without question. If he could walk, he would be doing everything in his power to get his leg back to full strength—to get combat-ready again.

"Do you really think he will be able to deploy again?" Meagan asked Reed as he walked her to her car.

"It wouldn't surprise me in the least. If there is one thing about that kid that I have learned, it's that he's determined as hell and a natural leader—a damn good NCO. It would be a shame if the army lost him on the line."

Meagan cringed inwardly at the thought of Brewer deploying. She had grown quite fond of him and his cocky ways over the last couple of weeks, and she didn't want to see him leave as much as he didn't want to leave. But more than that, she didn't want him to go back overseas. He was like her little brother, and he was hurt. She wanted to wrap him in bubble wrap and stick him in a padded room. But he was a soldier. Soldiers didn't know what bubble wrap or padded rooms were. They knew safety but disregarded their own to protect the safety of others. They knew how to risk their lives and didn't blink an eye or hesitate doing so. It's what they did— it's what Reed and Trevor and Kale and every other male she had ever cared about did, and it's what Brewer wanted to do again. She was used to the *hooah* mentality—but that didn't mean that she had to like their enthusiasm behind it.

Reed wrapped his large hand around the back of her neck, giving it a gentle squeeze. "Hey, where'd you go?"

She blinked hard. "Sorry. Just thinking about Brewer."

"Well, how about I get your mind off him? Let's go for a ride."

"I would, but I promised Eva I would scope out the nightlife tonight. We haven't gone out once, well, other than the time we met at Oasis, and she is itching for a girls' night."

Reed leaned forward and pressed his lips to her forehead. "All right." He pouted. She could hear the waver in his voice, like he was debating whether or not to protest her plans. He sighed. "But you're mine tomorrow."

"Is that so?"

"Yes."

"And should I be scared? You don't have any bungee jumping planned for a morning pick-me-up, do you?"

His brows danced up and down. "Do you need a morning pick-me-up?"

"Maybe."

"Don't tempt me."

She leaned into him and wrapped her arms around his waist. The rough fabric of his uniform scratched her chin as she rested it on his chest and looked up at him. "I'm not trying to tempt you, just encourage you."

"Well, all you are doing is encouraging me to throw your ass over the back of my bike and take you to my bed."

She pulled out of his embrace. Reed's bed had become one of her favorite places to be. Not only was it nice to be curled up in sexy, muscular arms, pressed against a sinfully gorgeous naked body all night, it sure beat the hell out of the air mattress in her apartment that was lacking the ability to hold air. But since the army finally took it upon themselves to deliver her and Eva's things today, she was fully looking forward to a much-needed comforter session with her own bed.

"So what's going on tomorrow?" she asked, knowing she should just back away now. The way Reed looked standing in his uniform had her imagining taking it off of him—and she had promised Eva a date. If she didn't get space between them, she was more than positive she would find her way back to his bed.

"Just some jet skiing and wakeboarding, more than likely a lot of beer drinking."

"Boating?" she said with a skip in her voice, an underlying tone of excitement rearing to life, distracting her from her previous thoughts.

Reed turned his head slightly and cocked his brows, looking at her from the side. "Yep, you in?"

"Yes."

"Good. I'll come get you in the morning. Be careful to-night." There was a slight threat to his words, a territorial rasp that equally tugged at her heart, and her body. She got the slight sense that he wasn't too keen on the idea of her hitting the bar scene with Eva. And she liked it. She knew some women hated the overprotective act from their man—but Meagan almost wanted it. She wanted him to want to punch any man who looked at her with just a hint of suggestiveness. She wanted him jealous and on edge, wondering if she was being flirted with or hit on. She liked the idea of him wanting her all to himself.

"I can come with you ladies, show you my white-boy dance moves."

Meagan laughed. She could only picture Reed and his moves out on the dance floor. If they were anything like the way he moved in the bedroom—she didn't know if *she* wanted anyone to see him dance like that.

"Sorry. You can't. That would defeat the purpose of a girls' night," she said. She rose onto her toes and slid her lips over his. He needed a distraction and she just needed him. Seeing him all pouty and disappointed that she wasn't going to be spending her evening in his bed was sexy—and tempting.

His hands latched onto her sides and he dug his fingers into her hips. She loved how every little touch from him had a way of letting her know just how much he wanted her. He didn't just hold on to her waist, he gripped her tightly with a force that walked the line of pain, but the good kind. The kind that was sexy. She didn't want to be touched, she wanted to be held, smothered.

Reed rolled his tongue into her mouth and the taste of him was like a drug. Her hands moved to his biceps, holding on to him as he kissed her—but then she pulled away. She had to. If she didn't, she wouldn't be able to hold true to her promise of a girls' night.

"That's not fair at all, sugar."

The muscles of her neck twitched as she pulled her mouth back in a frown. "Sorry."

"Oh, don't fucking lie, woman. You're not sorry."

Her cheeks split and he grasped her chin in his hand. "Night," he said as he hovered over her mouth. She waited. She waited for those perfect lips to caress hers one last time. She waited for the feel of his warm breath to be replaced by the feel of his warm mouth—but he didn't move. He just lingered there, so close she could basically taste him. Huh, he must think he's real good. . . .

She reached her hand down and pressed it over his cock, and no surprise, it was hard. It was a brief touch, just a quick, teasing pass—but it was enough to break his concentration and she pulled her face from his strong grasp. "Night." She smirked and turned to walk away.

Reed laughed, the luscious baritone ring saturating the evening air. She looked over her shoulder to get one last glimpse at the smile that was covering him when she saw a wicked glint flash across his eyes. He leaned forward and smacked her ass, hard, and she jumped.

"Ow," she whined, rubbing her butt with her hand.

He only laughed again. "Night, baby."

CHAPTER SEVENTEEN

Meagan had crawled in bed and died. The combination of beer and tequila shots, mixed with the oh so comfy familiarity of her bed that she had missed so much, had her passed out the second her head hit the pillow.

She was dreaming. And hell yes, it was a good dream too. The kind of dreams that were all chocolate and margaritas—hell, even a chocolate margarita—all your favorite book boyfriends popped into three-dimensional sex slaves for your dreamland vacation fantasy, mixed with sandy beaches and warm sun and a couple of mani-pedis thrown in there for good measure.

But said fantasy dream was cut short when she felt something brush across the bottom of her foot. It tickled. It was soft and it caused her to jolt so quickly from dreamland that she jerked awake. She kept her eyes shut, praying she would fall back asleep so she could get back to the goodness that was men and margaritas and foot massages. But then real life started kissing the back of her calves, igniting goose bumps to scatter across her bare legs.

Her eyes fluttered open when she recognized the feather-light touches. She lay perfectly still. She wanted to soak it all up, let her body absorb all it could. A rough pair of hands led a path for the mouth that was still taunting her body with sensuous kisses. The pressure was gentle—but anything but light. It was as if the fingertips were branding her skin with their personal imprint—bruising her without leaving a mark. She wasn't sure if she was awake or not anymore. . . .

The callused sensation traveled over her hips, giving attention to the exposed panel of skin between the bottom of her tank top and the top of her panties as she lay facedown on her cool sheets, her head still sunken in to the down-feather pillow.

She closed her eyes as she felt the warm flat of a tongue lick the same path the fingers had previously taken and she writhed as the wet stimulation aroused a layer of goose bumps that penetrated her skin, reaching her insides.

"Mmm." Teeth sunk into the fleshy skin of her side, right above her hip. "You taste sweet, just like sugar," he whispered, his words barely audible.

She smiled into the pillow, the bend in his scruffy voice setting off a chain reaction that started in her ears and dominoed throughout her body.

His hands raised farther up the bare skin of her sides. His fingers slowly crept under her, toying with the smooth flesh under her breasts. She felt the weight of his body press on top of her, but she continued to lie still, her eyes closed, and her breathing calm and even. She liked this, this sensuous, sweet side of him she was experiencing.

His lips fastened over the back of her neck, right in the

pillow-y spot where her neck and shoulder met. His mouth was warm. He sucked gently, then pressed a soft, chaste kiss. "Hey, baby, time to get up." His mouth hung next to her ear, his lips brushing the bottom of her earlobe. He slid down next to her, his body enveloping as much as it could around her as she lay on her stomach. She sleepily lifted her lids, opening them to see Reed staring straight back at her.

"Morning." He smiled.

Meagan felt the need to cover her mouth with her hand to prevent her morning breath from seeping out when she spoke. She lifted her hand to her mouth. "Morning."

Reed tucked his arm across her back and under her stomach, flipping her over and pulling her back flush against his chest. "Now, can I kiss you like this?" His lips barely brushed against the skin below her hairline, and a fresh patch of goose bumps scattered down her body.

"Mmm-hmm."

She felt his lips tighten into a grin as he continued to dot kisses along her neck, her shoulders, and the top of her back.

She squirmed her body back, trying to wedge herself in closer to him. She felt the swell of his cock press against her ass and a pleasing hum vibrated from his lips.

His hand left her stomach and slid between her thighs, cupping her through her cotton panties. She had a moment's thought, a mental note she tacked in her mind, to start wearing something a little sexier to bed.

Reed's fingers grazed her, never applying pressure, and the featherlight touch was torturous. It almost tickled, but in the way that made her crave more.

"God, I want to taste you," he mumbled against her skin as he continued to kiss her. His finger pressed against her, slightly dipping inside her through the fabric, her panties soaking up the wetness.

His hand left her abruptly. "Fuck, baby."

She rolled to her back as Reed stood up. He slid his arms under her legs and back and scooped her up. She giggled—a sound that was usually left for her tipsy moments.

He spun around and headed toward her bathroom. "You need to take a shower and get ready to go."

"How is that fair after you just teased me like that? Take a shower with me?"

Reed bit his teeth together and sighed. "Don't tempt me," he said as he stepped into her bathroom and placed her feet on the floor.

She hooked her finger in the waist of his blue and white board shorts and skimmed it back and forth. The muscles tightened under her touch and she smiled. "I want to tempt you."

He grabbed ahold of her wrist and pulled her hand away from his stomach. At first she thought he was angry, but then she lifted her eyes to him and saw nothing but the same wanton craving she was having staring back at her.

He lifted her tank top and she raised her arms, allowing him to pull it over her head. His eyes devoured her naked breasts as he hooked onto the edge of her panties and dropped to his knees. Her mouth parted slightly as he slowly and deliberately inched the cotton toward the floor. She felt the fine hairs on the nape of her neck stand up as his feverish touch set flames to her body and although she was warm and flushed, a tremble coursed through her.

She stepped out of her panties. Reed stood back up, and a small wave of disappointment crushed against her when the anticipated feel of his tongue tasting between her thighs vanished. But her disappointment didn't last long, because the second his mouth was in front of hers—it was on hers.

His kiss was smooth, controlled, and anything but the way she was feeling. It was like he was forcing her to be patient, teasing the eager part of her that was ready to wrap herself around his body. But she'd seen this side of Reed before. The in-charge, calm, and controlled Captain Porter—and she knew better. If she had to guess, the last thing he was feeling right then was calm, and the only way he knew how to strangle the agitated rush of arousal he was feeling was to feign his control.

She gave into him, lowering from her toes and then re-leasing the grip she suddenly had on his shirt. She broke their kiss, breathless and more than a little worked up. "You sure I can't change your mind about that shower?"

Reed ran his hand through his hair as he dipped his head toward the ground. Meagan pressed her lips together—her suspicion was spot-on, he wasn't the least bit in control. All she would have to do is reach out and run her hand. . . .

"Sanders is waiting out in the truck for us"—his eyes glazed over and his voice dropped an octave, giving Meagan the shivers, the good kind—"otherwise, I would have already had you pinned against the wall."

She swallowed hard as the lascivious image ran through her mind, but then it registered.

"Sanders is waiting for us now?"

Reed laughed. "Yes. You overslept. We were supposed to leave"—he pulled his phone from his pocket and checked the time—"almost fifteen minutes ago."

"Shit!" She reached behind her to turn on the water.

"You're staring," she said in a singsong voice when she turned around to a gawking Reed.

"I am."

"It's distracting."

He laughed, and the sound titillated her skin. "I'll wait for you in the living room."

"So, Meagan, have you been boating before?" Sanders asked as they walked down the side of the boat ramp to where Murano and the girls were waiting in Finn's boat, which was tied up to the dock.

"A time or two."

Reed saw Finn cup his hands around his mouth. "Hurry the hell up! You guys are late!"

Meagan's eyes darted to Reed's as a blush crept over her cheeks. "I'm so sorry I slept—"

He hooked his arm around her shoulders and pulled her against his side. "Nope, no apologizing. Besides, you're cute as hell when you sleep. I liked getting the chance to come wake you up."

She tilted her head back and looked at him. It was those sweet fucking looks that twisted him up. The easy, genuine looks that stirred something inside him that was foreign. She smiled and he leaned down and kissed her on the forehead.

"Think you can wake me up in the morning?" she whispered. And there it was—the sexy, teasing Meagan. He liked seeing that mischievous smirk on her face almost as much.

"I'd be happy to wake you up, as long as I get to put you to sleep too."

"I think that can be arranged."

They stepped up on the dock and Reed held Meagan's hand as she stepped down into the boat.

"Finn, this is Meagan," Reed said, climbing in after her.

Finn reached out his hand to her. "Meagan, it's nice to meet you. Welcome aboard."

"Okay, and you know Murano. And this is Tessa," he said as he gestured toward the woman with long, dark hair who was wearing a swimsuit that looked like it was from the forties. It was sexy. She and Finn had an on-again, off-again thing, but she hung around either way, so it was hard tell which course they were currently navigating.

"And this beauty is Hadly," he said, as she stood up and wrapped her arms around him in a tight hug. "Finn's little sister." She'd moved in with Finn a few months ago after she'd dropped out of college and her parents had stopped supporting her. She was feisty and hilarious. She had a rockin' body, more curves and meat to her. She also had the same taste in women as Reed.

"Hadly, this is Meagan." Reed attempted to suppress his smile as Hadly attempted to keep her eyes from roaming over Meagan, but what could he say? His woman was a knockout.

Hadly reached forward and shook Megan's hand. "Hi."

"Okay, now that all the introductions are made, sit your

happy asses down so we can get the hell out of this idle zone."
Finn started up the boat and backed it away from the dock.

Meagan plopped down next to Reed on the bench seat at
the back of the boat and flung her legs over his. His hand
automatically found its place on her thigh.

"I'm boarding first," Sanders shouted from the seat across
from him. They had passed the wake zone and the boat was
gliding effortlessly through the water, the wind blowing past
their faces, making it difficult to hear one another.

Meagan's eyes widened. "Are you kidding? Luke, you can
wakeboard?"

Sanders' eyes darted between Reed and Meagan. "Uh,
yeah. Why?"

"I can't wait to see that."

"What? Why?" he said, suddenly looking embarrassed or
worried—neither one an emotion Sanders showed often.

"You are huge, like, Hulk-Hogan-meets-the-Incredible-
Hulk huge. I just can't picture you standing on a tiny board,
jumping over the wake." Meagan laughed and when Reed
looked over at Sanders he laughed too. Sanders was grinning
ear to ear. "Something funny?" Meagan challenged.

"I was just trying to picture *you* wakeboarding. You
know, since you seemed to enjoy a visual of me on the wake,
I'm trying to get one of you. Actually I'm trying to determine
if you can even pull yourself up out of the water." He was
probably more than likely trying to get a visual of her tits
bouncing around on the wake instead.

Hadly reached over and slapped Sanders on the bicep
with the back of her hand. "Knock it off, Luke."

Meagan just laughed. She wasn't affected by Sanders' teasing, if anything it seemed to spark something in her eyes. "Hmm, guess I'll have to try it."

Reed squeezed her knee. "You wanna wakeboard?"

"Sure, why not?"

Luke threw his hands in the air. "All right, I'm giving up my call at first go. Meagan, it's all yours." He snorted.

Ten minutes later and the boat was sitting in the middle of the lake as Meagan situated herself behind it, the rope in hand.

Reed was kneeling on the bench seat, leaning over the back of the boat. "You good, baby?"

She gave the universal thumbs-up. Reed turned around and nodded at Finn, who wasn't known for his lack of speed. "Take it easy on her, man."

Finn just nodded before throwing the boat into drive, giving it just enough of a kick of speed to help Meagan get up easily—and she did.

"Well, look at that, Luke," Hadly said.

"Hell, man, looks like your girl's been boating more than we thought."

Reed watched as Meagan glided behind the boat with ease. She was even power sliding and lip sliding through the wake, which was pretty damn impressive.

Then she jumped it.

"No fucking way!" Murano laughed, standing up to look over the girls, who were sitting in front of him.

Then she did it again.

"All right, she has been doing this way more than she led

on. Where the hell's my phone? I need to video this shit,"
Sanders said.

"Oh!" Murano pointed at Meagan, who had started to
bend her knees. "She's jumping again!"

She slid across the water and jumped the wake, her
board going high in the air as she grabbed ahold of the front
of the board with her hand, then landed facing the opposite
direction.

Reed shook his head and smiled. "She just did a nose
grab 180."

He looked over his shoulder at Sanders, who looked like
he had just seen a monkey fucking an elephant. "You see
that, Sanders?"

"Fuck yeah I did, and now she wants Finn to go faster."

Reed turned back around to look at her and sure enough,
she was bouncing her thumbs-up in the air, signaling to go
faster.

Murano laughed. "She's gonna put you to shame, Porter."

"Hell no. I'm proud as shit right now."

The boat picked up speed and the wake got bigger. Reed
couldn't take his eyes off her. She was shocking the hell out
of him. She had a smile that lit up her entire face. And there
was something to be said about all of his buddies watching
his girl show them up out on the water—doing better than
half of them could. He fucking loved it.

"Oh!" everyone said in unison as Meagan jumped and
landed a 360 turn.

"I have a boner. Sorry, man. I have a no-shit boner right
now watching her tear up that fucking wake." Sanders

bounced from foot to foot, shaking around as if he was adjusting himself.

"Can't say I blame you. It's hot."

Then she had to go and flip. A front flip over the wake, landing on the other side like she could do it in her sleep.

"I fucking love her," Sanders said, taking a drink of his afternoon beer.

Murano lifted his hand in the air. "I second that."

"I third that," Hadly said.

"Hell, me too," Tessa chimed in. Then they all erupted with laughter.

"Finn, you're missing one hell of a show!" Murano shouted.

"So I can hear!"

A sweet, sexy woman who could lie soft in his arms, make him lose his mind in bed, and throw out tricks on the water like a pro—yep, he had his hands on a good one.

Meagan smiled and it was wicked. It was laced with confidence that ran along every part of her expression. She threw her hands in the air, releasing the handle, letting the rope fall into the water.

"She's down!" Reed hollered up to Finn.

They circled around and she climbed up the ladder on the back of the boat and grabbed Reed's outstretched hand.

"So, you've been boating before?" he asked as he pulled her into the boat.

"Eh"—she shrugged—"a time or two."

Sanders pulled a beer from the cooler in the floorboard and handed it to Meagan. "A time or two my ass."

She took the beer and tossed her sopping life jacket

against Sanders' chest. "Thanks, Hulk. Now let's see you get your ass out there."

The water dripped down Meagan's body and goose bumps pricked across the tops of her tits when the boat took off. Her nipples perked through the thin yellow fabric of her bikini and as badly as he wanted to pull that scrap of fabric aside and run his tongue across her soft pink nipple, he wanted to cover her up even more.

He wrapped a towel around her and sat down beside her, her legs taking up the space of his lap again.

"That was pretty damn impressive, sugar."

She winked. "Why, thank you. My parents have a couple boats. I grew up on the water. No matter where we were stationed, we went to the closest lake every chance we had."

"A couple boats?"

"My dad kind of has a thing for toys. Vintage cars, boats, motorcycles. He likes to buy them, fix 'em up, then flip 'em. More often than my mom would probably like, he keeps a few too."

"Sounds like your dad and I would get along just fine."

The corners of her mouth lifted a little. "I think you're probably right. Although he's not that adventurous anymore. He is in his seventies, you know."

"Aw, you're never too old to get on the back of a bike or drive a boat down an open lake."

She laughed.

"What?"

"That is exactly something he would say. Yeah, you two would get along just fine."

. . .

The party cove was packed. There were two boats tied up on either side of Finn's boat, and each had a row of boats tied up to them as well. The alcohol that Meagan had consumed throughout the day was settling in her stomach, making her nice and fuzzy around the edges, just the way she liked it when she was out on the water. A good lake buzz was the best.

The summer heat was torture, and the water was barely any relief.

"Found one!" she hollered as she straddled her floaty between her thighs. She was a little off balance and she swayed backward for a moment as she tried to scoot forward.

Reed kicked his legs beneath the water, wading his way toward her. "You gonna share?"

"If you ask nicely."

"Or how about I just take it?" he said, pulling her legs from their grip on the floaty and pulling her onto his lap. He swayed back and forth for a moment as he tried to steady his own floaty between his legs now that he was balancing her on top of him as well. They both laughed.

"Damn, that feels good."

She shifted her weight on his lap and locked her legs behind his waist. "Well, you better enjoy it because these cold spots don't last for long."

His eyes glassed over in that way that always seemed to trigger her inner pervert, and a not so innocent tickle moved between her legs.

"I wasn't referring to the cold spot."

She leaned in close to him and pressed her mouth against his ear. "I assumed as much."

She felt Reed's cock twitch against her and the look that was covering his face when she pulled her lips away from his ear was worth the little torture she was experiencing from his now hard cock, teasing her as she settled above it. She grinned.

"You're not right—you know that?" he said, reaching his hand down in between them to readjust.

Her lips puckered into a pout and Reed leaned in and latched onto it in between his teeth. Not the reaction she was going for, but she would most definitely take it.

He pulled her lip into his mouth and sucked hard. Her mouth molded around his when he released her now swollen lip before she leaned back and tilted her beer to the sky, letting the remainder of its contents trickle down her throat.

"I'm gonna go grab another beer. Do you want one?"

Reed emptied his beer into his mouth then submerged it into the water, the can filling up before sinking below the surface. "Yep."

Meagan released the hold she had around his waist, pushed herself back, and swam toward the boat.

After hurling herself up the ladder and clumsily flopping back into the boat, she decided that floating on one of the flat tubes would be a good change from floating on that tiny little foam board between her legs. Definitely a good change as her balance was in serious jeopardy this many beers in. Yep, flat tube sounded like a much better idea.

"Anyone else need a beer?" she shouted over the blaring music coming from Finn's boat.

The mass of people bobbing around in the water made her smile. Everyone was pink and wet, and the majority were drunk. She needed a day like this, she just wished Eva would had been able to come along. She would have loved it.

Hadly and Luke wanted a beer, as well as a few others she didn't know. She tossed them all beers, splashing them in the face with lake water as the cans landed short in front of them.

Luke snatched his beer before it floated away from him. "You throw like a girl!"

"Do you want to go wakeboarding?" she hollered back, a cocky smile set firmly in place as she hoisted her hands on her hips, balancing, although slightly unsteadily, on the back ledge of the boat.

Luke shook his head and laughed. "Well played, Meg. Well played."

The use of her nickname from him made her grin. She could get used to that big guy.

Meagan grabbed onto the rope that was tied from the back of Finn's boat and started pulling the giant black tube toward her. When it was close enough, she tossed two beers onto it and then jumped on, landing not so gracefully on her knees.

"Reed, I've got your beer," she yelled as she turned over and flopped onto her back. The sun was absorbing the tiny drops of water that still clung to her skin.

"Hang on to it for me. I'm gonna go swing off that cliff over there." He nodded his head toward the cliff behind him that had a rope that looked like a scrap of yarn dangling from a branch that could quite possibly be a twig.

"Are you crazy?"

"Ah, sugar. I thought we already determined that I was!"
As he started to swim toward the cliff, he flashed her a
crooked grin paired with a wink that, given any other cir-
cumstances, she would have melted—well, she still did a
little—but the fearless, cocky, more than tipsy smirk mostly
made her nervous. Reed didn't know the definition of dangerous. If she was to look up the word under the dictionary
via Reed, it would say: a pleasurable sensation of fright. Oh
wait. That's the definition of thrill. Reed apparently couldn't
differentiate between the two.

Meagan swung her legs underneath her and sat Indian-
style on the tube and watched as he and Finn pulled themselves up the shore, swaying back and forth as they tried to
keep their footing over the slippery rocks beneath them.
They wound their way up the overgrown path that led to the
top of the cliff and although Meagan was a good ways away,
she could still pick out his deep laugh. It was like listening to
the joy of a kid. It was sweet, and as much as she wanted to
suppress the damn feeling, she thought it was incredibly sexy
too. She hated to admit that there was a secret part of her
that loved how fearless he was and how playful he was.

"Oh my God, I can't watch this," Tess said, swimming up
next to Meagan. It was nice to know that she wasn't the only
one having a slight panic attack as she watched the guys
climb higher. All it would take was one little slip and they
would tumble down the jagged rocks. . . .

She turned her head toward Tess, who Meagan was ad-
mittedly jealous of. The woman was gorgeous. She was a doll
too. "I know, I think we snagged ourselves some idiots."

"Oh, there's no thinkin' about it. They are downright stupid for doing that." She laughed, but it was forced and nervous.

The guys got to the top and Reed maneuvered his body between the rocks to grab onto the rope and pull it up to a flatter spot, if there was even one. He gave it a couple of tugs, obviously attempting to check the safety of the rope, but given the look of it, it wouldn't hold a toddler.

A few of the stragglers who were bobbing around in the water made their way toward Meagan, trying to get a better look at the dumbasses who were about to swing off the cliff over a bunch of rocks and hopefully land in deep enough waters that they didn't crack open their heads or break their legs. Did she mention they were idiots?

Some guy swam to her tube and latched onto the side. Meagan had to hold her breath to keep from laughing. He looked like a lobster. He was so sunburned that it actually hurt her to look at him. If she could see past the angry skin, he was extremely attractive with a buzzed head—which was also the same red color as his face and shoulders—that showed the remnants of blond hair, and he had a prominent chin that jutted forward from his face with a small vertical indentation right in the center. If she pulled him up out of the water, she was almost positive she would see a six-pack nestled on his torso. He had those broad shoulders and a nice thick neck that gave the I-spend-all-my-free-time-at-the-gym look. She didn't quite know what was going on with all the good-looking guys here in Georgia, but she wasn't going to question it, her eyes were grateful. "Hey, I'm Adam," he slurred, and she smiled. He was tanked.

"Hi, Adam."

She turned her attention back to Reed. She met his eyes
and he smiled. It was one of those show-off grins. She rolled
her eyes, although she knew he couldn't see, and shook her
head. He held the rope with both hands, one slightly higher
than the other; then he leaned back into a squat.

Meagan held her breath. She wanted to close her eyes
but was unable to peel them away from him. After he got the
momentum in his knees, he jumped. It was in slow motion,
or at least that's how Meagan saw it. His feet left the cliff, and
the muscles of his arms flexed as he held on to the rope. It
swung out. "Let go," Meagan whispered to herself. All she
could picture was him not letting go in time and slamming
back against the cliff, or worse, letting go too soon or too late
and falling on the rocks below. If he made it safely into the
water, she was going to kill him when she got her hands on
him for making her witness this.

He let go.

His body made a beeline to the water below and the
show-off did a somersault right before he hit the lake. Meagan let out the breath she was holding and inhaled a much-
needed breath of fresh air, but it was thick and hot and it did
nothing to quench her need for oxygen.

She took another breath and waited for him to pop up
out of the water. And then she started to get antsy again.

"Where the hell is he?" She rose up onto her knees in an
attempt to get a better look but all it did was make her unbalanced.

"Eh, Porter will be fine. That crazy son of a bitch has

jumped off that cliff more times than I could count." Okay, so obviously Lobster Boy knew Reed.

"I don't care if he's done it a million times, it only takes one time for something bad to happen." She narrowed her eyes at Adam but all he did was smile and point. She followed the direction of his hand and saw a grinning Reed swimming their way—and she relaxed. She plopped back down on her back and sprawled out on the tube, reaching her hand down in the water to scoop some over her chest and stomach in attempts to cool her off.

"Scoot on over, I'll cool ya off," Adam slurred.

Meagan laughed once. "Thanks, but no, thanks. Besides nothing will cool anyone in this heat."

He placed his hands on the top of the flat tube and lifted his upper body onto it, his hips and legs dangling over the side. "Eh, you'd be surprised what a little wet body could do next to ya." Okay, so he was harmless, Meagan got that. He was just a piss-poor flirt, and he obviously hadn't picked up on the little fact that she was there with Reed.

She had opened her mouth to tell him, when he was jerked from the tube, his body submerging under the water.

Meagan sat up quickly, but her urgency faltered once she saw Reed looking at her. Her eyes shrunk from their what-the-hell look, and she smiled. He was starting to become a pussy over that fucking smile, but he didn't particularly give a shit. He winked.

"What the fuck was that for, Porter?" Adam whined

when he bobbed to the surface like a fishing lure, choking on water as he reined in his laughter.

"For trying to get your prick ass close to my girl."

His laughs tapered off. "This beautiful blonde is with your sorry ass?"

"Yes."

Reed knew Adam was drunk; he also knew that Adam was about as good of a guy as they came. And although he knew that Meagan would brush him off, and it had been nothing but innocent flirting from a drunk buddy, his body told him different. The moment he saw Adam lay on that thick smile at Meagan and try to climb up on the tube to lie next to her, he got tense. His fucking jealousy radar was blaring in his ears and he felt a territorial rush sweep through his veins.

"She's mine, just thought I should let you know," he barked, all the while a satisfied tilt to his head and a cheese-eatin' grin on his face worked its way into his expression.

Adam's drunken lids were starting to drop over his eyes. He threw his hands in the air at the same time as he tried to balance a Styrofoam noodle that he had just shoved in between his legs.

"I'm yours, huh?" he heard Meagan say behind him, the sweet, amused hum in her voice rattling him.

He turned around and pulled his upper body onto the tube like Adam had, and Meagan lay back down against the black nylon. Water dripped from his chin onto her tanned shoulder, his face hovering over hers. "I thought we had already established that, sugar."

"We had, but it was nice to see you go all knight-in-shining-armor."

"Yeah? You want me to do it again?"

She leaned up on her elbows, her damp hair matting together and tumbling down her back. "Nah, not this time. But you can say it again."

She wanted him to say it again, and he loved that. Fuck, it wasn't like him to want to shout it from the rooftops, but he was about ready to climb those damn rocks again and scream it out for the whole party cove to hear. She was his and his alone.

He deliberately lifted the corners of his mouth, slowly, just the way he knew would get a little rise out of her, and then he laid it on thick, accent and all. "You're mine."

She leaned over, wrapped her hand around his neck, and kissed him. He loved the way she kissed him when she was a little buzzed. She was eager, and nothing else was there—not her confidence that usually knocked him on his ass, not her shyness that made him want to pull her in his arms and do nothing but kiss her all night, and not her intensity that threatened his self-control. No, she was just eager and sexy—wanting nothing but him.

The kiss continued, and he almost forgot that they were surrounded by a shit-ton of his drunken friends, none of whom were used to seeing him like that with a woman, but they made their presence known when the whoops and hollers and perverted catcalls started streaming their way.

But Reed didn't give a shit, not when Meagan was kissing him like that. He just wished like hell they were alone.

CHAPTER EIGHTEEN

"You tell that little friend of yours I missed her today," Luke said through the window as Meagan and Reed stepped up onto the sidewalk.

"I will."

Reed grabbed onto her hand and led her up the walk that led to their apartment building. She was completely exhausted. The beer, the sun, the wakeboarding—she was sure she was gonna be all kinds of hurting tomorrow. Her arms already felt the familiar pull as her muscles tightened and began to ache. Her good beer buzz was long gone and it left a nice, sleepy residue in her veins. She leaned her head down on Reed's shoulder and he instantly wrapped his arm around her.

Meagan continued to walk past Reed's apartment, but he gave her a gentle tug as he halted his steps. "Sleep in my bed tonight."

It wasn't a question and he didn't wait for her to respond, he just scooped her up in his arms and kissed her. She would have said yes anyway, but he was quite convincing.

Somehow he managed to unlock the door with her still

cradled against his chest. He headed straight for the bathroom.

He set her down in front of the sink. "Arms up," he ordered, and she gladly obeyed.

"I've been thinking about this all day." he murmured as he lifted her tank top over her head.

She cocked her eyebrow. "About what?"

Yes, she wanted him to spell it out for her. She had never been a big bedroom talker. She didn't particularly go for the vocal man between the sheets—or at least none of the men she had been with in the past liked to give a play-by-play. But there was something about hearing Reed tell her—something about hearing word for word every delicious thing he planned to do to her body, every soft touch, every teasing kiss—that made her heart beat fast.

His accent wasn't bad either.

She liked knowing that he thought about it too. She loved the fact that he knew exactly what he wanted to do to her, exactly what little reaction he wanted to get from her, and she loved it when he told her his plans. It was hot.

His eyes seemed to take on more gold tonight, like they had melted, and he locked those seductive eyes on hers. A knowing glance filled them and she blushed. "I've been wanting to reach around your neck and pull these damn strings loose."

And he did.

His fingers skimmed across her stomach and wrapped around to her back; then they toyed with the strings that dangled down her spine. "I've wanted to untie this from your body so I could see you. . . ."

And he did.

Her breath hitched as his eyes drank in the sight of her bare breasts, but he didn't touch her. His hands hung loose at his sides and he just looked at her. His stare was torture—in the best possible way. It was causing an anticipation to pound against her chest, an anxious pressure smothering her as she waited and waited, wondering when he was going to reach out and relieve her from the torture his eyes were giving her. But he didn't.

She moved her fingers to the buttons of her jean shorts and clumsily made work of undoing them. She unzipped and dropped them, along with her bikini bottoms, to the cold tile floor.

His mouth parted, and his eyes journeyed over her. Her body heated up and her nerve endings seemed to stir and tingle as her body craved his touch. She took a step toward him and he smiled. Damn him. He was playing her.

"Reed," she admonished.

His lips pulled up tighter. "Yeah, baby?"

"I believe I've mentioned to you before that it's more fun to touch than to look."

"At this very moment, I might have to argue against that." His eyes left her body and met hers. They were glassed over with need. "You're beautiful."

This time she smiled.

"Thank you."

"I'm going to touch you now," he warned, and her pulse spiked.

His large hands reached out and grabbed onto her hips, pulling her flush against him. The soft cotton of his cutoff

T-shirt brushed across her breasts and her nipples hardened from the sensation.

His lips tasted the thin skin at the dip in her throat, licking a path over her collarbone and up the side of her neck, dotting featherlight kisses along the way. His mouth lingered next to her ear, his warm breath pricking her sensitive skin. "Let's take that shower now."

She nodded.

Reed pulled his shirt over his head and stepped out of his board shorts as Meagan turned on the water. She felt his body close in behind her. She melted against his chest and he wrapped his strong arms around her stomach, pinning her arms to her side. She loved the feel of him surrounding her like that, like a protective blanket.

He stepped forward, moving her along with him until they were both standing under the spray of the water.

He washed her. Carefully lathering her skin, running his soapy hands over her arms, down her stomach, between her legs—then he turned her around, the water rinsing the front of her body as he repeated his work on her back.

"Lean forward, sugar," he whispered against her neck as he pressed his body in tight to her back.

She leaned forward, the spray of the water pattering against the small of her back as she braced her hands against the wall. Reed's hands reached around and massaged her between her legs.

"Baby," he said. Then the next thing she felt was his cock sliding between her legs from behind. He slid into her, smooth and easy, and she felt his heavy sigh expand against her back. Her body tightened around him, and she dropped her head, hanging it between her shoulders.

He stayed slow, circling his hips, then slowly pulling out and slowly sliding back in. It was almost agony. A part of her wanted to tell him to move harder, faster, to alleviate the ache that was threatening to take her over. But a stronger part of her wanted to savor the feeling. She was powerless against him as he gripped her hips from behind, as he leaned his hard chest against her, and as he moved of his own accord inside her. It was sexy to be under his control. To be subject to his pleasure as he watched their bodies connect from behind. But what was sexier, what she loved even more, was that he was savoring it too.

Reed's hands bit into her soft curves; then he snaked one down her stomach, holding her tight against him, giving her an anchor to hold her down. His other hand lifted to her breast, the full flesh spilling over his palm.

He pressed his lips to the back of her shoulder, using his teeth to brush over the water that was spattering over her skin. She moaned—so he did it again.

He was struggling—hard. Every little shudder, every soft moan or airy breath, sent a jolt straight to his hips, giving him the green light to pound into her—to fill her body so completely that she wouldn't remember anything but the way his dick felt against her slick pussy, how the friction caused a tingling, pricking, almost numbing pleasure to un-dulate inside her. He wanted it. He wanted to lift her body to the edge, then make her free-fall all the way back down.

But not tonight.

Tonight he focused on the lines of her back, the dip of her curves. He watched as her hair absorbed the water, the sodden strands sticking to her neck. He memorized her tics—what caused her to tighten around him, what made her sigh, and what made her writhe against him. He memorized them, then utilized them—making her tighten and sigh and writhe again and again.

"Reed," she whimpered.

"Not yet, baby."

Her back arched and her ass pressed into him. "I can't—"

"You can."

His hands splayed across her stomach and he pulled her back until she was standing straight, her back molding to him. He withdrew from her, then turned her around and pinned her to the wall.

Her wet, naked body made a sweet little smacking noise as it collided against the warm shower tile—and she gasped, an openmouthed smile pulling a sharp breath into her lungs, and goddamn, it was sexy.

His weight crushed against her as he lifted her legs around him. Then he was back inside her. He held her in his arms as she arched against the wall and tilted her head up to the ceiling. Fuck, her sweet little responses to him were almost too damn much.

He slowed again, making sure to ride it out—to claim her pleasure as his own. He wanted her body worn and strung out—raw from delectation.

Her nails dug into his shoulders, so hard he was sure she

pierced his skin. She pushed against him, her shoulder blades the only part of her body in contact with the wall behind her as she forced her body to take all of him.

She was moaning. Every thrust received its own appreciative little noise, and each one got louder and louder. Reed's restraint was paper thin, he was barely hanging on, but every delicious cry that seeped into the steam of the shower clung to his body like dew—forcing him to keep up the slow, torturous rhythm.

"Reed." It was a plea. She needed to let go.

His mouth latched onto the side of her neck, her erratic pulse vibrating against his lips as he kissed the wet skin below her ear. Then he slowly pulled out of her tender pussy, the very tip of his cock lingering inside—then in one quick, hard thrust, he filled her completely.

Her head rolled against the wall as every muscle in her body tightened around him and she filled the room with the sound of her melodic voice crying out his name.

The smell of Reed's T-shirt was the most comforting scent her lungs had ever breathed in. It was clean and crisp and nothing but Reed.

She slipped the worn, gray cotton over her naked body, the spicy aroma encasing her. "I don't think a bed has ever looked this good." She could hear the exhaustion in her own voice as she crawled into the bed next to Reed.

"My bed *hasn't* ever looked this good, not until you were lying in it." He folded the covers down and opened up his arms.

Meagan didn't waste a moment before she was covered—by the blankets and by Reed.

"That was pretty smooth there, sweet talker."

He lowered his chin to his chest, his brows tightening, causing little creases to form between his eyes. "I'm not sweet-talking." He lifted her chin with his fingers so she was forced to meet his riveting stare. "I'm not. Seeing you curled up in my bed is a sight I never thought I would be so damn happy to see, sugar."

His words honestly melted her. She snuggled into the crook of his arm and let him hold her tight. She was falling—hard. And it was scaring the shit out of her.

His hand stroked her hair and the repetitious touch was tingling her scalp, relaxing her body even more than it already was.

His lips brushed against her forehead. "Come somewhere with me next weekend."

Her fingers raked over his bare chest, mimicking the movement of his fingers through her hair. "Where?"

"Panama City."

Her fingers stalled and fell against his chest. "Florida?"

"My parents own a condo there, I thought you might like it."

"Do you ever just stay home on the weekends and do absolutely nothing?"

"No."

She sighed, although it sounded more like a laugh. "I would love to go."

She would. She loved the Gulf and the beach. And the

idea of having Reed all to herself for an entire weekend was more than appealing.

He stretched his arms behind her, his legs straightening toward the foot of the bed as he yawned his response. "Why do I feel a 'but' coming on?" After his chest exhaled his tired breath, he locked his arms back around her and pulled her in tight.

"No 'but,' just some terms."

"What kind of terms?"

She laughed quickly at his worried tone. "I will go to Panama City with you *if* you promise to relax. No crazy sports, no terrifying stunts, no adrenaline-rush activities—unless they are in the bedroom"—she felt him smile against her cheek—"just a nice, relaxed weekend filled with lazy days on the beach and cozy nights on the couch. Think you can do it?"

"For you? Absolutely."

She laughed. "Yeah, we'll see."

CHAPTER NINETEEN

*I*t was almost dark when Reed pulled his motorcycle into the garage of the beachfront condo. Four hours on his bike with Meagan wrapped around him was the best ride he'd ever taken. Meagan, on the other hand, didn't feel completely the same.

He helped her climb off, her legs stiff as she straightened them. "My ass hurts and it's never felt so good to close my legs in my whole life. Words I never thought I'd say."

Reed pulled on her waist so she was closer to him. "Here." Gripping her ass, he started rubbing deep circles with the heel of his palm.

"Oh God, that feels so good."

He laughed and pulled away his hands, lifting them in the air in surrender. "All right, I can't be doing that, sugar. I'll end up fucking you right here on my bike."

"As fun as that might be, this ass is not getting back on that bike the rest of the night."

Reed pulled the keys out of the ignition, twirling them around his finger. "Here." He held the keys out for Meagan to catch and she cupped her hands so he could toss them to her. "Go on in, I'll bring our bags," he said, climbing off the bike to unhook the duffel bags he had strapped to the back.

"Okay."

"Reed?" He heard her holler from the living room as he stepped into the condo. He dropped their bags in the hallway and followed her voice. She was standing in front of the mantel, and Reed's heart sank into the pit of his stomach.

She turned around, her beautiful blue eyes shining with excitement. "Would you like to explain to me why I'm seeing double?" she teased, lifting a picture frame from the mantel and holding it out for him to see.

It was a picture of his family, taken on the beach a few years back. Gosh, Beck seemed so young as she stood between her brothers. Reed on one side and Mackly on the other. That seemed like a lifetime ago.

"That's Mackly," he said, walking farther into the living room. "My twin brother."

Meagan's smile split across her face. Her smiles always had a way of sparking this unseen ignition inside of him, roaring him to life—but this time, it just turned over.

"Oh my God. Two Reed Porters. If he is anything like you, I can only imagine the headache your poor mom had raising you." Her words were sweet and they were right. They had given his momma hell.

"A twin brother! Why didn't you tell me?"

"I don't know. He's not a topic that I tend to bring up

much anymore." Which was the truth. He didn't talk about Mackly much. It was a topic that lingered like the white elephant in the room. Occasionally Beck would bring him up, but Reed would just cut the conversation short.

He'd known bringing Meagan here would open up doors and windows and fucking black holes that led to his past—to his family. He knew he would have to tell her, and a part of him wanted to tell her. She had quickly become the most important person in his life—a title that, up until now, only his brother had held, and up until now, his brother was the only person he would spill his guts to.

She frowned and her face flushed with a guilt that she couldn't possibly understand and a guilt that she had no reason to feel.

"He's dead." The words seemed like acid coming out of his mouth. Although he'd said them many times before, although he'd finally absorbed the idea that his brother was gone, it still left a grainy coating in his throat.

Meagan placed the frame back on the mantel and paused, gauging his actions—more like his reaction. He kept his breathing even, and he held her eyes, not wanting to give her a reason to feel any worse than he knew she already was.

She didn't walk toward him. She didn't come to him to wrap her arms around him and tell him how sorry she was. She didn't dote over the fact that he had lost someone close to him. He guessed she was a pro at this kind of thing by now. Growing up around soldiers, working in the ER at a military hospital, he supposed she had earned a thing or two about comforting a loss.

He could see the pain on her face, pain for him, but she didn't smother him or ask a single question—and he respected that about her.

He walked to the couch and sat down, throwing his head down into his hands. When he looked back up, Meagan was sitting on the arm of the couch just watching him.

"It was three years ago."

"Reed—"

His named rolled from her lips in a desperation that forced him to meet her eyes. She pressed her lips together.

"You would have loved him. He was just as sexy and handsome as me." He lifted his mouth into a forced smile and she scooted off the arm of the couch and took the spot next to him.

"Yeah, I would assume so, considering you shared the same face," she teased softly.

"Yeah, but he was a hell of a better man than me."

"Reed—" She tried interrupting again.

"I'm good, baby." He reached over and squeezed her bare knee, trying to reassure her.

"We were inseparable growing up, we basically did everything together. We played all the same sports in high school—he could kick my ass in football, but I hands down had his ass beat in wrestling—we had all the same friends, fuck, I think the only time we were apart growing up was when we were out with a chick. Other than that, we were together." He smiled as the memory flickered through his mind.

"We were in our first year of college when 9/11 happened. We were both chomping at the bit to join the army so we got into the ROTC program together. Fuck, we both even went to OBC at Leonard Wood." He winked.

She smiled.

"He was supposed to meet me at the bar that night, ya know. If he had, I might not have brought you back to my hotel room because he would have been working his tricks on you the second he saw you."

"Well, lucky for me then." She nudged him with her shoulder and allowed herself to lean into him for a moment. The contact was soothing, even when he didn't realize it.

"After that we were assigned to different companies, different posts, but we tried to get together as much as possible.

"We were deployed at the same time once, which was hell for our momma, but it was nice having him there in that sandpit with me. Even if we weren't stationed at the same FOB, he was still there. It was like having a bit of home in hell. The army arranged for us to visit each other once—for our birthday."

He shifted his eyes over to Meagan, who was still listening to him patiently. For maybe the second time since he had known this woman, she let the blinders down that shielded her eyes—and he saw her sympathy. He saw the sorrow that ringed her big blue irises, and in the middle of feeling his past rising above his head, threatening to drown him when he was finally reaching the surface, he also felt her. Her eyes absorbed him, held him, and calmed him—and he could breathe.

"We got through everything together. Women, college,

deployments—between the two of us we had been through more shit than two people should be allowed to go through.

"Every year, no matter where we all were, the whole family would meet up for the Fourth of July." He swallowed hard. "It was my first year stationed at Benning, Mac and I had just gotten home from our deployment in Afghanistan not even a month before, and it was my turn for everyone to come to me. So I rented the cabin."

Her eyes widened.

"Mac had this new woman that he started dating shortly before he deployed. She was it for him. He had bought the ring, asked her parents, the whole nine yards. He was going to marry her."

"What was her name?" she asked.

"Karrie. She was good for him."

Meagan's mouth lifted slightly, but she stayed still next to him, not fidgeting—just listening.

"Every year Mac and I would meet up and ride our bikes to wherever it was that we were staying for the Fourth and make a road trip out of it. But that year he brought Karrie. She had a son. A three-year-old little terror." He laughed as he remembered that little guy taking over his family's complete attention that weekend. That kid broke more stuff and peed on everything, but it was fun having a kid around. And Mac loved him.

"So, they drove her car instead. I still rode my bike, though. It was tradition, and I kinda have a thing for traditions." He winked.

"It was a good weekend until my sorry ass got piss-ass

drunk and fell down the back deck stairs that led down to the lake."

Her hand flew to her mouth. "Oh my God," she muttered.

"Yeah, they were steep and narrow and they were made from the stone, built into the cliff. It hurt like a motherfucker."

He smiled when he saw fear cross her face while he assumed she was picturing his clumsy-ass fall. "I broke my wrist and got a pretty impressive gash on my head." His head dropped between his shoulders. "Needless to say, I couldn't drive my bike home."

Meagan sucked in a sharp breath as realization struck her, but he continued his story anyway. He wanted her to hear it.

"Karrie was driving me home, following behind Mac, who was driving my bike." He paused for a moment as the memory flooded his mind. He had had a headache from the recent temper tantrum Karrie's son had let loose. The little guy finally wore himself out and fell asleep and they had switched from listening to some cartoon on the DVD player to some girly song that was on the radio. His head was throbbing, but Karrie loved that song, and she was his brother's girl—family trumped headache. He remembered laughing at her as she spilled her Diet Coke down the front of her shirt. He reached into the backseat, grabbing around on the floorboard for something for her to wipe up with. Her foot lightened on the accelerator as she dabbed at her shirt with a T-shirt. Reed took her moment of distraction to change the station, laughing as she flung the wet, wadded-up shirt in his face. It wasn't but a heartbeat later that he looked up and saw a white SUV pull out onto the road. There was no time. Mac didn't have time to stop. He didn't know who or what divine intervention decided to play a part in creating distance between Karrie's car and Mac, but he knew if Karrie hadn't absentmindedly slowed down, she wouldn't have had time to stop either.

The sound of Karrie's scream mixed with the sound of the rubber skidding across the asphalt as she hit the brakes haunted him still, but the sound of his brother crashing at sixty miles per hour straight into the side of the SUV would stay with him for the rest of his life.

"Mackly collided with some ass that wasn't paying the fuck attention and pulled out in front of him." Pure hatred and anger dripped from his words. Forgiveness was something he was working on, but it wasn't something he thought he would ever be able to give. His brother was gone.

"You saw it?" Her voice was quiet and shaky.

"I saw every second of it."

Her eyes welled with the tears that Reed could no longer produce. "He died instantly."

"Reed, I'm so sorry." His head dropped between his sagging shoulders. "After all the shit we had gone through, after surviving IED attacks in Iraq and Afghanistan on more than one occasion and after being under enemy fire and watching our buddies die before our eyes, he came home and, three weeks later, was killed in a car crash."

He shook his head, trying to rattle the memory that was flashing the image of his brother, broken and bloodied—

dead—on the hot asphalt, from the forefront of his mind. He had spent a lot of nights seeing that image sweep through his dreams. But the image that burned into his memory, branding it with a guilt he didn't think he could ever come away from was the image of Karrie as she fell to her knees in a shattered heap of heartbreak as she cried over his brother's lifeless body. His brother's life was gone—his future, his chance at a family with the woman who was clinging to his broken body, would never be. It should have been Reed. He should have been on that bike that day—that moment.

Meagan reached over and grabbed his hand, lacing her fingers through his. That was his corrosion. That was what ate away a layer of him—it's what left the rough patch, the harshness that hung on his shoulders, that subtle difference that she could see. It was his brother, his twin, a piece of him that eroded away.

His eyes looked down at their entwined hands, and he twisted the ruby ring Meagan had gotten from her mother on her twenty-first birthday with his thumb. His spine bowed and his head hung heavy on his neck. When he lifted his eyes to hers, they were broken, lost, ringed with a guilt that broke her heart—and it was terrifying. He wasn't putting up his in-control demeanor for her, he was letting her see the hurt that lingered behind it all, and she needed to make it go away, but she couldn't. She knew there was absolutely nothing that would mend the break in his heart that the death of his brother had created. Nothing ever would.

"My parents barely talk to me now," he said out of the blue, breaking through the silence that had ticked away the countless minutes she just sat there next to him, holding his hand.

Meagan's heart found its way into her throat, clogging her words as she spoke. "They don't blame you?" Surely they didn't. It wasn't his fault.

"No, they don't blame me. But it's kind of hard to look into a face that reminds them of their dead son." His voice was broken and the small wave of detriment that stung his words burned the back of her throat. "They should blame me, though. I should've been the one on that bike."

She wanted to give him his space, she didn't want to wrap her arms around him in the hopes of easing his hurt, because she knew it wouldn't. But now, seeing the depth of his anguish etched in the pull of his brow, the set of his jaw, the catch in his breaths—she couldn't help it. She linked her arms around his neck and sunk her body into him. He sighed deeply against her as his palms pressed her tightly to him and buried his face in the curve of her shoulder.

"Life is just too short, Meg. Too unpredictable," he mumbled against her neck. "It can be gone in the blink of an eye."

"That's why you do it, isn't it?"

He lifted his head. "Do what, baby?"

"Everything. Your rush." Meagan pulled her feet up on the couch and faced him.

He grabbed her ankles and pulled her legs onto his lap, rubbing his hands up and down her smooth skin.

"I've always lived for the thrill, it was another thing Mac

and I shared." He swallowed hard, his Adam's apple rising and falling slowly. "But yeah, it makes me feel closer to him, and I want to feel every rush life has to offer."

Meagan didn't know what to say, so she didn't say anything. He was her Mr. Thrill, living for the rush, living life day by day, never slowing down. And now she understood.

He continued to glide his hands up and down her shins. The rough pads of his fingers softly scratched her smooth skin. Her lids started to feel heavy, but she kept her eyes on Reed, watching him breathe as his head rested against the back of the couch, his eyes drilling holes into the ceiling.

She blinked her eyes slowly, and when she opened them again, she was staring at the bedroom wall. She felt Reed's arms tangle around her as he pulled her back against his chest, wrapping his body against her. He stroked her hair that spilled out above her pillow and kissed the back of her head.

"I want to live as much life as possible, baby," he whispered softly, thinking she was still asleep. "You never know when it will be gone."

CHAPTER TWENTY

"You have got to be fucking kidding me," Reed said as Meagan walked out of the bedroom.

Her eyes shifted side to side before they landed on him. "What?"

His head weaved up and down as he took in her choice of swimwear. "You are trying to kill me, aren't you, woman?"

"Kill you? No. Impress you, turn you on, drive you crazy . . . yes."

He nodded, picked up his Red Bull and took a drink. He set the can down and looked her over one more time and winked. "Mission accomplished."

She ambled into the kitchen and stepped between his legs. Her bare stomach pressed against his warm, bare chest as she linked her arms around his neck. "So what's on the agenda for today?"

"To put you back in my bed."

He grabbed onto her waist and she pulled away, moving out of his grasp. Yes, she would love to slide back into bed with him, and this time naked, but after last night's mood that set the stage for their weekend away, she just wanted to get him out. She knew Reed. He was going to lose his mind if he stayed cooped up in this condo all day—even if they were tangled in the bed together.

"That sounds very promising but—"

His eyebrows pulled down as he pouted. "Promising? Are you doubting my abilities to deliver?"

Her nose scrunched as she shook her head. "Never."

He reached for her again. "Good."

"But I would love to spend the day on the beach," she said, quickly taking another step back. He had that twinkle in his eye, that devilish, playful smirk on his face that told her if she kept running, he would have no problem chasing her.

"In that bikini?" His deep voice rolled over the words, his tone implying exactly what Meagan had predicted.

She squared her shoulders as he stood and took a steady step toward her. She wanted to clear her throat, which suddenly felt clogged with anticipation, but she didn't want to waver in her confidence. It was already sliding down a slippery slope. She lifted her eyes to his and held them. "Yes."

His steps stalled and he tilted his head back and laughed. "You're killin' me, woman."

She cocked her eyebrow at him in question.

"How am I supposed to relax when you will be parading on the beach nearly naked all fucking day?"

She pushed aside the burn in her cheeks from restraining her smile. He was too cute when he was all playful and pouty and shirtless. Okay, *cute* wasn't the right word. He was sexy.

She hoisted her hands on her hips. "Not my problem."

His lips parted and she had that oh-shit moment. She had just lit the fire under his ass. "Oh, it'll be your problem when I won't be able to keep my hands off you," he said as he took slow, deliberate steps, closing the small space between them.

Her hands formed a wall between her and Reed as he slammed into her. She pushed against his chest but barely made a dent in adding space between their bodies. "Did you even consider that was my intention?"

"I like the way your mind works, sugar," he whispered as he leaned in to make her lose all relevant trains of thought as he pressed his lips to her neck. She knew how he operated and she leaned back, dodging his advance.

Meagan's phone buzzed on the kitchen counter, and she ducked to the side, Reed damn near falling over. "Go get ready," she ordered to Reed. He leaned back up and stretched lazily, reaching his muscular arms above his head. His chest expanded as he yawned. "You sure I can't get you back in bed?"

She laughed. "Not gonna work. Go."

She picked up her phone, sliding her finger across the screen to unlock it. It was a text from Eva.

How is PC
Good
Have u made it out of the bed yet :)
Yes
Too bad
Lol . . . what r u doing today
You mean who am I doing today ;)

Luke coming over?

Yes. He's on his way now

Have fun! Heading to beach now. ttyl.

<3

Meagan set the phone back down on the counter and started grabbing water bottles and beers out of the fridge, packing them strategically in her cooler bag. She had her head stuck in the fridge when she heard Reed's bare feet pad back into the kitchen.

"All right, I'm ready to go."

"Okay, just a sec. Let me put these . . ." She turned around, and Reed in all of his sexy-naked-man glory was standing in front of her. His feet were set apart, his arms hanging loosely at his sides, and an annoyingly addictive, lopsided grin was stretched across his scruffy face.

Meagan licked her lips and Reed's smile got even wider—if that was possible. Dammit. "I didn't realize this was a nude beach," she joked.

"Yeah, well, seeing as you are teasing the hell out of me, strutting around in your barely there bikini, giving me all sorts of ideas as to what I would like to do to you once I finally get you back in my bed, I thought I would return the favor. I forgot my lucky Speedos, so birthday suit was the next best thing."

"Mmm." She nodded, then turned back around to grab a few more beers. When she looked at him again his cocky smirk hadn't faltered—apparently her attempt at feigning lack of interest wasn't working.

His cock was hard. His body was hard. His jaw was set hard. The only thing soft on that man was his eyes. And not only were they looking at her with that playful gleam, they looked like they were penetrating her.

"Dammit, Reed," she snapped, then threw herself against him. She felt his lips hold their smile the whole time they were working their magic over hers. His hands wound around her and his cock pressed against her stomach.

He lifted her under her butt and she wrapped her legs around his waist. He carried her through the condo to the bedroom and fell against the bed.

He rained kisses over her entire body—her stomach, her thigh, her toes. He was all mouth and tongue and raw, hot need.

He ran his mouth between her legs and over the top her bikini bottoms before he settled his hips between her thighs. She could feel the swell of his cock pressing through the fabric that separated them.

"I knew I'd find a way to get you back in my bed."

"Yeah, yeah. You're sexy, and tricky, and I'm weak and horny. I get it. Now take my clothes off and have your way with me before I change my mind."

His forehead fell into the curve of her neck as he shook with laughter. "Yes, ma'am," he breathed against her shoulder. She shuddered.

Damn that accent.

Meagan was sprawled out on a beach towel, on her stomach, her ass perky and perfect and in complete view. The pink bottoms barely covered her ass cheeks, and the sweet, soft curve that met her thighs was making an appearance. And even though they were lying on the beach, in the middle of the day, with families and couples and drunken college kids surrounding them, he couldn't help the impulse he felt to lower his mouth and sink his teeth into the plump flesh—but he didn't.

Reed reclined back onto his elbows, the backs of his calves burning as they pressed into the hot, white sand. He could hear the soft sighs coming from Meagan as his head hovered close to hers. She was asleep.

Her face was clammy, and a sheen of moisture accumulated on her forehead and above her lip. Small beads of sweat rolled down the delicate dip in her back. Her shoulders glistened and her blond hair stuck to the back of her neck and the sides of her face. She was hot, and sweaty, and softly snoring—and she was fucking beautiful.

Reed reached his hand into the cooler bag and dipped it into the melted ice. He held his hand over the small of Meagan's back and let the ice water drip from his fingertips to her heated skin. She didn't even flinch.

He repeated his task, dipping his hand in, then cooling her with the cold drops. He did this to her back, her shoulders, her arms, and the backs of her thighs.

"Thanks, baby," she muttered sleepily.

"Did I wake you?"

"It's okay, it felt good," she said, rolling onto her back. The front of her body had the pattern from the cotton of the towel embedded in red on her skin.

He splayed his palm out flat over her stomach and laughed when she sucked in a quick breath. "Your hand is freezing!"

"Hey, look." He sat up and nodded out toward the water.

"What?" Meagan asked, pushing herself up next to him.

"Parasailing."

Her big baby blues widened and her mouth made a perfect little O shape, and the sight caused him to shift his body on the towel. "Oh no! Don't even think about it."

"A promise is a promise, baby." He stretched back out and laid his head on her lap. "I wouldn't."

She sighed and ran her hand through his hair. "But you want to?"

"It's fun. And the view of the ocean is completely different when you're hovering above it."

Her face pinched together. "Can't you just do nothing? Settle down for a little while?" she sneered.

"Why would I want to settle down? There're way too many things to see out there, too many places to go and shit to try. You're missing out, baby."

Her eyebrows pulled in and he could see her mind turning, like she was shifting through her thoughts, and whatever they were, they weren't sitting well with her.

"You thinking about it?"

She blinked, moving her eyes from the waves crashing into the shoreline in front of them. "Hell no. What if the line snapped? What if the parasail broke and fell into the water and I got tangled up in the sail? Not a chance in hell."

He laughed. "You're cute when you're ranting—you know that?"

"Because cute is exactly what I'm going for." She pouted. But something else was souring the light mood she had only moments ago when she woke up.

"You okay?"

"I'm fine," she said, her tone warning, and he knew he had said something to piss her off.

Her phone took that moment to buzz, along with his phone, which started ringing inside the beach bag. Reed grabbed his phone from where he had wadded it up in his towel. It was Sanders. "Hello?"

"We got a problem, bro."

"What?" he said as he laid his head back down on Meagan's lap.

"Murano's been at the bar since about two o'clock, Eva and I just picked him up."

Reed sat up. "Bridgette?" he assumed. She was the center of all of Murano's whisky binges.

"Yeah. It's not good."

Reed huffed a frustrated breath. "Goddammit. 'Not good' how?"

"Not good as in he's piss-ass drunk on my couch right now, threatening to go to her."

"Did you take his keys?"

"What the fuck do you think? Of course I did. But you know how he gets when he's fucked-up like this, he won't listen to me."

Reed turned his head to look at Meagan, who was texting on her phone. He saw Eva's name scrolled at the top. Meagan was more than likely getting the exact conversation he was. Dammit, he didn't want to leave. Something was up with her. He could feel it.

"Reed?" Sanders said when he didn't reply. He was distracted, and he couldn't help feel a sinking feeling burn in his gut, like sharp iron daggers were branding him on the inside.

"Yeah?"

"I'm just gonna throw him in my room and hope like hell he passes the fuck out."

Meagan looked at him and smiled faintly and stood up, grabbing her bag and the towel with her. "No, we're coming."

The ride back was the fastest fucking four-hour drive of his life. Meagan had slipped up this wall between them. She was putting it off, pretending she was fine, but there was a small hesitance to her—and he felt like he was losing her all over again.

A case of déjà vu swept over him. Just like when he left the cabin a little less than a month ago, he was driving home with the feeling that things had changed, and for the worse.

Meagan held on tighter to him than ever. She kept moving her hands over his chest and his stomach. She had even slid her fingers under the hem of his shirt and splayed her hands out on his bare skin. Even that felt off—somehow changed.

They pulled into Sanders' driveway and parked behind his truck. It was just now getting dark, but the fading sun did little to relieve the August heat and beads of sweat instantly started to form around his hairline now that the wind was no longer pounding against his face.

"I'll wait outside," Meagan said as she climbed off the bike.

"No, Eva's still here. Come in." He grabbed her hand and held it tightly in his as they walked up to the porch.

Luke opened the door before Reed's hand had a chance to touch the handle. "Hey."

"How's he doin'?" Reed asked, shouldering past Luke, pulling Meagan along with him

"Well, he's sobered up some, so he's at least making full sentences now, and he hasn't taken a swing a me in the last hour or so," he explained as they walked down the narrow hall that led to the living room.

Eva was perched on a barstool next to Murano, who looked like he had been run over by a semi and dragged down the interstate. His eyes were glassed over and it was hard to determine whether it was from the obvious hell he was going through or if it was from the empty bottle of Crown on the counter.

"Hey, my man."

Eva turned her head when she heard Reed's voice and popped off the barstool, but Murano just kept his eyes focused on the ground.

Reed dropped Meagan's hand as Eva came and swung her arm around her.

"Hey, babes, how was your romantic getaway? I told Luke we could handle tough guy over there"—she nodded toward Murano—"until tomorrow, but supposedly Reed is the only one who can talk some sense into his drunk ass."

"Nah, I just don't have a problem kicking his ass if need be."

"Well hell, I could have done that for you," Eva said.

Meagan laughed, and for some reason the sound was like fresh oxygen to his lungs. He was happy to hear her laugh.

"Murano," Reed coaxed, walking up behind him and slapping him on the back. "What happened?"

His face remained locked toward the floor. "I was at the gym this morning and she called, but I fucking missed it."

He sat down on the seat next to him and glanced back at Meagan, who was talking quietly to Eva. "Okay?"

"She left me a message, Porter. She said she was ending it."

Murano looked up at him and pure pain haunted his features. God, he was torn up over this woman. And she wasn't worth it. She was married, for fuck's sake!

"Look, I know you cared about her—"

"I loved her," he snapped, meeting Reed's eyes in a challenge Murano was in no condition to throw out. Luckily Reed knew to roll with the punches when Murano got this way. The guy was a good man, but he drank like a pussy-whipped prick and was quick to lash out when he was upset—and this woman had a way of fucking with him bad. Reed was partially surprised to see Sanders' place still intact.

"Okay, you loved her. But she's married." Reed could hear the accusation pressing against his words, so he cleared his throat and tried softening it down a bit. "You knew this day would come."

"Yeah," he admitted, lowering his head again. The poor sap was a mess. "I just didn't realize how much it would fucking hurt."

Reed's hand thudded on top of Murano's shoulder and he gave it a firm squeeze. "How's your head? Good?"

"Besides the fact that it's no longer fuzzy, yeah, it's good, man."

"Good, let's go."

"Where?"

"Out for a drink." One way to fix this drunken pity problem—drink more. Hanging around in limbo where he was drunk enough to lash out and start shit yet sober enough to still feel the pain he was obviously going through was only going to end badly on everyone's account. Tipping him over the edge so he was downright numb and could pass out until morning—that's what he needed.

"Reed, I don't—"

"What have I told you before? Life is too fucking short. No woman is worth this. . . ."

The moment the words left his lips he knew they weren't true. He thought back to the way he felt when he pulled away from Meagan that day at the cabin, when he thought he was doing what he needed to keep her.

Meagan was worth it.

He looked back at her and her eyes were glued to his. That same pounding filled his chest, like tiny little nails poking him repeatedly until the feeling burned in his stomach. She'd heard him. . . .

But then she smiled at him.

Her lips pulled up tightly and she sent him a wink. He returned her smile, relieved, then wrapped his arms around Murano's shoulder. "Come on, let's go get you drunk again."

"Lead the way," he muttered, standing up from his stool.

"Baby, I'm gonna take him to grab a few beers—"

She wrinkled her nose up and smiled. "Go."

He grabbed her chin and kissed her mouth. Her lips instantly relaxed around his and he slipped his tongue inside to get one last taste before he left. That should hold him over till tonight.

Meagan dropped her duffel bag by the leather sectional and plopped down on the chaise. She heard the soft patter of little paws prancing down the hard floor seconds before a big ball of black fur landed in her lap. Harry was her lover. Weasley couldn't care less if she was around or not—typical.

Eva dropped her truck's keys on the bar that separated the kitchen from the living room, and they chimed against the granite. "Well played, again, babe. You got that man wound up so tight he can't even see straight." The sarcasm lacing her words pissed Meagan off.

"Eva, I'm exhausted, and I'm really not in the mood for your word games. If you have something to bitch at me about then just fucking say it already."

She walked into the living room and stood in front of the couch. "You're calling it quits with him, aren't you?"

Meagan's eyes darted over Eva. "How the hell? Seriously, sometimes it's downright scary how well you know me."

She shrugged. "It's a gift." She flopped down on the ottoman next to Meagan. "Spill. What happened?"

"Nothing."

"I'm not buying it."

She chewed on her bottom lip, trying to pull her thoughts to match what she was feeling. It was a lot harder than it sounded. "I'm falling for him," she confessed as she rubbed the top of Harry's head like it was her life support.

"Yeah, can you tell me something I don't already know?"

Meagan's eyes darted up and she sighed. She never thought she would ever feel this way again. That head-over-heels love. The one she felt in college. The love that built her up and broke her down. She was falling for Reed. No, she had fallen—hard. And she couldn't be shattered again. One time was enough, and she knew that if she allowed it to happen this time—with Reed—it would be much worse.

"He's not ready to settle down, not in any aspect of his life. And that's okay. I can't just hope that someday he will want the future I do. I want a man who already wants it too."

"Mr. Safe," Eva uttered.

"Yes. My heart's torn. Torn between the future I want, and the man I want that future with"—she shook her head—"and I know I can't have them both."

CHAPTER TWENTY-ONE

Reed was wasted by the time Murano was ready to stop his pussy-pouting and leave the bar. He felt for the guy, though. Reed might not have agreed with his buddy fucking around with a married woman, but he hated that he was hurt. It sucked when a woman held that power over you.

He didn't bother texting or calling Meagan. She was probably asleep by now, so he just stumbled out of Sanders' truck, who had bitch-boy duty twice in one day—they were going to owe him big—and managed to stagger into his own apartment.

Stripping out of his clothes, he spread out on the cool cotton sheets and closed his eyes—and before he knew it, the sun was pouring in through the open blinds and Tiny's not so pleasant dog breath was panting in his face.

He reached over the bed and pulled his cell phone out of the pocket of his jeans. It was only nine in the morning, and Reed had gotten way too drunk the night before to be up that damn early.

"You need to pee, big guy?" he asked as he roughed up the fur on Tiny's head, which was resting on the edge of the bed.

Tiny let out a soundless bark, more like a breath-bark, and backed away as he pranced from paw to paw in excitement.

Reed pulled on a pair of gym shorts and sauntered into the living room and to the patio door, Tiny right at his side. Reed hooked his Newfie up to the leash and walked him barefoot out in the courtyard.

"Well, good morning, handsome."

Reed turned his head over his shoulder to see Eva sitting in her patio chair, coffee mug in hand.

He nodded his head. "Morning."

"I was talking to Tiny."

Tiny heard his name and spun around. His tail whipped back and forth when he saw Eva, and he all but pulled Reed to the patio.

Eva grabbed his oversize head in between her hands and smashed her face to his snout.

"You know he licks his balls, right?" Reed said, when Eva proceeded to let Tiny lap over her entire face.

"Yeah, and so would you if you could, so I don't want to hear it."

He laughed. "Where's my girl?"

Eva's eyes dropped. "Oh, she will be out in a minute, she went in for a refill."

Just then, the back door opened up and Meagan walked out. She was still in her sweats, her hair piled on top of her head, and she had a pair of huge black-rimmed glasses on her face. He loved when he got to see her in the mornings.

"Morning, sugar."

She smiled, but it didn't quite make it to her eyes. Not like the way she usually smiled at him when she first saw him for the day.

"Hey." The metal legs of the chair skidded across the concrete patio as she pulled the chair away from the small round table and sat down.

Reed's arm straightened behind him as Tiny made his way to the nearest bush to hike his leg. "How about I make you dinner tonight? Make up for cutting our weekend short?"

Meagan's eyes darted to Eva's, her lids widening enough for Reed's heart to make a quick, jerky thud against his chest. He fucking knew something was up yesterday, and her subtle little response just confirmed it.

Her eyes flitted to his. "Um, sure."

He could do two things at that very moment. He could call her out, ask her what the hell was going on, or he could suck it up and play it off—wait it out. Neither one seemed appealing, but he went with the latter, because there was this part of him that was stabbing him in the gut, telling him that if he asked her, he would regret it.

He put on a smile, hoping that it pulled off his usual reaction from her. "All right, baby. Come over around five."

She scrunched her nose, and the wrinkles that creased between her eyes as she told him okay gave him an ounce of relief, but just barely.

"*Y*ou're wearing that?"

Meagan turned around and glared at Eva, who had made her way into her room and sat down on her bed.

"I'm just saying, babe. You can't wear something like that when you are going to break a man's heart. That's not really playing a fair game."

"I'm not going to break his heart, Eva. Mine? That's a very strong possibility, but his, not so much."

"You're an idiot." Meagan narrowed her eyes and pinched her brows together. "What? Sorry, but I'm not going to add whipped cream on top. You're stupid if you can't see how bad that man has it for you."

Meagan went to the closet and pulled out a pair of pumps and dropped them to the floor. "It doesn't matter."

"And you're sure this is what you want? To give up what you have with him because he's a wild card?"

"I don't want to wake up five years from now, two years from now, hell, six months from now, and realize he's not it. Not when I already know."

She knew. She knew her heart was lodged so far into his that it was going to be hard to pull it back. She knew he cared about her—she didn't need him to tell her for her to know. But she also knew that the road he had mapped out for himself never intersected with hers. If she thought this was going to be hard now, how would it be down the road when she was too far gone to realize it? It would be impossible. She wasn't going to be blinded, not this time.

Meagan smoothed her hands over her yellow cotton tunic dress. It was casual, not too fitted, didn't show too much boob or too much shoulder (which was one of Reed's weaknesses), but it gave away a good portion of her thighs. She stepped into her peep-toe pumps, fluffed her hair, which was having problems holding any volume in this Georgia heat, and spun around toward the door.

"Wish me luck?" she lilted.

Eva sighed heavily. "Yeah, I'll wish you luck." Meagan felt the weight of Eva's eyes as her friend offered a sad smile. "You're gonna need it, babe."

Reed had worked out a plan in the last eight hours. Actually, he had worked out a few different plans, but he'd finally settled on one. He was going to act just like he always did. Not much of a plan, but it was the best one he had.

He heard the door open and the sound of Tiny scurrying down the hall as he was stirring the pasta.

"Meg?"

"Yeah, it's me! Okay, hi, Tiny, nice to see you too, boy."

He huffed a short laugh and shook his head. That damn dog was a pain in the ass.

Meagan rounded the corner and the way her pink lips parted into a smile when she saw him caused a chain reaction of panic to sweep through his blood. But he played it off.

"You look beautiful. Too good to be having dinner in my apartment."

Her hands fluttered to her dress, smoothing down over the sides. She was nervous. "Thanks."

"Wine? Beer?"

"You bought wine?"

"Nah, I've had this lying around the apartment from

when Becky visited the week her and Conner came to tell me they were getting married. Apparently, she was nervous."

"Becky? I find that hard to believe."

"Well, her big brother's approval supposedly meant a lot to her, and I had yet to meet the fucker who was stealing my baby sister's heart. Lucky for him, I loved the bastard."

She laughed and the sound settled over him and he relaxed. Her laugh had a way of doing that to him—even if she was only pretending. He could pretend too.

"Dinner's ready."

"What can I do?"

"Nothing, go sit down."

Reed fumbled around in the kitchen. He was no chef, that was for damn sure. The best meals he made were the ones he carried home in paper bags. The one and only thing, aside from throwing meat on the grill, that he didn't royally screw up was pasta—sorta.

He carefully dumped the pasta into a large bowl and carried it to the table along with a beer and a glass of wine.

"Dig in, baby," he said, setting the pasta down on the table and shoving in a large spoon.

Meagan's lips tucked under as she pressed them tightly together. Her cheeks turned bright red and the edges of her eyes pricked with a suppressed smile. "Mac and cheese?" She snickered, unable to hold back her laugh any longer. And thank God, it was like music to his ears.

Reed sat down next to her and spooned out a giant helping and slapped it down on his plate. "Hey, I offered to make you dinner, woman. I didn't say it was going to be fancy."

She tilted her head and looked at him from the side while she lifted her brows and spooned some pasta onto her own plate. "Lucky for you, mac and cheese is one of my staple food groups."

He reached out his hand and moved the strands of blond waves that were hanging over her shoulder to her back, exposing the side of her long neck. She froze and her breathing stilled.

Then he touched her—the way he knew she loved.

He ran the backs of his knuckles down the side of her neck and she closed her eyes and inhaled a deep breath. "Did I tell you how beautiful you look?" he said softly.

A pained expression hardened her face as she fidgeted her legs under the table. "Yes, and thank you."

Her pulse was pattering rapidly below her ear, her soft, golden skin infinitesimally rising and falling with the beat of her heart. There were her body's reactions to him—tempting him, luring him in without her even realizing it. He couldn't help himself. He leaned over and pressed his lips to her warm skin. Her scent filled his nose and sent a familiar signal to his groin.

"Reed . . ."

Her words trailed off. Her attempt to protest faded as she involuntarily rolled her head to the side, giving him a better path to take down the side of her neck. Her body could never lie to him.

"Yeah, baby?" he murmured as he skimmed his lips over the dip at the base of her throat, flicking his tongue out to taste her.

"I . . . we need to . . ."

His hands explored the inside of her thighs, making their way beneath her dress.

Her legs clamped closed, locking his hand in place. "Reed," she sighed, and his heart fell to the floor. Her mind's hesitance was clear, crystal clear, but her body still had a weakness, still was quivering under his lips and softening against the chair. And if his gut was right, if what he was sensing was true, he was taking her body's opening. He was going to remind her just exactly the way she felt beneath him. How she felt against him as he held her naked body in his arms. Her body could never lie to him—and he was going to use that selfishly to his advantage.

His fingers gently bit into her inner thigh, his thumb grazing over the lace that covered her, and her head fell against the back of the chair and her legs relaxed. He didn't waste any time crushing his mouth to hers. Her lips moved over his, it was desperate and gentle and completely new.

He felt an unfamiliar tug in his chest as her hands lifted and molded to the sides of his face. She whimpered into his mouth, but it wasn't from desire.

He scooped her in his arms and carried her back to his room, never once letting his mouth leave hers.

Meagan felt the cool floor against her feet as Reed lowered her out of his arms in front of the bed. His eyes held hers with a vise grip, and it was terrifying—terrifying because as badly as she wanted to break his stare, she couldn't.

His hands reached behind her and carefully unzipped her dress. His fingers easily unhooked her bra and then traveled up her spine, igniting every nerve in her body. The light touches—the simple, sweet, and easy touches, those hurt the worst. His hands continued to the nape of her neck, then fell around to her shoulders, pushing the fabric from her arms, allowing the dress to pool on the floor at her feet, followed by her lace bra.

"I could do this all day, you know."

"What?" she asked softly, her voice breaking.

"Look at you."

His eyes followed his hands as they traced the curve of her sides. His touch was light, but the rough pads of his fingers pressed into her like they were weighted down with liquid ice, leaving a burning trail of goose bumps as they fanned over her sensitive skin, and she shuddered.

He hooked his fingers under the waist of her panties and kneeled as he pulled them down her legs. She braced her hands on his shoulders for balance as he helped her step out of her heels.

His mouth leaned in, his tongue swiped quickly across the ache between her thighs, and her knees buckled from the surprise. Gripping her strongly around her waist, he stood back up.

Her lungs constricted and she felt like she couldn't breathe as her heartbeat seemed to stop. The look in Reed's eyes tore into her. They were intense but gentle. Raw but hard. Hurt but hopeful. The myriad of conflicting emotions penetrated her and knocked her heart from her chest. The only way she knew to smother the bereavement that was inevitably finding her was to get lost, and Reed had a way of doing that to her. Of rising her to a place that she couldn't touch alone, of carrying her to heights that terrified her until she couldn't do anything but feel his body inside her. And that's what she needed. That was the only thing that could lure her away from the heartbreak that was waiting for her on the other side. Right now—she wanted to feel lost.

She tore at Reed's clothes, eagerly peeling his shirt off over his head. She quickly unbuttoned his jeans, pushing them to the floor—then he had her on the bed.

Every single nerve ending in her body was on fire. Reed's hands touched her like he was feeling her for the first time. He was savoring every line, every curve, every dip. His mouth was easy—soft, dotting kisses over her neck, breaking away to crush against her lips before he would find his way back to her neck again as he held his weight above her.

"Reed . . . ," she mumbled against his jaw.

"Let me take my time with you, baby."

His hand slid between her legs and his fingers slowly sank into her—but it wasn't enough, it wasn't what she wanted. She needed him. She needed him to fill her, to feel his thick cock buried inside her, stretching her around him until she couldn't take any more. She needed to feel him—so she didn't feel anything else.

Her throat burned, accompanying the prick she felt behind her eyes. "Reed," she said again, only this time her words were strangled by the sob that was caught in the back of her throat.

The sound of his name struggling as it left her lips sent a pang of panic to his chest. His mouth left her neck and his eyes darted to hers. They were filled with unshed tears that gathered above her thick bottom lashes. He smoothed back the hair that fell next to her face.

He saw it all. All the hurt she was hiding, and he wanted to fucking drain the pain from her eyes.

Her hands wound under his arms and locked around his back as he hovered over her. Her legs lifted and she wrapped them around his waist.

"Please," she whimpered.

He searched her face, every line, every crease. He didn't know why she was hurting, he only knew she was. He didn't know the words that she struggled to say, but he had a damn good idea.

His forehead fell to the curve of her shoulder and she pressed her cheek against his head. Then he slammed into her.

Her back arched off the bed and her nails pierced his shoulders as a sharp gasp left her mouth. He pulled back, then thrust again. He wanted to go slow, he wanted to feel every warm muscle in her pussy clamp around him as he slid inside her, and he wanted to feel her grip onto his dick as he slid back out.

But he didn't.

She needed this. For whatever reason was muddling up

her beautiful mind, she needed this from him—and if she needed it, he would give it to her.

His hips rocked back then rammed into her over and over. Each thrust harder than the last, each roll of his hips deeper than before.

He raised to his knees then lifted her ass, her legs draping over his shoulders. She cried out as he continued his rhythm, and each grateful moan that rolled from her lips made him fill her harder, deeper.

Her hands clawed at the sheets, dug into his arms, clung onto his thighs. She was spiraling.

"Oh God . . ." She sighed as her body started to quicken and tighten around him.

He stopped.

Her eyes fluttered opened and fell on his. Her mouth tightened into a line as she inhaled a shaky breath, then squeezed her eyes shut.

Dropping her legs to the side, Reed lowered, sinking down on top of her. "Look at me, baby."

Her eyes opened, and a single tear made a path down her hot cheeks as they looked into his.

Then he kissed her.

His mouth saturated her with need. His lips tangled with hers and her tongue brushed his, evading him. Her kiss pleaded with him—he devoured her as her hands cradled his face, and a broken sigh vibrated from her lips and hummed in his mouth.

Reed lifted his hips, slowly pulling his cock back; then just as slowly, he inched back inside her until she couldn't take any more of him. Then he did it again.

And again.

Her teeth tugged on his bottom lip as a forceful palpitation rocked him. She clung to his shoulders, raising her body off the mattress, their kiss never breaking. Her body tightened around him one last time; then she fell back onto the mattress, and he collapsed on top of her. Their breaths and sighs mingled and mixed between them in a thick aroma of sex . . . and desperation.

That was what he needed. To bring her to that edge and make her free fall over the side with him.

Reed rolled to the side and pulled her against his chest, a thin layer of moisture clinging to their skin. He leaned down and kissed her forehead and she inwardly sighed at the way his lips felt—sweet, easy, right . . .

"Reed—"

"Don't," he interrupted.

She started to pull away but he tightened his arm around her. "Don't."

She lifted her head and looked at him. He held her eyes, a long, pained stare emitting from his brown eyes, the flecks of gold bleeding into the green rim as a layer of glaze covered the surface.

Realization slapped her hard. "You know."

"I feel you pulling away, yes."

She sat up, and he let her. His arms dropped like dead weights against the mattress as she pulled herself against the headboard and covered up with the sheet. "I need things you're not ready to give me," she blurted.

A switch seemed to flick and the gentle Reed who was holding her only a heartbeat ago transformed. He sat up and flung his legs over the side of the bed, his back to her.

"And you already knew all this about me, Meagan." He stood and pulled on his jeans, which were lying on the floor.

"Reed, I'm not willing to risk it. I need to leave before my heart won't let me." Her voice was weak, almost unsure, and when the sound of her plea—a plea to herself—met her ears, a weight she hadn't felt in a really long time, eight years to be exact, smothered her.

Reed whipped around to face her, his arms flailing out at his sides. "And what about my heart, huh? What, you just fucking use me as your goddamned stepping-stone until your future husband comes knocking at your door? What? Tell me, Meg! What was running through your head when you wrapped your arms around me and told me you wanted a go at this? Because I sure as fuck don't know anymore!" he yelled, the anger in his voice rolling over her, coating her with an extra layer of guilt.

"I don't know what I was thinking. I thought maybe you would—"

"That I would what?" Fear washed over her as he stepped around the bed, his strides urgent—determined. It wasn't a fear that he would hurt her—not physically, but a fear that he would break her, that his pain and his words would destroy her.

He placed his hands on the mattress on either side of her

and leaned in close, his ambrosial breath bouncing off her lips. His voice lowered, and she almost wished he was still yelling, because the rich control he inflected in his tone was much worse. "Change?" He got even closer—she swallowed hard. "Become the man you always wanted?"

She was trapped between him and the headboard, his arms caging her in. "Yes! Okay, yes! I thought that maybe I would be worth it, that maybe you would see the life I wanted and see it for you too—see it for us!" She blinked slowly and sighed. "That your plans would change."

Reed's hands lifted and he scrubbed them over his face as he spun around and walked toward his window. She quickly pulled her dress over her head and stood up.

"You heard what I said to Murano?" She nodded and his head fell between his shoulders. "You *are* fucking worth it, Meg. You're worth that and more." He faced her again. "I told you I couldn't promise you those things." His hands ripped through his hair. "Dammit! Don't you think I want to give you everything you deserve someday? I just . . . I don't . . . you need to give me time."

She felt the assurance she'd built up start to shrink. It was happening—his words were crushing her. But in the back of her mind, when she shoved the throbbing ache in her chest aside, she knew she had to do this. She couldn't let history repeat itself. "I can't, Reed. You don't know if there will ever be a someday for you, and that's okay. But I don't want to fall any harder. I don't want to learn down the road that you still don't see the future I see." She paused, her next words—words she had never said to him—were stuck in her mouth, which had suddenly gone dry. She swallowed hard. "I love you too much."

Her breath hitched as he took a single stride toward her, his step nearly completely closing the space between them. His body was a sliver away from touching her. If she inhaled too deeply, she would press against him.

He didn't reach out, he didn't touch her; he just stood there, staring at her like he could see straight to her heart. She closed her eyes, fighting back the sob that was working its way up her throat. "It would hurt too much," she whispered. "I don't want to hope that I will be enough for you, that I will be the one you want forever with." She opened her eyes.

"Don't do this, Meg. You know how I feel about you."

She knew he cared about her, she could see it flicker in his eyes, and she could feel how much he was hurting at that very moment. But it didn't matter. Reed was a wild card. He lived life with no expectations, and if she stayed—if she let herself fall any more than she already had—she would break. She knew what it felt like to love someone so fiercely that your life intertwined and locked into theirs. That when you saw the future, you saw them. She'd had that. She'd felt that. Then she felt the earth crack and crumble beneath her feet when that future was ripped from her heart. When Daniel broke her heart . . .

She couldn't give Reed that chance. She loved him too much to hate him if he broke her heart. Hating him would be worse than never having him.

She inhaled a shaky breath then took a step back. The

back of her knees hit the bed. "I know how you feel about me, Reed. But it's not enough."

"So you're cutting out early because you're scared." He wasn't asking her, he was telling her. . . .

"I'm not—"

He hovered over her as he leaned in. His hands fell to her shoulders, lightly brushing them down her arms until they reached her fingers. Lacing them together, he rested his forehead to hers and whispered, "You are. Sometimes, baby, the things that scare us the most are the things that give us the biggest rush."

She yanked her hands from his. "I don't want a rush."

CHAPTER TWENTY-TWO

Meagan should have known better. She knew loving a man like Reed would end in a sobfest and a broken heart. She just didn't realize she would be the one to cause it.

"Knock, knock," Eva said, pushing Meagan's bedroom door open. "How ya doing?"

"Well, all things considered, horrible," she said, wiping away the puddle that lingered under her eyes.

"Ah, babe. What can I do? Shot? Want me to go score you some medicinal marijuana? We can get stoned out of our minds like seventeen-year-olds and binge on Rocky Road and Merlot. Well, you can get stoned, I will just get drunk."

Meagan laughed. "Ugh, that surprisingly sounds incredibly tempting. But I'm just going to go to bed. I feel like death."

"A broken heart will do that to ya."

Harry jumped up on her bed and climbed onto her stomach, using her boobs as a kneading cushion. She scratched the top of his head. "Crazy cat lady," she mumbled as another pathetic tear found its way down the worn path on her cheek.

"You are not . . . it's . . . you . . . ugh!" Eva threw her hands up in surrender. "I give up, babe. Try to sleep. I'll see you in the morning."

Avoiding Reed over the next two weeks was easier than she thought. She fully expected to go back to their uncomfortable attempt at friendship. She'd assumed he would wave to her or try his usual flirty greetings—but nothing. She never saw him. She would occasionally hear his bike roar to life at the butt crack of dawn when he was heading to work, and she would occasionally hear him out in the courtyard with Tiny, but that was it. Her friend, the guy who made her smile and laugh—more often driving her crazy—checked out of her life. But whose fault was that? Hers. She couldn't have her cake and eat it too. Damn, she hated that expression, but it was true. You couldn't hold on to something after you had just let it go. It didn't work that way.

Plopping down at the nurses' station, Meagan lifted her feet onto the small ledge that ran the length under the desk.

"Hey, aren't you off?" Zoe asked, leaning over the top of the desk.

"Yes, but I'm so tired I just had to sit."

"Well, get your butt home and crawl into bed with a glass of wine—that will do the trick."

"You don't have to tell me twice." She stood up and all the blood rushed to her head and she braced her hands on the side of the desk as her vision darkened around the corners.

"Hey, you okay?"

"I think so," she said, standing back up.

Zoe eyed her, unconvinced. "Text me when you get home so I know you made it okay."

"Will do. See you next week."

"Pass over the Doritos, man," Murano said as he turned onto the highway.

Reed reached to the floorboard in the backseat of the jeep and grabbed the half-empty bag of chips, tossing them onto Murano's lap.

He shoved a handful of broken chips into his mouth. "Thanks for coming with me," he said around another mouthful.

"It's no problem. You need this closure, man. I'm glad you're finally ending it for good."

"Yeah, well, I can't play Bridgette's fucking mind games anymore. It's tearing me up."

"It's tearing up your liver."

He nodded. "Yeah, that too." He tilted the bag toward Reed, offering him some chips that were more than likely two months stale, but Reed dug his hand in anyway. "What about you?" Murano asked.

"What about me?"

Static seeped through the speakers and Murano pressed the button on his steering wheel, shifting through every bubble-gum station until he finally stopped on a good country song. "You have your closure?" he asked, taking a drink of his Mountain Dew.

"I'm pretty sure I got my closure when she looked me in the eyes and told me I wasn't enough."

"But she told you she loved you?"

He laughed once. "Yeah."

"Women, I swear," he said after a heavy sigh heaved from his chest.

"But she was right."

Murano shifted his eyes to Reed for a moment before looking back at the road. "Says who?"

"Says me. I'm not ready for the things she wants. Not a chance in hell. And who the fuck am I to keep her from them?"

"I feel like you're talking in code, man. Keep her from what?"

"That happily-ever-after shit."

He nodded his understanding, although Reed knew that if Bridgette gave Murano the chance, he would marry her, play the stepdad role with pride, and probably create some dark-skinned spawn of his own—and he wouldn't blink a fucking eye about it either.

"But you love her?" he asked.

Reed kept his eyes on the gray asphalt that stretched before them. "Yeah, I love her."

He loved her, and he hadn't even realized it until the words had left his mouth. Which was exactly why he needed to just let her go.

The door slammed shut, causing Meagan's heavy lids to flutter open. She was sprawled out on the couch, her jean shorts lying on the floor, her cotton-panty ass facing the ceiling, her forehead pressed into the leather and a small trace of drool on the corner of her mouth.

She had come home and died, falling asleep like she hadn't slept in days.

"What the hell are you doing?"

Meagan started awake at the sound of Eva's bitching. Stretching her body like she was doing the downward dog in yoga class or something, she eventually sat up. "I fell asleep."

"In your panties?"

"I was hot."

"What if I'd had Luke with me or something?"

"Then he would have gotten a nice show of my granny panties. What's with the third degree?"

"You're awful snappy today, princess." She set a large paper bag down on the counter.

"Sorry. I'm just tired." She yawned, moping her way off the couch and into the kitchen.

"Well, are you hungry?"

She sat down on the stool in front of the bar. "Yes."

Reaching in the paper bag, Meagan pulled out a foil container of her favorite meal—an overstuffed burrito. The smell of grilled chicken and onions smothered in queso assaulted her nose and her hand instantly flew to her mouth as she stumbled off the stool and made a mad dash to the bathroom, barely making it to the toilet in time before she doubled over—and puked.

Eva ran to the doorway, her lip curling and her nose wrinkling as she recoiled and turned away from the bathroom. "Are you okay?" she asked on the verge of a gag.

Meagan lifted her head from the toilet and flushed. "Yes," she said, her words muffled as the back of her fingers ran across her mouth.

Turning on the water, she leaned down and ran her mouth under the faucet in the hopes of rinsing the aftertaste from her tongue, but all it did was make it worse.

"I think I've got the flu."

Eva turned back around, her face still a little pale. She was such a sympathy-puker. "I think you're pregnant."

Meagan's panicked eyes flashed to Eva, who was as serious as a heart attack. "No . . ."

She wasn't . . . was she?

"I should be starting . . ." Her head lifted toward the ceiling and her lips moved silently as she counted backward.

"You should have started shortly after your Florida trip. You're always a week after me," Eva cut in, interrupting her panicked attempt at counting backward from twenty-eight.

"Oh my God, Florida."

Meagan rushed to her bedroom and pulled a pair of yoga pants from her bottom drawer.

Eva followed. "What?"

"I forgot to take my pill the night we got home from Florida," she said as she pulled the black cotton up over her hips. "I was exhausted and worried about . . ."

"The break-up?"

She nodded. "Oh God, Eva. I didn't even realize it until I went to take my pill the next night, so I doubled up. That's happened to me before. Hasn't it happened to you? You forgot to take your pill so you just doubled up the next day?"

"Well, yeah, but—"

She sat down on the edge of her bed. "I slept with him that day." Her eyes widened as she stared up at Eva, who was standing surprisingly calm in front of her.

"When?"

"The night we broke up. Oh my God, Eva. I'm two weeks late. Is it even possible to get pregnant that close to your cycle?"

"Do you need Sex Ed 101?"

Her shoulders slumped and her neck jutted out as she widened her eyes at Eva. "Be serious," she snapped.

"Did you have sex?"

"Yes."

"Money shot?"

"Yes."

"Then it's very possible."

Eva tossed Meagan her flip-flops that were on the floor. "Didn't you notice you were late when you went to start a new pack?"

She stood up and slipped her toes between the thin rubber straps. "I never refilled. My mind's just been elsewhere."

Eva gave her a knowing glance and locked her arm around Meagan's. "I know, babe. Come on, let's go get you a test before we start freaking."

They walked out the door and started toward Eva's truck. She realized that normal women would be bawling their eyes out at that very moment if they thought they might be pregnant by a man they just broke up with, but the very thought that she might have a tiny little life growing inside her was enough to keep the tears away.

As she passed Reed's apartment, she paused, and the first ounce of sadness reached her. She should be rushing off to the store with him, she should be jumping up and down, sharing this possible happiness with him—but she couldn't.

Two giant glasses of water and four pregnancy tests later, Meagan sat on the edge of the bathtub, staring at four identical double lines—officially pregnant.

"You gonna call him?" Eva asked, sitting on the counter next to the sink.

Her eyes never left the white sticks that lined the linoleum floor in front of her feet. She was afraid, no, she wasn't afraid, she was terrified. A faint nausea came over her—but it wasn't the pregnancy, it was her nerves. All she seemed to do was go back to that night—that night eight years ago when the man she loved took her world and flattened it between his hands along with everything she thought was true, along with her future.

And now she was faced with the extreme reality that it was going to happen all over again. She knew Reed didn't want this, that he wasn't ready for this—ready to settle down with a family—and she needed to prepare herself for that. If she could, then maybe she could brace against the destruction that would claim her heart.

She inhaled a deep breath, then let it out slowly, lifting her head. "Yeah, I'm gonna call him."

This gas station should had been condemned. Reed could piss anywhere, but he wasn't about to get his dick within aiming distance of that fucking urinal. It had shit growing on it that hadn't even been discovered yet. Not to mention the entire place smelled like it was the inside of an overflowing Porta-John in the dead of summer. He lifted the crook of his arm to his nose and backed out.

The setting sun glared off of his sunglasses as he walked back toward the jeep. "Don't fucking go in there."

"Why? Don't be a pansy—it can't be that bad." Murano said, tossing Reed the keys as he put the cap back on his gas tank.

"I'm telling you, man, don't say I didn't warn you." He hopped in behind the wheel as Murano shrugged and headed toward the bathroom.

His phone vibrated against his thigh and he dug his hand in his pocket, retrieving it. The picture that popped up on the screen stalled his heart. The blond waves that were blowing across her face and the way her nose was scrunched up as her lips perked together, blowing a kiss, sent a longing through him that he was trying desperately to shut out.

It was Meagan.

Clearing his throat, he pressed the Accept button and lifted the phone to his ear. "Hello," he said, sounding a little more excited to hear from her than he would have liked.

"Hey, Reed. Uh . . . it's Meagan." The nervous hitch in her voice caught him by surprise, but it made him smile anyway.

"I know, sugar."

She sighed.

"You okay?" he asked when she didn't respond.

"Yeah. No, I'm fine. How are you?"

She wanted to know how he was? What the hell? They lived next door to each other and she hadn't spoken to him once in the last two weeks and now she wanted to call to see how he was? He might not understand it, but he sure as shit was happy she called. Her voice alone damn near brought him to his knees, and if he wasn't sitting down, it probably would have.

"I'm good."

"Good. Um, I was hoping we could talk." There was that nervous crack in her words again and he could picture her twirling a lock of her hair from her nape around her finger. God, he missed her.

He smiled. "We can talk anytime. All you have to do is call, or hell, stop by."

"Okay." Relief flooded her voice. "Would now be a good time to pop over?"

"Damn, you weren't fucking lying," Murano said, coughing as he climbed into the jeep. Reed shot him a shut-the-fuck-up glance.

"I'm out of town now, sugar. I'll be back tomorrow night, though. I can stop by when I get back if you want."

"Okay, yeah."

There was a pause, a silence between them that for the first time since he had known her was awkward. He felt that she wanted to say more, so he sat there in silence letting her work through it.

"Talk to you then?" she finally said. He was slightly disappointed, hell, more than slightly. He hadn't heard her voice in fourteen long-ass days and he wasn't ready to hang up, especially when he could tell something was off.

"Sounds good."

She sighed and he could feel the smile that she had pulled across her face through the phone. "Bye, Reed."

He had the urge to call her *baby*, to let the word roll from his lips, to let her know that he still needed her that way, but he didn't.

He shut his phone and pulled the jeep out of the gas station.

Murano propped his feet up on the dashboard. "Who was that?"

"Meg."

"Yeah? What did she want?"

Reed's grip tightened on the steering wheel, suddenly anxious. If it wasn't for Murano, he would have whipped a U-ey and would already be on his way back to Benning. "Hell, I don't know. I haven't heard from her in two weeks."

Unfortunately, his friend was privy to the emotions he was failing to hide. His hand clamped down on Reed's shoulder. "What'd I tell you, man? Once you found that one— you'd be crawling back to her every chance you got."

"I'm not crawling, I don't even know what she wanted."

"But you'd go crawling if she gave you the chance, wouldn't you?"

His eyes darted to Murano before they fell back in line with the yellow dashes stretching out in front of him. "I'd crawl, scoot, roll, skip—fuck, I'd fly if I could."

Murano's hand tightened in a squeeze before it dropped from Reed's shoulder. "Welcome to love, my man. It fucking sucks."

CHAPTER TWENTY-THREE

Meagan woke up early. Then she went back to sleep. Then she woke up.

She was restless to say the least. Reed had texted her the night before, saying he wouldn't be stopping by because he and Murano wouldn't get home till late and he had to be at work at five in the morning—so he wanted to talk today instead. And the waiting was killing her. It was like she was replaying every possible scenario in her head over and over and it did nothing but make her more anxious than she already was.

She showered, shaved, shampooed, and contemplated repeating. But instead, she got out, tried on three different sundresses, blew out her hair, brushed her teeth, threw up a couple of times, brushed her teeth again, and finally took a nap. And it was still only eleven thirty. . . .

Finally, after attempting to eat lunch but not being able to stomach anything—whether the baby or Reed was to blame she didn't know—she decided to just go to him. He'd always told her she should come out and watch him jump. Better late than never, right?

To her surprise, there were a lot more people at the landing zone than she thought. It looked like mostly girlfriends and wives were there, but there were a few parents present and a handful of kids running around. She could see the planes flying above and she was glad she hadn't missed it.

She saw Luke's truck parked a ways away, over by one of the pits that had smoke rising from it. She stepped up closer—still a far ways away—but she could clearly see his huge body leaning against the bed of his truck, his massive arms pulled his uniform tight across his chest as he rested them over the side. She couldn't help herself. She sent him a text.

Lookin good big guy

She watched as he pulled his phone from his pocket, then scanned the crowd of people. She raised her hand in the air and waved—he nodded with an annoyingly cocky smirk that only Luke Sanders could pull off.

Hey. What u doin here?
Came 2 talk 2 Reed & watch him jump
Cool. He'll b glad 2 see u

Yeah, she wasn't too sure about that.

Has he jumped yet?
Nope getting ready 2 now. He will b the
first one

Knowing Reed would be the first one out of the plane made the anticipation even more nerve-racking. But it was nothing compared to the way she felt when she saw the doors open up and his body jump out—it was terrifying.

His body whipped out of the plane at a speed that was incredible, and as quickly as he whipped out, his chute jerked him back. Thankfully his opened up perfectly. Reed had told her about how Brewer's chute got twisted up, a cigarette roll is what he called it, and if she saw something like that, she would have lost it.

He floated quickly to the ground. She was a little surprised how fast it went. Before she knew it, he landed— hard—and her hand flew absentmindedly to her mouth. But then he got up, and when he stood, her heart sank to the pit of her stomach.

She lived right next to him, yet she hadn't seen him in two weeks, and the sight of him in uniform, jogging to Luke's truck, sent an unwelcome shot of desire through her. She'd always had a weakness for men in uniform—hell, you didn't grow up around soldiers without gaining an appreciation for the sexiness that was a pair of ACU pants and a tucked-in tan shirt with dog tags hanging against the chest—and she found herself wishing she could slide off his ACU jacket and see exactly that.

Reed threw his pack in the back of Luke's truck, then followed Luke's outstretched hand that was pointing right at her. She felt like a teenager. She had that giddy burst of excitement coursing through her as he lifted his lips into that award-winning smile that she loved and hated all at the same time. But the second he started jogging toward her, that giddy burst exploded into fear.

It took him a minute or so to cross the distance to her. He stopped in front of her, his breathing slightly heavy. Sweat dotted his forehead underneath his dark hair. He smelled like outside and sweat, with a touch of the clean, spicy Reed scent she loved.

He smiled again—and she melted. Seriously, she felt that she was in a sopping puddle at his feet. The perfect bow of his upper lip twitched as the corners lifted and his teeth flashed. His eyes gripped hers and drank her in like she was able to quench his thirst.

Then he talked.

"Hey, sugar." Yep, that was all he said, and the rich sound of his accent vibrated against her skin, leaving a tingling sensation in its wake.

"Hey."

His hand reached out like he was going to run it through her hair or cup her face—something—but then he dropped it back to his side.

His eyebrows danced and his smile morphed into a smirk. "Enjoy the show?" And just like that, the playful Reed that reeled her in so long ago was making an appearance. Thank God, she missed that Reed.

"Well, I had a mini panic attack—and then I almost peed my pants, but, yes, other than that, I enjoyed the show."

His laugh erupted around her, smothering her and strangling her—in the best possible way.

Then his face fell, and his lips softened around the edges,

his eyes penetrating hers. "God, I've missed you." His words came out soft, desperate, and incredibly sexy—and she panicked.

"Reed, I'm pregnant."

Something happened. He wasn't exactly sure what it was, but it was something.

He felt his pulse start to pick up, his heartbeat thrashing in his ear. A heaviness crept into his chest, one different from any other. His shoulders tightened, and he felt the sensation of his clammy hands tearing through the short hair on top of his head—but the action never registered to him. He was standing in front of Meagan, his eyes focused on her—on her high cheekbones, the pink pout of her lips, the shallow crease between her eyes and everything felt as if it was rushing past him. He could hear his men giving the "all okay" in the distance behind him. He could smell the smoke from the pits. He could hear the sound of light footsteps running up and down the metal bleachers in the staging area. But beyond that, nothing penetrated his mind. Not one single thought—until he watched the first tear pool over the bottom of Meagan's lashes to stream down her cheeks. Then it hit him with a force that damn near knocked him on his ass.

She was pregnant.

He didn't hesitate one moment longer, not when the woman he loved was looking at him with tears in her eyes and fear-driven panic saturating her expression. It didn't matter that he felt his world spiraling in the opposite direction, all that mattered was Meagan.

Reaching out, he wrapped his hands around her waist, pressing into the small of her back. He pulled her body flush against him, and the familiar contact seeped into his pores like a good memory. She lifted her chin, her eyes filling with tears, and he kissed her.

Her lips thawed against his and his tongue pressed against hers, the taste of her tears mixing with the sweetness of her breath. Her body weakened against him, molding to his, her legs buckling beneath her—and he just held on that much tighter.

She whimpered into his mouth; then he broke their kiss—he had to. The quavering sound that vibrated against his lips was about two seconds away from causing him to pick her up and carry her to his bike and drive off with her. She needed him—he could see it, and it fucking killed him that he had to go.

"I've got to get back, but I will come over tonight," he said, leaning his forehead against hers.

She didn't say anything, just held perfectly still in his arms. He ran his hand through her hair, then pressed his lips to hers one last time.

"Tonight?"

She nodded, then walked away.

The look on Meagan's face when she told him she was pregnant skirted through his memory as he jogged back to Sanders' truck, and it mirrored the way he was feeling at that very moment—scared.

Sanders leaned away from the truck and took an urgent step toward Reed as he got closer.

"What the fuck, Porter? Is everything okay?" he blurted.

"No."

His eyes widened. "What? God, you look like you got kicked in the balls, what happened?"

"Meagan's pregnant."

Sanders' back fell against the side of the truck as he leaned his weight into it. "Fuuuck. What are you going to do?"

"I don't have a clue."

CHAPTER TWENTY-FOUR

There's something to be said about initial reactions. Meagan was starting to develop a sixth sense for them. You could always tell from that split-second look in someone's eyes how they really felt, before they had a chance to put up any walls to camouflage the truth with what they wanted you to see. It was natural to be apprehensive, to feel fear or excitement, or to feel joy, but a lot of time our insecurities mock us and trick us and tell us to feel things we don't truly feel. But it was in that one moment, that first instant reaction that was the most honest—that's the one to trust.

And the look on Reed's face when she told him couldn't lie. He was scared, confused, hurt—but the one emotion that flashed over him, trailing the end of the others, was anger. And that alone said it all.

Despite the August heat, Meagan was freezing. She had wrapped herself up in a blanket and wedged her feet in between the cushions of the couch, her body heat warming the leather. Cramps settled low in her stomach, and she swallowed as her mouth became increasingly moist, nausea settling in her throat—and she was tired . . . so tired. How a baby the size of a peanut could make her feel like she had just run a marathon while PMSing and coming down with the flu was beyond her, but that's exactly how she felt. Oh, not to mention heartbroken. Just icing on the cake, right?

A knock on the door sent a wave of panic through her veins and she sat up. It was Reed.

Eva peeled her eyes away from the TV to look at Meagan. "You want me to get that?"

"Tell him I don't want to talk right now."

She nodded her understanding, stood up, and went to the door.

Meagan didn't want to see him, she didn't want to go through the hell of feeling her heart shatter any more than she had earlier. She didn't need to hear the words come out of his mouth, they were already plastered all over his face when she told him—and that was all she needed to know.

Hiding out in her living room, she heard the sound of the door open and Reed's lush, thick accent waft into the apartment. "Hey, Eva." His words were flat, his tone calm, and she knew that his in-control facade was set in place.

"She doesn't want to talk, Reed."

There was a pause, and Meagan pictured him running his hands over his head, working the muscles in his jaw.

"Please," he said, trying to reason with her. "Let me in."

"No." The shift in Eva's voice took on a more forceful approach as she stood her ground. In the midst of it all, Meagan smiled to herself—she had one pretty amazing overprotective friend.

But then her smile fell the second Reed's voice seeped into the room again. "Dammit, I just need to talk to her. Meagan!"

A sob raked through her as she clutched the blanket tighter around her.

"Just go. Give her time."

"But—"

"Go."

She heard, no, more like she *felt* Reed's heavy sigh before the door clicked shut.

Eva walked back into the living room, her ACU pants dragging around her green, socked feet. "That was rough, babe." She plopped down next to Meagan and shoved her small body under the blanket with her. "You can do this, ya know," she said, leaning her shoulder into Meagan. "You won't be alone, you've got me."

Meagan laughed, rolling her head back against the couch. "Oh God, that's almost scary."

"What? I'm good with kids."

"Yeah, if you consider good betting your eleven-year-old nephew fifty bucks that he wouldn't shave his seventeen-year-old brother's eyebrows off, then, yes, you are the perfect role model."

"How was I supposed to know that he would actually do it? The little shit."

"Yeah, and you gave him a hundred bucks."

A smile covered her freckled face. "What can I say? I was proud."

She shook her head and slouched down into the corner of the couch.

"You can't shut him out forever, babe. You know that, right?"

"I know." She sighed.

She knew she needed to talk to Reed, she just needed to find a way to detach her heart from him first, because she was afraid that he was going to detach himself from her, and their baby—completely. She needed to be ready for that. She had to be.

The next morning was fucking hell. Reed hadn't slept at all. He lay in bed and thought about all the ways he had fucked up with Meagan in the short time since she had found her way back into his life.

But he was going to make it right—he had to.

His life was about to change. Nothing would ever be the same again, and he didn't have a damn clue what to do. The only thing he knew for sure was that he needed to see her. He needed to talk to Meagan.

His gray army T-shirt was sodden from sweat as he climbed off his bike and walked back toward the apartment building. His men were all cussing him out right now, he knew they were. He had pushed them during PT this morning. He made them run farther, harder—and the thick Southern air secured them in a humid bubble that enclosed them all in an inferno. Yeah—he was going to have to take it easy on them tomorrow, but he needed the push today. He needed to feel the burn in every single muscle of his body. It helped.

Reed stopped in front of Meagan's apartment. He had full intentions to shower and wash the foul perspiration off his body before he talked to her, but before the action registered with him, he was knocking on her door.

He heard the soft smack of bare feet padding across the floor before the door cracked. Her sleep-ringed eyes shot open when they fell on his face.

"Reed. What are you doing here?"

Her tight tank top clung to her body, graciously hugging her full, bare tits that settled underneath it. His eyes trailed down to her body, homing in on the thin cotton boy shorts that barely covered her.

"You always answer the door in your underwear, sugar?" he asked, trying to lighten the mood.

Her eyes darted down, realization crossing her face. "Shit. Sorry. I was asleep." She bit her bottom lip nervously and Reed couldn't help feeling the need to pull it from her mouth. God, he needed to touch those lips to his, to kiss her again.

"I didn't mean to wake you up, I just wanted to see you before I went back to work."

"Reed—"

"We need to talk," he said quickly, interrupting her before she had a chance to tell him to fuck off. "Can we just talk, Meg?"

Her lips pressed together as her chin trembled. Fuck. If she started crying he would lose it. He had seen her eyes fill up with tears twice now, and the sight tore at his insides and stabbed him in the chest. He couldn't see it again, especially knowing he was the one to cause it.

She inhaled deeply then released it quickly. "Yes."

The muscles in his shoulders relaxed—but only slightly. "Good. Come over around eight?"

"You're not going to make mac and cheese again are you?"

He laughed. "I'll make whatever you want."

"I'll eat before I come." She yawned.

"Go back to bed, sugar." He had an uncontrollable need to wrap her in his arms and carry her back to her bed, pull the blanket down, and cover her body with his. He wanted it, and he needed it more than he fucking realized. "See you at eight," he said.

She smiled, but it was forced, and the hope she instilled in him vanished when she shut the door.

Meagan rolled over in bed, attempting to untangle herself from her sheets. Reaching over, she grabbed her phone from the nightstand. It was after one. She was instantly thankful that she worked three twelve-hour shifts a week, because if she kept feeling like this, she was going to sleep her entire pregnancy away.

She forced herself out of bed and ambled across the cold floor of her bedroom and into her bathroom. She needed to put her big-girl panties on. She was thirty years old, she was a grown-ass woman, and she needed to stop filling the pity party that was taking up residence in her mind.

She also needed to call her mom. God, what was she going to say? She knew about Reed, she knew that Meagan had fallen, but that as quickly as she fell, she'd gotten up and walked away. And in typical mom fashion, she'd comforted her. But now Meagan was pregnant with his baby, and she couldn't help but wonder if her mom would be happy. So this wasn't the five-year plan she had anticipated. She wasn't getting the picket fence and the perfect husband, but she was getting the baby. And regardless of the pain she felt hovering in chest—she was excited. She was going to be a mommy.

She turned the shower on, pushing the nozzle over, hoping that the warm water would help relieve the cramps and soothe her tired body.

She stripped out of her clothes and stood in front of the bathroom mirror. She ran her hands over her full breasts, which were covered in white lines from being hidden from the sun, and down her smooth, golden stomach until her fingers grazed the soft flesh below her belly button.

Her palm flattened against her stomach, a smile fanning across her face as she imagined her body swelling from her baby. Her baby. A flutter tickled her chest, filling her lungs and heating her heart. Her baby.

She stepped into the shower, the heat of the warm water trickling over her skin, relaxing the tension that seemed to cling to her muscles. After a few moments, she filled her hands with soap, rubbing them together until a thick lather coated her palms. She rubbed her arms, her chest, washing her breasts and her stomach, and then her hand slipped between her thighs, lathering herself. She lifted her hand, grabbing the bottle of soap from the caddy against the wall— and she froze.

Red suds bubbled over her fingers, across her wrists.

Her head jerked down, her eyes falling to her legs as a trickle of blood skidded down her inner thigh, mixing with the water at her feet.

Her mind seemed to go black at that moment. Thoughts couldn't penetrate the fear that morphed into terror and sorrow, suffocating her. She clutched her stomach. The life that she had always wanted, the life that she was so close to, the life that was inside her, was disappearing.

She stepped from the shower as a sharp pain ripped apart her lower stomach. She cried out as her hands latched onto the sink for support—blood flowing heavily down her legs.

She grabbed her phone and sank down to the cold floor. Her wet body shaking from the cold, from the pain, from the deep crevice of sorrow that had formed a new fissure in her already broken heart.

Without thinking twice, she dialed the one person she needed—but he didn't answer. Reed's playful voice sounded through the phone as his voice mail picked up, and a new wave of heartbreak coursed through her.

She hung up and dialed again.

"Hey, babe, what's up?" Eva asked when she answered.

The tears that were glazing across her vision finally fell from her burning eyes. The sob that she was trying desperately to hold back raked through her, her body trembling as it shook through her back, escaping from her lips.

"Oh my God, Meggy, what's wrong?"

"I need you to come get me," she managed to choke out.

She pulled her knees to her chest as she sat against the bathtub, the shower still running, filling the small room with a haze of steam. She tightened her arms around her naked body as the towel beneath her soaked crimson. "I'm losing the baby."

The time at the hospital felt like a fuzzy dream. One that you knew you were having, one where you could see the events taking place in your mind, but they were blurred around the edges, preventing you from seeing clearly. That's how she felt—blurred.

She lay in her bed, Harry and Weasly both curled up in a ball at her feet, Eva sitting next to her, her fingers softly raking through Meagan's hair, gently pulling apart the tangles.

Her eyes burned. They were swollen, and puffy, and raw. Her nose felt hot, the skin red and sensitive. And her face felt sticky with the remnants of her tears. Her body felt—empty.

Time faded. The seconds into minutes and the minutes into hours. She didn't know how long she lay there, just staring at the white walls beside her, but it seemed like eternity.

She startled when an oh so familiar knock gently pounded against the front door. She lifted up her phone—it was eight thirty.

"It's him, babe."

"I know." She knew he would come when she didn't show up at his apartment.

Eva gave her a warning look. She knew Meagan had surpassed her breaking point, but that was the thing; she couldn't possibly break any more than she already had.

Meagan slowly climbed out of bed.

"I'll be in my room if you need me, okay?" Eva said carefully.

A fresh batch of tears pricked the back of Meagan's eyes and she nodded.

Her feet felt weighted down as she made her way down the hall, through the living room, and to the front door. Wiping underneath her eyes with the pad of her thumb, she took a deep breath and opened the door—a smiling Reed staring back at her. His face fell and concern molded into the creases of his eyes as he looked at her.

He reached out his hand and cupped her face, and it was everything she had in her not to throw her arms around him. "Meg," he said softly. That single word pulled her tears to the forefront of her vision before they spilled over her lashes. "Dammit, baby. What's wrong?"

She swallowed hard and clutched onto the hem of her T-shirt—Reed's T-shirt, one she had taken from him after spending a night wrapped in his arms.

She blinked. "I lost the baby."

His feet staggered back a half step and his shoulders slumped forward. The look that covered his face shattered the last bit of control that she was clinging onto, and her heart felt as if it was caving in all over again—something she would have never thought possible. But when a sincere look of complete sadness reached his eyes, she crumbled. The tears came, and they didn't stop, and she didn't hold them back.

Reed didn't speak a word—he just pulled her into his

arms and held her. His strong hands pressed into her lower back, forcing her body to mold to his chest. Her cheek rested against the thin material of his shirt as it absorbed her tears. He just held her there in the doorway for what felt like a lifetime. He didn't move. He didn't try to calm her. He just let her come undone in his arms.

Her sobs turned to cries, and her cries faded to tears until eventually there was nothing left in her. Tired and crushed and broken, Reed picked her up and cradled her against his chest.

"I'm here," he whispered as he pressed his lips to her forehead.

He carried her through the apartment and laid her down gently in her bed. He peeled off his T-shirt and stripped down to his boxers, then climbed in bed, curling himself around her.

She knew she should tell him to leave, give him the out that she knew he wanted—but she didn't. At that moment, she was going to let him hold her, and then maybe she wouldn't completely fall apart.

CHAPTER TWENTY-FIVE

Reed stirred. Something in his subconscious grabbed him by the balls and forced his eyes to open. It was still dark out, the early-morning sun was still tucked away nice and tight, giving him a few more hours of sleep. His hand reached out, the bed that stretched out next to him was empty, and the sinking feeling that he was getting used to having over the last few weeks found its way back in.

Stepping out of bed, he pulled his jeans on and walked out into the living room.

"Meg? What are you doing?"

She was dressed and waiting on the couch with a small duffel bag on the floor next to her. Panic washed through him when she looked at him.

"I'm going to go stay with my parents, get away for a little bit."

"Meg—," he started but she stood up and pinned him with a sad stare that wiped whatever words he was going to say right from his mind. All he could focus on was the pain in her eyes—eyes that never showed him their secrets before were screaming at him loud and clear.

She headed toward the door and stopped when Reed called out her name again. She placed her hand on the doorknob and turned her head over her shoulder and looked at him, grief saturating the circles under her blue eyes.

"I need this, Reed. I need to sit by the ocean and clear my head and my heart from everything that has happened these last few weeks."

He pulled in a breath as an invisible thread that was wrapped around his heart tightened between them, threatening to snap. She was leaving. Maybe not for good, maybe just for a little bit—but the reality of the matter was, she was leaving him.

He walked to her, knowing that he was walking on thin ice, stepping over shards of glass, but he made his way to her anyway. He couldn't just let her walk out. He did that once already and it was the worst fucking thing he ever let happen.

He saw the plea in her eyes, telling him not to come to her, begging him to stop, but he knew it was now or never.

A sad smile tugged on her lips, her once bright eyes now dim, and he felt the need to run to her—but her words stopped him cold.

"You're off the hook now. You can go back to the way things were, the way you want them. And I can move on."

There was no malice in her voice, no longing, no hatred, no guilt—no emotion at all.

"Go back to the way things were? Meg, that's not possible." His hand ripped through his hair as his eyes shifted toward the ceiling. "Don't do this," he pleaded, looking back at the eyes that would haunt his memory for eternity if she walked out that door. He stepped toward her again, his feet making quick work beneath his legs. His hand folded on top of hers, covering the doorknob, preventing her from walking out that door.

"I'm so sorry about the baby. I'm sorry you're hurting, and I'm sorry there is nothing I can do to fix it. But I'll try. I'll try like hell." He stepped into her, weaving his fingers though her hair. He needed to touch her. "I'll do everything in my power to fix this. Just tell me what to do."

Her fingers flew to her mouth as she shut her eyes and shook her head. "Let me go, Reed."

Let her go. The words held a different meaning than he was ready to accept. Even if he let her walk out that door, he would never let her go. He was too far gone.

"I can't let you go, not again." His hands dropped to her back and he pulled her against him. He wasn't letting her go.

Her hands flattened against his chest and she pushed herself out of his arms. "Good-bye, Reed." She choked, unable to meet his eyes as she grabbed the handle again.

Going against everything he wanted, he stepped away from the door. He didn't want to—but he did.

And she left.

The heaviness he felt in his chest traveled through his body—weighing him down. He wasn't whole—he hadn't been for years, but now another part of him was missing, a part he never knew he had or wanted.

It had happened again. A life, a piece of him, was taken away from him in a single breath, without any warning. And that same piece of him had been ripped away from Meagan too. He knew she wanted that baby, and he knew that losing it damn near crushed her. But he didn't know that he would feel the same. He didn't realize how that brief life had healed him until he felt himself break all over again.

That familiar yearning that was layered in a thick coating of anguish flowed through his veins as it pumped from his damaged heart.

He fell to his knees.

Not only was he no longer whole—he was empty.

CHAPTER TWENTY-SIX

Meagan spent two days lying on the beach, doing absolutely nothing but soaking up the end of summer—and she needed that, she needed that time with her parents. With her mom.

Her mom stepped up beside her, her tiny body covered in a long, sheer dress over her swimsuit. She plopped down in the sand next to Meagan and handed her a Diet Coke.

She smiled. "Thanks."

"Now you finish that, then get your butt back home."

Her head snapped to her mom. "What?"

"You heard me, sweetheart. I know you're going through something that I can't even possibly imagine, but you have to go back. You can't hide out here forever."

"Why not?"

Her mom laughed and it shook her boney body. "Oh, sweetie, I would love it if I got to see you every day, and so would your dad, but running away never solved anything."

"There's nothing to solve, Mom."

"Oh, there is, sweetie."

She stretched her legs out in the sand, the warm grainy texture digging into her legs. "Okay, care to elaborate? Share your motherlike wisdom?"

"You know how badly I wanted children—"

"Mom—"

"No, no. Let me tell you. I couldn't wait to start a family, and if I would have had my way, I would have tried to get pregnant the first year your father and I were married. But he wanted to wait. He was a free spirit—he wasn't ready for all that, like your Reed."

Meagan picked up warm, white sand and poured it from hand to hand. "You never told me that."

Her mom sighed. "Meagan, our lives pan out how they should, not always how we plan them. And I'm sorry for putting that pressure on you."

"No, you were right." Her mom told her she needed safe, and she was right. Falling in love with Reed was proof enough. That fall had landed hard, and it hurt.

"No, I wasn't—"

"Mom—" She tried to interrupt again. She almost hated seeing this vulnerable side of her mother. The woman was always so strong, so sure.

Her mom placed her hand on top of Meagan's and the sand spilled to her feet. "I love your dad, and the years I spent following him around, carefree and reckless, were some of the best of my life, and they led me to you."

Her eyes filled up with the threatening prick of tears.

"Now go talk to him."

"Mom," she pleaded again. She didn't think she could

face him. Not now. Not when she could still feel the break in her heart and the phantom emptiness in her stomach. She knew with time, Reed would be back to traveling the world, checking off his crazy bucket list, and living his life the way he wanted. She saw the hurt in his eyes when she left, but it wouldn't last long. He would go back to the way things were before she came along and threw in a kink. She needed to figure out a way to keep it together until he did.

Her mom uncurled her tiny hand from hers and patted her arm as she stood up. "Your bag is in your car, your dad filled up your gas tank, and there is a fifty in the ashtray. Now go."

She didn't want to go. She had forgotten how much comfort her mom could bring her and she wasn't ready to give up that comfort. But if that wasn't a shove in the ass, Meagan didn't know what was.

M eagan walked into her apartment after driving the long drive home and set her bag down by the front door.

"Hey, buddy," she said as Harry wound in and out of her legs.

The apartment was quiet. Eva should have been home from work by now, which meant she was either at the gym or out with Luke. It was Friday night, so chances were Meagan had the apartment to herself.

She made her way into the kitchen to find a giant pitcher of margaritas sitting nicely on the bar. She smiled to herself.

If there was one thing about Eva that she loved the most, it was her way of knowing exactly what Meagan needed, when she needed it. Eva wasn't even there, yet she knew she would need a drink after a visit with her mom, even if this particular visit was much needed.

She picked up the Solo cup that was sitting next to the pitcher and started to pour herself a glass when she saw a folded-up note that had been underneath the cup.

A note? Seriously? Who did that anymore?

> *Hey, babe,*
> *Pour yourself a margarita and get your cute*
> *little ass out to the pool. Oh, and bring the*
> *pitcher!*
>
> *XOXO*
> *Eva*

Eva was plotting something. She knew it. Eva didn't leave cute little notes under margarita cups unless she had something up her sleeve, and Meagan was bound to go bat-shit crazy if that something started with Reed and ended with Porter. Meagan didn't think she could handle that right now, although she didn't see his bike in the parking lot, and she had looked, thoroughly, so she was probably safe.

She just needed to get heavily wasted with her best friend, pass out on whatever surface of her apartment seemed the most comfortable or the most convenient, wake up tomorrow with a hangover from hell, wear it off by watching a stream of Channing Tatum movies, all the while eating grease and or fried foods all day long. That pretty much sounded perfect.

Meagan kept her shorts and tank top on, not caring to get in the water, and picked up her glass and the pitcher and made her way to the courtyard. It was empty, as per usual. These apartments were some of the quietest she had ever been in. She still wasn't convinced that the landlord wouldn't off her in the middle of the night if she was out here alone.

"Meg! You're home!" an overly tipsy Eva shouted from the water.

"Yep, I'm home. And I found your little note. What the hell stunt are you pulling, my friend?" she asked as she walked through the gate that surrounded the pool area, setting the pitcher down on one of the round tables.

"Hey, Meg."

Meagan's head whipped to the side as a familiar voice said her name and she damn near dropped her margarita.

"Trevor!" she shouted, as he stood up from the pool chair and opened up his arms to her. She flew into them.

"What are you doing here?" she asked as he sat her back down on the ground. She moved her arms from his neck to his waist and hugged him tightly.

He kissed the top of her head. "It's good to see you too, Meg."

"I get Best Friend of the Year Award for getting his ass here, right?" Eva lilted.

Meagan winked. "Yes, thank you.

"But really, what are you doing here?" she asked again,

taking a step back and lifting her cup to her mouth. She was surprised she had managed not to spill it all during her giant Trevor hug.

"I wanted to check on you."

Her eyes dropped for a moment before she lifted them back to him. "You know?"

He nodded. "Yeah. I'm sorry, Meg. You okay?"

She shrugged but then nodded her head as her mouth tilted into somewhat of a smile. She was good. She had to be. It still hurt, she still felt the sadness clench her heart whenever she thought about the tiny life that was only briefly inside of her, but she was good, as good as she could be.

"I'm okay," she said in attempt to reassure Trevor as he looked at her like she was about to break into one of her legendary snotty sob fests, ready and willing with a shoulder to snot on.

He lifted his brow to her and cocked his head. Jeez, he was as bad as Eva.

"Truly. I'll be fine."

"What about the guy?"

"What about him?"

"You still love him?"

She glared at Eva and pressed her mouth into a tight line. She didn't keep things from Trevor. She never had. But Trevor had a tendency of going a little overboard with the big-brother role he had taken on, and when it came to men and her heart, he was lethal.

"Hey now, don't get pissed at her, I basically threatened it out of her."

KELSIE LEVERICH

"Yeah, because Eva is intimidated so easily," she mocked, rolling her eyes.

Trevor folded his big arms across his chest. "You still love him?" he repeated.

"I would just like to get trashed with my two best friends tonight. Too much to ask?" She walked to the edge of the pool and sat down, sinking her feet into the warm water, dodging the question. It wasn't that she didn't have the answer, she just didn't want to admit it.

"How long are you here for?" she asked as Trevor sank down next to her, grunting.

"I've gotta leave here pretty early in the morning, around nine or so."

"That's no time at all!" She pouted. She just got him here. She didn't want him to leave so soon.

"I know," he said apologetically. "I tried to get a pass but no such luck, it was too short notice."

Her brows furrowed. "Wait. Then how . . . Trevor! If you get caught this far from post without a pass, you'll be AWOL!" she snapped, punching him in the shoulder.

"Easy, Meg. I'm not gonna get caught. And the worst they would do is slap me on the wrist and stick me with extra duty."

"But—"

"No buts. Eva said you needed me, so here I am. End of story. And you better enjoy me while you have me, Cinderella, because I won't be here long."

She sighed and weaved her arm through his. It felt so good to see him again and even though he could potentially get in deep shit for being there, she was glad he was. "So what's new with you? Anyone good fall into your bed lately?" she asked.

He laughed and the sound was infectious, causing her to lean into him and laugh against his shoulder. He wrapped his arm around her and pulled her into a side hug—pulling her into his safe bubble—the place she had escaped to more times than she could count. He was always good at just being there when she needed him, and she definitely needed him now; she didn't even realize how much until that moment.

"Eh, no one in particular. I've got a thing for feisty red-heads. Know any?" he teased, bouncing his brows up and down at Eva.

"Gross," Eva said, splashing him in the face with water. "I wouldn't have sex with you if my left tit depended on it."

Meagan's face split open as she laughed until her side hurt. God, she needed that.

Eva's mouth pulled back, causing the tendons in her neck to bulge as she sucked in a breath. "Don't look now, but 'the guy' is walking this way."

And just like that, the small little bubble that Meagan had stepped into popped.

The sweet sound of Meagan's laugh rang though Reed's ears and shot out an addictive pull that kicked his adrenaline into overdrive. His eyes found her instantly, and as quickly as he felt that surge of excitement, that instant gratification from hearing a sound that was like heroin to a drug addict, another surge swept through him when he saw her arms tangled with another guy's.

His body didn't give him a choice. He was going to her. The little tick of jealousy that seemed to cause him to see red wherever Meagan was concerned was about ready to send him over the edge without his reserve lined up.

She looked the happiest he had seen her in weeks. The happiest he had seen her since before they left for Florida. . . .

The selfish prick inside of him boiled, but the other part of him, the one he was trying to bring to the surface, told him to be happy for her. Seeing her smile should make him happy. But knowing that he wasn't the one to give it to her pissed him the fuck off.

If she was going to move on without him, then he damn sure needed to make sure she knew how he felt first.

Her head turned over her shoulder as he stomped toward the pool and her face flushed. Yeah, seemed like he was still able to spark a little reaction from her. Good to know.

"Hey, sugar," he said, stepping inside the pool gates. He tried to sound normal, but the accusation forming his words spit from his mouth—and he hated the way it sounded.

The guy got to his feet and Meagan scrambled up after him. His jaw flexed and his body straightened. He was being protective—territorial—and it pissed Reed off even more, fueling the fire that was already igniting inside him.

She stood tall, her shoulders back, and her eyes firm. But he had learned to see through her facade, and he could see the subtle increase in her breathing as she looked at him— affected. He only needed an inch. . . .

"Hey, Reed."

"You're home."

"Yeah, I just got ba—"

"Who's this?" he said, nodding at the guy who had now taken a step in front of her, damn near blocking his view of the woman he so desperately needed to see.

Meagan sighed, apparently irritated, but he didn't care. "This is Trevor. Trevor, this is Reed."

He saw movement out of the corner of his eye, but he didn't look—he didn't take his eyes off of Trevor, who was staring back at him like he was ready to strike.

He felt a hand pat against his back. "Easy, killer." It was Eva. "Trevor's our *friend* from Fort Drum," she said, making sure to emphasize the word *friend*.

Reed nodded. He didn't care to pussyfoot around this guy. Okay, he was her friend, simple. But part of him cringed at the word. He didn't want to just be her friend, but he couldn't help feel the twinge of jealousy toward the man standing next to her. He had her trust—something Reed no longer had.

"Meagan, can we talk?" he said, shifting his eyes to hers.

"She doesn't want to talk to you, man."

His teeth bit together and his hands tightened into fists at his side. He didn't want to get into it with this guy, but with every beat of Reed's heart, his adrenaline spiked. "Meagan?"

Trevor stepped forward.

Wrong move.

Reed stepped forward, matching Trevor step for step until their chests were a breath away from touching.

"Trevor," Reed sneered, biting back the venom he was ready to spit out. "I'm going to talk to my girl now."

"Your girl? I don't think you can claim that title after you broke her fucking heart."

Reed's voice lowered. "I get that you are playing the big-brother role, and I can respect that, but I fucking swear to you right now, if you don't back the fuck away and give me a minute to talk to her, I will not hesitate to break your fucking jaw."

A slow smile tightened the corners of Trevor's mouth until the jackass was grinning like an idiot. Breaking his jaw was sounding more and more like a very strong possibility.

"Oh my God, is this seriously happening right now?" Meagan shrieked, shoving her hands in between them. Her palm pressing against his chest instantly calmed him and he was tempted to wrap his hand around hers and pull her against him. Christ, it was eating at him. She was right in front of him, so damn close he could smell the sweet scent of her perfume lingering on her neck—but he couldn't touch her. She was the one dangling on the tightrope now—it was close to breaking, he could see that. And once again, he was the one breaking it.

"Reed, I don't have anything to say to you right now. You look like shit. Go home and go to bed. Trevor, go inside the apartment and wait for me. Eva, help me clean up this mess."

She shot him a look that ripped the vocal cords from his throat followed by a frown that almost killed him. He'd hurt her again.

CHAPTER TWENTY-SEVEN

Meagan stood next to Trevor in the parking lot in front of her building, waiting for the taxi to pick him up and take him to the airport. She wanted to drive him, but he was being his stubborn-ass self and refused to let her. He was probably afraid she would break down and cry in the middle of the airport if she went with him. Which wasn't too far of a stretch. She felt like she could break down and cry at that very moment.

"I hate that you're leaving so soon," Meagan said, when she saw the taxi pull in. She wrapped her arms around his waist as he encased her in a hug.

"Me too."

Wiping her eyes with the back of her index finger, she pulled away. "All right, go before I jump on your back and make you take me with you." She sniffed.

He winked. "Jump on, honey."

Eva playfully shoved Meagan aside. "She's not leaving me. Get it out of your head now," she said, pressing her tiny body against Trevor's side.

His large body enveloped her in a hug. "Nah, I wouldn't take her from you. Besides, I think that guy, Reed, would hunt my ass down."

Meagan rolled her eyes.

"He loves you, Meg. And I hate to say it, but I kinda liked the guy. I'm pretty sure he would have had no problem taking a few swings at me." He laughed. "He was definitely ready to fight for you, Meg."

She closed her eyes briefly and sighed. Of course this would be the one guy he would approve of. "You're supposed to be on my side."

He wrapped his hand around the back of her neck and kissed the top of her head quickly. "I am on your side."

Lifting his duffel off the ground, he swung it over his shoulder. "All right, I've gotta go."

Meagan hugged him one last time; then he slid into the backseat of the taxi. She turned away before he drove off, and headed back toward the courtyard. She was glad he came, but saying good-bye always sucked.

"Trevor's right, you know," Eva said, stepping up beside her. Eva didn't agree with Trevor very often. She much preferred to argue with him. He could tell her that her hair was red and she would argue, so the fact that Eva was saying Trevor was right about something got Meagan's attention.

"About what?"

"Reed loves you."

She shook her head feverishly. What happened to her two best friends being on her side of things? What the hell happened to her wingman? She didn't need this from Eva, too. "It's over between us."

Eva laughed and the mocking sound was like nails on a damn chalkboard. "This is what you always do, Meagan. You self-sabotage," she argued.

Her steps halted in the middle of the courtyard. "What do you mean?" she muttered, her eyes finding a way to glare at Eva from the small slits in her lids.

Eva swung around to face her, her green eyes ready and willing to fight. "You can tell me till you're blue in the face that you want your forever—that you want Mr. Safe—but you don't. Why do you think you have always dated Mr. Bad, Mr. Sexy, and Mr. Unavailable?"

"And why's that?" she snapped, throwing her hands in the air, then dropping them to her bare thighs.

Eva shook her head like it should be written plain as day on her face, which was worse than her accusing laugh. "Because you knew there was no forever with them, you knew there was no risk. That's why you gave into Reed so easily after declaring your so-called plan—because you thought he wasn't safe either. You told me he was everything you usually went for. Sexy, funny, carefree, silly, reckless. You thought it wouldn't last, and that's why you chose him—because you're afraid of safe."

"That's ridiculous." A laugh escaped her throat as she stalked back toward her apartment but Eva wasn't the slightest bit fazed by the little outburst. She just fell in step right next to her again.

"Is it? Let's take Jax for example. You said yourself that you never saw yourself marrying him, it was just sex. Moving on to Joey, that man—sexy as he was—was nowhere close to husband material, not for anyone, and we all knew that. Then there was Kale—"

"I cared about him—"

"You did, but you also knew the score. He laid it all out there for you, nothing more than sex. There was no fear for the future because you knew there would never be one with him." She paused, her voice going soft when she continued. "You knew that Reed wasn't one to settle down, to slow down. But then you fell in love with him—and you ran."

Her feet froze midstep as Eva's words rang through her ears. She turned toward her friend, who was telling her everything she didn't want to hear, but everything she needed to know. And it pissed her off—because it was true.

"You're right, I ran!" she shouted, and it felt good. "I've been in love before, Eva. I know what it feels like to love someone so much that you can't see straight. I also know what it feels like when you find out that the man you love, the man you saw when you saw your future, doesn't see you. And I know what fear and anger look like when I look into that man's eyes when he finds out he is going to have a baby that he doesn't even want. Twice, Eva. I saw that same fucking look twice! So maybe you're right, maybe I don't want safe, because when you let yourself feel safe, that's when you get hurt." She swallowed hard, trying to soothe the sudden burn in the back of her throat. "I was right to run, but it still didn't prevent history from repeating itself, did it?"

She shouldered past Eva, quickly walking back toward the apartment. As far as she was concerned, this conversation was over.

"He's not Daniel, Meggy!" Eva hollered from behind her. If there was one thing Eva could say to shake her—that was it.

Meagan's feet sank into the grass as she turned on her heels in front of her patio. "Dammit, Eva. Let it go!"

"No," she said, her eyes drilling holes in Meagan's as she stalked toward her. "He's not Daniel." She stopped in front of her. "Daniel broke your heart. I get it. But Reed didn't. You did that for him."

Meagan's heart was racing. "Because he didn't want it! He didn't see me." She was shouting and part of her felt guilty for yelling at Eva, but that same part of her needed to shout. She needed to scream out all the anger she had at letting herself feel this way again.

Eva's eyebrows darted up and she crossed her arms over her chest. "Did he tell you that? Because from where I stood, he may not have realized it yet, but the man had that move-heaven-and-earth kind of love for you."

"He didn't need to tell me," she said, her voice cracking from the strain or a sob, she couldn't be sure. "I saw it written all over his face when I told him I was pregnant. That told me everything I needed to know."

"Well, did you know he sold his motorcycle?"

The voice was only vaguely familiar, but even then, Meagan recognized the icy tone that fell over her.

"Becky," she began as she turned around. But the first person she saw wasn't Becky—it was someone else, someone she'd seen before. She couldn't remember where, though, or who she was—but she had seen her before, she knew she had.

"Did you know?" Becky repeated, but the icy tone had melted some.

Meagan forced her gaze to meet Becky's. She expected to see anger and disdain, but she only saw sympathy. "No, I didn't."

Becky tucked her short hair behind her ears. "Well, he did. I never in a million years would have thought he could part ways with that motorcycle. So when he called me to make sure I was okay with him selling Mackly's bike, I knew something was going on with him."

Her eyes widened. *Mackly's bike?*

Becky nodded, answering the question that was apparently not only running through her mind but written all over her face. She sucked in a sharp breath as realization struck her, stealing the air that was previously in her lungs. The day Mackly died he was driving Reed's bike. Reed's motorcycle was his brother's. She didn't know how she didn't realize it sooner.

"You had just told him you were pregnant and he was getting ready to go see you." A smile cracked across her hard face. "He didn't think you'd be too keen on strapping a baby to the back of the bike, so he traded it for an SUV. He said he needed something baby friendly."

Meagan's heart stalled before it worked its way into her throat. He gave up his bike, his brother's bike, for her baby? She just stood there, staring blankly at Becky, trying to find something to say, anything. Becky frowned and the tension in her eyes softened. She was sad. Hell, Meagan would rather her look angry. Sad was hard to handle right now. "I'm so sorry, Meagan," she said softly. "I can't even imagine—"

Meagan raised her palm in the air to stop her. "Thank you." That was all she could say—she couldn't go there, not at that moment.

"You may not believe me, but I was happy when he told me. I've never seen my brother look at a woman the way he looked at you that weekend. And I never thought I'd see the day he let go of some of his guilt and actually live his life instead of burying it with thrill."

Meagan's brow furrowed. What guilt? Reed wanted to live life to its fullest, not bury it.

"I don't understand."

Becky looked to the woman standing next to her as if the words she was about to say would somehow reach out and pierce her. Meagan wanted to beg her to just say them, to tell her what she meant. She felt like she was standing on the edge of a cliff looking down, just waiting for that moment when her feet would slip out from under her and her world would fall away with her. It was the waiting, not knowing how bad it would hurt when it happened, that was the worst. She just wanted to rip it off like a Band-Aid, but something in the way the woman's eyes fell to the ground made her step away from that edge. Meagan was staring at a woman who was in love. A woman who was in love with a man that she no longer had. She was looking at a broken heart.

Just as a stream of reasons why this woman was here for

Reed, brokenhearted, penetrated her mind, she stepped forward.

"He thinks he should have died that day, Meagan. He blames himself for Mackly's death. He feels like it should have been him instead," the woman said softly, barely able to get the words out.

Meagan's heart wedged its way into her throat, constricting the burn that was forming. She felt the need to run to him at that very moment, to wrap her arms around him and tell him how wrong he was to blame himself.

Meagan's eyes refocused in front of her when she felt a hand brush across her arm. When she looked up, the woman smiled faintly, pain etching deep in the facets of her eyes. "When Becky told me that Reed had fallen in love I didn't know whether to cry happy tears"—she laughed once through her smile—"or check my hearing. I never thought he'd let himself have love, let alone a family. But then when she told me the woman he had fallen in love with, the woman who was pregnant with his baby, was Meagan Mitchell, I didn't need any more confirmation."

Meagan's brows pinched together as she stared at her. Her blond hair was long and straight, her body was sun-kissed a dark golden brown, and she was curvy in all the right places. She was beautiful. But she wore a pained smile on her pink lips—a pained smile that mirrored the pain Meagan had seen tug through Reed's smile. Reed was broken, but so was she.

"Who are you?" she asked, once again tearing through the file folder in her memory that might help her remember where she knew this woman from.

"I was Mackly's girlfriend."

Meagan's eyes widened as the heartbreak that was written across her face registered. She had lost the man she loved the same day Reed had lost his brother.

"My name is Karrie. Karrie Jo. But you might know me better as Jo."

As the name reached her ear it was as if the proverbial lightbulb went on in Meagan's mind. Her feet shuffled back a step and she latched on to Eva's arm, which was suddenly and conveniently in her reach. A coldness slammed against her, leaving her gasping for breath.

She walked to the patio and pulled the metal chair from the table and sat down. She was afraid if she didn't, she would crumble to the ground.

Karrie . . . or Jo . . . or whatever her name was, followed her to the patio and stood in front of her. Meagan looked up at her and the familiarity she saw in her before transformed into recognition. She could see the beautiful blond cheerleader who was part of the reason her heart was a damaged mess. No. That was a lie. Jo wasn't the one who broke her trust and shattered her heart. Daniel did that the moment he made her believe she was his forever. He shattered her the moment he got Jo pregnant . . .

Her hand flattened against her chest. "Oh my God, the little blond boy Reed told me about . . . that was . . . you didn't . . ." Her mind was going in every which direction, preventing her from forming a clear thought, scrambling her words in her mouth.

She shook her head as a single tear skidded down her

cheek. "No," she said. "I didn't terminate the pregnancy. Daniel wanted me to, but I didn't."

The tears that were accumulating above Meagan's lashes finally spilled over, accompanied by a burn in the back of her throat as she forced down the sob that was raking through her body. "I'm glad," she whispered.

"Me too." She pulled out the chair next to Meagan and sat down. "Reed and Mackly were a lot alike, you know. If the tables were turned, I know without a doubt in my mind that Mackly would have wished it was him instead of his brother too. When you love someone the way they loved each other, you just can't watch their life slip away without watching a piece of you die right along with them." Another tear spilled from her eye and she quickly brushed it away with her finger. "That's why you can't give up on Reed so easily, Meagan. He doesn't think he deserves it. He closed his heart off to the idea of love and a family a long time ago, but you somehow found a way to open that back up for him. And don't think for one second that he didn't want your baby. He did."

Meagan closed her eyes. "That's where you're wrong."

"No," Becky said as she stepped onto the patio. "That's where *you're* wrong. He was scared. And I can count three times that I've ever seen my brother scared. And two of those times were because of you."

Biting her teeth together as the overprotective little sister started to shine through, Meagan crossed her arms over her chest. "Look—"

"But I realized something," Becky said, interrupting her. "Other than you, the only person in this world who had ever scared him was Mackly. The day my brother died was the first time I ever saw fear in Reed's eyes. The second time was when he watched you holding my daughter. And the only other time I have ever seen him scared was when I sat next to him last night as he told me that he lost you . . . and his baby."

Meagan's hand flew to her mouth as her unshed tears started falling from her eyes, making a path down her cheeks until they fell to the ground, waiting for the next to follow. The ache around her heart was spreading and her chin began to tremble beneath her fingers. Meagan lifted her head, a new crevice finding a place in her chest as Becky's words carved out a place for it to slip in. Her memory flickered over Reed's face as she told him she was pregnant—then to his face when she told him she had lost the baby. She remembered his own pain. He had lost another part of himself, and she was too wrapped up in her own grief to see it.

"You're the only other person who has ever held that power over him. When Murano called and told me that Reed was a zombie at work and he hadn't left the house in days, I knew he was hurting, but I never expected to see him like this."

"What do you mean?"

"She means you ran that man through the fucking ringer, Meg. He's no-shit broken and it's because the woman he loves is scared to love him back," Eva cut in. Her eyes softened and her voice lowered. "You're scared, babe, because this time you were wrong. This time you found Reed . . . you found your safe."

Meagan brushed away the wetness from her face and forced a smile. "You know, if this army thing doesn't work out for you, you could always be a shrink."

She threw her head back and laughed. "Oh, hell no. I couldn't get paid enough to fix people's problems. You, my love, don't need fixing. You need Reed."

CHAPTER TWENTY-EIGHT

Reed had just gotten out of the shower when he heard Tiny's thunderous bark ricochet through the apartment. He hadn't had one in two days and he was starting to gross himself out.

It was probably Sanders coming to give him the "don't be a pansy" pep talk, or Murano giving him the "life's too short" speech—both of which he'd invented himself, he just didn't realize at the time how fucking pointless they were. And if it was Murano, he was kicking his ass for calling his baby sister to come pick him up off the ground. And she'd brought Karrie. He sure as hell didn't want Karrie seeing him like this. He needed to get his shit together.

He pulled on a pair of gym shorts and waded through his apartment, which was starting to resemble his old fraternity house with all the pizza boxes and beer cans littering almost every inch of flat space. He'd smelled like hell, he looked like hell, and his apartment was turning into hell. At least he knocked one of those out by taking a shower.

The last thing he fucking expected was to open the door

and see Meagan standing on the other side looking beautiful as ever. Her hair was pulled back away from her face, a long blond strand of hair draping across her shoulder from the nape of her neck, ready and waiting to be twirled around her finger. Her pink lips parted slightly and her eyes shyly held his—and it was sexy.

"Hey," she said, a small smile pulling at her lips, but it wasn't the smile he wanted. He was aching to see that big, flirty smirk. The one that flashed her pearly whites and let loose the sexiest laugh he had ever heard. He fucking missed that. Seeing her in front of him made him realize that the longing he had felt for her was nothing compared to standing there next to her and knowing that she wasn't his anymore.

"Hey, sugar."

He stepped aside and she walked in, Tiny assaulting her with wet kisses.

"Hey, big boy," she cooed, holding Tiny's big head in between her hands.

"He missed you."

She lifted her eyes and frowned, and he wanted to kick his own ass for making that look cross over her face. "I missed him too. And you."

Every muscle in his body tightened as he forced himself to stay where he was, to not reach out and wrap her up in his arms and bury his face in her hair. He needed it so fucking bad he almost gave in, but he didn't want to push her away, not when she was finally standing in front of him.

"I miss you too, sugar," he replied, letting himself soak

up the way her breath seemed to catch in her throat, her chest slightly expanding as she blinked slowly.

"I saw Becky," she said as she walked farther into the apartment.

"You did?" *Fuck*.

Meagan laughed, and whatever he did to make that sound escape her mouth, he wanted to do it again. He needed to hear that sweet laugh almost as much as he needed to touch her.

"You can wipe the 'oh shit' look from your face, Reed. Her claws remained in the entire time."

"You sure it was my sister then?" he teased, walking into the living room behind her. She looked around at the mess and frowned.

"I saw Karrie too." The slight crack in her voice rattled him and he went to her. He didn't care at that moment that his head was barely above water. She was hurting and he'd deal with the consequences later. Right now, he was going to hold her.

He stepped into her and she sucked in a quick breath as his body pressed into hers. He didn't wait to see the look that crossed her face, he was almost scared to see it. Instead, he just linked his arms around her and held her tightly to him.

Immediately her shoulders relaxed and her forehead fell to his chest.

"Dammit, Meg. I'm so sorry," he whispered into her hair. He couldn't fucking help it. "Karrie told me. I know what happened." She tensed in his arms, and if knowing what the fucker did to her, and to Karrie, wasn't reason enough to hunt him down and break his jaw, then the way Meagan's body froze in his arms sure as hell was.

She lifted her head and a sad smile pulled on her lips before she took a few steps back. "Small world, huh?"

"Very."

She sucked her bottom lip into her mouth and closed her eyes briefly, but it was long enough to know that she was turning something over in her mind. "Becky told me you sold your bike."

Shoving his hands into the pockets of his jeans, he nodded. "Yeah."

Her head lowered to the ground for a moment before she looked at him again and whatever torture she was putting herself through was tearing him up. "I'm sorry, Reed."

"For what?" he asked, taking a step toward her again.

"Because you sold your bike, because I left you, because I lost the baby. Take your pick." Her eyes started to glaze over. He couldn't see her cry.

His steps were quick, and the very next breath he was in front of her. He lifted her chin, forcing her to look at him. "Don't you ever apologize for that, you hear me? That was not your fault."

Tears rolled down her cheeks, splashing small, warm drops on his hand. "No, but it was my fault that I didn't even stop to think how you might've felt when I lost the baby. It just hurt too bad."

"You want to know how I feel?" he asked, pulling her against him again. "I feel like I don't deserve you. Why should I be able to have the life my brother should've had? He had a woman he loved and a kid he loved. Then in an instant he was gone and I was still here. It should have been me." His mouth lowered to hers, hovering above her lips. "You walked back into my life and I fucking fell so in love with you that I started to forget how bad it hurt that he was gone." Reaching his thumb up, he smoothed it over her bottom lip. "You want to know how I feel? I feel guilty."

Her eyes closed. "Reed," she breathed across his lips. It was a plea.

"I feel guilty because I want it. I want you. And I want to be the man who gives you everything."

She lifted her arms and threaded her fingers through his short hair as she whispered over his lips, which were tempted to press against hers. "I ran because I love you, but I'm done running. I want you, Reed," she said as she pressed up onto her toes, inching her body in tight to his. "I want everything with you, I always have."

That was all he needed to hear.

He had her body pressed against the wall behind her before she even blinked. Then his mouth was on hers.

Her lips fell in step with the rhythm he set in place, molding her mouth to his, swirling her tongue in and out and around as they tasted each other.

"God, I've missed you," he murmured, breathing his warm breath against her lips.

She moaned her response, and that was all the encouragement he needed to wrap her legs around his waist and pin her arms above her head.

There was something about holding her this way, using his

body to crush her against the wall, her legs gripping his waist, her hands locked above her head—completely helpless beneath him. It was because he felt completely in control like this, and with Meagan he needed that control—because she sure as shit had a way of slipping it away from him. Her sweet, sexy, confidence made him weak, and her shy, needy responses made him lose his resolve. But when he had her like this—he was in control. Her body couldn't move—only her mouth, and only where he wanted it. She was his—her hands were his to confine, her lips were his to consume. And he did.

"Reed, you know we can't have . . . ," she whispered against his lips, which were still moving over hers.

He pulled away, leaving one hand to keep her wrists confined above her head, the other hand molding to the side of her face. She leaned her cheek into his palm and he sighed. "I know, baby. I just needed to feel you like this again."

Her teeth tugged on her bottom lip, and she nodded. "Again . . . please . . ." she said breathlessly.

He sealed his lips over hers and kissed her like it was the last thing he would ever do to her. He put every emotion he had ever felt for her into that kiss—hoping like hell she could feel it.

His hand left her wrists and found their way to her sides, feeling the soft skin that was exposed as her shirt lifted. Her hands wound around his neck, her fingers pulling through his hair.

Peeling her shirt from her body, he trailed his tongue above the lace seam of her bra, following the delicious path it made over the full swell of her tits, the dip in her cleavage, and then back up the other side.

Her neck rolled to the side, and he loved seeing her soft, erratic pulse tickling the thin skin below her ear. He lowered his mouth, his tongue flicking out to sample the quivering vibrations as she continued to expose her neck to him.

His tongue retreated, and he fastened his lips over the assaulted patch his tongue had just explored. She whimpered and shook, a hot rush of excitement coursing through him as she rocked her hips into him, forcing the center of her pussy to roll against his dick—only two layers of frustrating material preventing them from connecting.

The sensation was familiar and foreign all at the same time. The way she nestled into him was gratifyingly familiar but the yearning twitching in her muscles as her thighs clung to him, allowing her to press harder against him, was new—and it jolted him from the inside out.

His hand snaked beneath her and toyed with the soft flesh below her ass. He desperately wanted to slip his fingers up the leg of her shorts and find the wetness between her legs that he was so desperately craving—but he knew he couldn't. Her body still needed time to heal.

Instead, he carried her to his bed and gently laid her down. Seeing her slender body sprawled out above his sheets was a sight he never thought he'd see again.

Her blond hair tumbled behind her while her eyes descended over him, patiently waiting—for him.

Reed's body lingered at the edge of the bed as she lay there. She needed to feel him press her against the mattress, she needed to feel his weight crushing her, stealing the oxygen from her lungs, making her blind with desire. She needed him.

"You're staring." She smiled and watched his expression morph from serious to playful then back to serious again in the blink of an eye.

"I know."

"We've gone over this before," she teased. She just wanted him next to her, holding her, kissing her. She had put herself through hell and back in the last few weeks they were apart, and she needed to make up for lost time.

"I know, baby. But I'm still a little surprised that I've got you back in my bed again. I just needed to make sure you weren't going to disappear on me."

"I'm not going anywhere."

His shoulders relaxed and he sank down on the bed next to her. His arm wound around her and he pulled her on top of him. Every part of her fell over the length of him, her legs lying on top of his, her stomach and chest pressed against his, and her fingers laced through his.

His mouth found its way to hers and although she was only an inch away, the desperation in his touch as his lips dusted lightly over hers made her believe that they could find their way to her from anywhere.

He pulled away, breathing hard, and flipped her beneath him. This was want she needed, to be overwhelmed by him. . . .

"Meg," he said, smoothing her hair from her face. "As badly as I want to strip you down and kiss every inch of your body that has been burned into every good dream I have had in the last two months, I need to figure out a few things."

"I know," she whispered. But this was the hard part. Their attraction for each other was the easiest part of their relationship. It was giving each other over to the other that was the hard part.

"I wanted you, because deep down I knew you weren't the one for me."

He winced, pulling his eyebrows down and she smiled, running her thumb over his jaw—feeling the muscles beneath her fingers relax. "But I left you, because deep down, I realized that you *were* the one for me."

His deep baritone laugh bounced across her face and she inhaled the scent of his clean breath as it lingered in the space above her. "That's some twisted, contradictory, philosophical conclusion right there, sugar."

She sighed. "Tell that to my shrink."

"You have a shrink?" His eyes widened but the contented smile never left his freshly shaven face.

"In the form of a spitfire best friend, yes."

Reed sat up and pulled Meagan onto his lap. Her legs fitted around him and their bodies melded together as he cradled her to him. "I'm not so different from you, ya know." His palm left her hip and pressed flatly to her lower stomach—she trembled, but only from what no longer was. "We both wanted everything, I just didn't realize what everything was until you. You're my forever."

His look—his words—melted her.

She leaned in and pressed her lips to his. Her tongue

skimmed over the perfect arch, that delicious Cupid's bow, and a growl emitted from his chest.

"Have a mentioned that I've missed you?"

"A time or two." She crawled off his lap and stood in front of him. "Go somewhere with me?" she asked, hopeful.

He winked and stood up. "Anywhere."

Twenty minutes later, Meagan was pulling her Volkswagen Bug into the airfield, and Reed instantly sat up straight— well, as straight as he possibly could crammed in her tiny car.

His eyes flashed from side to side before his vision singled in on the plane. "What's going on, baby?"

"I want you to take me skydiving," she lilted.

"No, not a chance in hell."

"Why?"

"Because it terrifies you, and as much as I would like to feel you gliding through the air next to me, you're not doing it. You're not ready. This is crazy, you have nothing to prove to me, baby."

But she did. She had everything to prove.

She stepped out of the car, Reed walking around, meeting her near the hood. "I'm gonna say it again. You have nothing to prove to me."

She pressed up on her toes and kissed him and he wrapped his arms around her, trapping her between him and the car.

She smiled. "I'm ready to feel the rush, Reed. And I want to feel it with you."

"Baby, I've never felt a better rush than the one I felt falling in love with you."

He pulled her away from the car and led her by the hand to the plane. She might be crazy, which was a very valid argument given the last few weeks. But one thing was for sure. She wanted to jump, she wanted to fall, she wanted to throw caution to the wind and feel the rush—because she finally knew she had a safe place to land.

EPILOGUE

$\mathcal{I}$t was the day after Meagan's thirty-first birthday, and the thick July air was slowly blowing across Reed's face as it made its way over the still lake. He stood next to the water and stared up at the cabin where she was getting ready—keeping him out there waiting in the evening summer heat. He watched as the lights in the room turned off, leaving the top level of the cabin dark.

This was it.

His chest constricted around his heart and gave it a tight tug. He loved that woman, she had given him more in the last year than he had ever known was possible. When his brother died, he'd lost a piece of himself that he would never get back, but Meagan helped him feel whole again.

Sanders stood next to him, his eyes traveling over to Eva, who was standing on the other side of the dock. Their little fling hadn't lasted long, but Reed was almost positive Sanders wouldn't mind starting that rendezvous back up again.

He wished like hell that Murano was there. He'd come down on orders and left Fort Benning before Christmas, and although he tried like hell, he couldn't make it back down there. His unit was deploying in the fall, and he was busy in the field every other week training.

As Reed scanned the length of the dock, his eyes fell over his parents. He knew how incredibly hard it was for them to be there, all those memories of the last time they saw their son swimming to the surface of their minds, but they came. Things were still a little shaky between them, but he didn't expect things to change overnight. Baby steps.

He felt a hand clamp down on his shoulder. "There's your girl," Conner said as he stood next to him. He was more than likely enjoying the hell out of seeing Reed sweat it out. He wasn't nervous, though. Fuck no. He was anxious. He couldn't wait to call that woman his wife.

He didn't need to see her to know that she was smiling. He could feel it like it was a tattooed on his chest. But the moment he saw her, his body jolted to life. He had never seen her look more beautiful. Her hair was down, the waves cascading over her shoulders. Her skin was its summer shade of golden, and her face had the most perfect fucking blush spread over her cheeks. He pretty much lost all time from that moment until she was standing in front of him. She had a way of stealing his thoughts. She had the ability to consume his attention without even trying. She had become his life.

*R*eed's eyes hadn't left her from the moment she walked down those steps. And she was grateful. She needed to see him. She needed him to hold her together.

"Hey, baby," he said, leaning forward and pressing a kiss to the corner of her mouth. It wasn't enough. She had experienced the intensity of playful Reed, sexy Reed, gentle Reed, and sometimes even pissed-off Reed over the past year—and no matter which Reed she got, it was never enough. She would always want more of him. And she was finally getting it.

"I understand you want to recite your own vows?"

Meagan's eyes left the man who had roped her in so many years ago with that same playful smirk he was giving her at that very moment, and they shot to the pastor next to her.

"What?" she asked as panic swept through her.

Reed laughed, along with their handful of guests.

"I wanted to surprise you," he said in between his laughter.

The back of her hand found his chest. "I didn't prepare anything," she bit out between her teeth, trying to keep her voice low.

"Eh, so you'll wing it, sugar." Damn that accent. "You could recite the alphabet for all I care, as long as you say *I do* at the end."

And just like that, she melted, again. She thought that accent was his trademark. But his ability to turn her into a sopping puddle at his feet had taken it to a whole new level. It wasn't just his trademark. It was his secret weapon.

"All right," she said, raising her brows at him. "You get to go first."

"Gladly, baby."

Reed looked back at the pastor, who nodded the go-ahead, and Reed picked up her hand and pressed her knuckles to his lips. The pitter-patter in her chest was still there every time he looked at her, every time he touched her.

"I still love the way your body can't lie to me, sugar." He smirked.

"Well, hurry up so we can start our wedding night then," she teased, earning a round of cheers and whistles from their friends. She could hear her mom's distinct whistle meshing in with Trevor's voice hollering out who knows what.

"It's nice to know where your mind goes." He smirked. Then he stepped closer to her, if that was even possible, and laced his callused fingers through hers.

If ever there was a moment where time stood still and the rest of the world faded—it was that moment. The moment he looked at her and she saw everything she had ever wanted staring back at her. Nothing else mattered in that moment. He roped her in, just like always.

He laughed softly before running his thumb across her bottom lip; then with that luscious baritone voice that she loved, he started.

"I will start your car when it gets cold. I won't complain about the clump of hair in the shower. I will put my toothbrush back in the holder, and I will try to remember to put the seat down. I will wrap my hands around your toes when they are cold, and I will gladly remove your clothes when you are hot. I will do the dishes on nights you cook . . . I will do the dishes every night. I will kiss your stubbed toes and smashed fingers. I will tickle you . . . a lot. And pin you to the wall . . . a lot. I will be soft, but I will also be hard. I will go fast but also remember to take it slow. Sometimes. I will hold your hand at the movies and push your chair in at the restaurant. I will convince you to wing-walk. Someday. Not today. Not tomorrow. But someday. I will encourage you and push you. And when you need me to, I will hold you. And when you don't need me to, I will hold you. I will play, I will laugh, I will cry, and I will love—all with you."

He rubbed his hand over the large swell of her tummy. The tears were already pooling in her eyes, but that little touch sent them rolling down her cheeks. She looked down at his hand that was splayed across her stomach, and she folded her hand on top of his. His eyes were like liquid gold when she looked back at him. Liquid gold with flecks of green that reflected the ripples of the water below them.

He smiled.

"I will hold her finger and brush back her hair as she falls asleep in my arms, I will look into her eyes and see the love of her mother looking back at me. I will cry when I drop her off at preschool, and I will laugh when she burps or farts or does any other unladylike thing—and then I will high-five her. I will attempt to fix her hair, and I will kiss her scraped knees. I will hold back my temper and refrain from hurting the boy who ever breaks her heart. I will be there to kiss away the tears. I will open her door and look at her soundly sleeping every night before I climb in bed with you.

"I will fall asleep to the sound of you breathing as your head lies on my chest. And I will wake up and do it all over again—with you—forever."

ACKNOWLEDGMENTS

First and foremost, I have to thank my amazingly patient and helpful husband, who claimed chef duties, bath time duties, some nights bedtime duties, cleaning duties (but let's face it, that was just barely), and all the other mommy duties that he took on while I hid away and wrote this book. I love you. You are my inspiration, my motivation, and my encouragement. I couldn't have done this without your help during the day, and without your arms to crawl into at the end of those long days. Thanks, baby.

To my monsters, you make everything I do in this life meaningful. Love you both to the moon.

My little sisters, Jordan, Maddie, and Rylee, my biggest cheerleaders of all. I love having three sisters to turn to when I need advice—and when I don't like what one says I have two backups to turn to. Love you crazy ladies!

Jordan, your support and encouragement through the release of *The Valentine's Arrangement* and through the whole process of writing this second book have been amazing. I can't even begin to explain the way it makes me feel to have my little sis so proud of me, bragging about me, and shouting from the rooftops (or Twitter) about every little move I make with my novels.

Mom and Dad, thank you for your support. You never let me down. And, Dad, again, I would just rather you not read this book.

Grandma, thank you for letting me take over your recliner and living room until all hours of the night so I could work in peace without the distractions of my rugrats.

Michelle Valentine, you have become such a great mentor and friend! Thank you for taking me under your wing and guiding me through all my panicked questions. It was great to have you as a cheerleader, and it was fun to tackle our books together—knowing that there was someone else walking through all the madness with me!

To all my Chixx, THANK YOU! Having you ladies as a support system on this journey has been invaluable! Your support, guidance, encouragement, and listening ears truly helped me more than you could know. I love you ladies!

Denise Tung, I love you, girl! You have been such a huge support. I can't thank you enough for reading for me when it was crunch time. You're the best. *Tackle hug*

Bobbie, I love having a friend who lives all the way around the world. When I'm up at three in the morning working and I'm having a moment or I need to bounce an idea around, I know I can count on you. Your friendship means a lot to me, babe!

Stacey, my redheaded, beautiful friend. I lean on you for your opinions, and you are always willing to give them to me honestly. It means so much to me that you are excited to read my work and offer me feedback. It's so fun to have a friend to share the excitement with!

Heather, what would I do without you? You read more than me, and you are one woman who knows her smut! To have you read my work and get excited about it is amazing. Thank you for answering my panicked calls and for bouncing ideas around with me. I couldn't have done it without you.

To all my friends and family—I am fortunate to have so many I can't possibly list you all, but you know who you are— THANK YOU! I couldn't possibly follow my dreams without ALL of you.

To all the authors and bloggers I have met along the way, thank you. Thank you for your advice, support, encouragement, and, most of all, friendship. Seriously, none of this would be happening without you!

To my agent, Jill Marsal, thank you for making my transition from indie to traditional publishing smooth. I had a million-and-one questions and you were always there, willing to answer them all and offer your support and guidance along the way. I'm so lucky to have you. Thank you!

To my editor, Jesse, thank you for reading and loving *The Valentine's Arrangement* so much that you took a huge leap of faith and took on this series with me. You have my novel's best interest at heart, and working with you on this book has been a wonderful experience. Thank you for the long phone calls, talking things out with me, for answering all my questions, and for just being there if I needed advice. You have made my experience with traditional publishing seamless. It has truly been a great, and fast, journey. I can't wait to tackle book three with you!

And as always, thank you to our military men and women and their families. You are the backbone of this country, and I will be forever grateful to you and your service.

Don't miss Kelsie Leverich's
next Hard Feelings novel,

A BEAUTIFUL
DISTRACTION

Available from Signet Eclipse in May 2014.

PROLOGUE

Fallon Kelly walked slowly out to the middle of the stage. It was dark. She could see them—they just couldn't see her.

Not yet at least.

Looking around the club, Fallon listened as the voices hushed, and watched as the mingling exuberant eyes shifted their focus to the stage—to her. She always loved that part. Commanding a room like this. Sure, her lady goods on display were an enticing incentive for their attention. But even then, the dominance she wielded while on that stage was worth it—breasts out and all. She didn't doubt for one second that if she said *Jump*, the room would shake with the vibrations of shoes landing back on concrete.

She'd been dancing at Velour for the last six years, and even now, the terrifying feeling of being on that stage still rang through her body, like it did the very first night she had danced there. She didn't know how to describe it. It was a complicated contradiction of emotions, but they went together hand in hand—each not complete without its counterpart. Nervous yet satisfied, powerful yet scared, confident yet a tinge of diffidence. It pulled and pushed her in every single direction—and she loved it. Her skin felt sensitive under the lights, and her stomach fluttered and rolled. But at the same time, she was hyperaware of every pulse of her heartbeat, as a warm feeling of contentment spread through her veins.

Fallon adjusted her weight on her feet, the tulle from her tutu brushing against the bare flesh of her upper thigh, which was exposed between her white lace thigh-highs and her briefs. This wasn't the typical dance for the club. Pointe shoes and tutus weren't characteristically burlesque attire. But this was her dance. She danced this routine for herself— no one else. Even if she did get a high from the crowd's admiration, the high she felt when she slipped back into those pointe shoes was even better.

The music started to play, and the dim spotlight flicked on and hit her face.

Now they could see her.

This routine was her signature. And she didn't do it often. It was too real, too intimate for an audience. But every now and then, she needed it.

Growing up, Fallon had excelled at ballet. She'd been her mother's shining star, her prima ballerina—an additional step in her mother's climb up the social ladder to hell. And Fallon loved to dance, which made her resent the appalling little fact that her mother loved her dancing too—she just loved it for the wrong reasons. Fallon hated that she enjoyed something that increased her mother's flagrant prestige. She was merely an aesthetically valuable pawn in her mother's game.

After she'd lost her burlesque virginity to the stage at Velour, six long years ago, she'd gone to the basement studio, where the dancers choreographed and practiced their routines. And she'd bawled her eyes out. For the first time in two years, she'd cried. She'd cried for what she had done in her past, and she'd cried for what she had done on that stage. The feeling of baring your body to a roomful of strangers for the first time almost felt as if it had debased her value as a woman.

Almost.

But the reason her tears had fallen that night wasn't because she felt ashamed, but because dancing felt liberating.

So she'd stood up and danced. She'd moved in silence for hours, well into the early morning, staring at herself in the mirror—watching her body move like she hadn't seen it move in a long time. She'd danced every torturous emotion that was suffocating under the thick skin she'd grown, and it was powerful. It was freeing. And she loved it.

As the music ended its angelic melody, preparing to break into the passionate quick-beat tempo, Fallon refocused her mind from the past, closed her eyes, and carefully rose onto pointe. The club was crammed to near capacity, but not a single noise could be heard above the music—and Fallon knew, without needing visual validation, that everyone was fixated on her.

Her hands fluttered to the bodice of her costume. It was cut low and allowed her breasts to spill over the top, accentuating the perfect amount of cleavage. Sensually skimming her fingertips down her sides, she pulled the tulle of her skirt between her fingers. The volume of the music rose and drummed through her body, and she raised her arms and lifted her leg into arabesque. As she held her position, the music started to pick up and she spun around; throwing her body into the air, she leaped across the stage. The audience hollered out, and their approval of the beauty of ballet always surprised her. She loved the little shock factor she received when the club's patrons became animated over a grand jeté and a few pirouettes.

Her body began to feel the comforting familiar pull in her muscles. The vibrations against the stage from the music ricocheted through her bones, as the speed held a steady tempo—the instrumental sounds were almost scary, intense, and seductive. Her hands found the clasp of her skirt as she pushed off into a sequence of fouetté turns, and with every turn, her skirt spun off her body until she was covered in only her corset bodice and briefs.

The crowd cheered as the layer fell to the stage the moment her feet left the ground. Slowly, knowing that the act of undressing was more arousing than the result, she easily and deliberately untied the ribbon attached to the back of her corset, all the while circling the stage in piqué turns. She looped the ribbon around her wrists and unsnapped the hooks down the front of her corset, as she stood with her leg extended in the air. Then she let her corset fall to the ground, exposing her breasts, which were covered in a scanty leather bra. The crowd praised her again, as she used the movement of her body, paired with the beat of the music, to slip her briefs to the ground, exposing matching panties that covered little of her bottom.

Then, as if he had spoken her name aloud, her attention was drawn to an unfamiliar man sitting at a table close to the back of the club. Even from a distance, she could see the rich, luxurious softness inked into his dark stone irises. He returned her stare, holding her captive in his trance. His posture was lax, his thumb running across the rim of his glass, and his breathing controlled. Yet she knew she was affecting him. Not by the movements of his body, but by the way he was commanding her attention—refusing to release his eye contact. She felt the even, steady beat of her heart jerk into a jagged rhythm, her body melting under the smoldering heat of his gaze. Apparently, he was affecting her equally as much.

His eyebrow cocked and a slow, intentional smile pulled unevenly across his face, as if he could see the increase in her pulse and feel the flutter in her stomach—as if he was intensely aware of the way his attention had affected her.

His lips staggered upward a little higher, impishly lifting, as he continued to watch her. It was different from the other attentive eyes on her.

It was distracting.

A familiar rattling along with a swooshing sound blended with the music, breaking the visual spell she was under. She knew the curtain was pulling open, cueing her to the final part of her dance.

A gold pole was revealed in the middle of the stage. No one else used this pole but her. Their routines weren't based on the stereotypes of strippers and poles. But the pole—she loved it. The power and strength it took to maneuver her body up and down the pole, spinning and gliding with only her hands and thighs as support was, for lack of a better word, addictive.

Wrapping her hands around the cool metal, she leapt into the air, using her upper-body strength to keep herself gracefully spinning. She slowly flipped and rolled her body into an arabesque, using only her thighs to keep her in position high up on the pole, while she extended her arms and legs. The lithe way she could elongate her body, while holding on to the metal and elegantly pose, made her feel like she was a prima ballerina with wings.

Only she gave the prima ballerina over to seduction.

And it felt powerful.

CHAPTER ONE

The previous night

Rafe Murano's boot slipped from the bottom rung of the barstool, landing with a thump on the grimy concrete floor of the dive bar he'd been frequenting the last few weeks, more often than he was proud to admit. His body swayed unsteadily at the unintentional shift in his weight.

"Easy, killer," Trish said from behind the bar, where she was wiping the slick remnants of beer and liquor clean with a rag.

Rafe lifted his head from where he sat studying the slow burn of paper from the cherry of his Marlboro. He watched as Trish shook her head at him, attempting the illusion of disappointment, when he lifted his lips and flashed his teeth.

"You know that shit doesn't work on me. A pretty smile from a sexy man does nothing for a woman when she's repulsed by penises. Now, put that smile on a blonde with a nice pair of tits, and I'm putty."

"I get a blonde with a nice pair of tits tonight, and I'll share her with ya. How does that sound?"

Trish smiled, then squatted down to the floor, out of Rafe's line of vision. He could hear her fumbling around, then heard the distinct sound of glasses clinking together. When she rose, she had two glasses in one hand and a bottle of Angel's Envy in the other. Trish not only shared Rafe's love of women, but she also shared his love of whiskey. And Angel's Envy was like drinking nectar from the gods.

Silently watching her, Rafe sealed his lips around the filter of his cigarette and pulled the smoke into his lungs.

"Rafe, baby, I love you. But I don't share my women. And you—you don't strike me as a man who likes to share either," she probed. She poured the golden liquid into the glasses and slid one over to Rafe.

He wrapped his hand around the glass and pulled it in front of him.

"I take it by your lack of response that I hit the nail on the head?" Trish pried, cocking one of her thick brows, then lifted her glass to her mouth and took a leisurely sip.

Putting his cigarette back to his lips, he took another long drag, then stubbed it out in the ashtray next to him, releasing a cloud of smoke from his lungs. Picking up his glass, he met Trish's eyes and held them stolidly. "I don't share what's mine."

Her other eyebrow darted up as well. "And if it's not yours?" she asked cautiously.

"Then it's not mine to share in the first place, so it doesn't really fucking matter then, does it?" he barked.

"Watch it," Trish admonished. "I see that I struck a chord, but I don't put up with drunk ass-hat soldiers. I'm warning you now."

Rafe could feel the tension in his body like it was a visible limb attached from the inside out. He emptied the contents of his glass into his mouth and swallowed, then slid his glass back to Trish. She absentmindedly refilled it with more whiskey, never taking her eyes off him—as if she was waiting for a verbal strike—then slid his glass back across the worn wooden counter.

"I'm good, Trish," Rafe assured, running his thumb over the rim of his glass. He propped his black boot back up on the bottom leg of the barstool next to him. This had seemed to be his nightly routine as of late. What the fuck else was there to do now that he was back? After being deployed for the last twelve months—living every minute of every day on a mission, serving his country—the normalcy of civilian life wasn't so normal anymore. He went through this every time he came off deployment, though; attempting to adapt to life without carrying his M16 over his shoulder or transporting in armored vehicles or sweating his balls off in over-a-hundred-degree heat in full battle rattle. It made most men appreciate the ease of civilian life, and it sure as hell made Rafe appreciate it too. But there was always a part of him that missed it. Missed the constant missions, the uncertainty of every second. The way it took him over. He was fully focused and committed to his squad, and he didn't have time to dwell on anything other than his job and their safety.

"You'd better be. I wouldn't want to have to kick my favorite customer out of my bar. Plus, our big-boobed blonde is heading this way. I may be calling dibs on this one, big guy. She looks sweet enough to savor."

Rafe smiled, grateful for the mood-lifting ability that Trish possessed. He looked over his shoulder at the short blonde who was meekly approaching the bar, and then almost as quickly, he turned back around.

Innocence.

It basically encased her in an invisible protective shield. Rafe didn't fuck with those ones. In every sense of the word. The sweet ones had a tendency to slip under the radar and find a way to screw with his mind. These days, he kept his dick on the straight and narrow—as long as that straight and narrow led to the pussy of some chick who neither wanted nor expected anything other than a good time—and one time only. He wasn't about the repeat offenders either.

Rafe pulled the last cigarette from his pack and lit the end, inhaling deeply. His focus returned to Trish, who was close to salivating. And goddammit, seeing Trish get hot over a woman sent the alcohol-infused blood in Rafe's body rushing toward his dick. Trish was a knockout. Long, lean legs covered in black pants that adhered to every inch of her from hip to ankle, and her hair was jet-black with streaks of blond flashing around her face as she moved.

Rafe followed Trish's gaze back to the blonde behind him. Her hips and thighs were curvy, with a little additional padding, but her waist was small. Her jeans were snug and hung low on the flare of her hips. The purple shirt she wore clung to her body like a second skin, showcasing a flat stomach and an incredible pair of tits, with a generous amount of cleavage peeking over the deep V-neck. Her long hair was tied back away from her round face, and a soft blush spread across her neck when she noticed Rafe watching her.

"I'll have a Bud Light," she told Trish, as she stepped up to the bar and leaned her forearms over the counter. He knew Trish was getting an eyeful, and he knew she was loving it. Trish might not have been into sharing, but maybe he could talk her into letting him watch. . . .

"I knew your sorry ass would be here."

Rafe resisted the urge to roll his head back on his neck and groan. He didn't bother to look at who had suddenly taken up residence on the stool next to him. The irritating tone of his voice, warning of a near if not current lecture lingering on the surface, told him exactly who had made an appearance.

"What's up, Carter?" Rafe asked, exasperated. He noticed the slight lag in his words and looked down for confirmation at his near-empty glass before taking another hit from his cigarette.

His focus turned to the rows of liquor shelved in front of him. Carter was a good guy, but a little over-the-edge eager to be the one who jumped on the moral high horse. Not particularly a guy Rafe was interested in throwing a few back with. Rafe's moralities were somewhat unbalanced at the present.

"Saw your car here, *again*," Carter stated with an undertone of accusation.

Rafe's head turned to the side and he glared at Carter from the corner of his eye.

Carter's eyes darted past Rafe and behind the bar, and he nodded, apparently to get a drink from Trish, which meant he was sticking around. Son of a bitch.

"Look, man," Carter started, and the subtle uncertainty in his voice drew Rafe's attention away from the order of the liquor bottles he was memorizing back to Carter. He looked Carter in the eyes.

"I'm not trying to interfere with the apparent binge you've been on for the last few weeks—to each his own—but if you need to talk to someone . . . I'm . . . Shit, Murano . . . if you're not dealing with—"

"What are you trying to say, Carter?" Rafe questioned, having a pretty good idea as to where Carter was going with his current lecture.

Rafe had been deployed four times since 9/11, and he'd easily seen his share of fucked-up and could add a list of things that he'd done overseas that exceeded the definition of fucked-up, but he compartmentalized it all in the recesses of his mind and dealt with it. Rafe's rampant bender had nothing to do with his job, his duty as a soldier.

If anything, he wanted to go back, to use his missions to fill the void and distract him from his fucking ravaged heart. He yearned for the fight, the constant sharp edge of combat; the adrenaline that would invade the vacancy in his heart as it surged through his veins. He needed it. Without the distraction to ferment his heartache, it swelled, and the whiskey kept his shameful pang muted down to a simple, dull throb. So yeah, he'd been milking this shithole of a bar for every drop of liquid oblivion Trish would serve him, and he had no intention on stopping just because Carter felt the need to intervene.

"All I'm saying is . . ." Carter trailed off, sitting up straight as he met Rafe's challenging stare.

Deep down, Rafe could appreciate Carter's concern, but Rafe was three sheets to the wind, and Carter didn't know the first damn thing about what was going on in his head. And it lit a fuse.

Rafe's fingers parted over the ashtray and his cigarette landed in the accumulating ashes. "You wanna play Dr. Phil, go elsewhere. You're trotting way off course here," he said, his voice low and menacing.

"You need to calm the fuck down."

Wrong move. Rafe could feel his impending outburst lick up his spine, working its way to the surface as Carter's words rang through his mind and triggered his adrenaline to start pumping. Alcohol was like gasoline in Rafe's veins. All he needed was a little spark and he would catch fire.

Standing up and latching onto the edge of the table for support, Rafe leaned in closer. "One thing you should have already learned about me, Carter, is that I don't take orders, and you're walking a thin fuckin' line, my friend."

"Yeah, well, we're not in Afghanistan right now, *Sergeant*," he said mockingly, apparently not giving a shit about his chain of command, "and I'm not putting up with your bullshit, man. You're piss-ass drunk. You seriously want to fuckin' do this, Murano?" he hissed between clenched teeth. "I have no problem laying your ass out right now."

"Whoa, boys," Trish said, appearing next to Rafe. She

stepped in front of him and pressed her palm to his chest. "Look at me," she commanded.

Rafe slowly lowered his gaze until he was looking at the hauntingly dark irises staring back at him. "You're drunk, and whatever the hell made you snap, you need to rein it in and get ahold of it, because I'm about two seconds away from using your balls as a bottle opener." Her hands moved to his shoulders and she gave him a gentle squeeze and smiled.

There she went again, shifting his mood with the snap of her fingers.

Rafe sat down and blew out the air that had collected in his lungs. "You need another?" he asked Carter, who was watching him with incredulousness.

"Dammit, Rafe," he sputtered, sitting back down on the barstool next to him. "You're fucking bipolar—you know that?"

"I never claimed to be sane—that's for damn sure," he said, and tipped back the remaining contents of his glass of whiskey.

"Guess I'll leave your dumb ass to its own devices, then."

Rafe looked at him, watched as he took a long pull from his beer while his eyes focused straight ahead. "Yeah, I'd say that's a pretty good decision," Rafe finally replied.

Carter shook his head. Rafe knew better than to think he was in the clear from Carter's meddling. "Look," Carter pressed, shrugging his shoulders. "We may not know each other that well apart from our deployment, but I recognize that look in your eyes, man. I've been there. Women got a way of sucking the life from us."

An exasperated sigh heaved from Rafe's chest. Sucking the life out of him was one thing; he could handle that. It was the constant battle of missing her and hating her and wanting her that engulfed him, confining him within the depths of his depravity.

Nodding, Rafe finished his glass, enjoying the smooth, cathartic burn as the alcohol coated his throat. "I get that you're trying to help. I do. But the whole point of this"—he raised his empty glass—"is so I don't have to think about the woman who broke my goddamn heart," he admitted, flagging Trish down with a tilt of his head.

Rafe didn't want to think about Bridgette. He didn't want to think about the way his body craved her or the way her taste would assault him, deluding his senses at the simple thought of her mouth on his. And he definitely didn't want to think about the way she eviscerated him from the inside out until he no longer recognized the man he used to be. No, all thinking about it did was piss him the fuck off.

Picking up his beer bottle, Carter stood and gripped Rafe tightly on the shoulder. "All right, man." He gave Rafe's shoulder a squeeze, then drifted toward the pool tables, leaving Rafe to refocus on his attempt at becoming numb. At this point, the amount of alcohol infusing his blood would have him detached from his self-inflicted torment in no time. . . .

A couple minutes of silence later, the blonde who had caught his attention when he first got to the bar a few hours ago somehow found her way onto his knee. He wasn't going to protest. The alcohol had taken care of his mind, and if he played his cards right, this woman would take care of everything else. He'd found that the best way to smother that damn ceaseless pang in his chest was to bury himself inside a warm, eager pussy.

He slinked his arm around her waist, his fingers brushing across the small amount of flesh that was exposed between her jeans and her shirt. Smooth. He liked that.

"What's your name?" he asked as his fingers toyed with the top of her jeans.

She tilted her head over her shoulder to look at him. "Amber," she said nervously, which shocked the hell out of him, considering she'd hopped up on his lap like he was Santa Claus.

"You want to get out of here, Amber?"

A faint smile tugged at her glossed lips. "Can I bring my friend?" She nodded her head to the side where the curvy blonde was sitting, flirting with Trish. Rafe laughed. Trish was going to be pissed as hell when he took that little bombshell away from her.

Grabbing onto her hips he lifted her off his lap and stood up. "You can *absolutely* bring your friend," he replied.

Amber's smile widened, and he watched as her shy, nervous persona shifted. Her lids lowered slightly, her brows arched, and her shoulders straightened. He liked this game.

*K*nock. *Knock.*

Setting the stack of papers back down on her desk, Fallon uncrossed her legs and swiveled her plush office chair around to face the door. The chrome clock on the wall read three in the morning, and it was as if the visual time triggered her internal clock, making her yawn with exhaustion. Sleep was something Fallon got little of, and she welcomed the ache of fatigue like an old friend. Sleep meant dreaming, and the dreams that seemed to like to follow Fallon around weren't filled with fluffy bunnies and cotton candy, like they were when she had been a child.

"Come in," she hollered.

The heavy metal door pushed open, and a dark head of hair popped into her office. Jade's short brown hair waved around her face, and her round blue eyes were lined black on her top lid, and ringed with long dark lashes. She was stunning. A subtle, innocent beauty. But she only looked innocent. That was the thing that was most appealing about Jade. Her innocence was alluring, but her experience was enthralling.

"Hey, I'm heading up. Everything's locked up and George is getting ready to head out. He wanted me to see if you were ready for him to walk you to your car?" she asked.

Fallon stretched her arms out in front of her while another yawn filled her lungs and escaped in a long sigh. "No, tell him I'm gonna crash here tonight."

Jade eyed the vintage crushed-velvet sofa that was pressed against the back wall of the office. Fallon could see the protest on her face before her mouth even opened to speak. "Fallon, this makes the third night this week you've stayed here. Get your ass home and crawl into an actual bed."

Fallon loved her house. She'd bought it three years ago. The first home she had ever purchased. And it was magnificent. Large and spacious, with an open kitchen and a wrap-around porch. It was her sanctuary. But some nights, the small confines of her office comforted her more than the familiarity of her own bed.

Her office wasn't a typical office to begin with. It could easily have classified as a loft apartment, for most. It had a sitting area carved out in a little nook in the back wall of the room. She had a full bathroom with a vintage bronze pedestal sink, complete with a deep claw-foot tub. A vanity sat opposite her desk, in deep mahogany wood.

There was a small round table the height of a bar that sat in the back corner with two barstools, and next to it was a mini fridge and a fully stocked built-in floor-to-ceiling wine rack. Since Fallon rarely ever drank, the wine went virtually untouched.

She had everything she could need right here in this one room, and the simplicity of that was hard to resist. That along with the ability to drown herself in busywork.

"I have to go over a few inventory shipments and look through some things for my accountant, and then I'm going to make myself comfortable on the couch and pass the hell out."

Jade rolled her eyes and made sure to overdramatize the heavy sigh that she released from her chest. "Fine. I'll be upstairs if you need me," she offered.

Fallon not only owned Velour; she owned the entire building, and when Jade had nowhere else to go, Fallon had insisted she move into the loft apartment above the office. She'd been living there for almost two years now. Lord knows, nowadays Jade could afford any swanky condo she could get her paws on. But Fallon had grown accustomed to having Jade so close, and she was pretty sure Jade felt the same way. It was especially nice to have her around on nights like tonight when she had a mound of disorganized paperwork on her desk to shuffle through. Jade was always willing to take her place and help George close up. Maybe tomorrow, Fallon would drive to that little boutique downtown and buy that new Gucci handbag Jade had her eye on.

Fallon smiled. "I know. Thanks."

Jade flattened her palm against the door and gave it a few pats. "Get some sleep, princess. Tomorrow night is going to be packed."

"Friday nights are always packed."

"Yes, but tomorrow night our VIP will be full of those dirty little politicians. I hate when they come."

Fallon groaned at the realization and leaned back in her chair. "Shit, you're right."

Every other month, a handful of the state's top dogs would show their faces and sleaze up her VIP with their holier-than-thou attitudes and their overflowing wallets. It wasn't uncommon to find a few "headliners" as they liked to call them—the athletes, the politicians, and the occasional celebrity—on any given weekend. Fallon's club was the most exclusive, luxurious club in Denver. Its reputation spanned far and wide across the states, and she had even hosted a few elite private parties—for the right people and the right dollar amount, of course.

But tomorrow's headliners were a group of immoral,

crooked bastards who wore their political status in their pants. She hated them the most.

"Thanks for reminding me. I will call George and have him pull a few extra guys to work security, and we'll bring Ace in as another bouncer."

Jade yawned and nodded. "All right. I'm going to bed. Good night. Oh, and by the way, Dex is coming tomorrow night," she said quickly as she started to shut the door.

"What?" Fallon replied before Jade had a chance to escape.

Pushing the door open, Jade stepped a foot in. "He and a few of his friends are coming to Denver for the night and are gonna swing by the club." Jade's head lowered infinitesimally. She knew this little tidbit of information would not make Fallon happy. At. All.

"You know the rules," Fallon stated calmly, needing no other explanation. The tension radiating between them was explanation enough.

Lifting her head so she could see into Fallon's eyes, Jade frowned. *Ah, great.* She was going to try to win over the friend side of Fallon that was lurking around somewhere. Somewhere that was usually unattainable when her club was involved.

It's not going to work, Fallon thought when she saw Jade's eyes soften around the edges.

"Come on," Jade pleaded, and Fallon was pretty sure she saw her bottom lip pucker out a little bit.

"You know I don't allow boyfriends in my club, Jade. Ever. No exceptions. If I let you, I would have to let all the other girls, and I'm not doing it. I'm sorry. Those were the rules long before I enforced them."

Jade's back leaned against the doorframe and she sighed. "Take me off the lineup tomorrow," she proposed. "I'll work tables."

"The headliners love you. I'm not taking you off the lineup so you can play footsie under the table with your boyfriend." Fallon hated being a bitch, but rules were there for a reason.

"Please."

"No."

Fallon watched as the wheels started spinning in Jade's head while she shifted through her schemes to get off the lineup. Fallon would give her credit for trying.

"Take my place? You know the headliners would rather see you than me anyway." She stepped all the way inside and shut the door behind her. "If you actually would let yourself have a man in your life, I would do it for you. No questions asked."

"I would never allow my boyfriend to come to my club, knowing the rules in the first place," Fallon retorted.

"Dammit, Fallon. Quit being such a hard-ass and let me off the damn lineup."

Fallon inhaled a deep breath and closed her eyes, accepting defeat. "Fine," she started, and Jade's eyes widened and a smile broke out on her ivory face. "*But*, as far as the other girls are concerned, I did *not* give you permission. And I took you off the lineup as punishment and docked your pay for the evening."

"Deal." Jade beamed and opened the door.

"And, Jade," Fallon said before Jade stepped out, "you know that if there are any problems—any—I will instruct George to haul their asses out of here by their shirttails, right?"

Jade smiled. "I wouldn't expect anything other than that from you, babe. But there won't be a problem. I promise."

"I hope you're right."

Jade rolled her eyes and started pulling the door closed. "Night," she sang.

Sighing, Fallon shook her head, hoping to God she hadn't just made a huge mistake by allowing Dex and his friends to come to the club. "Night," she replied, watching the door click closed.

Fallon slipped her peep-toe Mary Jane stilettos from her feet and curled her toes. She had just purchased the sexy deep purple Prada pumps a few days ago, and the arches of her soles ached. A few more times around the block and those puppies would be good and broken in. She stood up and made her way barefoot to the wrought-iron wardrobe next to her vanity and pulled a satin slip from the lingerie drawer.

She had on one of her favorite wrap dresses. It was cut low on her chest and the tie cinched at her waist, leaving the skirt of the dress to flow easily above her knees.

She pulled on the tie and the dress fell open, allowing her to slide her arms out. It gathered at her feet and she slinked into the satin slip, before stepping out of her dress and kicking it to the side.

Sitting down at her vanity, Fallon reached behind her

neck and unclasped the thin gold chain that rested along her collarbone. She dropped the necklace into her palm. The small, delicate pendant felt heavy in her hand as she brushed her finger over it before placing it in its designated spot in her vanity.

Her lids began to feel heavy, weighted down. She had a bit more work to finish, especially now that she needed to make sure everything was in order for her headliners tomorrow, but instead of sitting herself down at her desk, she fell onto the sofa and curled her legs up on the soft velvet.

She pulled the throw blanket from the back of the sofa down over herself and wedged herself deep into the back cushions. Hopefully, sleep would find her tonight.

Kelsie Leverich is the *New York Times* bestselling author of *The Valentine's Arrangement*. She lives with her husband, two children, and their three pets. When she's not writing, you can usually find her out on the lake with friends and family or snuggling on the couch with her kids and a good book. She loves stories that can sweep you off your feet, make you fall in love, break your heart, and heal your soul.

CONNECT ONLINE

www.kelsieleverich.com